After The Fairytale

by

Angie Hulme

PUBLISH AMERICA

PublishAmerica
Baltimore

First printing

At the specific preference of the author, PublishAmerica allowed this work to remain exactly as the author intended, verbatim, without editorial input.

ISBN: 1-4137-7076-2
PUBLISHED BY PUBLISHAMERICA, LLLP
www.publishamerica.com
Baltimore

Printed in the United States of America

There are so many names, it would take a book of its own to thank you all.

So I give this to all who have inspired and encouraged me.

To everyone doing their own thing to make the world a nicer place.

To those who show me my faults, and allow me to do with them what I will.

To everybody who listens to, answers and generally deals with my random ramblings and musings with an indulgent smile.

To those who point me in the right direction when I lose my way.

To all who showed me things about people and friendship that I never believed were real.

To everyone who makes me smile and fills my heart with love every day.

And, of course, to Cinderella…

Chapter 1

Bring him to me!" the Queen commanded shrilly.

A man was dragged into the courtroom by two armored guards in red cloaks, and thrown to his knees.

"Cinderella, my dear..." began the King feebly.

"Shut up, Osmon," she snapped and glared at the whimpering wreck below her.

"Samson Smithson!"

He raised his head, eyes fearful, "Your Highness..."

A guard stepped forwards and pinned him to the floor with his boot, "Shuddup," he snarled and stepped back. Samson continued hugging the floor.

Cinderella continued, "You are charged with treason. Do you have anything to say?"

Samson blubbered, "Your Highness, I-it was a joke. It meant naught. I love you, my beautiful Queen."

"Enough," She snapped her fingers and the guards dragged him to a wooden block, ten feet to the Queen's left. They laid his head down, threaded a chain through loops on either side and pulled. Samson's head hit the block with a thud.

"Die by Fire and be a lesson to all," she proclaimed, raising her hand. The executioner raised his sword.

Fire reflected the lights as it hovered.

Cinderella dropped her hand.

An instant later, Fire dropped, a head rolled and the court was silent.

Cinderella clapped twice, "Clean him up!"

Three cleaners came; one grabbed the head and stuffed it into a sackcloth bag to be spiked on the castle wall. -The second rolled the body into a thick cloth and dragged it away. The third began to mop up the blood from the floor. She left the block itself to dry. It was already red with old blood. The Queen preferred it that way.

"The blood of all my traitors," she might say, "Is always there to remind me that they, also, are always there."

Once done, the third cleaner followed the others out and the court shuffled awkwardly, anxious for dismissal.

"Any more business?" Cinderella called.

Nobody responded.

"Good. Blessings to you all. You are dismissed."

The court emptied rapidly with low murmurs and the sound of hurrying feet.

The executioner remained when all but the King and Queen had left. He laid Fire at Cinderella's feet and knelt, "I christen Fire, as always, in the blood of those who would betray you, and in your name, my Queen."

Fire glittered deep orange and blood with the lights in the courtroom. Forged a thousand years before of the strongest wizard metal, filled with light and dark magics, beat by the greatest blacksmith, blessed by the greatest sorcerer. Never to rust, blunt or fail its owner in battle.

"Thank you. Your 100th, if my count is correct."

"Yes, m'lady."

"Then you are discharged, as I promised. Fire will be returned to your King."

The executioner unbuckled his sword belt and laid it on the floor. He cleaned the drying blood from the blade with a crimson cloth and sheathed it.

"It is returned, m'lady. But I'd like to stay, if you'll let me."

The Queen laughed, "A taste for killing, eh? Well, it is better that than for thievery, Barett."

Barett was once a master sneak. There was nothing, he boasted, that he could not steal—and return—without detection. Until he set his sights on Fire—a handsome blade for a thief, and a handsomer ransom to be got from its possession.

He never knew how the Queen had known his plan, though he guessed bitterly that Jerne, her spy, was involved.

She had come herself, flanked by Palace Guards—the highest knights in the Kingdom, pledged to protect the Royal family and all they owned. They took him as he fled the castle, blade in hand.

He had expected death, yes, but his own.

Instead, Cinderella had left him in a dungeon cell while she plotted a punishment for him.

And the time was not wasted. He was brought before her, pale and ready to die. But she had laughed and handed him Fire.

"No death for you, thief," she had said, "But 100 lives you shall take for me, as my executioner—and using Fire, the blade which was your downfall. And as a thief, lover of darkness, mystery, once with a shadow for a face, this mask you shall wear until you die."

She produced a black metal mask in two halves, one to fit over his face, the other over the back of his head. The court blacksmith was already standing by; hidden in the crowd of nobles, and at a nod from the Queen, he stepped out and bolted them together over Barett's face. The eyelets were small and gave him tunnel vision. To another, looking from the outside of the mask, he may have had black holes for eyes. A slot over his mouth allowed him to eat and drink, room at his chin and neck allowed hair and beard to grow out and be cut.

It was cramped and uncomfortable, dark and sweaty. Yet Barett had come to love it. He was the ultimate sneak; no one would ever know his true face again.

Taking his first life, he had hesitated. Yet failure meant a worse fate and he paused only to remind himself of such. Before he reached double figures, it was becoming easy to shut off the part of his mind that complained.

Now, reaching 100, Barett felt he could do nothing less than serve the Queen who had spared him by generously allowing him to behead those she named traitor.

Also, he had to admit that the rush of power, the whistle of the blade, the clunk and thud as the head was severed and hit the floor, gave him a feeling he had never known even in his heyday of thievery.

Besides, his Queen was good to him.

"Aye, m'lady," he replied now, "I have my taste for taking life—and for protecting my Queen.

"Then you shall stay. But Fire must still be returned—100 deaths were all I gave you from it. More than that, you choose to do and I am pleased. Now your punishment is over, you will receive regular payment that fits your work," she handed him a bag of gold coins, "Use it to have my blacksmith forge you a blade."

"I will see him immediately. Thank you, m'lady. You are good to me."

"Go then," she nodded him away.

When he was gone, she retrieved the sword and brought it to her husband, "Osmon, your sword is returned."

"Aye, and 100 deaths the better off," Osmon commented dully.

She laughed, "You sound unhappy."

"A little. Many a good man I have watched die by your command, my dear,"

"Traitors, each one."

"A harmless joke? An idle comment?"

"Aye, those, but also plotters, would-be usurpers."

Osmon sighed, "Yes, dear. I know you see your ways as justice. But such varied punishment at times, and so little leeway. This creates more murmurs and better hiding places, not loyalty and devotion."

"A murmur unchecked rises to more, Osmon. And varied? Perhaps. Barett was an unusual punishment, but look what we gained. I spare those I see may be useful to me."

"Well I remember, Your Highness," Another voice spoke from behind them.

"Jerne," Cinderella smiled at the noseless head of her spy guild.

"M'lady, m'lord King," Jerne bowed low to Osmond.

"I will go," Osmond predicted the next command from his wife, "It has been too long since I held Fire," he buckled the sword on his waist and strode off in the direction of the training grounds.

"You disposed of the town's best smithy," Jerne spoke freely when in the company of only the Queen.

"He spoke treason."

"Your Highness, he got drunk, swore he would have you lower taxes even if he had to storm the castle to do so. A comment hardly worth losing a head for. The people do not like this."

"Oh, is that so? Maybe I'll have all their heads!"

"Every head in the Kingdom?"

Cinderella frowned at him, "Does this visit have a point, Jerne? I wish to visit my stepsisters."

"I simply wished to express my opinion. I have no important news."

"Then come again to see me when you do. Honestly, I sometimes regret taking your nose—it is not the prettiest of sights."

"I am reminded of this every time I glance in a mirror," Jerne agreed, "But I have not spied on you since. My nose—or rather my whole face, now, has been firmly poked into the business of everybody else."

"You are loyal, I think, for now at least. You tell me even those things that you wish you had never heard. And I sense you do have a point after all, get to it."

Jerne inclined his head politely, "As you wish. I would see myself rewarded suitably for my services. My spies are everywhere and report to me, but I am everywhere also. They are forced to look for me and it takes time. Things are missed, delayed. If I was in one place, only leaving for more important matters..."

"You wish for land," Cinderella finished for him.

"Yes, m'lady. And any title that may come with it."

The Queen studied the short man in ragged black clothing. '*He dresses down to attempt my sympathy,*' she realised with some amusement.

"I have earned it," he told her.

"You have earned nothing. You do this so I do not cut off the rest of you, not because you have love or loyalty."

"I am sorry, my Queen," Jerne backed away, "I will return to my duties."

"Wait," the Queen commanded, thinking. Jerne waited, "Earn it and you shall have it. I release you from my service. Show your true faith, spy."

He bowed and exited rapidly before she could change her mind.

Cinderella watched him leave, frowning. '*He grows demanding,*' she thought, '*I give him life and a career, and he makes requests as though I owe it to him. He must be watched carefully, a spy has no loyalty but to his own neck.*' She turned in a flurry of gown and exited the throne room.

The main street in Lamsonia was a bustling place. Roads were wide to accommodate horse-riders, pedestrians and market stalls. The sides were lined with slums, taverns and abandoned lots.

In the center of the town square stood a bronze statue of Cinderella Reah. She stood 15 feet tall; one fisted hand was raised towards the sky, the other placed over the center of her chest—the traditional Lamsonian pose of love and justice. Two of her corrupt City Guards, dressed in blue and grey, permanently guarded the statue. Behind it, facing outwards to a clear space was a stage used for Royal speeches and town meetings.

On either side of the statue were two cages. They measured ten feet square, with bars of thick iron and floor of wood.

Inside each, one figure sat hunched close to the center—away from the reach of most passersby. At their feet was a tray, empty now but for a cup. On these was placed their daily meal. One cup of ale, one chunk of bread, one chunk of sheepsmeat. Occasionally, when Cinderella caught herself in an especially kind—or playful—mood, a slice of cheese or butter may be offered.

Regina and Melina were the names of the two captives. They were tattered and filthy. Their hair strung greasily around their shoulders, and their clothes hung ripped and loose on scrawny frames.

Once, they were twins of sharp beauty, but the cruel nature learned from their mother had made them heartless towards their stepsister.

Once, Cinderella had been their servant. Once, she was tattered and filthy, scrawny, beaten and underfed. Once, she slept in the cinders by the kitchen fire.

But, a 'Faery' gave her a dress, a carriage, an invitation to Prince Osmon Reah's ball. Midnight struck and Cinders had run from the besotted Prince, leaving behind a slipper of fur with which he found her again.

Later, when they wed, Cinderella spread tales of a glass slipper, not fur. Glass, she thought, was nobler, womanly, sharp and unmovable. Like herself. She had a glassblower fit her such a shoe and displayed it, now, in the throne room.

For eight years now, she had been Queen. King Santai had left his body behind one evening after a terrible illness. Fine the day before, one afternoon he was taken by a strange sickness. He stumbled and fell to the ground. Unable to use his legs properly he was hurried to his bed by panicked servants close by. Trembling, with ice-cold hands and feet, he begged for water but failed to keep it down. Before the morning, he had ceased to breathe.

This left Osmon, Cinderella and their then year-old son, Cinamon. Queen Asheyi had passed away in childbirth, Osmon knew no mother but his beloved Nanny who weaned him on goats-milk and told him stories of great deeds and romantic trysts.

Regina and Melina had been imprisoned the very day after Cinderella and Osmon had married. The twins and their stonehearted mother, Danzae, though surprised at a warm invitation to the wedding with promise of spacious quarters, had shown themselves. They were resentful and jealous, but showing only love and support for their servant-turned-Princess.

Cinderella's father had died years earlier—driven (so Cinderella told herself) to death by his second wife.

The morning after the wedding, Regina, Melina and Danzae woke to a noisy invasion by palace guards. They were locked in separate dungeons while three cages were constructed, then placed in the town square just as they were now—though the statue now towering over it was not commissioned until Cinderella took her place on the throne.

This capture and public humiliation was the wedding gift Cinderella had begged of King Santai. The King was unhappy, but tradition and Honour would not let him refuse anything in his power that was asked of him by his new daughter-in-law.

Cinderella entered the town square now, riding in a litter carried by four Centaurs. Each wore red cloaks lined with gold; bronze chainmail glittered underneath. The litter itself was large enough for three, decorated with purple, yellow and red livery. Each curtained side was emblazoned with the crest of the Royal House. On a bronze

ANGIE HULME

background, a Crown crossed underneath by a longsword and a Staff of Peace.

Inside lounged Cinderella, nibbling plates of meat and fruit and giving off waves of thorough boredom.

The street cleared as they approached and silence fell. The Queen, it was known, disliked reminder of any previous life, including the poorer citizens of her Kingdom. The last villein who publicly approached her to offer good wishes had been staked to the ground and lashed to death on her order.

The litter stopped sharply, jerking Cinderella forwards. She cursed under her breath and, once lowered, climbed gracefully out.

"Which of you?" she cried. The centaurs knew the question meant banishment for he who owned up or for all if they remained silent. They bowed their heads and said nothing. *'Those cursed creatures!'* she thought to herself, "Very well," she told them quietly, knowing they could hear her well enough, and not wanting any lingering subjects to hear, "Once you have returned me to the castle the four of you will be escorted to the Centaur's Forest."

Centaur's Forest was full of banished and wild-bred Centaurs. The Queen was strict and vengeful, during the years since she had taken the Royal title hundreds of Centaurs had been banished to a patch of land set aside for this very action.

Far from punishment, however, the palace-bred horse-men longed for this life. Freedom to hunt, live and breed in a loosely wooded area banned to poachers on pain of death.

Loyalty and Honour, however, dictated they do the duty assigned to them, silent and uncomplaining, until the Queen grew angry at some small mistake. For, some 600 years ago, an army of Lamsonia had liberated 12 Centaurs from slavery on one of the neighbouring Islands. In return for this, and failing to foresee such a future as Cinderella had brought, the species had gratefully bound themselves to the family.

Now, mistakes as small as lashing a tail at a fly while in presence of the Queen were grounds for exile, though it was generally agreed that to be cast into a dungeon and fed stale bread and water forever would have been a welcome relief from the usual treatment doled out by the Queen. Mistakes made on purpose, however, were ignoble and would cause the rest of the breed to cast aside the one the oath-

AFTER THE FAIRYTALE

breaker. However, it all mattered little; for every Centaur knew, they would be free eventually. None had perished while in service to the palace since Cinderella had arrived. Therefore, they allowed the Queen to see banishment as painful for them. Thus, they grew up knowing they would one day be free—officially in disgrace with the Royal family, but allowed to return to their natural state.

Once free, keep could be earned in the towns. Pulling loads, training horses, protecting landowners. In return, spare food and bow and arrows were left for them, and medical treatment was given free.

Now the four Centaurs kept their heads bowed. One pawed the floor, eager to leave. The Queen took it as a sign of frustration and sadness, and she smiled as she turned away and walked to the closest cage.

Melina, seeing her stepsister approach, scuttled to the far side of the cage and crouched, trembling. Cinderella smiled warmly, revealing her hatred only by the iciness in her eyes.

"My darling stepsister," she spread her arms wide as she reached the bars, "How are you, Melina? Well, I hope. You look better than last time I saw you. Nasty cough that was, best hope the next Great Cold is not quite so…cold," she reached into the folds of her gown and placed a lump of cheese on the floor inside the cage, "Come on, Melina," she cooed, "Come get the cheese."

Melina shook her head and cowered.

"Come on…I can see your mouth water from here. Come and take the cheese, sister. Would you disobey your Queen? You know what happens when people do that…" her voice was as sickly sweet as her smile.

Melina knew better than to disobey, and the reminder of what Cinderella could and would do to her took away the rest of her cowardice. She crawled slowly towards the edge of the cage, where the cheese lay. Stopping just within reach, she tentatively stretched out her arm, touched the cheese, and then snapped it back expecting…something to happen. Cinderella had not moved, now she motioned once more to the cheese and smiled widely. Melina reached once more, snagged the cheese, and raced to the corner once more. She watched Cinderella carefully as she gnawed.

13

Cinderella waved and moved on to the second cage. Already, Regina was edging out of her corner, ready to grab her cheese. When she was edging to within arms reach, Cinderella produced a chunk and held it up. Regina edged closer still, almost able to stretch and grab it from Cinderella's hand. Cinderella waved it gently in the air and smiled the same, wide smile. Regina moved closer, closer, made a grab.

Cinderella whipped the cheese away and laughed delightedly as Regina hit the floor of the cage with a thud. Realizing some game, realizing she was within reach, Regina tried to run, but Cinderella grabbed a clump of hair and twisted. Regina cried out, a hoarse, dull sound. Inside, her mouth was empty where her tongue should be. Only a stump of the muscle still flapped uselessly towards the back of the throat.

While Regina struggled, Cinderella withdrew a knife from her dress. Feeling the steel on the back of her neck, Regina froze, mouth hanging open, and slowly a line of yellow liquid ran down her leg to create a small pool on the floor.

Cinderella saw this and laughed some more. She moved the knife gently down Regina's back, stopped at the base of the spine, then dug in and snapped her arm upwards, letting go of the hair as she did so.

Regina hit the floor, bleeding from a skillful cut just to the right of her spine, barely missing every nerve. Cinderella clapped, loosing droplets of blood from the knife, and giggled. She cleaned the blade with a scrap of cloth from a pocket, carefully replaced it in the scabbard and walked away.

"Doctooor!" she cried like icicles, looking for a response. A small, round man came forward; the City Guards reluctantly let him pass unhurt, "One of my dear, beloved sisters seems to have injured herself. Do take care of her. Do not attempt to enter the cage, or to bring her out of it. My Guards will make sure you treat her well," she gestured to the two burly men, scowling hatred at the small man and flexing their muscles, "Thank yoouuu," she threw a gold nug into the air and it landed at the doctor's feet, more wage than he would usually receive in a month. He grabbed it and scurried off to fetch his tools, shouting at his assistant to go staunch the blood flow as well as he could.

Cinderella sighed happily and sat back into her litter, "Remember," she called to the Centaurs, "Once we return—you are to be escorted from the Palace. Say your good-byes speedily."

The Centaurs allowed themselves inner smiles as they pulled the harness once more over their heads to rest on their backs, turned and trotted—almost as gently as they could—to the castle.

Chapter 2

Lady Mueren looked out from the window in the top of her tower. Beyond her was a vast sea, turbulent with foam that crashed onto the cliff, at the top of which stood the Tower of Pyrone—named for the God of the Sea.

The surrounding farmland was bleak. Food could not grow in the poisoned ground, nor animals be grazed. Instead, the mud was packed downwards with the tread of countless soldiers who had trained here.

It was said the Gods of the people in the Land Outside cursed the ground, once upon a time. It had been this way for so long, even the sorcerer Lady Mueren—by far the oldest known person—could not even remember tales of it.

Still, the land was hers and the Royal Guards paid well for its use three moons of every ten. Lady Mueren watched, sometimes, as the recruits trained. The noise was difficult to ignore, and somehow watching the swordfights, bow and arrow contests, and battle training was as calming as watching the sea. But she had not ventured from the Tower for some years.

Now, the grounds were deserted apart from weed and wild grass. So Mueren watched Pyrone send his white horses to play upon the rock face of the cliff.

Disturbed by a shout from below, she walked across the large, circular room, bare apart from a bed in the center, and looked out.

"I have your goods, m'lady," cried a merchant, pointing to a wooden horse-trailer attached to a sunken grey mare.

Mueren nodded and signaled her to wait. She left the room and descended the steps—300 of them, too many for an old woman, she told herself again. Once the door was open, the merchant brought the packages inside and laid them on the floor in the large main room.

"That'll be 3 'n' 7, if it please m'lady," she said when all was unloaded.

Mueren handed her four nugs from a purse, "Accept the extra as a token of my goodwill. You are blessed, Ivory, for making this journey at the behest of an old witch."

Ivory pocketed the coins and bowed, "It be my pleasure, m'lady, though you're not so old."

Mueren fingered her grey hair, the lines creasing her face, "You make an old lady happy, young Ivory," she told her, "I will thrice bless you within a circle once I put the delivery away."

"M'lady, you're too kind. I'd ask my God, Zheledor of the Harvest to bless you."

"You have my permission and thanks. Zheledor and Pyrone are friends, after all. You may go."

Ivory bowed once more and left, closing the door.

Mueren unpacked the delivery slowly, examining with care the packed herbs and magical aids. Once done, she fed her owl—Gamma—her only link to the main towns. He took orders to merchants, who returned him with parchments of news.

Remembering her promise to bless Ivory, she spread a circle of powdered red snath and stepped inside. There, she raised her arms.

"Pyrone, master of waters and sea.

"Bringer of fish that feed the hungry and stallions that gallop along the waves.

"I beg thee, thrice bless the lowly.

"The merchant, Ivory, is a godly villein. She is good to your humble servant. I would see luck brought her way.

"Let it be as you wish, but hear my cry."

She slowly sank to her knees and ran a finger through the snath, breaking the circle to allow her prayer to go free.

After short meditation, she struggled to her feet, joints cracking and aching. *'I am too old. I cannot do this forever. Pyrone, give me death or cure.'*

The snath was now little more than a pale pink. Its power spent, it was no longer poisonous or of magical use. Mueren swept it onto a thing strip of iron and set it aside. Once fermented in water, snath was a sought after cure for forms of insanity. Few could produce a mix as potent as Mueren; she made a good livelihood from its sale via her merchants.

Puttering in her small kitchen, making food, Mueren's thoughts often turned to her past. Near 250 years she had lived, taking on roles of guardian, godmother, sorcerer and others. Mueren was the reason that, 100 years ago, laws were passed to create distinction between dark and light magics. Mueren practiced both—few sorcerers kept only to the one side or the other, but most used both only for good. However, the law had stopped the automatic execution of anyone suspected of sorcery, and for this, she was proud and pleased.

Today her mind turned to the day of a wedding between a Prince and a servant.

Mueren had arrived the morning of the wedding from her then-home, set just apart from the closest village. Far enough to give her privacy, yet visible enough to allay the suspicion caused by her status of sorceress, and close enough to allow her easy contact when necessary.

In her finest outfit of black and green, woven with deep crimson, Mueren arrived by carriage bearing gifts. Cinderella had spotted her immediately and hurried over. After seeing the gifts handed carelessly away, Mueren found herself led into a private, unfurnished room.

"Godmother!" Cinderella embraced the woman she knew as a radiant Faery.

"Greetings, Princess Cinderella," Mueren replied, smiling.

"I'm no Princess yet," Cinderella shot back, "I'm not even properly learned in the speech."

Mueren, though, had noticed the new clip in her accent, the improved enunciation—spoiled only by use of the words of the lower caste. These, presumably, were the wrinkles still to be smoothed.

They ran through the small talk of 'how are yous', Cinderella setting a fast pace through the niceties, Mueren too curious to slow down.

"My new father has allowed me a gift," the younger woman said, finally, "I begged for two, but he can only permit me one for myself.

So I chose…well you will see soon, Godmother, how those who still call me servant and Cinder girl fare for their trouble.

"The second, though, the King has asked me to present to you in his name. In return for bringing me and the Prince together."

'Well, well,' thought Mueren, shifting her weight, "And the gift?" she asked, politely.

Cinderella clapped her hands in excitement, "King Santai let me choose an area of land which he wishes to present to you—with a title."

Mueren tensed, knowing she should be pleased but sensing the gift would turn out to be a false boon.

Cinderella took the hesitation as pleasure and smiled widely, "You'll be closer to that water God of yours, Godmother. I have given you Pyrone's Tower."

Mueren hid a frown, "M'lady, the lands around the tower are poisoned," she smiled to show good nature.

"The Army pays a lot to train there, Godmother, whoever owns that land can never go poor," Cinderella's voice was suddenly stern.

'They'll make a true Princess of her well enough.' Mueren thought. *'She is already taught the attitude of a Royal.'* aloud she said; "And you present this land to me, as a gift. M'Lady I give thanks."

Cinderella clasped Mueren's shoulders in an affectionate gesture, "All the privacy you want, enough income every seven moons to let you live well. And you will be named Lady before the wedding ceremony—so you may journey to your new home before dark."

Mueren took a step back, "You wish me to leave before you are married, m'lady."

Cinderella flapped her hand, "You came, did you not? I simply wish for you to settle in your home as soon as possible.

'Aye, that or hide me from your new court.' she thought to herself. *'I wonder of her plans for those who treat her wrong, if this is gratitude for my part in her current pleasurable situation.'*

Cinderella stood, awaiting a reply, so Mueren smiled and curtseyed, "You honour me, m'lady."

"Then come with me, Godmother, you are to be made a Lady."

Since that day, Mueren allowed herself few lapses of thought. She told herself Cinderella was truly trying to give a gift, not trying to keep her away. But sometimes, in the dark, when the shutters banged with the wind and the snow pushed its way through and floated silently to the ground…sometimes, Mueren found in herself a bitterness she had not known before.

When the light of morning came, however, it was easy to dismiss those thoughts and ignore the news that would come of Cinderella's treatment of those she was once lower than. Mueren had to be honest with herself by admitting she did enjoy her home. She felt closer to Pyrone when she stared out at the sea, though she was really no closer to Him than when she lived inland. Sea and rain came from the same God, after all. And the empty spaces around her were welcoming, when to most they would feel lonely.

Mueren spooned her food onto a tin plate and sat in her main room, taking a book of spells to study while she ate.

Prince Osmon threw himself inside, slammed shut the door and slipped the latch home before he turned to face the occupant.

When he did, it was with a warm smile, "Royston…"

"My dear King, this hiding and running really is growing rather tiresome," Royston replied by way of greeting and handed Osmon a drink with a kiss on the cheek.

Both were of similar size, though Osmon's upper body boasted the girth of an accomplished swordsman, Royston's narrow chest showed lack of physical exertion, while the fine cloth covering it hinted at inherited wealth. Osmon's dress was dark and drab—that of a villein—though to the eye of a knowledgeable observer its bruised appearance was obviously contrived.

"Oh, Royston," Osmon scolded lightly, "Please save me from this conversation, just once."

Royston held up a hand and tossed his head, "I merely wished to remind you, oh King o' my heart, that the fabulous lifestyle of the modern doll, such as myself, was made acceptable by your very own Grandfather."

Osmon sighed, resigned, and sat on a chair, "Yes, but unfortunately for this doll, adultery—especially in a King—is still frowned upon by most. I also have no wish to be the first Monarch exposed as an adulterous dolly."

"Yes, it is a knotty problem," Royston agreed, moving gracefully behind Osmon and smoothing his hair, "And I still profess it a shame your little plan failed."

"You hated my plan," Osmon reminded him.

"Yes, but only in comparison to mine."

Osmon dropped his head backwards and looked upside down at Royston, "Which was for the two of us to publicly express our love and hope the entire Kingdom was as understanding as my Grandfather evidently was?"

"It still left you the option of abdicating and crossing the sea with me to find new life," Royston pointed out, and then shook his tousled head, "Instead…" he gestured.

"Instead…" Osmon groaned, "I brought the first poor girl I found into my palace. I offered her marriage, power, riches, and the freedom to take any lover. In return for which, she would attend as my Queen, give me patronage of her first bastard and allow me to keep my very own true love right where he belonged," Osmon rose and spun around to face Royston, "How could I know? Two weeks in the castle and she was no longer an innocent, grateful girl who I would enjoy befriending and teaching. She laughed in my face and told me no. When I suggested I therefore find me a new wife, and give her land and money in return for secrecy—she told me if I so much as thought of you again, every being in the Kingdom would know their beloved King Osmon was a 'back-tickling, shirt-lifting, wand-polisher.'" he held Royston gently by the shoulders, "What was I to do?"

Royston gazed into his eyes, sadly, "You could have been honest. At least we could then have been together. My King, my love, I can do this no more. Nigh on 15 years I have loved you behind locked doors. And every day of it broke my heart a little more," Royston fell to his knees and wept.

Osmon fell too; eyes wet, and gathered Royston into his arms, "My heart breaks too, with every second. If it is what you must do, then damn me for a coward and I shall never return to darken your door! I have done my best to follow the way of my Father and Grandfather. As peasants, we would have been wed, a true family, and few would blink an eye. But as King, I fear the reaction of so many. I am afraid,

I have not the courage of those before me to do what is right and take the consequences. I do not know how to be the first Doll-King."

Royston looked up, streaks on his cheeks, eyes red, "Perhaps you would only be the first to be open."

Osmon stared for a moment, then, "Explain?"

"How many Kings, Queens and Royals in history?" Royston asked, "Does not mere chance say that some must have felt attraction for their own?"

Osmon stared more, shook his head slightly in wonder, "I see what you say, but not where you are going."

Royston fell back into a cross-legged sitting position, "Did you never wonder, Osmon, why your Grandfather passed those laws? Why he so publicly released the imprisoned from jails and hospitals. Why he personally talked to so many who disagreed. Why he fought so hard for people to see that dolls—and tabbies for that matter—are the same as anyone?"

Osmon slumped downwards, "I truly never did…you believe my Grandfather was a dolly?"

"Maybe," Royston agreed, "He or some close friend or relative, certainly. Why else?"

Osmon opened his mouth and shut it again. Royston knelt once more in front of Osmon and took his chin in one hand, "You think yourself a coward, Osmon, because you fear. Only a fool knows no fear, and fools live short lives. Bravery is to do that which is right no matter the fear of what consequences may be."

"But my only fear now, this moment, is of you leaving," Osmon whispered.

"I could never do so, not truly. You make my soul complete and if I must spend my days living in darkness, then so be it. The light that comes from you is all I need. Even were I a world away, I would be with you."

"I will tell them," Osmon promised, the lump in his throat making him hoarse, "With you always by my side, I will tell them and take whatever the return may be."

Royston considered, "Sometimes on the path to bravery and truth a speedy horse may sit idling by the wayside…it is no shame to accept a quicker way along the path," he smiled wickedly.

"Ooh, I see my lover has a plan," Osmon smiled back.

Royston nodded, "Later, we may talk. Now, my King, I have hungers that lay unchecked these past 2 moons."

Nine-year-old Cinamon, Crown Prince of Lamsonia, had run away. Again.

Or rather, he had walked coolly out of the Palace and planned to be gone for some time.

He was short and dark-haired with tan skin and chocolate-brown eyes. He currently ran no risk of laughter lines as he aged, for he rarely smiled. In fact, he rarely made any expression and only a privileged group learned how to read behind the deadpan.

That group was the banished Centaurs of the forest. More accurately, a large field with trees, Cinamon nonetheless liked to come here whenever possible. The Centaurs told him tales, took him for rides, taught him things he never learned from the stuffy old tutors at school. They also listened when others ignored or scoffed, understood when others laughed or scolded. Cinamon knew them all well, he made a point of visiting new exiles and helping them adjust to life outside the Palace, with so many strangers, and with his help each soon became as much a part of the group as any other

Today he had come for two reasons. Word from the Palace Centaurs told him of four new exiles. In addition, he had questions to ask one of the elder Centaurs, questions about what Eera had told him on his last visit a week ago.

A week only because the Queen had, as she always did after his disappeared for a time, set Palace Guards to watch him day and night. This only ever lasted for a few days before other duties forced a lapse. Cinamon was just glad his mother seemed to believe his vague references to nature walks. If she ever knew he visited those she had banished, she would likely hop up and down with anger before throwing him in a dungeon for inventive punishment, while sentencing the Centaurs to their doom.

So Cinamon traveled in a roundabout way—through the thickly weeded fields behind the castle, around a self-created, barely visible trail, across the Kone River and into Centaur forest at the side farthest from the city.

Arriving now, he walked up to the nearest Centaur and greeted her with a friendly pat on the flank—a playful greeting no other Human but he could get away with, "Hi Arison."

"Cinamon!" she tossed her silvery mane and kissed his cheek, "How good to see you—the new Herd are arrived," she guessed the reason he was here.

Cinamon nodded, "May I see them?"

"Of course," Arison set off with a flick of her silver-grey tail, Cinamon by her side.

Unlike Cinderella, Cinamon had little care for the respect and power his Royal status should accord him. When his mother was not around, he preferred people to greet him with a simple 'Hello' or nothing at all, than with respect yet unearned. Besides, he was fully convinced that groveling was pointless for all, painful for many and degrading to both parties—breeding resentment among peers and elders alike as they bowed their heads and told him what he wanted to hear.

Being nine, of course, Cinamon had not yet the words or quality of speech to express this fully, usually phrasing it as 'Groveling's stupid.' or 'Stop lying just 'cause I'm a Prince.'

Cinderella, of course, knew of this abomination, but was forced to quietly seethe or risk revealing—and therefore losing—her spies. Therefore, she chose to seethe with anger and jealousy as her son somehow commanded more respect with friendship than she had ever gained from fear.

Arison and Cinamon now approached the four ex-litter carriers, Cinamon a step behind to show he was a friend and respected them well enough to require introduction.

'My new friends, please meet the Prince Cinamon.' Arison said, grandly. The four bowed and Cinamon took the time to take in their features. All from the same litter, he decided, for all four boasted a white crest in their heads and copper-flecked fur and mane. Their tails, however, were variously black, white, gold and red-brown.

As they rose, Cinamon bowed also, "Greetings, I heard of your banishment and came to befriend you—as is my custom."

"We have heard great things of you, sire," one said, "Please call me Jonae. These are my litter-brothers, Missn, Zaoreth and Oomyu," as he indicated the three standing around him each inclined their head politely.

Cinamon inclined his head back, and drew himself up, "I offer my apologies for my mother and your unfortunate disgrace, and my friendship for the four of you. I am long a friend to the Centaurs of the Forest and hope to continue this with you."

The four Centaurs gave a similar offer of friendship, and the formalities were finished. Eera chose this time to reveal himself from within a nearby crop of trees, "My young Prince," he crooned silkily, flicking Cinamon's nose with a smile, "I was expecting you."

"Eera," Cinamon hugged him. Eera was the oldest Centaur, the first banished, and Cinamon's favourite of all. He was sheer black once, though now he showed faint flecks of grey hair, making him look as distinguished as he indeed was. The Centaur life-span is anything from 50-150 years, when pushed Eera tacitly admitted himself as '80 or so'. He was full of lore and legends and Cinamon often spent hours listening to stories of old, then turning them over in his head at night to find the intelligence and lessons behind each.

"Eera, I would speak with you if I may," the boy said.

Eera nodded.

"Excuse me, my newest friends; we shall talk more in the future," Cinamon took his leave and followed Eera into the trees.

After a minute or two Eera stopped, shook his whole body out and sat on his haunches in a small clearing. Cinamon sat opposite him and waited.

"My boy, you have questions from our last conversation," Cinamon nodded, Eera went on, "I told you that you have the inner power and wisdom to be a great wizard, if only you were taught how," Cinamon nodded again, "Ask questions, my son, and I shall answer as I can."

Cinamon thought carefully, what was it he truly wanted to know? That he had power, Eera had told him, and he believed it. That he had wisdom, he also mostly believed. That he needed teaching before he could become great, this he realized, but knew not who or how. These were the questions he asked.

Eera listened and contemplated, furrowing his bold brow in concentration, "There is a sorcerer," he said finally, "An old witch, who has done great deeds, who's power has not faded with age. Alas, she hides herself in a Tower by the sea, surrounded by poisoned lands. She once did a great thing for your mother, who in return gave her this Tower to remove her from sight. It is possible, maybe, to persuade the Queen to send you to this woman for teaching. Though the lady herself has been known a recluse these past 10 years and would need incentive, persuasion, something…"

"My family has riches—" Cinamon began.

"No, my son," Eera shook his long neck, "This is a witch with no such simple desires. She values kindness, intelligence, friendship above all other. I knew her as a younger Centaur and never saw a gold coin turn her head."

Cinamon stood and walked up and down, kicking at loose grass and leaves, "Then how can I ask her to teach me if she does not want the only thing I can give her?"

"You have more than gold, my son," Eera chided gently, "You have intelligence, kindness, bravery, and the inner strength needed. I will journey to this lady's Tower and ask her to take you in. I pray she remembers me."

Eera stood, effectively ending the conversation, "I must journey soon. Return to me in some days and I will provide you, I pray, with a positive answer. Your mother should be persuadable once the lady witch shows willingness."

Cinamon bowed low, "Thank you. If you can do this for me, I give you my word I shall become the greatest wizard you have ever known. And I shall never forget the Centaurs, or what you have done for me," he said.

Eera hugged him, "My son, I ask no repayment but to see you blossom into a great man."

Cinamon smiled and departed, waving hurriedly to the other Centaurs as he returned to his room to accept his punishment, and daydream the time away.

Chapter 3

Eera approached Arison and brought her away from the group, offering polite apologies, "Arison, I must make a journey. One of great importance to myself, to young Cinamon and, I believe, to the future of our Kingdom."

Arison pawed the ground, "You cannot travel alone. Wherever it is you must go, I will send a guard to protect you."

Eera shook his head and flicked his tail, "I would visit the sorceress, Mueren, in Pyrone's Tower. She is a recluse of some years. I cannot greet her flanked by swordsmen. I assisted her, once, we were friends. I hope to beg a boon, so I must go only with gifts."

Arison flexed her legs and stood proudly, "Then I shall be your guard. I have lost no tournament in my lifetime, and I am female—therefore more welcoming for a human female. I shall bear your gifts, also."

Eera nodded and embraced her powerful upper body. She patted his furred back playfully, "I am sure you have a few more years in you yet, old wise Eera. I intend to see you live them."

Eera smiled, "Ah, but to be young again...the haste and foolishness would be a small price to pay for that. We leave soon; I will gather potions from the village as our tribute. We will be far away by nightfall," he looked at the sky as he spoke, seeing the sun just past its peak.

Arison, having little of the knowledge Eera learned and passed on to those so inclined, simply nodded, "I will inform the Herd and be waiting for your return."

They parted for now. Arison watched Eera trot towards the milling village. *'And what boon do you wish, Eera? For the good of the Kingdom, you say, and I believe. Yet what can a Drou offer us in false magic?'*

Arison shook her head and cantered away. Skeptical she may be; Drou was the word for witch used by those who did not believe in magic. But Eera was wise and knew more of the world in all its forms than any other Arison had known. She kicked up a clump of dirt as she sped up and galloped towards the cluster of wooden Shaa huts hidden between crops of trees—used for storage and shelter from the rain—to fetch her weapon, armour and all she would need for the journey.

Eera chuckled to himself as he trotted towards the magic shop he knew Mueren once used, before she left the village. *'The sorceress will make a believer out of young Arison.'* he swished his tail and waved to the villagers he passed.

Eera had bred no young in his long life. He had spent his Palace days engaged in study and teaching, and had now passed the years where he wished for carnal pleasure. His banishment happened not long after Cinderella ascended to Queen, she saw no use for a Centaur Master and had cast him out, taking his Links—one forged for each step of knowledge he had taken. He had kept to his profession, teaching those of the Centaur who wished for knowledge, and though Arison had been a warrior from birth, he looked upon her kindly. He would have wished for no other to protect him, and keep him in good company, as he traveled.

The shopkeeper looked up as Eera entered and smiled, "Eera. Good to see you, what can I do?"

Eera trotted over, his hoofs clattering on the stone, "Basha. I have need of supplies—any you can spare—as a gift to an old friend."

Basha nodded and moved around the shop. He was one of the many allies Eera and the Centaurs had made in the village. Eera himself had carried the midwife to the birth of Basha's daughter, without his help both the wife and the daughter would surely have died. Basha vowed debt to Eera for this, and now hummed softly to himself, as he was finally able to fulfill it.

"How is your daughter Basha?" Eera enquired.

"Well, sir," Basha replied, according the title 'sir' though Eera was no knight, nor any longer a Master, "She grows well and happy."

"This is indeed good news. When I return, I invite you and your family to visit with the Centaurs."

"I thank ye sir, we'll be happy to dine with ye," he dropped a bundle of vials and bottles onto the counter, "I can spare ye some potions an' herbs," he brought out a cloth bag from underneath and began to fill it, "I just got some charms in too; who does your witch pray too?"

"Pyrone. Though I have no wish to bankrupt you, Basha."

"Aye, but business is good nowadays. And I've not forgot I owe you me wife and me daughter," Basha replied, retrieving a silver charm from under the counter, "'Ere, the charm of Pyrone," he handed it to Eera.

The charm was small, drowning in Eera's palm. It was made of silver, with two triangles placed together, one facing straight, the other turning at an angle from the corner of the first.

Eera took it graciously, "You are kind, Basha. This charm will protect me on my journey."

"A journey, you say?" Basha asked, surprised.

"I must travel to visit my friend. I intended to do so with but the one guard—our warrior, Arison. With this charm, I now have two."

"Arison, eh? To see a witch?" Basha shook his head in amusement, "The lady still backs away whenever I show my mug to her."

Eera smiled, "Skeptical she is, but cautious also? Arison is indeed more intelligent than I imagined."

Basha grinned, "Well, here you go, sir. These should make your witch happy to see you." he came around the counter and handed the bag to Eera who laced it around his waist to balance comfortably over his back.

"Thank you, Basha," Eera made a small bow, ducking his head and bending his front legs, "I must take my leave. May the Gods bless you and all you love."

"Might they keep the thieves from you on your road," Basha replied, "Safe travels, old friend."

When Eera returned to Centaur Forest, he found Arison at the center of a large group. All of the Centaur had gathered to bid farewell to their favourite fighter, and the man many thought of as a second father, or grandfather, and all knew as a mentor and friend.

"He returns," Arison called as he drew near. She was splendid in her armor. A sword hung on her side, engraved with the insignia of the Centaurian warrior god—Throu. She bore a chestplate, dyed deep green, and a cloak of twilight fastened with a Centaur-shaped iron clasp. On her four legs were black leather shields; draped over her torso was a cloth of indigo, speckled with white. Wrapped around her tail were gold and silver bands. The silver, one for each tournament battle she had won. The gold, one for each real battle won, Arison was not only the greatest tournament fighter, she was also one of the Centaur guards who watched at night for predators, each individual or group of them she downed would count as a victory. There was little left of her tail to see.

Arison looked a true warrior, and Eera felt both proud and humbled as he walked gracefully into the circle. Arison bowed—respect due to the leader and elder from a warrior. Eera touched his head and placed a hand over his heart—respect due to the warrior from a teacher.

Around them, the other Centaurs touched their breasts also and raised their tails in salute. One stepped forward, a brown female with strong features, to conduct the traditional blessings.

"Eera, Arison," Kanama bowed, "We bless you and your journey. May your task be easy and free from pain or sorrow. In the name of Sanachae, the Mother, go with love and return with peace," she clasped the wrists of each briefly, and returned to the circle.

"My friends," Eera returned, "May the Mother bless you and keep you well until our return. You shall never be far from our thoughts, and always in our hearts."

Arison now drew her sword from its scabbard with her right hand, and rested it over her left wrist, "In the name of Sanachae and Throu, I pledge my life and my blade. My ward shall remain unharmed so long as my heart shall beat."

Traditional blessings given, the circle broke and hurried to wish the two well. Only when everyone had embraced and uttered good-byes did Eera and Arison step away. With a wave and salute, they trotted away from their kin towards the deep forest and the Tower of Pyrone.

They spoke little until nightfall, the first rush of enthusiasm spurring them on to cover as much ground as they could. Eventually, though, the twilight began to dim the forest trail and Arison cut away the grass and shrubs to create a makeshift campsite.

Used to sleeping on the ground and under stars or leaves, neither had brought bedding, so the remaining gloomy light was used to collect the slow-burning wood and grass that would keep the fire glowing until morning.

Sitting on her haunches, comfortably close to the heat, roasting a flayed animal on a wooden spit, Arison felt at ease and shyly asked Eera to tell a story.

Eera laughed, "Well, well, young one. I had believed such things far below you."

"Truth is, Master, I used to make the little ones retell the stories you told them," Arison smiled wryly, "I was to be a warrior—interest in fairytales was no help to the path of my sword."

"I see," Eera sounded amused, though his fire-lit face showed nothing, "But your God—Throu—my God of Learning, Weisen, the Mother and all others. Are not these, in a way, fairytales? Myths without proof, names without faces. Concepts, without substance."

Arison had almost dropped the spit. As she spoke, she held onto it tightly, "Our Gods are what hold us; they keep us safe and hear our prayers. Weisen may allow such talk, but Throu would surely throw me to his three-headed dragon, were I to speak so."

"'Tis true, young one," Eera sighed, "Weisen's nature encourages questions as so few Gods do. But I do not mean to say there are no Gods. It seems there are too many—or one, with a thousand names and species. However, I forget you are not a student, a story you asked for—not a tree of thought."

"Yes, Master. My warrior brain would surely collapse, were I to consider such weighty things as you," Arison kept her face hidden in the guise of splitting the animal in two. Her voice was bitter, though, and as she passed the crisped meat to Eera, her eyes danced spitefully.

Eera had no words to calm away insecurity, he so he simply began his story.

'Long ago, the world was black. There was no light, no life, only solid, unchanging matter. Mother Sanachae saw this and mourned the void, which went unfilled.

'She cried tears which fell onto the world and created the seas. Still there was no life.

'She called to her Flamius, God of Light, and bid him strike flint for fire and set the fire to roll around the black orb. However, there was still no life.

'Mother called to her Icksnat; God of Metals, Zinon; God of food, Python; God of Water and Footarn; God of Animals. She bade them create metal, food, rain, currents, all the animals and more. Still there was no true life, no sentient beings to advance and create.

Mother called to her Mushin and Quaar — the brother Gods of Free Will and Evolution. But Mushin and Quaar were bitter rivals. Each created a species, similar but different, and neither would compromise.

Soon, Mother tired of their quarrels and ordered a decision — on pain of death. Quaar bowed his head and submitted. Mushin's race was to be created.

Mushin formed a creature, covered all over in hair, with two arms, four legs and a tail. He placed them on the world and called them 'Centaur'.

But Quaar, while Mother and Mushin were distracted, had modified his species and formed his own race. Two arms, two legs, sparse hair. He instilled in them the will and determination to master and control each other and everything else. These he called 'Human', and he set one above all others and called him King. Then he told King to divide the rest into rich and poor.

When the Humans were discovered, Mother and Mushin were incensed. They violently destroyed Quaar, scattering him in a million pieces all across the sky to shine down at night and remind the Centaur that they were created in love and equality.'

Arison applauded, the near-argument forgotten for a moment, "That was fabulous! None of your children could ever tell a story like that."

Eera smiled.

Arison suddenly looked sad, "Maybe I truly am inferior. I have no such tales, nor such thoughts as you do. I am more Human than Centaur. I know only how to kill," She flicked her tail around and looked disgustedly at the bands which covered it. She stood and kicked the bare bones of the animal away, then sat once more.

"You may lack tales of Gods and heroes," Eera said, softly, barely audible over the crackling fire, "But you are one of those heroes. The takes will one day be about you, and they could neither be created nor passed on without protection by great fighters such as you," Arison tried to speak, but Eera raised a silencing hand and continued, "You can be both warrior and wise, my friend. Now you know the sword, you long for the knowledge of deeper things. So now, maybe, is the time to learn of them."

"If you would teach, I would learn," Arison whispered.

Eera reached over the fire and rested a hand on her shoulder, "I would teach, Arison. I think you will learn well. Yet I tire, and tomorrow is soon enough."

Arison smiled, "Yes. Old men must sleep. I will sit for a while. I will not disturb. We move on when the sun drapes through the trees."

"Sleep well, friend," Eera said, sleepily. He moved a little away from the fire and pawed the ground into shape. Then he folded downwards and his head dropped into sleep.

"Goodnight, old man," Arison said, too quiet for anyone but herself to hear. She looked now into the fire and tried to think deep thoughts.

Chapter 4

As Osmon and Royston slept, they heard no sound. But between the door and the jam, there slipped a thin strip of iron. It moved upwards, nudging the latch from its home. The door opened quietly and Cinderella stepped in, carefully replacing the strip back into her purse.

For a moment, she studied the sleeping figures in the bed before her, intertwined in each other's arms and oblivious to her presence. Then she daintily kicked the door shut.

It slammed home, jerking the lovers from slumber. Osmon shot out of the bed, scrabbling for clothes.

"You forget, Osmon, I have seen it before," Cinderella said, icily.

Royston sat up, covered by the sheet, and looked levelly at Cinderella, "Queen Cinderella. An honour. Excuse me if I do not rise, my clothes seem to be somewhat elsewhere," He said with mild politeness.

Cinderella shot him a deathly cold look, "Osmon, give him some clothes."

Osmon, one leg half in his breeches, snatched Royston's clothes from the floor and tossed them to him, "Cinderella," he gasped, struggling with his belt, "How did you…? We were just…"

"You forget my spies, Osmon. I know every occasion that you have met with this…person. Pray tell, husband, you were just what? Just…chatting over a tumbler of ale and a game of cards when you accidentally dropped your clothes and fell into bed?"

Osmon opened and closed his mouth, dumbfounded.

"So why now?" Royston asked, coolly.

Cinderella ignored him, "I warned you, Osmon."

Osmon pulled on his tunic, leaving it unfastened. He drew back his shoulders and stood as tall as he could, "So what now, *Cinders*?" he exaggerated the hated nickname, "You tell the world? Try to stave off the embarrassment by making yourself a martyr? Go ahead."

Cinderella screwed her sharp features into a frown, "And when they come after you, with flame and pitchfork?"

Osmon spread his hands, "Then I leave. Royston and I will leave for one of the Islands and make a new life. I care for your heavy, shrewish hand no more."

Cinderella allowed herself an impish smile, "And be known as the King who abandoned his family in their need, leaving a young child to fend alone?"

Osmon took a step back, "Time of need? You and Cinamon have no need. I do not wish to abandon my son, he may come if he wishes, or visit later. As for teaching him, what he knows from me is all I have to teach, anything more is to be learned from others. Need? What needs could a Queen, owner of all the lands and riches, ever have?"

The Queen rested a hand on her stomach, "Not me, husband. Nor Cinamon. There will be another who needs guidance from you."

"No..." Osmon stepped back again. This time the backs of his knees thudded against the bed and he sat, heavily.

"Yes. I am with child, Osmon. My moon blood has been absent two months. The doctor saw me this morning and confirmed my fears."

Royston leaned against the wall, pale. He raised his face to Osmon, "Osmon...you and her...still," he spat the sentence.

"Yes," Cinderella said with a polite smile, "Once a month I would bring him to my bed for those five minutes of dreary boredom. Once a month, or I could legally cast him aside as no true man and take the Kingdom from him. I see now that would have been the best course, but no matter," she beckoned to Osmon with a long, manicured finger, "Come. Now is the time to grow into a man. I will banish him, if the temptation is too much for you."

"No!" Osmon leapt to his feet, "After these 10 years I can take it no more! I never loved you, nor you me! I will tell my people the truth and give them the privilege to decide whether it negates my worth as King. Either way, oh Queen, we are no more."

Cinderella laughed and clapped her hands, "Oh, Osmon. For years, I prayed you would grow a backbone. Now I see I should have asked for a brain to go with it! Your people will run you over the water."

"Maybe," Osmon stepped to Royston, rested shaking hands on his shoulders and looked into deep, brown eyes, "But if my man will still say yes, I care not which side of the water I live on."

Royston nodded, "I still say yes. Oh, Osmon, I would follow you anywhere if it meant we could be together for real."

Cinderella ground her teeth, "Very well!" she turned on her heel and threw open the door, "Let it be known," she shrilled, "Tomorrow at noon there will be a King's audience in Market Square. All must attend!"

Outside, a hundred villagers scurried to spread the word, discussing in hushed voices what may be wrong.

"There, husband. I hope you are well prepared," Cinderella told him over her shoulder, "I suggest you pack tonight and bring your fastest horse tomorrow," she pulled the door shut with a crash as she stalked out.

Osmon fell onto the bed with an agonised groan, "Tomorrow at noon…"

Royston perched by him and pulled him close, "It has been many years since your Grandfather. Dolls and Tabbies are barely blinked at, now."

"Yes, but I am a coward, Royston. I fear I have little wish to test the faith, fickleness and prejudice of my people."

"If you still fear too much, I will not stand in your way tomorrow. If you announce, instead, the coming of a new heir, rather than the test of love, I will not contradict you. I will be in the crowd; it is up to you what you choose."

Osmon looked at him, "And if I balk, if I say the easy words and choose the emptier of two hard lives?"

Royston looked away and stood, "Then I leave tomorrow, for some Island where I will be welcome. I would give my life to be with you, but I cannot make your choice or toughen your spine," Royston kissed him quickly and hastened to the door, "You will see me at the front of the crowd as you stand by your Queen," he opened the door,

"Whichever you choose, Osmon, know I will love you. In this life and every other," he closed the door quietly and left.

Arella opened her door to the knocking and saw a bedraggled Osmon, shivering from the rain.

"Oh my, Osmon, hurry inside!" she fussed around, bringing a towel and hanging his tunic over the fire, "What were you doing out in the rain, young one?" she asked as she set a pot to boil over the hearth.

Arella was small and fragile-looking, as she always had been in Osmon's memory. Now, though, she was bent forwards a little with age, and lines cut her pruned face into the disturbing pattern of a hard life.

Osmon regretted, now, his lack of visits. As a boy, she told him stories, sang songs, bathed his wounds and wiped his tears. Suddenly Osmon wished he had done more than shut his old Nanny away into a house with a nice monthly allowance. '*On my soul,*' he vowed. '*I will do more for this woman. Wherever I finish up, I will see her remaining days pass well.*'

"I need help, Nanny," he hung his head and watched the water drip onto the bare wood floor.

"Yes, I had guessed this. What can I do to help you?" Arella sat across from him, noting with pride his proud stance and intelligent eyes.

"It's Royston…and Cinderella. I wish to tell the world of my love for Royston. Yet I fear, still. I fear more now than before. Cinderella is with child."

Arella thought as she poured hot water into a cup and added a touch of wine, "Drink," she told him, "It will stave off sickness."

Osmon sipped gratefully, "She's always known of Royston and only now has decided to reveal this. There is to be a meeting tomorrow where she has dared me to confess my true desires. Am I to depart, or leave my son and my unborn child, risk my own people running me from my own Kingdom? Nether path is easy, but one is easier to say than the other."

"Child," Arella began sympathetically, "You never had the courage of your ancestors. Always, you ran from a fight and bowed to the will of others. I suggested you marry Cinderella, when you came to me for help, hoping it would spur you into admission. I see now it was foolish, but here is your opportunity to do this thing anyway. I haven't answers for you, Os, you can only do what you can. If you're brave and confess your love for dear Royston, then you'll have him whichever city you're in. If not then, for the sake of your children, you'll have to stop this affair and be a father."

"Royston will leave, to live on one of the Islands, if I choose Cinderella. I understand why. He is braver than I have ever been. Why is it his love makes him stronger, but mine only makes me weak?"

Arella shook her head, sadly, "I don't know, Os. All I know are my stories and ballads, where love and honesty win through always. But this is life, and this I'm unfamiliar with. Only you can decide if your love is stronger than your cowardice," she patted the hand that trembled on his knee, "When you stand tomorrow to make an announcement, you'll know what you have chosen as you say it. I can't help you this time, Os."

He sighed and put down his mug, "I suppose I know this. Only I can choose my own path. I have two destinies, laid out before me. I feel I will only know which I follow when I my speech tomorrow lays me upon its road. Nanny, I love Royston. I do, more than anything. Yet my cowardice…it is easier to announce the new child and try to forget—though both paths would be hard if I walk them," he stood and gathered his tunic, "Thank you, Nanny. I hope you will be there tomorrow, and I hope I can be brave enough."

Osmon buttoned his tunic and knelt before Arella, "You raised me well, Nanny. If I can live up to that, I will be happy. If not, then I will never be sorry enough. I never wish to let you down."

"Ah, son, you have never let me down," she promised, embracing him though her joints creaked with the effort, "Go now. Search yourself. Tomorrow brings hope for the future."

Osmon rose and exited into the dull gloom of the heavy rain.

Royston listened to the water slap his wall and rattle the shutters. Though a rich son, he lived in a wood house only a little more extravagant than that of a successful merchant. Rich, he might be, but extravagant showoff he was only occasionally.

His tears hit the floor as he puttered back and forth, slowly packing. In one corner, that which would journey with him wherever he should go tomorrow. In another, those things which he would have brought to him later. In a third, a pile to be given to the poorhouse, where the homeless and orphaned slept and begged food, clothes, or work.

'*Just in case.*' he was telling himself. '*Just in case the people aren't too pleased.*' He pretended not to consider the other possibility—if Osmon yellowed to the eyes of the crowd and forsook his faithful lover.

Finished, convincing himself that he was now prepared to happily transport over to the Palace—once Osmon introduced him and the people accepted. Prepared, though a little less, to take his things and transport himself and Osmon to the dock. Unprepared to take them to sea alone. Royston tried to read, tried to write, tried to sing and play his flute. Tried to sleep, tried not to think and tried to think about other things.

He fell into an uneasy sleep, somehow, after dawn, and awoke to the town clock's chime.

He listened, "Eleven already!" he leapt up, flattened his hair and shrugged as it stuck up. Flattened his clothes and shrugged as they wrinkled. He threw open the door and ran towards the market square to assume his place close to the stage, leaving the door open in his haste.

The square was packed and overflowing, Osmon saw from his litter. He shared it—one last time, he swore—with Cinderella and Cinamon—the former smiling sardonically, the latter crouching in a corner, sensing wrongness.

The clock chimed 12 times and the litter was set down behind the stage.

Together, Osmon and Cinderella walked up the steps, with Cinamon between them glancing worriedly around.

Osmon dared not look around until he stood still, at the top. As the applause from the villeins died out, the King saw Royston, just to the right of direct view. With shock, he noted the pale face, rumpled hair and creased outfit of his lover. The man's pain read clearly on his face.

'*What have I done to him?*' Osmon forced a smile, but the horror flickered momentarily across his eyes. He remembered a younger Royston, less hollow with stress and pain, less haunted, less carved with fear and sorrow. *'I have turned him into something else.'* Osmon realised. The crowd before him watched their King expectantly, unable to penetrate his thoughts.

Cinderella moved swiftly, knocking Cinamon into him. Osmon jerked his head as if surprised to find himself there, then he shook it a little and his eyes cleared.

"My people," had he been less practiced at public speaking, he may have halted, stuttered, paused to check the words before they marched out. Alas, all his life had been spent training or doing this, so without consideration or thought, he plowed on smoothly. What he said would only register once it was done being spoken.

"Me beloved people, I stand before you a humbled man. I hope I have not read you so wrong if I say you have loved me, since I was no more than a prince-in-arms. I know I say no lie when I say I have loved each one of you from the moment I knew you were here.

"My family can boast many great people throughout history. Brave and strong, in battle and leadership. I, however, was born without such iron strength.

"However, my friends, today I must finally show the strength I did not know was hiding in me.

"For I, my loyal citizens…am to father my second child by the fair Queen Cinderella."

A stunned silence. Osmon balked and gaped at the words now spoken. He searched the crowd for Royston; saw his head swimming away through the throng.

Then cheering, whistles and cries of happiness. Osmon realised Cinderella had smiled and confirmed the child she carried.

The blood fell from his face and the crowd seemed to push him into the ground. Osmon stumbled back to the litter; fell upon one of the new Centaurs.

The Centaur, a black-as-night, burly male, picked him up and placed him gently inside the curtain. On-stage, Cinderella was apologising for Osmon's behaviour—he was excited, the pleasure and celebration too much for him—she tinkled merrily with the crowd.

Osmon realised that the black Centaur had whispered in his ear. Before he could understand, though, Cinderella and Cinamon were climbing in to join him.

Osmon tucked it away for later, and tried to feign sleep as Cinderella gushed and the litter arose and lumbered back towards the palace.

Royston entered his house in tears, barely registering the now-closed door until he saw the empty room. Shaking his head, *'I am mistaken!'* he raced through the house.

He found nothing.

'I am lost.' he wailed inside. *'Ruined. My clothes, my food, my money…my love, my heart…oh, to lie down and die is my only wish.'* he lay on his bed and stared at the blank wall.

'But no!' he cried, leaping to his feet. 'I vowed to leave and live again, and so I shall! My things stolen? Well, and all the better to travel without encumbrance!" The seed of betrayal and hatred was planted already and it spurred him on. *'To the docks.'* he decided and picked up his heels towards the sea air and a job as a ship hand on the first vessel sailing out.

Chapter 5

Osmon hurriedly locked himself in his study. He wandered the shelves of books and scrolls, seeing nothing but the back of a head...bobbing away, breaking his heart.

Tears were not a thing Osmon shied from, but neither did he welcome them. After the initial fit of wailing, sobbing, tearing anguish, the eyes were dry, and empty.

'What have I done!' it was no question; he knew what he had done. *'How did this happen? I was ready to speak true! What traitor tongue spoke those words that end my life? She has won, Cinderella. I am broken.'*

He fell, exhausted, into sleep on a rickety old chair in a dusty corner. Blessedly he did not dream, but awoke hours later feeling the touch of darkness outside. On his lips was the phrase uttered by the Centaur who placed him so kindly into the litter.

"But what do the sounds mean?" he paced, hardly realizing his thoughts were aloud, "I was barely there, just noises, no words. What was I told?"

As he paced, faster and faster in agitation, the urgency grew. He must know! It was certain to be something of great importance. In his mind, the half-remembered syllables gained mythic proportions. They were a way out, amends, something to settle the inner fire. All knew the Centaur were wise, what did this one know? What did the black half-man say!

Finally breaking, ready to do anything, Osmon raced to the Centaur stables. Oblivious to anyone who saw him, wide-eyed and pale with blazing misery in his eyes, he burst inside.

"Centaur—black Centaur! This is your King," somehow, he felt ashamed to invoke such a royal demand and changed his tone, "I wish, please, to speak with he who helped me to my litter this afternoon."

Shuffling and mutterings in the barely-adequate torchlight. Then a Centaur stepped forwards. Sheer-black fur and skin glistened majestically as he trotted outside ahead of Osmon. Once there, he bowed.

Osmon felt himself bow also, surprised at such a show towards a lesser beast such as a Centaur is—or so he had been told by Cinderella for many years, "Centaur, give me your name," he spoke the King's demands again, as if compensating for the bow, confused that he felt almost humbled by the presence in front of him.

The Centaur pawed uncomfortably, "I cannot, my liege. A name is sacred to a Centaur, and none may know but the Herd."

Osmon waved it aside, "Very well. No-name, repeat to me the words you spoke in my ear today. I would find peace in them, if peace is to be found, and if you do not tell me...the Queen shall know of your bold insolence and she shall banish you surely as day banishes night."

Osmon cringed as he spoke and began to apologise, but the Centaur suppressed a frown and only flicked his tail in annoyance, he was an understanding sort and sensed the agitation of the King— plus he had seen the earlier events and knew of the King's pain. So he let it pass, "My liege, there is no peace in words alone. Only in following their path."

"Then repeat to me the path I must take," Osmon's voice had grown soft, again as if to compensate for his lordliness.

The Centaur gave a small shake of his hindquarters and bobbed his head, "I believe I offered you the likely name of the ship your man would board to cross the water."

Osmon reached up and grabbed the Centaur by the shoulders. The black figure flinched and pulled backwards with a stifled cry, "Sire, I beg your grace, but do not touch me."

Osmon dropped his hands to his side, finally cowed by the noble creature in front of him, too desperate for news of Royston to care, "Please, Centaur, accept my apologies. I am...in a strange mind tonight. I must know the ship's name."

"It is the Peregrine, sire, though I fear it has already departed with the last tide."

"No, no, no, no…" Osmon whispered, somehow wailing in that small voice. He almost saw his only chance slip away with his hope, "Please, I beg you, help me find him. I know not why I spoke those cursed words, but I know now if I have him back to me, I am a coward no longer."

The black Centaur bent close and whispered, "Go to Centaur Forest; see those banished by your Queen. Ask to speak with Master Eera—and describe he who sent you as Night-Sky. If there is still hope, Eera will find it."

"Thank you!" Osmon felt a sudden urge to hug the strange creature in front of him, but stopped before he did—remembering not only the aversion to touch, but finally once again own rank as well, "Whether I am given hope or not, you have helped me. Name any wish and I shall grant it."

Night-Sky bowed graciously, "If I may, I will save this wish. One of the Herd, perhaps I, perhaps another, may need it at some future time. When that time arrives I hope you will still honour us."

"Yes, as you will. Thank you again. You truly are a fine creature," Osmon politely showed him back into the enclosure before half-skipping back inside the castle and to his bedroom.

'There may be hope yet.' he dared a small smile as he lay. *'Peregrine, you carry my hearts true love. Keep him safe and treat him well for my arrival.'*

He slept well, if not soundly, exhaustion saw to that. Now the banging on the cabin door roused him, aching, from his bed.

"Royston! There y'are. The Cap'ns been lookin' for ye. We got workin' hours ago, mate."

Royston nodded groggily, "I apologise. I am unused to the hours and exertion. I promise it will not happen again."

"Aye, I believe ya. 'Ere—I got some scrubbin's for ya. Eat 'em and gerron deck—yer on sail cleanin' duty," Samson darted off after dumping a plate of food into Royston's hands. He was nimble, for a man his size. Standing six feet tall, he lost no girth for his height—though his hair seemed to have receded back into his skull leaving not so much as a shadow to give it away.

"Thank you, Samson," Royston called after him, though he was probably out of earshot by now.

The sailors and deckhands treated him well. They knew high-birth when they saw it, and any who might have resented him for such were put to rest by the Captain. Dane was a kindly old fellow with a bushy grey-white beard. He had forwarded Royston some of his pay to buy clothes more fitting to the work. Then, after instructing Samson to take care of him, had informed the ship that Royston was an aristocrat. Tired of the pretensions forced upon him, he had come to travel and work for a time. Of course, he said it in the coarser words Royston thought of as 'sailor-speak'.

Now, grateful for Samson, who had indeed cared for him these past 3 days, Royston wolfed down cold meat and potatoes as he brushed his hair and put on his mottled brown clothing and cap.

So attired, he headed speedily out of the door to the top deck and the—apparently—dirty sails.

Cinderella found Osmon moping as usual in his study. He seemed intent on whatever lay on the table before him, so when she touched his shoulder lightly he jumped up with a yelp of surprise.

"Cinderella!" he gasped, heart slamming against his ribs. He rolled up the papers he was poring over and slid them into a desk drawer.

"Plotting something, husband?" she asked in her silkiest voice, "You have barely shown your face to me these few days since…the announcement," she spoke tenderly but her eyes glinted with malice.

"Nothing you need concern your head with," Osmon cared little to conceal the frostiness in his voice, "Now tell me the real reason you invade my sanctum. I know you are not simply worried at my absence."

"True," she trailed her finger along the desk as she walked a full circle around it. She drew close to Osmon and put her lips by his ear, "I merely wondered how you were coping with the loss of your precious toy doll."

He gritted his teeth and stared ahead blankly, offering no reply. Her laugh grated like blunt knives in his head.

"My dear husband…" Cinderella pushed her breasts against his arm and slipped a leg around his front, kneading his crotch rhythmically. She caressed his face and smiled, "Ah, I see you are not dead where it counts. Like a true man, you respond to the touch of a woman," her knee was replaced by a probing hand.

Osmon flung it aside roughly and stepped back, "A man's rod may respond to many things. A man's heart and mind are not too easily fooled by a skillful hand."

"And yet so often both are cast aside when the ramrod lifts its head," she darted forward and squeezed the half-erect lump hard. Osmon gasped in the pleasure and pain of stimulation.

"Get your poison hand off me, evil harpy," he cried and wrenched her arm away.

She laughed her sharp laugh, "Very well, husband. It is a thing barely worth my time anyway. Just remember who owns that traitorous muscle."

Osmon turned away, flushed despite the hatred that welled up. *'Royston used to tease me so.'* he recalled, *'Though he was never so cruel — I don't think he could be if he wished to.'*

Cinderella came close again and Osmon stiffened, ready to throw her advances. Instead, she whispered from behind, "You are safe until our child is born. Wax your candle with thoughts of your doll until then. But one day you shall share my bed as a proper husband, as you chose.

"And think not of finding your mincing doll. I dare say he works as hard as a slave after all his belongings were stolen the day you betrayed him…and I dare say each callous that appears on his hand only deepens his hatred for you."

Without pausing, without thinking, Osmon whipped around. His hand, raised, caught the Queen a cracking blow to the side of her head. She dropped like a stone to the floor. Osmon almost apologised, almost begged forgiveness, but instead his eyes grew cold.

He stared down at the woman before him, suddenly seeing in her sprawling form the pleasant-but-poor girl she once was. But even as he recognised this, it vanished; replaced by the calculating bitch he had created himself.

"You stole all he had…you left him a beggar and a ship's hand," It began a question, but ended as a cold statement. He knew. The dancing glint in her eyes told him. The pleased smile and the lit-up face told him.

Finally, the laughter told him. Hammering at his soul like a smithy on metal. This was not the Queenly tinkle, nor the girlishly cruel giggle. This was the happy, insane, roaring laughter of a woman crazed by the power of her own intelligence.

Osmon grabbed her arm tightly and hauled the laughing heap to the door. He opened it and tossed her out bodily. As she hit the wall, he slammed the door. Yet still he could hear the laughter as she walked away.

When the noise was gone, when the echo of it faded from his mind, Osmon realised one fist was clenched while the other scratched at his face, as if to tear out the awful laughter. Blood oozed from deep scratches on his forehead, and from crescent shapes in his palm. Osmon barely noticed the sting that would later turn into a dull throb as his skin stiffened with drying blood. He would have relished it if he did.

All he could think was of Royston. Penniless and scrubbing some ship. Surrounded by dirty, coarse men who would resent his soft hands, beauty and birth.

But as he slid to the floor in a near-swoon, another image occurred. Of Royston, and the cracked, weather worn face of a young sailor. Alone in a cabin, and screwing with obvious pleasure as Royston cried out a name that was not Osmon.

With this thought agonizing in his head, Osmon let himself fade gladly into dark sleep on the cold stone of the Palace. The Palace where Royston should be, by his King's side.

Waking again, a short time later, Osmon rose unsteadily and wobbled to his desk. In the top drawer was a custom-made flask. He took a long nip and shook his head to clear it.

For a moment he stood, debating. Should he continue examining the scrolls he had hidden from his wife?

The last three days had been spent in study of the Centaur traditions, greetings and way of life.

He turned from his desk, deciding there was little more to be gleaned. He thought that maybe he understood the breed at least a little, could greet and make polite conversation with them. The Centaurs, however, were always a secretive race. Little was known other than the things any patient person could watch from a distance.

As for their possible reaction to Osmon—King and husband of the woman who banished them—this he tried not to imagine.

'*Just try.*' he told himself, changing into clothes less regal. He assumed that appearing in royal dress could help him none, and possibly even harm his chances. The scrolls had told of their equal society, none above another, with but a small number who grew into natural speakers and could tell of decisions made by the whole Herd, so he dressed in the clothes of a respectable citizen, but not a King. Blue long-sleeved shirt, threaded with black. Pale grey trousers and boots polished to a matte grey.

As he locked the study door behind him, a dim vision returned to haunt his weary brain. Royston and the sailor…Royston and the sailor…

Osmon hit the side of his head sharply, as if he could shake it out by force, earning a sidelong glance from a passing servant.

He smiled, amiably. She curtseyed, eyes down. He assumed she would enjoy telling the other Palace servants of his strange behaviours and scolded himself; '*Act like a sane man! No Centaur is likely to help a mad King. And a mad King can only finish up as a mad, overthrown prisoner.*'

Thus fortified, he ambled down the corridor, feigning relaxation and looking to all the world as if he was stepping out for a leisurely stroll. Inside he churned and wished for a God to pray to—if only to share the burden a little. He did the best he could. '*Please, Eera, help me. You are my one hope, and I need him. Help me.*'

He whistled jauntily as he waved to the guards at the gate and tried not to speed up until well out of sight.

Centaur Forest was only a short walk away. Today it took Osmon almost two hours to reach the grassy edge where—he judged—town traffic would be minimal. At every step and turn there seemed to be a villein, merchant, acquaintance darting to shake his hand and offer congratulations and prayers for the new baby.

Still, he walked stolidly on at the highest speed he could while remaining polite. Finally, he arrived and stepped onto the grass with a glance around. There was nobody in this corner to see him. Ahead, he saw Centaurs talking, chewing grass, and playing. Osmon took a deep breathe and started towards them, holding his head confidently in the air—though confident was far from what he felt.

Cinderella's laughter had died away before she reached her chamber-cum-study. She allowed the familiar, scornful fury to rise in her face until the door was bolted and she knew she was alone.

Her head throbbed and the pain flared sharply with every movement. She stood before her mirror and put her hand to the tender spot where Osmon had connected with his ring. The flesh was dented, and no doubt bruising, but not torn. Fortunately, the ring had been a plain gold band. For perhaps the first time, Cinderella was glad her husband lacked the showmanship to wear gem-encrusted jewelry.

Sighing at the bruise she was sure to have for a while, mentally etching into her subconscious instructions not to lie on it and to be careful when brushing her hair, Cinderella sat down on her soft bed. Later she might visit her physician for a pain remedy, now she felt strangely listless and troubled.

Bubbling in her mind was a memory. Her stepmother, catching her once stealing bread for her starving stomach. Danzae had screamed unintelligibly and smashed the nearby water jug over the young, slender cinder-girl's head.

Cinderella had drifted in various stages of dazed half-consciousness for a while. Feeling the sting, the drying blood in her matted hair, and the shards of pottery digging into her skin as she lay.

Nobody had come to help. Eventually, Cinderella had pulled herself to all fours and cleaned up the pieces, scrubbed away the blood. Only then, did she dare stumble to the water pump and then back to her kitchen with a sloshing bucket of cold water. She washed the wound and treated it with a little cheap wine—not enough to be noticeable (for such would surely earn her another injury), but enough so her eyes watered and she bit down on her own hand to still the cry of pain.

The Queen, now far removed from the scene of that crime—and many others, some worse, some the same—sank gently down onto the bed and tried to sleep the all-too familiar dizziness away.

'All I ever wanted was a happy family to love.' she remembered, giddily, before sinking into disturbed slumber.

One by one, the Centaurs broke off and turned to look at the figure striding towards them. From the side, one set off at a trot to intercept, subtly signaling the rest to stay where they were.

As she approached, the human figure came to a stop and waited. The rusty coloured Centaur slowed to a walk and halted a few yards away, waiting for the visitor to move first.

'The King.' she realised suddenly and held back a bitter smile.

Osmon tucked left hand under right, placed them on his chest and bowed deeply from the waist, "Noble Centaur," he spoke clearly, but with a slight tremor, "*I come to you an equal. I am Osmon, and wish your blessing and leave to speak with one of your Herd.*"

The red Centaur clasped her hands and bowed similarly, "You know the traditions well, Osmon. My blessing you have, for you earn it. I am Red-Huntress, to you. Who would you speak with, and why?"

Osmon let his hands fall behind his back and hold each other, "One of your Herd who calls himself Night-Sky gave me hope of palaver with Eera—Centaur Master. I would beg his advice and assistance in a matter that pains my heart and soul," He added the last words without thinking, the natural speaking talent that betrayed him earlier this time remembered the Centaur's value of heart and soul above all else.

"I am sorry, Osmon—for your pain. Also, I am sorry I cannot take you to Master Eera. He is away. Return in a few days and then I believe he will see you," Red-Huntress felt a stab of sympathy as the concrete-set face of Osmon fell with an almost audible thud. Before he could speak, she stepped closer and continued, "I hear rumours, Osmon, of a new child and a broken King. A lover betrayed and a coward who hides his pain badly. If you come for help with your lover, I believe I can help you more than Eera. He is a wise creature, but in many ways I am the wiser in these matters."

Osmon stared up at her. His eyes glistened and tried to spill tears as he spoke through the lump in his throat, "Red-Huntress, would you help me? I will give you anything—I swear."

"I will hear you, Osmon. If I can help I shall."

Osmon nodded and smiled, for the first time feeling a slight lift inside, "What is your wish?"

"After your tale, if I can be of help, I will offer you a bargain. Your lover for my wish. It is then up to you to accept or deny. Is this agreeable?

"Yes, Red-Huntress, this is quite acceptable. Where might we talk?"

Red-Huntress motioned for him to follow and he did. She nodded gently to her fellow Centaurs—watching warily—and they nodded back. She led Osmon into the same enclosed clearing Eera had used to speak with Cinamon, only a few days earlier. She sat and he sat opposite her.

When settled, he told the fast version of his courtship with Royston and marriage to Cinderella. Then, able to express himself freely for the first time, he told the story of events since Cinderella had woken he and Royston with a slam of a door.

When he had finished, it was dark and the rusty fur of Red-Huntress twinkled merrily in the moonlight coasting down beneath the canopy.

"I believe I can help. Return tomorrow at nightfall and I may have a way to bring you and your man together. I must talk with my Herd, first to gain their blessing before I can strike the promised bargain. Then to build a strategy."

Osmon rose, grimacing at the stiffness that had settled over him while he sat, "Thank you, Red-Huntress," he executed another bow. It was returned by the Centaur who left him to make his way back to the Palace while she trotted to her Herd and called a meeting.

Chapter 6

Arison stopped and pointed at the line rising faintly on the horizon, "The Tower?" she asked.

Eera squinted and shrugged, "You have younger eyes than I, but it must be the Tower for there is nothing else nearby."

"Will we make it today, then?"

"Tell me, young one, how many hours of light remain?"

The first thing Eera had taught his new pupil was gauging time by the sun and moon. Now, Arison studied the yellow orb for a minute, "I think, maybe, three until dark."

Eera looked up himself, "Good, you have learned well. Shall we walk until dusk, then press on to the Tower for arrival tomorrow morning?"

Arison looked doubtful, "I have little wish to spend another night at the mercy of every passing band of miscreants."

The two nights since they had left the denser forest close to their home, walking at a soft stroll, had been anything but restful. Twice, the two Centaurs had been set upon by bands of thieves.

The first—a large group, and vicious—had run after the loss of their leader and a few more injuries. The second, a smaller crew, had made haste with Arison's sword to their behinds after a quick tussle.

Neither Arison nor Eera was injured, none of their possessions stolen, but Arison was loathe to test their luck to breaking point.

Eera, however, shook his head, "There are no brigands in this area. No food grows, very few journey here—only those bearing supplies for the sorcerer ever travel this far. And any who bring trouble...well;

I have seen the punishment wrought on any who attack a being under the witch's protection. We are safe here; within sight of the Tower, none would dare harm us.

He set off walking again and Arison followed a moment later, "What option do I have but to believe you?" she told him, cynical as ever of magic.

Eera smiled, "I will be drawn into no more quarrels about magic—and its existence or lack thereof. I say the lady will show you the truth. You say you will uncover the sham behind any trick she attempts. Let us leave it there and see what the future brings," he held out his hand and Arison shook it in agreement.

"I still say it's a fraud!" she laughed and galloped away, leaving Eera playfully shaking his fist.

Arison stopped and waited for him to catch up, "Sorry, old one. I should not flaunt my youth and speed," she grinned.

Eera reared, front legs kicking high, "Let us see who has the youth!" he cried and took off, covering the ground with ease.

Arison fell in beside him, "What, this is the youthful speed you talk of?" she teased and let herself hit full speed.

Eera sped up a little, watching as Arison slackened bit-by-bit as her stamina began to run low.

She stopped and turned back, glistening with sweat and laughing breathlessly at Eera, now thundering towards her.

He skidded to a halt, hardly out of breath and smiled.

Arison gaped, "How…how do you run so far…" she panted, "and hardly breathe?"

Eera smiled wider, "Speed is commendable and good for a short burst. Stamina, however, must win over any lengthy race."

'Another lesson.' Arison realised. *'He finds teaching in everything.'* she nodded, breathing slower now, "Is it possible to have both speed and stamina?" she asked.

"Indeed I would recommend it," Eera said, "You are a great warrior, Arison, but you can be surpassed in any strenuous battle. Stamina will help you become greater—but not unbeatable. Remember that, never unbeatable."

Arison bowed her head to her teacher, "I will remember well, Master."

Eera patted her shoulder, "Come, I think we can make good distance before dusk. Tomorrow we will arrive early to visit my old friend.

'*And I pray she remembers me.*' he thought to himself. Doubts had plagued him throughout the journey. Would she remember? Would she help? Would she still be the dear friend he had once loved, or embittered with loneliness, as he feared?

These doubts he had kept silent, hesitant to show fear to his young student. '*Or to admit I am afraid, unsure, imperfect.*' he added, part of him scoffing at his foolishness even as another part welcomed it.

Arison stopped suddenly, looking warily around.

"What is it?" Eera asked quietly.

She pointed at the ground. Barely discernible on the dry, packed mud were paw prints.

"A wolf?" Eera guessed. Tracking was a subject for hunters and fighters, and so something of which he knew little.

Arison shook her head, "Maybe…but larger than any I have ever seen."

They stood for a moment, looking around them.

"There are tales…" Eera said, "Of an animal breed unlike any other. Born when Footarn became jealous of the human and Centaur rights bestowed upon them by the Mother—to rule over his animals."

"I think I know this tale," Arison thought hard, "Footarn combined wild dogs, dragons, bears, and giant cats to make a new breed of animals—meant to terrorise the two favoured species."

Eera nodded, "Yes. Generations and battles, so says the legend, eventually killed all but one—though at great expense of life. Perhaps…we should continue travelling until within reach of the Tower."

Arison nodded, "These animals…I recall now a description. Large and yellow as a golden sun, fire dances in a circle around their faces. They have deadly sharp teeth and a deafening roar. Yes, I think we would be well to journey on until we arrive. But I also think it worth waking your Drou when we do, rather than dying within feet of our destination.

"I will not risk her distemper. The Tower, if I know her, has a protected perimeter around it. Scoff, if you will, but I believe we will be safe once in it's shadow."

"All the same-" Arison began to argue.

"No," Eera told her, sternly, "I will sleep well outside its walls and I will not chance disfavour by forcing an old lady from her bed."

Arison stilled her tongue. *'If she is so powerful, can she not already see us? Can she not halt or pause fatigue?'* she thought to herself, knowing she was being childish but for the moment, uncaring.

Eera was watching her as if he read her thoughts, so she changed them and nodded submission, "Very well—I trust you will not complain if I choose to sit guard tonight."

Eera shook his head, knowing this was the best he could hope for, "If it is your wish. Shall we walk?"

Arson nodded and plodded along in sullen silence.

Cinamon trundled heavily into his room and slung his small bag of school-things into the far corner.

His maid, (Cinamon refused to call her Nanny) appeared in the doorway opposite his bed—from the rolled up sleeves and rag in one hand, the boy deduced she had been cleaning.

"Oh, Master Cinamon where've ya bin! I was worried blind, so I was—what yer mother'd say I don't know! Out at all hours..." she enveloped him in a bosomy embrace, "Are ye well, Master Cinamon?" she loosed him and dabbed at her brow, leaving a dusty smear.

"I went for a walk," he told her, sitting down on his rocking chair.

"For so long? School put out hours ago!"

"I felt like a walk," he repeated, stubbornly.

Vanesi took the hint and tucked her rag into a pocket of the dirty apron she always wore. She disappeared into the next room and brought out a bucket of dirty water, "Well, so long as you're well..." she eyed him.

Cinamon gave her a shiny smile, "I'm fine."

"Okay Master Cinamon. Don't stay up too late, y'hear?"

He rolled his eyes but nodded amiably, knowing she had his best interests at heart. Vanesi curtseyed clumsily, slopping water over the floor, and hurried out shutting the heavy oak door behind her.

Cinamon rose and slid the bolt home. Then he sat back on his chair and rocked gently.

It soothed him, since he was a baby the smooth motion had calmed and softened him. He sat in it most nights, scribbling homework on yellow paper with an inkwell by his side. Or reading a book, losing himself in tales of pirates, sailors and sea. Or, like now, rehashing the events of the day.

He was too young, yet, to understand the compulsive reliving of events. Too young, also, to hate himself or others—though that was fast approaching. He simply accepted that he would go over things, invent new endings, or simply trouble himself with those things already past.

Today was a day he almost felt the dark, bubbling hatred that may one day cripple him from within. For today had been a very bad day.

There was to be a school dance—an event done numerous times every year at the slightest excuse. This one was to celebrate the coming of a new Royal child.

In his own way, the nine-year-old boy knew and understood he was already jealous of the new child. He knew he would be expected to fawn and gush, all the while being ignored in favour of the new delivery. He had no memory of his parents taking the time to play and teach him; only Vanesi had ever done that. Rocked him to sleep, wiped his tears and sympathised over cuts and grazes. In fact, he knew his parents very little, and in some corner of his heart he would resent them for not being around, and he would resent his new sibling for taking the spotlight in any family moments soon to come.

So from the moment the dance was announced, it was a bad day. Always people expected him to be the polite and slightly dullish young Prince. At school events, he was forced to greet parents and smile angelically. And now, a dance in celebration of a forthcoming addition to his family? He dreaded it from the very start.

Still, best to show a brave and handsome face. Even at nine, he knew he should enter properly, in Royal dress with a shimmering partner on his arm.

So he decided to find a partner as fast as he could, before all the girls who would be acceptable were taken. Also, so he could then forget about the dance for the next month or two—until it actually happened.

He thought little of it when he was turned down each time. He knew, of course, that their polite excuses were just that—excuses. That, Cinamon was not used to—though only because he made no habit of asking girls to dances. Still, it hurt only for a second and once the blush faded he shrugged idly and forgot about it.

The girls themselves, however, were not quite so forgiving or easygoing. Within two hours, everybody knew. He could see them. He could hear them. Snickering behind their hands, halting conversations as he drew near. The bolder ones would shout a comment at his back, and already have ducked out of view by the time he turned.

'*You're not paranoid if they really do hate you.*' he realized, now. Then directly on its heels, '*And they do hate me...just for being born here.*'

"I don't have a single friend," he told the wall, which was moving up and down as he rocked more vigorously, "They only put up with me to my face because the Queen'll chop their head off if they don't."

This new realisation sent a jolt through him, forcing his spine to straighten. Like a lightning bolt, another thought came.

'*Well maybe I can hate them too!*'

Another;

'*I can hate them too!*'

And another;

'*But no, they know nothing, know no better, they are pawns and I am a Prince...*'

Suddenly exhausted, the brain fever faded, leaving only a bright imprint in Cinamon's mind to show the thoughts had been there at all. Cinamon shook his head and chuckled to himself. The sharp hatred had disturbed him, but the memory was already beginning to fade into a feeling of slight foolishness.

Slightly bewildered, Cinamon yawed widely. He cast a cursory glance at the school parchments lying in the corner, shrugged, and decided to leave them until the weekend.

Yawning again, noisily, he blearily stumbled to his closet, changed clumsily into an oversized nightshirt and dropped into bed.

By the time he had drifted into sleep, the thunderous new thoughts were forgotten. Stored away, accessible, growing. But, for now, forgotten.

Arison watched the sun rise slowly over the sea. She shivered and moved faster, now cantering around in a wide circle to keep her warm. She guessed they were no more than three hours from the Tower, at their set speed of frustratingly slow—which now loomed somewhat ominously in her view.

Soon, Eera stirred, grumbling at the aches the cold stirred in his bones. They sat close together, eating the meat saved from the animals Arison had been hunting.

When the sun rose high enough to cast a shadow, Eera rose, stretched and promptly sat down again with a thump.

"Eera, are you injured?" Arison was already rooting for the soothing balm the Centaurs used for injuries, a solution taken from the healing tears of the Phoenix.

"No, Arison. I fear I simply grow old. Sleeping out in the cold like this…is not good for a Centaur my age."

Arison looked at him, worried, "Where does it hurt? Perhaps the balm will help. Will the old Drou be able to help you? Can you make the return journey?"

Eera smiled painfully, "It hurts in my bones; the balm cannot help the spread of age. My old friend may be able to help. If so, the journey will be easier—if not I may ask for an even slower pace and longer rests. But I will make it."

Arison nodded, "Of course. You should rest now, for a while. The sun will warm us shortly."

He shook his head, rose and flexed each joint gingerly then with more confidence. He forced the pained look from his face and nodded, "So, I improve already. Let us walk—the stiffness will fade."

Arison walked beside him, keeping a slow pace, "I think once we return it is time you took a Shaa."

Eera bowed his head in weary submission. The Shaa were the huts the Centaur built in their forest. Some were used for storage of weaponry, food and other things; some were kept for the old or sickly to sleep. Mostly the Centaurs slept out in the field under the stars, but when illness or old age showed itself in one of them, they would be given a Shaa to recover, or live, in.

"Perhaps," Eera said now, "I shall miss the field, but a roof to keep out the wind, a fire to warm the room…these I would like to have," he sighed heavily, his whole body seeming to droop, "It is a sad thing, to admit infirmity."

"I think you have many more years, Eera. Your mind is as sharp as in your youth, but the body is a fragile thing. If taking care of it means acknowledging age, then I feel it is a good compromise. The Herd—

and I—are not ready to find you frozen in the field one cold morning."

"I am no more ready than you," Eera smiled, "I will take a Shaa—the Herd will allow me, I know this. And now, let us make good pace to the Tower and hope we find our lady in a pleasant mood."

"How did you know her, Master? And why do you not use her name—she is human, after all."

Eera bobbed his head, "She us human, yet I consider her one of the Herd. Presumptuous, perhaps, but this is what she means to me. As for how we met…" he smiled at memory.

"I was a youngster then, a little younger than you, Arison. I was on errand for my human Master, my teacher, Salzark. The lesson was to be magic, and I was for the magic shop with a list. It was owned, then, by a surly fellow. A paranoid man, though he knew more of magic than some sorcerers did, he thought people laughed at him for selling magic supplies when he could do no magic himself. Such things make men unhappy.

"I hurried through my list and went at speed through the door—trying to outrun his sullen stare—and I crashed into the lady we now journey to see. In apology, I bought her a meal and a drink. We became friends, and I often enjoyed helping her when she had a special project.

"Our Queen, you know, was one of those. Tell no-one, Arison, what I tell you now."

Arison held one hand to his mouth and the other to his heart—to his breed this said 'I pledge my heart I will tell no soul.' Eera smiled.

"Cinderella was a scullery slave. She slept in the cinders from the fire. She was a slave to her stepmother and stepsisters after her father died. They treated her…rather as she herself now treats our breed, though with much more violence and force. Men could sleep with her for a copper or two—friends of the family. She was beaten at any provocation—real or imaginary—forced to abortion…I know not how many times. I find it a miracle she remained fertile.

"The sorceress did good deeds for people like her, people who needed help. She was a caring person who wished no harm for anyone and gave poor souls a better life.

"Cinderella, she told me, was the worst, the most lowly and badly-treated, person she had ever been able to help, and only something big would make amends.

"The legend is changed, now, by the Queen herself. But this is what truly happened.

"It was the day of Prince Osmon's 20th birthday ball. The lady took herself down to near-death by meditating close to the house, and then she sent her apparition to Cinderella. She gave her a gown, fur shoes and a golden carriage—which I pulled to the Palace myself. She was ordered to return by midnight—when the clothing and gown would revert, and I would take the carriage away. I realised only afterwards that part of the plan was that Cinderella would leave in a hurry.

"The girl enchanted the Prince, and missed the deadline as the sorceress planned. She used her magic to remove a shoe and keep it as fur, though the rest had reverted, and she placed it in the Prince's path.

"The rest you know. Osmon went to every house, made every maiden try the shoe. Cinderella forced herself into his eyeline when he reached her Stepmother's house, and away she was whisked to marry the Prince."

Arison marvelled, "Your lady sounds an incredible one."

Eera nodded, "Yes. I do not try to read minds, but I believe my banishment and the lady's gift of this far-off Tower were part of Cinderella's purge of her past. Even the few good memories would serve only to remind her of the bad, so she purged those also."

"And now you hope she will do one more good deed for you, her old friend."

"Yes. Cinamon has magic in him; I believe it may be for the good of the Kingdom for him to have the ability to use it."

"And if she refuses?"

"I do not know," Eera admitted, "My knowledge is limited; the boy needs a true teacher. I feel that without his magic, the Kingdom may be in danger. I know not where from, but I believe it may be dire."

"What if he learns too slowly for this thing he is needed for?"

Eera smiled softly, "I believe the Gods will give him the speed to learn, if it is needed."

They walked on in silence, watching the Tower grow larger with each step.

When they reached its shadow, the sun was warm and Eera developed a slight sheen upon his skin—though this was mostly from nerves. *'Please, Great Mother.'* he prayed. *'Let her remember me and fondly. And let her wish to do good, ever-present those years ago, remain for this last deed, long and hard though it may be.'*

He steeled himself, accepted an embrace of confidence from Arison, and knocked on the stout door of the Tower.

Chapter 7

Mueren was drinking mulled wine and reading a book of verse when she heard the knocking.

She rose and cocked her head. *'Did I order and forget?'* She looked at her owl, who stared back placidly, and set her book to one side.

She leaned out of her window at the top of the Tower and called down, "Who knocks?"

Two Centaurs stepped back and looked up, "M'lady," said one—older, with frosted grey hair and fur. He was paler, and the lines of age on his face had deepened, but his face was still one she knew.

"Eera!" she cried, "By the Gods—stay, I am on my way down."

The Centaurs waited patiently. *'She remembers me—and fondly, it seems.'* Eera let one of his worries slip away.

Arison stood respectfully behind him as the door opened to reveal a grey-white haired woman, her face made young by a beaming smile.

"Eera," she said, holding out her arms. He stepped forward and they embraced with the gentleness of those who know the pain of old age.

"This is Arison," he said, "The greatest warrior of my Herd."

Arison stepped forward and executed a clasp-handed bow, "It is an honour, m'lady. Eera speaks highly of you."

She smiled and bowed in return, "It is a pleasure, Arison. I thank you for the gift of your name, I will keep it safe."

The Centaur were protective of their true names, only giving them to their Herd and a very few privileged others. The name, they believe, is connected to the soul and therefore holds great power of good, evil and identity. For an outsider to be given it is a gift, and a message of friendship and trust.

Mueren realized, then that Eera would have kept her name a secret, "I offer you my name as a gift. I am Mueren."

Arison smiled, "I will keep it safe."

Mueren knew well the customs of the Centaur, having been instructed over many nights by Eera in the time of their friendship. To keep a name safe meant giving it to no other, and never cursing or allowing ill thoughts of a person to become connected to it. To do so endangered the soul and the mind.

All knowing, now, that they were three trusted friends, Mueren brought them into her ground-floor room. She took the softest pillows and cushions from her furniture and piled them on the floor to make seats for her guests

"I am sorry, Mueren, for not visiting before. The journey is a long one, and I dislike being so far from the Herd. Also, as I grow older…things become more perilous…," he trailed, a little embarrassed.

"I know, Eera," Mueren smiled, "I bear you no grudge, you were always my friend, absent or not. What brings you now? I know it must be important."

"It is," he shifted his weight and grimaced painfully, "First, old friend, if you have any potion that might relieve the aches of old-age I would be glad of some. I will pay you, of course, but it would make the return journey so much more bearable."

"Of course!" she rose and reached into the cupboard on the wall behind her, "I need no payment, please, accept it as a gift," she gave him a vial of faintly blue-tinged liquid, "Take a capful in the mornings—I will give you the recipe for when this runs out. It works well though, I use it myself."

Eera took the lid off the vial and saw it was hollow. He filled it and swallowed the liquid with a smile, "As always your potions taste delicious."

She smiled back, "Makes it easier to take, I find. If you would stay tonight, I have one spare bed, which I think you deserve Eera, and straw enough to make a bed for you, Arison. I know you are eager to return, but a night of good rest would no doubt help your bones."

"We will, thank you," Eera nodded at Arison, who remembered the gifts she carried on her back. She passed the bag to Eera, who handed it to Mueren, "We brought these, from the magic shop."

Mueren sorted through, flustered, "Well-I-this is too kind…" the sentence drifted as she discovered the amulet of Pyrone. It reflected the candlelight, making it look as mystical as it supposedly was, "These amulets are rare…expensive…Eera this is…too much."

Eera frowned a little, "The shopkeeper gave it as if it were a commonplace trinket. If it is valuable—in coin and magic—then I owe him a debt. And I beg you, keep it, for all you have done…and maybe, will do."

Mueren missed the hint. She was examining the silver triangles minutely, "This is…a very rare and valuable amulet. It is said to hold the power of Pyrone himself! But it has been lost for so long…most believe it only a myth.

"You see, each of the Human Gods created a handful of these each—a sigil which they put a portion of their power into—and secreted it away. They were to be found and used only in a time of great crisis. Now it is thousands of years later, and even the ones who believe the tale have lost all hope of finding any intact.

"Your magic man must not know its worth—he would not part with it if he did. I cannot keep it."

Eera refused to take it back, ignoring the outstretched hand the offered the amulet, "It has come to you for a reason. Keep it, I will tell the man and pay the debt in favours over time. But it has found its way to you, Mueren. This is where it must stay."

Mueren accepted this with resignation. Removing a brick from the floor, she wrapped the amulet in cloth and secreted it there, replacing the brick carefully so it was flush with the rest.

"Now, Eera," she said, smiling, "Tell me the reason you are here. It must be grave business for such a long journey—and such gifts!" She smiled at the new vials of magical tools and concoctions.

Eera nodded, "I believe the Kingdom may be in danger. I do not know where or who—I do not know for sure it is true. The Gods, though, they speak to me sometimes in dreams, and they sent me a message I have worried on for some months…something will happen, something big, something to change everything. We need something of our own to stop it, or the world we know may be no more."

Mueren bowed her head, "This is grave indeed. I fear I am too old to fight a powerful being—the amulet, which I'm sure you believe involved, would likely kill me if I attempted use it in a fight. But this you know, so I must assume you have a solution?"

"I believe so. The Royal son, Cinamon, has a great power inside him. I have sensed it since he was born. I believe he is our best hope, but I know little of magic and have even less inside me," he stopped and waited.

He did not wait long. Mueren threw back her head and laughed, "You want me to teach the boy! You really think Cinderella will allow him near me!"

Eera set his face, somewhat chagrined, "I think we have to convince her somehow."

Mueren's smile faded, "I apologise, old friend, I do not laugh at you. Only...you know as I do the Queen's loathing of reminders. She will never allow her son here. The excuses may be of school and duty, but the reason will be the same one that gave me my poisoned wilderness. She will not let him come here."

"Maybe she will," Eera recounted the recent events of the town meeting and concluded; "And now there are rumours we gleaned on our travel, the King is depressed and acts strangely, there is a betrayed lover taken to sea, a new child..."

Mueren considered, "If Cinamon wants to come, she may be distracted and persuaded—if these events work in our favour."

"Return with us," Arison spoke up suddenly, reminding the other two of her presence, "Return with us and help cause the distraction. When done, Cinamon can quickly break her down and you can both leave in haste."

"Return? To the Queen? My dear, even if the journey would not near kill me, I am unwanted. My presence close by can only hinder."

Arison rippled her strong back, "You are light, Mueren, and I strong. I will carry you. Then you can take a Shaa in our field—the Centaur will not refuse you once Eera and I explain. The Queen need not know of your presence until the end—if at all. And the boy will need a companion to ride with."

Eera watched them both. *'Arison hides her skepticism well.'* he marveled, "If Arison is willing, I see no reason why a Shaa may not be available to a friend of our Herd. You can remain hidden easily, only Cinamon visits us. We can plan as we journey and move to action once we arrive."

Mueren stared at the two of them for a moment. Then she broke into a resigned grin, "I seem to have no choice! So be it."

"Excellent," Eera smiled, "We start with sunrise tomorrow."

Cinderella tapped her fingernails on the table and sighed impatiently, "You," she shrilled, and a ragged young servant ran over and curtseyed, "Go fetch my son! And make it quick, I am trying to have a family meal!" the girl turned and ran out of the hall.

The dining hall was almost large enough to be a ballroom. A long table sat in the center, and at either end sat Cinderella and a gloomy Osmon. One place was laid but, as yet, empty in the center.

The hall was cold, a flickering fireplace in one corner gave no heat and the candle-chandeliers were too high up for their small flames to help. Around the walls were various banners—the Royal sigil over the main entrance, plus the icons some of the more wealthy lords and loyal knights. This was a new, but rapidly becoming common, decorative trend—introduced by Cinderella to the walls of all the rooms used for public gathering.

Today was a small event—a family lunch. The hall looked empty, each word or movement echoed off the walls and the carpet under the table did little to muffle sound. Cinderella's nails hit the tabletop and echoed repeatedly.

"Honestly," Osmon realised she was talking, "He was told yesterday! That boy will turn out a shame to us all, just you wait!"

"Your confidence inspires me to great depths, mother," Cinamon replied bitterly, crossing to his chair.

"Take that tone again, boy, and I will have it whipped out of you!"

The boy ignored her and sat down, "Father," he greeted amicably.

"How are you, son?" Osmon asked, painfully aware of two things. First, that Cinamon was sure to have heard plenty of embellished rumours over the past few days about Royston. Second, that it took him a moment to recall the boy's name—and a moment longer to recognise the boy he was supposed to know. This sent a pang of shame through him. '*My own son, I would hardly recognise him on the street!*' he thought. '*Oh to be more like my own father…*' but Cinamon interrupted.

"I am well. The school is to hold a dance to celebrate my unborn sibling; I am to be the guest of honour."

"Guest of honour indeed?" Cinderella tittered, "You might take that look from your face first. It seems you need instruction in the art of being a Prince."

"No, mother," Cinamon tried on a princely smile, "See, I am practiced well."

Cinderella relented as a steaming plate of food was placed in front of her, "As you say—though you might practice it a little more in the presence of your parents."

Cinamon bowed his head dutifully. '*What? My shrew of a mother and my coward of a father? Call it the art of false respect and leave it be.*' But he smiled still and began to eat as quickly as was polite.

"So how is school, son?" Osmon affected what he hoped was a fatherly smile, remembering how they used to thrill him when they came from his own attentive father, and received a cynical glance that hurt him.

"It's…school. Lessons, work, teachers, kids, nothing changes."

"What lesson is your favourite?" Osmon tried harder.

Cinamon shrugged, "Depends."

"Answer your father properly," Cinderella ordered between dainty mouthfuls.

"No, dear," Osmon replied, "The boy is simply acting like a boy."

Cinamon gave him a sidelong glance of surprise. '*He stood up to her? I never saw him do that!*'

Osmon caught the look, but pretended not to see. '*Gods, what my own son thinks of me. I am a shame as a King and a father.*'

Cinderella, meanwhile, was glaring at her husband, unused to being countered. '*What, the man found a knob of backbone?*'

The meal was quickly finished in silence. Cinamon waited patiently to be dismissed. '*Every six months…a family meal—it always ends the same. Why keep on? I'll never force my kids into these things!*'

Cinderella rose and nodded a stiff dismissal, then stalked out before the other two had a chance to rise.

Cinamon moved fast and almost made it out of the room.

"Cinamon," Osmon caught up, "May we talk?"

"Maybe later?" the boy tried, hopefully, and was dismayed to see his father's face drop.

"Okay, son. Whenever you have time," he failed to force a smile and turned away instead.

"Father," Cinamon caught his robe, "We could go for a walk—in the garden?"

Osmon's smile lit up his face. 'Probably the first time he's smiled properly in days.' Cinamon realized, leading him out of the nearby door.

The garden sat in the very center of the castle. A large circle, tended carefully by three gardeners, it bloomed always with never a weed in sight. In the very center rose a Bjortree—the symbol of the God of natural life, Bjornden.

Most notable families had a Bjortree in the center of their garden. It provided both a focal design feature, and good growth for the plants. Those who took Bjornden as their patron God would pray at their tree—he could provide plant and herb growth, sometimes sun or rain, and his leaves could assist with lung and chest afflictions.

Osmon himself had little to do with the Gods he had never believed in as anything more than a metaphor, but left others free to worship in his absence.

Cinamon, though still in the more innocent stages of youth—believed that perhaps the Gods were there to be used as an excuse and comfort, but whether they were real or not, they were all good. Later was time enough to find out different, and choose a patron—though he secretly preferred the Centaur Gods to his own.

They crossed now and sat on a wood bench underneath the Bjortree. Osmon fidgeted a little; uncomfortably aware that beside him sat a practical stranger. Cinamon waited with the patience of the young, and watched the flowers sway.

"Son…" Osmon began finally, "I saw you today for the first time in a number of days. As you know it is often weeks between contact, and then often an obligatory visit and no more," he paused to find words, "I saw you in the dining hall and…I realised you were a stranger to me—as I now know I am to you," he looked at Cinamon who gazed back calmly. Osmon sighed, "I never wished for our relationship to be so distant, so forced. I wish to apologise for the first nine years, and I would like to be allowed the opportunity to begin again. I would like the chance to be your father, as mine was to me."

Cinamon smiled—a little mischievously, Osmon thought, "Then tell me some things," he said, his voice expressionless.

"Ye-es?" Osmon braced himself.

"Are you really a doll—like everyone says? If so, are you really a coward or do I miss an important corner of the story?"

'He speaks as a man already.' Osmon realised. *'I am sure he thinks as one too...therefore the painful truth it must be.'*

"Yes, son. I am a doll. I am also a coward. I have spent 15 years afraid to admit the love I have for one man, and finally I drove him away with my weakness," he hung his head, "Not quite the father you wish for, am I? You need stay no longer, son."

Cinamon touched his father's hand gingerly, and then held it, "Father...why are you afraid? If you love this man, then surely...how could you let him go?"

Osmon squeezed the boy's hand, "I know not, son. If I was a coward ten years ago, I am a broken one now. You should not have to hear this, but son, your mother has broken me down. I finally had the perfect opportunity to tell the truth, and I shrunk away and hid behind her as I had from the moment we met."

Cinamon smiled, "Have no fear, father. My mother could cow even the mythical Dog Knight—all 17 feet of him!"

Osmon laughed, "No son," he tried to scold him but gave up and threw his free hand in the air, "You have the truth, what can be said?"

"Father," Cinamon asked, serious again, "Why do you not go to find him?"

Osmon glanced around furtively and leaned closer to lower his voice, "I am attempting to enlist help. I return tonight to the Centaur Forest, I hope they can—and will—help me."

Cinamon grinned widely, "Of course they will—especially if I come too!"

"You are acquainted with them?" Osmon asked in surprise.

"I certainly am! I am one of their Herd, I have their names," the boy drew himself up proudly."

"Well…by the Gods, you are a surprising young fellow!" Osmon shook his head and grinned, "My own son, one of a Centaur Herd,"

"You won't tell mother?" Cinamon pleaded.

"Not a word—and likewise for my secret?"

"Not a word," the boy mimicked.

"I hope we can be friends, son," Osmon said, "And I would be honoured if you would accompany me to the Centaur Forest at sundown."

"I hope so too—and I would love to," Cinamon stood, "Which means I ought to finish my schoolwork now."

"Of course. I will meet you here, when the sun falls below the treeline," he said.

Cinamon nodded, "Until then, father."

"Until then, my boy," Osmon waved. '*And what a surprisingly fine boy he is, too. Perhaps my absence has done more to raise him well than my presence could.*' he thought wryly, and shook his head as he stood to walk back to his study.

Chapter 8

Cinderella watched the garden from a mid-floor window, peeping slyly through the wood-slat shutter.

'*What do they speak of, so caught between laughter and seriousness?*' she narrowed her eyes as Cinamon's hand took hold of his father's. '*A son and father, so estranged until now…what secrets do they plan?*'

She watched until they both left to their separate rooms. As she turned, someone coughed and she whipped her head towards the sound, "Jerne."

The one-time leader of her spy guild leaned against the wall.

"What do you want?" she hissed.

"Hardly a greeting for a loyal—and recently freed—citizen," he smiled and lit a cigarette.

"My apologies, Jerne. What can I do for you?" she forced a smile, though it physically pained her to do so.

"I have news—I thought it may interest you."

The smile turned real in an instant and the anger in Cinderella's eyes was replaced by cunning, "Then join me in my chamber in ten minutes. I may have a reward…" she winked suggestively and rested a hand on her chest, 'for useful information."

Jerne ogled her unabashedly, "I believe you will be satisfied," he took a last look and vanished into the shadows, leaving no trace but a smoking ember on the floor.

'*It has been too long…*' Cinderella walked quickly to her quarters. '*Too long without Jerne's news…and too long without his other…talents. He may have no nose,*' she reflected, closing her door and unlacing the front of her dress, '*but, well, there are other things to make up for that.*'

She reclined on her bed, dress pulled open slightly, leaning her head on one palm.

A moment later, the door opened and Jerne slipped in, locking it behind him.

"You used the door, how different," Cinderella remarked.

The palace, like many of the buildings built in the more paranoid older times, was riddled with secret rooms and passageways. Jerne often boasted knowledge of them all, and seldom lost an opportunity to prove it.

Now, he simply smiled and sat on the bed beside her. She pouted her lips and let her dress fall open. Jerne smiled.

"First, tell me your news," she whispered, teasing him gently between his thighs.

"Your King plans to use the Centaurs to find his lost love," he said plainly, "He returns to the Centaurs tonight—with your son, who has long been their friend."

Cinderella's eyes flicked wide in a moment of surprise, "Well, well. The news we hear…I can trust you to keep me informed?" she accentuated her point by deftly undoing Jerne's breeches and letting her hand hover inside.

He licked his lips, "Of course."

"Good boy," she whispered and pulled him close.

"We can help," The Centaur said, as soon as she, Osmon and Cinamon were seated inside the leafy enclosure.

"Red-Huntress, I do not know how to thank you," Osmon told her, honestly. The Centaur just smiled.

"Red-Huntress?" Cinamon chuckled, "It suits you."

Osmon glanced at him, "I assume you know her true name?"

Cinamon nodded.

"I see no reason you should not, now," she told Osmon, "As Cinamon can vouch for you, and as a seal of my promise to help. I am Mossan."

Osmon smiled, "Mossan…" he tasted, then remembered, "I, er, I will keep your name safe," he promised.

Mossan smiled, "Thank you, Osmon. I will tell you our plan, and then offer you the bargain we spoke of. Then it is your choice—and yours alone—to accept or to not," she waited for assent. Osmon nodded, "Good. The plan, then. We know the ship is the Peregrine. We Centaurs have birds that can fly faster than any ship to give messages to our friends on other islands—some other Herds, some humans, some…other things.

"We will ask them to return word of the ship—to let us know when it arrives, or if it has already—and if any crewmen remain behind. We will give them a description of your man and they will let us know where he disembarks, then watch him and know where he is.

"Once he is found, it is for you, Osmon, to board your own ship and follow him—our friends will lead you to him once you hit shore. From there, I cannot control.

"Once you see him again, it is for your two hearts to decide.

"I must warn you, though, that he is surely hurt. You betrayed him, and he may hate you. I can offer no guarantee further than that we will find him."

Osmon looked at the floor sadly, "I broke his heart…even if he hates me; all I need is a chance to try. If you find him, then your work is complete."

Mossan bowed her head, "I hope he loves you still, that hate has been left behind."

"Thank you, Mossan. And…the bargain?" Osmon looked up

"Yes. In return for completion—which we have agreed on as presenting you with the location of your man—you must fulfill your promise upon your return. If you give it, you must return to do so."

Osmon nodded, "Anything. If you find him again, I will do anything."

Mossan smiled, "I hope so. In exchange for your man, you must set the Centaurs of my Herd free of their royal bondage."

Osmon gaped, "Cinderella…will go mad!" his mouth turned into a fierce grin, "I will do it! I give you my word! You tell me where he is, and your Herd shall go free!"

Mossan smiled wider, "My word also—I will find your man and give you his location. In return, you will set my Herd free."

She cleared a space in the leaves and drew a small circle in the mud, "The Centaur tradition calls for a blood bond," she explained, "My blood and yours join in this circle, linking us until each side is fulfilled."

Osmon nodded and Mossan took a hunting knife from her waist. She drew it across her palm and let the blood run into the circle. Then she wrapped her hand in cloth and handed Osmon the knife, and another strip.

Osmon hesitated. Cinamon squeezed him arm. Osmon gritted his teeth and resisted the urge to cry out as he pulled the knife across his own hand. The blood dripped and combined with the pool already there.

When the circle was full, and the outline a moat of red, Mossan nodded and Osmon took back his hand. He wrapped the slightly oily-textured cloth around it and immediately the burn of pain was replaced by a cooling sensation.

Mossan laughed at the surprise on his face, "Before you came, I soaked both rags in a balm we make to heal wounds. Keep the cloth on tonight, by morning it will be almost healed."

"Thank you," Osmon whispered, not just for the soothing rag.

Mossan smiled, "We both are set to receive our dearest wish. Tonight, I pray to the Gods. Tomorrow, I will dispatch the birds to each of the Islands. Now, you must both return before you are missed."

Osmon gave her a detailed description of Royston, filled with emotion and the eyes of love, and then the three of them exchanged good-byes. Mossan watched the two humans until they were lost in the darkness. Then she trotted to the waiting Herd.

"It is done," she confirmed, "We send the birds tomorrow. Once we have the man's location, our Herd is to be freed at last upon Osmon's return."

A cheer erupted all around as Centaurs—many who had known the cruel captivity of Cinderella, and the less cruel but still degrading captivity of earlier rulers—went wild in anticipation. 600 years of bondage, and all that remained to bar freedom was a single man's address.

Osmon put his good hand on Cinamon's shoulder as they walked, "Son, would you accompany me on my trip? Officially, I will still be King—simply paying a friendly visit to keep alliances strong. What better thing than to bring my heir to learn the complexities…plus, it is simply unfair to force you to remain with your mother in my absence, though there may be no Kingdom left to inherit, should she have full reign."

Cinamon sighed, "Father, I would love to join you and Royston—I truly would. But I have another thing I must do, just as you must do this.

"The reason Eera, the one you were sent to see first, is away is because he is visiting an old friend. A powerful sorcerer. He believes I have power in me, and I think he thinks I'll need it. He wants his friend to take me in and teach me."

Osmon walked in silence a while, "You truly wish to go to this woman, to become a sorcerer?"

Cinamon nodded, then realised they were in a dark street, "Yes, father. I believe I must...and yes, I do want to learn. I feel...I feel I could be a great wizard."

Osmon smiled to himself. *'If only I had my own son's strength...'* Aloud he said, "Very well. We will make your mother accept...or not. Either way, you shall go. And her formidable temper will make no difference."

"Father..." Cinamon fought for words, "If you do not return, mother will have nothing to control her."

Osmon sighed, "True enough. And I know I must return—alone or not, for I have a vow to fulfill. And whichever his answer may be, when I return I will divorce her, take both my children and leave her powerless with money enough to live on, and no more."

"I see you're practicing your bravery already," Cinamon chuckled.

Osmon laughed, "It would seem so, son. I only hope my supply is not limited...and that I remember how to use it."

They walked the rest of the way in silence, each contemplating their own possible futures.

Cinderella awoke, still lying next to Jerne. She nudged him until he rolled over sleepily and opened his eyes.

"Jerne," she whispered. He grunted in reply, "It is night, Jerne. Time for you to gather more news for your beloved Queen," she ran a finger down his chest.

"Not tonight," he grumbled.

"Yes, tonight," she gripped him gently beneath the covers and smiled when she felt a reaction.

"Not tonight," he sat up and pushed her hand away, "Not tomorrow," he rolled out of bed and looked for his clothes, "Not ever," he stood up, having located them, and eyed her darkly.

Cinderella slowly slipped back the sheets, climbed out of bed and languorously stretched her naked frame. From the corner of her eye, she saw Jerne's eyes widen and his penis begin to rise.

He looked away with obvious effort, "No more, Cinders," she stiffened at the name and felt his eyes swivel back towards her, gleaming, even though she faced the wall.

"I showed you. You set me free, and I returned with information. I showed you I can be loyal, in exchange for other things."

Cinderella sucked the tip of her index finger girlishly and batted her eyelids, "I thought you had your reward…"

Jerne forced himself to look at the wall. Cinderella slid closer, tracing the curves of her flesh.

"I want land. I want a title. Give me these and I'll be your spy — yes, and your bed-buddy — all you want."

Cinderella blew gently in his ear and whispered; "How about you be my bed-buddy and be happy to keep your head…" her hand moved south, "both of them," she squeezed quickly and released.

Jerne, flustered, breathing hard, pulled away, "Not this time, Cinders."

The name gave her only a small pause; she overcame it and followed him until he was backed against the wall.

"I think…every time," she whispered, grasping him again and sliding her practiced hand up and down.

Jerne tried to duck away, but Cinderella blocked him, grabbed a tuft of hair and pressed his mouth to her nipple, "Go on…take it…" she ordered, "Take it, just this once, any way you want it."

Cinderella gasped and smiled as she felt Jerne's mouth close around her.

"Good boy…" she breathed, "Now isn't it better to…play along?"

Jerne nodded and added a muffled affirmation.

'*Mine again.*' she applauded herself. '*Men are such simple, easy playthings…*'

Royston took a long swig of ale and slammed the mug on the table, "Alright, Swanson, I raise you 3 nugs," he dropped three gold coins on the pile.

Swanson bit down on the end of his cigar, "A'right, right boy. Three nugs—I meet yer and call. Flip 'em picture up, boy."

Royston grinned at the rough-hewn sailor across from him and threw down his cards, face up, "Full House, my friend."

Swanson swore under his breath and dropped his own—a flush, "Damn yer and yer family," he growled, but he was smiling, "Yer got a good card face there, richie. Now take yer winnin's and scram. Time for this old groaner ter rest."

Royston left with the two other players—Archoke, a fresh-faced youth who came on deck at the last port, and Samson, now a fast friend of Royston.

Archoke bid them goodnight and sidled off to his cabin.

"Where yer off to, lad?" Samson asked.

"I thought to go on deck and look at the stars awhile," Royston told him.

Samson laid a beefy hand on his shoulder, "Lad, I know yer asked me not to pry...but if yer tell me yer woes it may 'elp some."

Royston smiled sheepishly, "I fear my woes may put a barrier between us."

"Look, lad, I know yer a doll. Yer told me. So what is it? Some lubber back yonder still givin' yer brain the old heave-to?"

"Something like that," Royston agreed, after taking a second to translate, "I suppose it may help me to speak of it. Shall we go on deck?"

"That's meh boy. Up we go, then."

They walked silently to the bow of the ship, where a once golden— now chipped—peregrine spread its wings across the waters."

"So what is it, lad? Yer runnin' from 'im, or did 'e send yer packin'?"

"Both, really," Royston watched the water as he spoke, "He is, was, a powerful man in the Kingdom. We were together 15 years. 10 years ago, he married some girl; he was afraid to be honest and thought it best. So, he picked a low class girl and tried to strike a deal—mutual freedom if she became his wife in name. He picked the wrong girl...the past 10 years she's beaten him down into a pulp.

"We'd been meeting on the sly all this time, and it turns out she knew. Only now she's pregnant—by Osmon, she says, apparently she made him take her bed once every month to keep the marriage consummated.

"She told him to throw me over, or tell the truth—if he saw me again she would do it for him.

"I thought he was finally going to be brave and cast the shrew aside. Instead, he said in front of the whole city how proud he was to be having another child…

"He cast me aside instead, after he promised—swore—he could not.

"All my things were stolen—I had packed in anticipation of moving in with him and I left my door open. Somebody took it all.

"So, I came here, to a ship traveling to one of the Islands, and begged for work," Royston hung his head, "I loved him, Samson; I still do in a way. But…I think I hate him for what he did. Either way, I can never go home, surely everyone knows now—and…well, I-"

"Yer might be tempted to take revenge if yer saw 'im again," Samson finished, his rumbling voice momentarily soft.

Royston nodded and leaned over the edge, resting his elbows, "I want revenge," he said, watching his tears fall onto the wing below and slide off to be lost forever in the sea.

"Who was 'e, lad? This fella, this god-cussed yellow-spine. Who was 'e?"

Royston gave a short laugh, "You really wish to know?"

"Aye, lad, I do."

"King Osmon," Royston whispered into the wind, "His Royal Highness Himself," he stood now, and shouted it, "The Royal Coward! King Yellow! May the Gods curse his every hour!"

Samson put his hands on Royston's shoulders, "Now lad, be wary of what yer sayin'. The God's 'ave a way of listenin' out 'ere."

"I know what I say, Samson," Royston's eyes blazed as he realised that, for the first time in years, he knew exactly what he was going to do, "I've sat on this ship and drowned in my own tears for that…that…coward! Well no more! I will take revenge, Samson. One day. One day when I have made myself a man again," he leaned into the wind, "Do you hear me—if you Gods listen, hear this! I vow on every one of you that I will break this man as he broke me! And I will see him cast down onto his own filthy streets if it takes my death to do it!" he laughed maniacally.

When he calmed and turned, Samson was gone, "And God's curse you too," he spat, "I'll have nothing more to do with cowards."

'At next port.' he decided, *'I will leave here and start anew. And one day, that cursed coward will see my face and know what it is to be destroyed by the one you once loved.'*

Chapter 9

Cinderella awoke to an empty bed the next morning. Humming merrily to herself, she rose, dressed and poured some wine from the decanter on her dresser. She sipped daintily and opened the shutter over the large window.

The room faced the public courtyard and Cinderella often sat and watched the people below. When doing so, she often made up stories. Here, a well-dressed man and young girl—father and daughter, he on the run from his wife, she innocently enjoying a holiday. There, a Centaur conversing with a short, dark character—plotting theft of purses under the blind eyes of the City Guards.

Other times, she might pick out points on each—some real, some imaginary—and create a gruesome picture in her head.

Sometimes, she simply laughed silently at the beggars as they asked help from a cruel world and were turned away with the toe of a sturdy boot and a burst of raucous laughter from the blue-grey Guards.

Today, she turned from the throng in disgust and ventured through the door adjoining her bedroom and study. She sat, with an idle glance around. Even the expensive ornaments could not cheer her today.

Giving up, not bothering to act as if she could concentrate on a book, she sat back in her chair, fingered the animal hide and allowed her thoughts to slide.

'Jerne grows too bold. He can be turned easy enough, he will never be strong enough to refuse,' here, a narrow smile touched her lips. 'Yet *what to do? I have need of his news, but no patience for his selfishness each time we meet. Maybe I could give him something…but the only place distant enough, and little-traveled, is the Tower of Pyrone…and I wish even less for the company of the old witch.'*

She mused, lost in her thoughts, until she felt eyes boring into the back of her skull. She remained motionless, waiting.

The figure took a step, slow and silent, but she heard.

"Stop where you are, husband," she smiled, sensing the stiffening surprise, "Why do you sneak so?"

"You sat so still that I wondered if you slept—I do not wish to disturb your beauty rest."

"Tut, tut, Osmon. Never imply that a lady is anything less than perfectly glamorous."

"I know that, wife. I merely assumed it applies only to actual ladies—rather than those with a mask…" the sentence trailed slightly, making it seem more sensible than it was. Osmon scolded himself inwardly—as much for the barely sensical insult as for succumbing so easily to temptation, "We need to have a small talk," he said, rounding the desk and pulling up a stool. So perched, he smiled pleasantly.

Cinderella watched him, expressionless. *'Oh yes? A talk…mayhap my husband plans a trip away from his loving wife.'* she smiled as amiable as she could and spread her hands invitingly, "Talk away, dear husband. My ears are yours to occupy."

He blinked at the unexpected niceties. She was obviously uncomfortable with them, so why was she trying?

"Two things, in fact. Firstly, I fear I may soon have to undertake a journey," he noticed her smile falter slightly, "Relations with one or two of the Islands are a little strained, due to my long absence, and one or two other troublesome events of which I have heard only rumours. I feel a diplomatic hand may yet be needed, if so then in the next few days I will likely need take a ship and leave for a time."

"As you wish. Relations with the Islands are important," Cinderella nodded and smiled on, *'Relations, yes, but with no Islands. Fine, he may go, but he will not be alone. And he may not return.'*

'What? She sits and defers to me? The woman plots, I know it.'

"And this second thing, Osmon dearest?"

He winced, "Your tone is strange, Cinderella. I think…yes, it is a new one to me. I hope you are well."

Cinderella laughed merrily, "No, husband. I simply wish to make our marriage a marriage. With that awful man gone, we have only ourselves and our children," she rested a hand lightly on her stomach, "We must be a family."

Inwardly she smirked. *'I am a better actor even than I thought! Perhaps…I should let him go find his loverboy. Surely the doll loathes him now. He may return a dutiful man…'*

Osmon watched her carefully. *'Oh, to see those thoughts, ye grand bitch. But very well, you wish to play — and you think you run circles around me? We shall see.'*

"Wife, our son has expressed a desire to leave for a time. Mueren — she who so blessedly brought us together — may take him and teach him magic. It is thought Cinamon has great power. He talked with me; his desire to learn these things is strong. I would let him go, but we are a family, as you say, so I ask your opinion."

'The old witch wants to take my boy away?' Cinderella thought for a moment. *'Maybe…maybe a sorcerer as my heir would be a useful thing, if he were on my side.'*

Osmon cleared his throat, bringing Cinderella from reverie. She smiled sweetly, "Of course he may — on the promise that the old sorceress keeps him learned in the other subjects. If it is his wish, then, as his mother, it must be mine also."

Osmon smiled broadly and stood, "Good. He will be pleased."

"So I may lose both my men within a matter of days," Cinderella tried on a mournful expression.

Osmon matched it, "Will you be lonely?"

"I think I can console myself, for a while," She rose and kissed Osmon's cheek, "Of course, I shall be eager for your return."

"Let us see, first, if I must go," he fidgeted, uncomfortable at such close quarters.

Cinderella smiled and gave him a small wave, "I think, perhaps, you should take a walk, or a ride. You seem to have an excess of energy."

"Yes, I think…yes," Osmon flashed a smile and scurried out.

Cinderella shut the door and turned. On her chair sat Jerne.

"Nervous old fellow, isn't he?" he was examining his nails carefully, hobnail boots on the table. Cinderella moved swiftly and knocked them off.

"You're filthy!" she exclaimed, wiping mud from the surface and eyeing his normally neat, black clothing. It was now mud-spattered to his chest and stained somewhat green.

Jerne looked down at himself briefly and shrugged, "I was in the swamp earlier—before dawn. Best place to catch sun-flies. I use them often to light my hole-in-the-ground, to make it a little more homely. I have a colony, in fact, but many of them died because-"

Cinderella cut him off with an angry sigh, knowing he lived in a warm house with plenty of homely treasures, neither caring nor knowing if he used torches or sunflies.

"Oh, sorry, of course," he smiled, "Yes, I have further news. Osmon will shortly be taking a trip to whichever Island the Centaur's friends find Royston on," he looked at her, expectantly.

"Yes, I know," she told him, gleeful at the surprise and frustration on his face, "He was here to tell me that relations with the Islands may need cementing—so he may have to take a trip."

"Well..." Jerne fumbled, "I also have news of Cinamon."

"He wishes to learn magic from the old hag, Mueren?" she suggested, suppressing the urge to laugh in his face.

"Well...yes..." he stammered.

"Osmon again," she told him sweetly, pretending not to notice his agitation.

"The two Centaurs that went to visit the witch should return in a day or two. I believe you know one of them...he pulled a very special carriage for you one evening...he was the first you banished," Now Jerne was smiling smugly, seeing her off guard he continued, "Oh. Osmon also made a deal with one Centaur. If they provide him with Royston's whereabouts, Osmon will set all your Centaurs free."

"WHAT!" the lady screeched, causing Jerne to block his ears and squint.

'Not so nice to be taken a fool, is it?' He thought. *'I'll have my land and title from you, even if I have to play the loyal spy forever.'* He contented himself by explaining the sexual weakness of last night—and other times—as part of his plan to get his demands by cunning. Only in a

corner of his mind did the truth lie—and that corner was generally locked.

Cinderella was pacing and talking to herself, fists clenched, scowling. *'Looking thoroughly un-queenlike.'* Jerne mused. *'Strange, for one so obsessed with appearance and facade.'* He shrugged, deep thoughts were often best thought over a few pitchers of ale, and in company of oneself.

He rose, silent and sleek, and pressed a spot on the underside of a bookshelf. A rectangle of dark appeared in the wall beside it, and he slipped through.

It closed, silently, as Cinderella whirled to look for him. By the time her eye reached that wall, there was nothing left to see.

"Curse that bastard of a spy," she growled then returned in her poisonous thoughts to Osmon, "Free my Centaurs, will he? Well…we shall see, Osmon. Free them, yes, but the land they live on is my land. I will have them back. And you, Osmon, for this you may die on that Island. Preferably, in the slender arms of your beloved dolly."

Mossan checked each bird carefully. This was a species raised in the wild by Centaurs, trained over hundreds of years to be messengers and friends to their protectors. They were special birds, sent by the Gods, and held special powers deep in their breasts.

They were large, standing up to 2 feet tall, but light. Feathers varied in colours and patterns, blue to yellow, swirls to spots. On each, attached painlessly to their left leg, was a message pouch.

Each Phoenix stood in a line, patiently awaiting the off. Each knew their destination and purpose. And each would return, in time, with a reply—or die in the attempt.

Satisfied that the messages were secure, and that each Phoenix was healthy and happy, Mossan nodded to their chief trainer, Xyntu.

Xyntu nodded back and walked along the line, touching the tail of each. One by one, they took off and soared into the distance, a flock of speeding colour.

"Farewell, my friends," Xyntu called, "Return soon—on one of you rests the freedom of our Herd."

"Now we wait," Mossan said, "Thank you, Xyntu. I am certain your flock will prove their worth," She smiled, a little uneasily, and walked away.

'*And if a hunter fells the wrong bird? If they lose their way on such a long trip? If the reply falls loose? If Royston is not found? If-*'

She was interrupted by a polite cough, "Mossan," said Jonae—one of the four recently banished from the Palace.

"Yes, Jonae? You seem worried," she said, gently.

"A little…I worry about Osmon—about our Herd. I worry he is no more decent and honest than Cinderella. I worry that even if he is a good man, that she will prevent the release. Or inflict worse upon us all," He shook his head, "I think too much, this I know, but with Eera gone I had no other to allay my fears."

Mossan looked at him sadly, "I fear I am not Eera. No Master, philosopher or scholar am I. Whether he could bring you peace, I do not know, though he is an honest man and judges character well. He will soon return, perhaps then he can do what you ask."

"You also fear, then?" The young Centaur asked, somewhat surprised.

Mossan gave him a rueful smile, "Sometimes I think I fear more at 47 that I did at your age. I dread another 100 years of this—if I live so long. Yes, I fear also. But I do believe the King will try—he and his son are our friends, I believe this."

But…?" He asked, observing the shifting of Mossan's eyes.

She sighed, "But…Cinderella is a cruel and disturbed human. Whatever her reasons may be…I know little of them, but what I do know I sympathise with. She was treated worse than a gutter-sprat. Yet…her past does not give her excuse—she chose to be who she is. And so…I have hope that we shall be freed, though I think we will not live in peace. We may have to fight for our freedom."

Jonae braced his shoulders proudly, "Fight, Mossan? That I can do."

Mossan smiled warmly. '*He is a good man, growing strong and intelligent. 25, come this mating. I think…I may have found my mate. If Cinderella allows us so long a life.*'

Dane Weathers sighed heavily, "I'll be sorry to see you go, Royston," he shrugged his broad shoulders, "You're a good worker, and a good man."

"It is what I wish, sir," Royston replied.

"I know. But it's still a damn shame," he patted Royston's shoulders, "I had hopes you'd mebbe sleep here, someday," he gestured to his cabin.

It was twice the size of the normal cabins, and furnished with a bed, desk and sideboard—plus cupboards on the walls. In one desk drawer sat maps and tools, most of the other space was filled with Dane's many belongings. He liked to pick up trinkets, toys, and other miscellany, wherever he went. Though invariably, they would be sold a few ports down the line to make room for more.

Royston nodded, expressionless, "I am sorry, sir. It would be good, to be a Captain, but I am afraid it is not for me. I am a land man, an entertainer and gambler, yes, but I prefer my home to be still."

"Aye, I know. We hit the next port tonight. I altered the course to take us to Giizintaan. We normally only hit it coming back, but you seem eager to be away. And I think you'll be welcomed there and find easy living. Play that pipe of yours, son, the Giizintaans will appreciate you."

"Thank you, sir," Royston almost let himself feel touched.

Dane shook his shaggy head and took his time lighting a pipe. When finally done, he puffed smoke to one side and looked Royston in the eye.

"Lad, I dunno what really brought you to my ship. I dunno what's happened to turn you from a friendly young lad into…something cold and distant. Samson won't talk; you…won't crack an expression. So I won't even try. But whatever it is, lad, I don't like it. I don't like that new look in your eye or that new stride what used to be a stroll. And I don't like that feeling that follows you now—it's dark, and it bodes evil.

"I'll let you go at Giizintaan tonight, lad, but I'm gonna make sure you go with one bit of advice.

"Drop it. Whatever it is that's done this, whatever you're planning—or think you're planning. Drop it. No good'll come of it. I guarantee you that.

"But I'll always be your friend, lad, and if I can help you out someday, I will. You're a good lad, and I don't want to see you come to a rotten end."

Dane watched, hoped for a reaction. Royston simply stared through him with his new eyes—once light blue, now a darker grey—and did not stir.

Finally, Dane felt himself shudder and, suddenly repulsed, he snapped, "Get out, then. Whatever you are, you're not the lad I met back there and did a good turn for. Get out, and get off my ship this eve, and don't lemme see your face again 'till it's your real one, not this…mask," And he turned his back on Royston, expecting any second to feel pain—or death.

Instead, the cabin door closed with a soft murmur. Dane collapsed into his chair, exhausted, and poured a glass of whisky from the bottle he kept in bottom draw in his desk.

'*Gods help the lad.*' he thought, knocking back the first glass and pouring a second. '*Gods help him before he loses himself completely…if you can.*' he shuddered again, still crawling with the dead gaze, and decided to finish his bottle. It was his last, but he could easily buy more tonight, perhaps a case.

He knocked back the second and filled the glass, settling comfortably on his bed for a long day's drinking.

Royston entered his own cabin and shut the door. '*Fool.*' He scoffed. '*The man is a fool. How did I ever see him as brave and intelligent?*' He looked around, seeing his few things packed up and stacked in a corner.

"Well, well," He laughed, "This time I shall not be robbed of all I own."

Satisfied all was ready, he left—making sure the door was locked by jiggling the key and shoving a little. He smiled, acknowledging his cautiousness, and left to take the deck and look for land over the calm, cool sea.

Chapter 10

Royston waited until dusk before he left the boat. By then, everyone was ashore and he could sling his bag over a shoulder, trot down the ramp and immerse himself in the crowd with no one trying to say goodbye.

Dane hid given him his pay—had slid it under his cabin door as he lay reading, but though hungry and thirsty, Royston knew the alehouses would be packed with sailors. So he walked for a while, enjoying his land-legs again and taking in the foggy atmosphere here.

Giizintaan was a calm place, made of equals. No Monarch or select group controlled all; no rich landowners paid little and gained plenty. No special interest groups were favoured. No hierarchy or class system was in play.

Each village worked separately, friendly with the rest and joining together when needed, but organising and living within their own community. Each citizen had a voice, and each worked his or her job only a few hours a day—because here, everybody worked. There was money on Giizintaan, but shared. The workers were paid well with no higher class trying to keep it all, and prices were low, as each citizen had done their part with no one higher trying to take all their money away.

The people were fulfilled and felt both responsible and respected. To Royston, a once rich nobleman in the arms of a King, used to special treatment and people below him, it was the sort of hellish equality his parents had told him of, that he had barely believed existed. Until he finally came to the Island they spoke so fearfully of.

He stopped a short, middle-aged gentleman with grizzled hair and moustache, wearing a bland sort of suit and whistling to himself as he walked, "Sorry, sir. I only just arrived, but I plan to stay awhile. Tell me, where is a place I may sleep?"

The man looked at his surroundings, "Well, there's a visitors house 'round that next corner and down a ways. It's the…well now, I walk past it every day and I can't remember the name…it has a sign…."

"No matter." Royston smiled companionably, "I will find it and stay tonight. Tell me, sir, where might I find a job and proper residence?"

"A job?" the man pulled on his moustache, "Well, that all depends on what you're good at."

"I regret sir; I have never worked a job. I am-was a nobleman of Lamsonia."

The man 'hmm'd and looked Royston up and down, "Well, I dare say you're a bonny sort. There's a house or two that might put you up for the use of your body to warm their bed. Nice ladies—or gents, if you prefer."

Royston laughed, "I had heard there was no law against payment for favours on this Island."

"Well, of course!" the man stuck his hands in his pockets, "There's no such thing as a consensual crime in this place."

"Hmm. Interesting policy. Still, I think…I would not be good at that sort of work." Royston smiled.

"Hmm. Well, is there anything you are good at?"

"I do play the pipes—well, I am told…"

"Well, well. As it happens, I'm a musician myself. There's a buskers circle every afternoon, we're a man short right now and I've not heard pipes for many a year. We play a half-hour each, then split the takings. The folks around here are inclined to be generous to a talented player."

Royston grinned and rubbed his hand together, "Is there hope I could try my hand tomorrow?"

"Indeed there is my young friend! And there we just answered your question of lodging. The players and me, we have a house—been home to the buskers circle for 80 years or so. I'm off there now, if you care to join me we'll get you settled in and introduced."

"That would be…thank you." Royston raised a hand for shaking, "I am Royston."

"Good to meet you, Roy!" the man shook his hand with gusto, "I'm Ellis Boway."

"What do you play, Ellis?" Royston asked, falling into step beside him."

"Moonstone." he replied.

"Moonstone? I believe this is new to me."

Ellis grinned, "I'm not shocked, Roy. It's a rare thing, is a moonstone. They find them occasionally on the shores of Queanton—my home. It's a silver rock, in the shape of a half-moon, hollow inside. We put holes in it and blow. Like the pipes, except just one—and it sounds completely different." he laughed.

Royston laughed too. *'I think I might just bear it here.'* he thought. *'As long as this fool keeps out of my way. I can save most of the money and be away from here soon enough.'* So he walked on in the mist, smiling and feigning interest in Ellis' friendly chatter.

Cinderella found herself unable to rest. She walked her study in circles, barely able to form coherent thought. There was a lot to plan—Centaur recapture, Osmon and Royston's assassinations, Jerne's newfound self-worth…

Today was her father's birthday, were he alive he would be 50. He was a good man, at least she remembered him so. He once told tales of his first wife, Cinderella's mother. And had comforted her when the realisation finally came that her mother had died giving birth to her.

She never knew or understood how he came to marry Danzae. She was an evil, spiteful woman all the time Cinderella knew her. He looked sadder every day and gave up fighting quickly; Danzae soon controlled him and laughingly walked all over him. The only thing he would ever speak harshly of was the bad treatment Danzae and her two daughters gave to his Cinderella.

Danzae, of course, simply became clever. She put fears into Cinderella so well that the young girl could barely look at her father at all. Then, they simply made sure he was in his study—as he invariably was—before laying to with words and stinging fists.

When he died, the young Cinders knew Danzae had been the cause. Only later did she suspect actual foul play—when the symptoms of hemlock poisoning were seen and recognized in later years.

Now Danzae was dead. Given the criminal's funeral of hot flame. Only her stepsisters remained, in their cages, savage and cowed.

Finally giving in, Cinderella decided to visit them in the morning. She felt it was time they be removed from display in the Square and talked with—before she decided final punishment.

"Yes." She nodded, pleased, "Tomorrow my stepsisters will be brought to my dungeons, and we shall talk…" Now satisfied, she felt her mind ease a little and became absorbed in planning revenges. So much so, that she did not sense the listening presence behind her study wall get up and leave stealthily, smiling to himself all the way.

Early the next morning, Regina and Melina were brought—dragged—in chains to the Palace and locked in a small dungeon cell.

Three hours later, Cinderella ventured down, holding a flat-bottomed torch, humming happily to herself after a pleasant night's sleep. She ignored the various groans and cries coming from behind the metal studded doors—prisoners awaiting sentencing. Those left to die slowly were on a level below, chained to the floor to be eaten by rats, or unchained but given no food and waiting to starve to death.

Some, those whom Cinderella disliked intensely, those who were known to her before imprisonment, were taken to a special prison. It sat atop a high cliff, cells hanging out over the rocks and frothing waves. Each cell had a five feet square hole in the center, around it was a ten feet wide walkway for them to sit and sleep on. They were fed, given cheap wine and stale food, but whipped daily, given no bedding, blankets, new clothes or medical aid. They were lifetime prisoners, and were reminded every day that there was no escape. Water usually dripped through the roof—made badly for the very purpose—and the cold sea wind came up beneath them constantly. Left to themselves to stew in their misery, pain, and cold. Staring down from their prison, knowing the only escape in their lifetime—the only escape from the beatings and loneliness, they invariably concluded that the only way out was down, a quick death on the jagged stone below before washing out to sea to be eaten by the fish.

Cinderella smiled at the nervous young guard who fumbled his keys and took a few seconds longer than usual to open the door, "Thank you. I will call you when I am ready to leave. You may go."

He nodded, bowed stiffly and made a show of hurrying to the far side of the long corridor.

Cinderella entered and squinted into the gloom. She saw the two ragged shapes, chained hand and foot to the wall, and set her torch down close by, their faces flickering gloomily in the shadows. For a moment, she studied them.

They stared back, faces blank but eyes afraid, remembering her past cruelties—and their own.

"Good morning sisters." she said at last, cheerfully, "Tell me first of all, did your tongues grow back or are you still unable to speak?"

"Ugg." grunted Regina. Melina shook her head, ratted hair sticking to her grimy face.

"Good." she smiled sweetly, "Then I will have no rude interruptions." she stood still, an arm's length away, and looked at each in turn as she spoke.

"You should know why I have had you brought from your cages. The time has come to end this play. You have spent ten years in the Square. You saw your mother die. You have been cold, wet, hungry, injured—stared at and ridiculed. You have experienced some of those things that you made me go through. I, though, was a young innocent, while you were never more than cruel, envious demons.

"Now, however, I tire of such games. You will be put to death by fire—as criminals and the dark sorcerers of old. For you, the pain and misery will soon end—I consider you fortunate. I live every day with memories of what you did. I see the scars you gave me, I feel the wounds you opened up inside. I remember and dream. There is no end for me until I die by the hand of the Gods. For you, the end comes in two days. You will be washed, dressed as Royal sisters, branded in the cheek with the black circle of the damned. But this means your misery will be soon over, the Gods will know of your deeds and they shall destroy your souls the moment they leave your bodies.

"You should thank me, sisters, though I know you will not. What I offer is a mercy, compared to what you offered me." She finished and studied the two closely.

Barely human, now, unrecognisable as the sharply cruel but beautiful and weak creatures they once were. They stared back, still expressionless, eyes dancing between fear and hatred.

Cinderella stepped forward and half-embraced them both, being careful not to dirty her dress.

She took a handkerchief from her pocket and wiped off her hands carefully, her top lip upturned in an unconscious sneer of disgust.

"It was my father's birthday, yesterday." She continued after dropping the now-filthy rag into the torch flame and watching it burn, "Today is the anniversary of the day you and your mother gained full control. You had beaten me before, but on this day…

"I truly recall only some, but I do recall weeping over my father's death. I do recall the three of you entering, smiling gleefully and laughing at my grief. I do recall being stripped naked and held to the floor by you both while your mother whipped until every inch of me black and red. I recall my hair being cut away in clumps, and I recall the laughter. The rest is dark, until some days later when I returned from my first fugue. The first of many you joyfully imposed upon me.

"I remember everything. The first time one of your uncles visited. I was in the kitchen, preparing cold supper for him. I heard low voices, then laughter. He bellowed 'A'right, I'll give you a tug for it.' Then I heard the copper coin hit the floor.

"He came in alone and grabbed my shoulders. I tried to turn, he would not let me until I swore, through sobs, that I would do as I was told—or live forever with his sigil burned to my face in wax.

"He lay with me, on the table. He made me call him 'Big Knight' and lie still while he grunted and groaned like a bear.

"Once done, he left, without a word, leaving me curled in my cinders, bleeding, crying.

"I believe it was then that I began to forget my own name. It was all you had left me, my name and my fantasies of a better place. But that day…they began to slowly slip away until I was less than a shell of whatever I may have been.

"Once, you beat me and I did not cry—I could cry no longer, or barely feel the pain. You punished me for that, holding me down and scoring a tear into my back with a red-hot knife. From that day, I cried, I wailed, I struggled, and the more I did so the faster you left.

"Oh yes, sisters. I learned every trick. I made noise so you were quickly satisfied. I learned to take a man in every way possible, and in groups. I learned the right moves, noises, muscles to flex to make them leave faster.

"Oh yes, I learned them all and played you as mummers until I was taken away and given all this, this which I only deserved.

"Fortunately, the numerous children you flushed from my belly before birth, the pain, the misery, the humiliation…through all this I kept one tiny piece of me. I had no name but that which you called me—Cinderella, Cinders, for where I slept and belonged. But I kept that one, small nugget of myself, locked away, waiting. When the opportunity arose, I used it and broke free. And once free, that nugget grew and I became whole once more.

"I was always better than you. Prettier, cleverer, faster…everything you had, all your mother bought. Clothes, hair, suitors, manners, everything you had she bought—and you hated me because I was better than you even as I lived in the cinders.

"And now, there you both are. Chained in the Queen's dungeon. And I am the Queen." she smiled nastily. Her mouth was dry with talking; her head swam with memories trying to draw her in.

"Sisters…before I go. You should take with you two thoughts.

"Firstly, I know you murdered my father. Oh, not until later, no, at first I merely thought the three of you had driven him to his grave. My knowledge that you had grown tired of waiting and decided to take a more active stance, in the form of hemlock, came only when I witnessed the same symptoms from Osmon's father, the late King Santai.

"How did I recognise them, do you wonder?" Cinderella's smiled turned genuine for the first time since entering the cell, "Well, my sisters, I gave the late king a dose of hemlock wine.

"I knew the truth, the irony, immediately as he grew sick those last few hours. Cold hands, heavy wheezing breaths, dizziness, vomiting…yes, I knew them right away and laughed at the coincidence that we should both use this rare plant for similar means.

"My sisters, the only other thought I leave with you is this. There are those who take a chance, seize their own destiny and make it great. There are those who were never more than a talking sewer rat with a high opinion of themselves.

"I am the first. You are the second. So now you die, criminals soon to be forgotten, souls to be destroyed. While I, Queen, will go on—and before the Gods take me into their paradise my name will be remembered for eternity.

"This, my dear sisters, is justice. I hope you enjoy your brief visit."

She gestured around, as a host showing a fabulously decorated room. Then she picked up her torch and left, calling for the guard to lock the door as she marched back up to the light, smiling grandly and feeling very pleased.

The guard locked up and went to fetch the cold, brown, lumpy dishes of offal, and the watery, urine yellow beer that passed as breakfast for the imprisoned.

Then he left a dish each by Regina and Melina, close enough so they could lean over—chains at full stretch and grating on bone—and lap at it like clumsy stray cats.

Once gone, the sisters fed greedily, noisily, until Regina, sensing a presence, looked up and grunted in surprise.

Melina's head rose and her eyes widened at the figure standing above them, coming from nowhere, with a ruined face, but bearing a light—a clear jar with sun-flies inside—and holding up keys to their chains.

"You will come with me." Jerne told them, unlocking the iron and leading them through the passageway.

Once the entrance closed, he continued, "I heard every word. I can help you to regain everything, to look and be as ladies once more. If I do this, and before you are presented once more to the world, you must give evidence to a high court of Cinderella's regicide, and her patricide…" he raised an eyebrow questioningly, sure they would be willing to down Cinderella for the murder she had not committed as much as for the one she had.

Both sisters nodded vigorously.

Jerne smiled, eerie in the dull flicker of his dancing sun-flies, "Good…good. We will have the harpy thrown onto a bonfire, then oust that cowardly doll Osmon and his pathetic son, and banish them to the Islands.

"Then, my new friends, the throne is ours and a new Age of Lamsonia will begin."

This time his smile showed teeth, like a predator preparing to strike. Melina shuddered, Regina nodded vigorously.

Jerne set off again through the narrow corridor, torch held high, and his two freed and grateful new friends followed, half-smiling, close behind.

Chapter 11

Jerne led the two women through a maze of underground tunnels. Though they were unable to speak, he answered their questions with unnerving accuracy.

"The tunnels run under most of the Kingdom." He explained, pausing at a junction to check his bearings then heading down an identical path to the right, "I know every one as well as I know my own face. The legends speak of a mass of tunnels leading to every building. Of course, they stopped being built some time ago and now there are newer buildings in the Kingdom without a passageway yet. The story says that for 50 generations, the Lamsonian Royals set their slaves and captives to creating these places using only primitive tools. The stone coating you see now was only added later to hold in the earth, to stop it collapsing and killing the working slaves. Of course, the family was likely more concerned that each time a tunnel collapsed they lost labour and time in rebuilding it.

"They were made both to hide in, should escape be needed, and to travel and spy in secret.

"The maps were lost when the last line of Royals died out—or, rather, were murdered by the current line.

"I spent most of my life following and mapping them, never on paper. Each tunnel and route is listed in my head only. Even my spies only have knowledge of but a small amount."

The continued in silence for a time, turning corners through a maze of dark tunnels, lit only by Jerne's jar of sunflies. Then he spoke again,

"When you see my face proper, please try not to be alarmed. The Queen...relieved me of my nose after I was careless. I was a spy and a thief, and I grew too sure of myself. She caught me stealing from the Palace vaults.

"I was hurried, afraid—I had never dared steal from the Palace before, but I wished for a large heist. Wealth on which I could, perhaps, retire and live in comfort.

"As I threw gold into bags, I heard the vault open and I hid. They would never have found me—never thought to look—but I had left open the door to the passageway. I had thought myself too cautious, leaving the door open for a fast escape. I know now I was foolish.

"They saw the door, guessed I was still inside and searched every inch until they found me.

"I knew many secrets, things that I would tell if threatened with death. Also, I knew my ways out of the dungeons—as you two can tell. So I was allowed to live in service to the Queen, but my nose was taken.

"I had expected to lose my hands—as a thief, it would have been more fitting. But the secret things I knew angered the Queen more than did my attempted theft. So she thought to teach me to keep my nose out of business—except that which she wished to know herself, of course.

"I was freed from bondage recently. I asked for land and a title— only what I deserve for the good work I have done. Instead, she freed me and told me to bring back secrets of my own volition—which would prove my loyalty.

"But all the bitch wants is my services for free—as spy and lover. She never will present me with what I ask for and deserve.

"So, I wish to take them. All I wanted was a small castle, some acres, and a sir before my name. Now, I believe I am no worse a being than she. And I can rule a Kingdom better than she ever will.

"And you two may rule with me. A trio, partners." He stopped and turned to them, "This door leads to my home. Once you enter, you cannot break our partnership—or I will kill you. So tell me now, yay or nay.

"You will give evidence to all that Cinders killed her father, and King Santai. Once she is dethroned, we will expose Osmon and banish him and that wimp boy of his forever. Then, we shall take the throne. You two as its closest heirs, me as your trusted companion. And together we shall rule. We shall bring the Islands under our banner—by force, if we must—and make this Kingdom as great as it should be."

He directed the lamp of sunflies into their faces, watching carefully as their dulled brains processed.

Regina smiled and nodded yes. She took his hand and shook it with surprising strength, for one so frail and wan.

Melina nodded assent, eyes darting around. Jerne took her hand and forced her to look at him. She nodded yes once more, and he shook her hand, smiling gleefully.

"Good decision, sisters. Now let us enter my humble abode and find you some water, food and clothes. It will be a short road to recovery, I think. You cannot speak—but there are others who are deaf or mute—you will learn their language of hands. It is crude, but will express most things you wish to say. You should also carry parchment and pen at all times—to express things you cannot express in the language of hands, and to speak with those ignorant of it.

"Soon enough we will be ready to remove the harpy from her cursed throne."

He smiled briefly, turned and pushed a brick. The wall opened smoothly, and he led them inside to his home.

There was but one spacious room, with a corner shut off for a bathroom. It was well furnished, mostly with articles stolen, bribed or 'found.'

Jerne's servant was Spitter—a green-skinned, black-haired, black-eyed Rumaze, imported at cost from one of the more exotic and far-flung Islands—Rumazane. He spoke English, though little more than was needed to serve Jerne and Jerne was happy keeping it so. All the easier to talk in front of him.

The Rumaze were a quiet race, in general. They fed by spitting on their prey. Once in contact, it quickly absorbed through the skin and into the bloodstream, poisoning the animal in seconds. Though as of yet Jerne had not found the right opportunity to test it's potency on humans, he kept a jar of the green spittle on his poisonous substance shelf, and lived forever in hope.

The floor was laid wall-to-wall with thick, expensive carpet. On the walls, hung rare paintings and the more costly shielded fire-torches cast a cheery, flickering, orange glow on the mahogany, antique or otherwise kingly furniture.

In one corner, a space had been cleared of small, ornamental bric-a-brac and Spitter had laid down large blankets and soft mattress for the sisters to sleep on.

Jerne smiled brightly at the look of twin awe on the faces of his guests, "It's not much…" he began, then clapped his hands and guffawed, "Actually, it is indeed a lot. And it is my—and now your—home. I should be able to provide you both with beds within a week—I have called in some…favours." Here he smiled nastily, "But for now, I am certain you will be much more comfortable on the mattress than you have been over the last ten years or so."

Spitter, meanwhile, had produced three steaming plates of fish, potatoes and rice—accompanied by bread and wine.

Jerne led his guests to the table—a dark, intricately carved telling of an old legend about gods and mortals—and sat them on highly polished bronze chairs.

Once he seated himself, Spitter poured all three a glass of wine, left the bottle and retreated through a barely-visibly door off to the side.

"Eat, drink." Jerne motioned to them both and began shoveling food into his mouth, "You may bathe after you eat." He told them around mouthfuls, "Then we shall talk some more."

Regina tucked in with a hearty appetite, matching Jerne morsel for morsel, drink for drink, and between the two of them the wine and food was soon no more.

Melina ate well, but listlessly. Playing with each bite, chewing thoughtfully, seeming barely to know there was anyone else in the room.

Jerne and Regina, wrapped up in themselves, failed to notice and went on grinning wolfishly at each other over their empty plates.

Eera, Arison and Mueren returned that afternoon. Tired, dusty, happy to arrive and rest themselves.

The Centaurs gathered to meet the stranger riding on Arison's back, and paid their respects to all three.

Eera gave a quick account of their journey out, conversation, and uneventful return. Then he asked for two Shaas, one for Mueren during her stay, one for himself to rest his aging bones.

After Mossan updated the returned semi-heroes on Osmon's pact and the goings on between him and Cinderella, all three retreated to rest. Eera and Mueren to neighbouring Shaas, Arison to a peaceful, warm corner of the large paddock.

All three slept soundly through the night, waking within minutes of each other in the late morning.

Cinamon, able to escape Cinderella more easily than his father, plus it not being a school day, was already waiting for them to awake. He broke off his idle conversation and ran over to Eera and Arison, foregoing polite bows and hugging them both in turn.

Then he straightened himself and bowed as Eera introduced himself and Mueren by name.

"I have heard much of you, Cinamon. I am pleased to make your friendship, and look forward to teaching you." Mueren smiled at him. They stood almost the same height. She, wizened with age, had barely half a head on the boy.

"I cannot wait, Mueren. If you're as good a sorcerer as Eera tells me, then I am blessed indeed to have you as my teacher, and owe you a great debt."

"All you need do, my boy, is try hard. Seeing you into a powerful wizard will be payment enough for me."

'A nice boy, I think.' She studied him casually. *'Bit disturbed…most likely Cinderella's doing. I hope he is too young to harbor much hatred. Eera was right; he has much power and I have no wish to create a destroyer.'*

Cinamon studied her less obviously, from his peripheral vision as he had been taught. *'Nice lady. I think I'll like learning from her—she's not like the teacher at school. Expecting me to be the perfect Prince, being so wounded when I perform badly on a test. Yes, I think she is better. Magic, too, should be enjoyable to learn.'*

"We have, together, produced a plan to make Cinderella let you go." Arison smiled proudly.

Cinamon shook his head and grinned, "She has already granted me permission. I have packed, and am ready to leave whenever my teacher sees fit."

Arison's proud smile faltered, to be replaced a second later by a relieved grin, "Oh the gods saw fit to save me!" She laughed at Cinamon's questioning look, "I was to cause a public ruckus and embarrass the Queen—in relation to Osmon's affair. At which point, you would be mightily upset by the backlash and beg for escape."

"It may have worked." Eera mused, "But, thank the Gods, we need never know."

"Mother would have taken your head, Arison." Cinamon told her, quietly.

Arison nodded and shrugged, "One head, for the sake of such a powerful wizard, for the greater good of our Kingdom. In the light of the things Eera feels may happen, I would give it twice were I able!" She flicked her gold and silver-banded tail and stomped her hooves to show her courage and resolve.

Cinamon looked at the ground, touched and embarrassed, unable to put into words just what Arison's willingness meant to him. Articulate and princely he was and could be, but only as far as his Royal training had taken him. For now, expression of self was a muddy-brown area of inadequate understanding and limited suitable vocabulary. But Arison saw, knew, and smiled tenderly, feeling love for the awkward, almost pitiable, young child.

"As the situation has changed," Arison continued, "I think it would be well if I returned to the Tower with you both and remained. I will not be trouble, but I think I can help in case of…unforeseen problems."

"Well said, Arison. I agree," Eera looked to Cinamon and Mueren for reactions.

"It sounds advisable to me," Cinamon nodded, "But it is Mueren's home; the final decision should rest with her."

Mueren cracked a toothy smile, "So, the old hag gets to give the orders for a while—to a Prince and a Centaur warrior, no less!" She guffawed once, and then nodded, "I think I would like to have Arison around. I can feed us three, but you might have to entertain yourself. I have libraries and ample space…"

Arison nodded, "I like to read, also I can walk, exercise, train. I think I will be well enough. So it is done?"

Mueren nodded.

Arison smiled, "Then I shall collect together my things, and when you are ready, old hag," Arison winked at Cinamon who hastily moved his hands to his mouth to unsuccessfully hide a giggle, "I will be ready also. I think, too, that the boy will take a horse?" She looked at Cinamon who composed himself.

"I'll borrow a lightfoot, Harse," He confirmed, "He'll return to the Palace when I tell him, mother won't let me keep him away I know that."

"Then Harse and I shall alternate pulling a cart with our belongings and Mueren on it."

Mueren opened her mouth to argue, and then sighed, "Yes, I am forced to admit I am likely unable to make the trip afoot," Her shoulder slumped slightly, and then she brightened, "May I call out orders and brace you with a sturdy whip?" She kept her face straight.

"Only if you wish great pain, m'lady," Arison touched her sword and gave a slit-eyed sneer, which sent Cinamon into fits of giggles.

Eera interrupted, smiling widely himself, "Then all is settled. Mueren, whenever you feel ready, you shall depart. When a Phoenix returns, I shall have it sent to you so we may be in contact."

Mueren nodded, "That would be most welcome. I believe we should start tomorrow morn."

With this agreed, Cinamon took leave to update his father with the news, leaving the two to rest and prepare, and Eera to visit with young Centaurs happy to have their teacher, friend and storyteller home.

Chapter 12

Royston, lost in the mournful sound of his pipes, saw none of the entranced audience surround the square, heard none of the coins clatter to the floor in front of him, building up the already sizable pile.

His eyes closed, swaying gently to his rhythm, he saw scenes from his past.

Osmon laughing…Osmon talking…Osmon looking into his eyes lovingly. Osmon telling the crowd there was a new Royal child on the way, and he was so proud.

Tears ran heavily down his cheeks, and in turn the cheeks of his bewitched listeners.

His fellow musicians—Ellis the moonstone player, Taton the hand-harp player, Hesuit the viola player, Zane the sitar player and Dijn the singer—stared in astonishment, their own eyes prickling with tears of their own.

This was Royston's second performance. Last night's had been a dark, fiery number—disturbing all with its jealous emotion. Tonight's cry to the Gods touched the hearts of all who listened, and they wept silently for their own memories and loves lost or soured.

Even the children—who would normally tire quickly of such tunes and run off, laughing and happy in the knowledge that they would surely never know such sadness—sat or stood still, hypnotized by the anguished despair the pipe described.

Royston finished and lowered his pipe, astonished first to find his own tears, then again to see all the others.

As he walked with his comrades back to the house, he ignored their joyful talk of all the money made. Ignored their raucous compliments and occasional fluttering of notes and arrogant solos.

They would be well off, wealthy, and all thanks to Royston. But Dijn noticed his silence and dropped back to walk beside him. He said nothing, merely walked. Royston glanced at him, but did not break the silence. Dijn, he knew, had words to speak, and he would not be hurried into saying them.

When they arrived at their house—a homely place full of chipped paint and wobbly-legged furniture. But also warmth, music and cheerful friendship. Dijn left the others to go inside and touched Royston on the arm.

He pointed to a bench almost invisible in the permanent foggy gloom, "Sit with me a while."

Royston nodded. He liked Dijn, more than the others and their mindless, loutish yelling. He was soft-spoken, intelligent, not drunk on dreams of things that would never be true except in his music.

"The songs you played these two nights," Dijn began, "The first told me of anger, hurt revenge. A storm in your mind that will not die down.

"Tonight you spoke of broken hearts and misery, love lost and a soul crushed.

"There is a story to you. Something more than a bored nobleman. I will not ask," He smiled gently, seeing Royston's face harden defensively, "I will never ask. But I will always listen."

"I would tell you a tale. If I may," Royston nodded, resigned to a pathetic story of some maiden fair and Dijn's bravery in overcoming her deceit.

Dijn nodded, seeing his thoughts but saying nothing. He settled himself more comfortably on the bench and spoke into the mist.

"Once upon a time, I was 21—6 years ago, now. I was born and had lived in the Island Yassa. I do not remember life before the dictator Dunkat—I only remember his coup.

"You should know, my family survived intact. My parents immediately bent their knees to Dunkat, helping to sacrifice their King, and forced my brother and me to do the same. But that is not my story.

"For when I was 19, I met…was wooed by a young man-"

"You're a doll!" Royston gaped a moment then laughed, "I should've known!"

"Just as I know you are," Dijn told him, "This man, Dentoi, showed me why I had no interest in girls for more than friendship. He made me happy in that way, and all others.

"But he was the son of an aging bigot. A rich man, with thick distaste for Dunkat, and a lot of stored anger.

"For two years he raged at me and Dentoi, threatened and cajoled, tried bribery, violence…everything short of actual murder.

"He would have, gladly, but my parents were some of Dunkat's most loyal, and ranked high in His police-army. They would kill for little or no reason. And I was one of Dunkat's occasional news-bringers—in other words, I spied for him when he had things he wished to know. But—though Dunkat had no love for such as me, and may target a doll more viciously if given reason, he did not himself condemn just for something even he admitted was nothing but another natural form of love.

"If the old man were to harm me, Dunkat would iron-clap and torture him to death for it. The old man knew this, as did Dentoi and I. So his raging threats gave us no mind. Or so I thought.

"Dentoi became paranoid. Thought the old man was plotting to kill him. He had lost faith that my protection would extend to him.

"He grew worse over a short time, weeks really. Eventually, without a word, he wed one of his father's whores while I cared for my mother who was sick. When she recovered, I ran to see him and found him bedding his girl—with his eyes closed, no less, and a look of concentrated self-loathing on his face.

"He followed me as I ran to the kitchen. I killed him with a knife I found there, without waiting for him to speak.

"The girl had followed, and I killed her too.

"Then I awoke the old bastard and pinned him down, whispering to him what I had done. I cursed him to the hells and raised my arm to kill him…and he laughed. He looked at me, laughed, and told me 'Look what I have made you become!' I killed him, but that laugh and those words have never left me.

"I went right away to my father and told him the events. He told Dunkat who banished me without another word. I could go where I liked, but could never see my home or my family again.

"I received word of my mother's death; she passed just days after I had left. Suicide—with a dagger.

"My father, four years ago, died too. After he quit the police-army when I was banished, he simply sat in his house, eating, drinking, sleeping—willing himself to die. Eventually he did.

Dijn stood and stared about, "If I'd stopped, if I'd not killed them, I would not see my parent's faces each time I sleep. And if I'd waited, planned, been clever…I may have found a way to quench the hatred I still bear for all three of those demons, "His face twisted a moment, then cleared, "Or, I may have come to my senses and made a new life for myself without them. Or persuaded Dentoi back to me, where I knew he wanted to be," He smiled absently and shrugged, "I can help with any option, should you need me," He scratched the back of his head with one finger, nodded, and went inside.

Royston stayed on the bench, not minding the damp cold—it seemed to suit today's maudlin mood. He searched the story, looking for the hidden lesson or moral. All he found was a tale against ever falling in love.

So he moved past it, to the end of Dijn's speech. Revenge could make the quenching of hatred sweeter and more permanent. Or it could leave him forever unfulfilled.

Forgetting, moving on, could leave him with no thirst quenched, but the need…the need might die. Taking Osmon back was no choice for Royston, but the others…

And for both options, he had a friend who wished to help. Someone who did not judge, only wished to see Royston through— whatever his decision may be.

So, the choice was his. He had made his vow for revenge, countless times renewed since that night over the sea. To give it up now may condemn him to his God, and to himself, "But…to release it; let it go, live again…if this was possible…"

Royston took up his pipe and played to the grey swirls and silhouettes on his deserted street.

'*Krammol, God of music, hear my prayer.*' He thought, seeing the words drift upwards on the music. '*Tell me what I should do. I am your servant, guide me.*'

Royston sank to his knees on the floor, bowed his head in meditation and continued to play, waiting for an answer.

Soon, it came. Sounds in his head, words flowing through his pipes.

"The decision is yours, not mine. You are my child, and for your music you shall be mine always.

"I feel by walking on, you will not forget, but will become easier as you find other happiness. I also feel you will never be completely fulfilled if you do not complete your revenge.

"Neither choice is perfection. You may never be truly happy— though I cannot say for certain. Guilt on the one path, emptiness on the other.

"The third choice, the one you dismiss so readily, may be your only true salvation.

"But it is your choice my child, not mine."

Royston played a while longer, hoping for more, for one more syllable to cast light on the murky, triple-forked road before him.

He gave up, lowered his pipe, and pictured them. The left, empty of everything—people, things, space, time, everything. The right, crawling with thorns and hot coal. The middle...no, he would not show himself scenes like that to break his own resolve.

He scoffed. '*It is no real choice. Nothing weighed against much, what more to be considered?*'

Melina was the first to rise the next day. For hours, she simply walked around the house and looked out of the windows at the world. It was all so different when not viewed from the inside of a filthy, smelly cage.

Spitter entered from his side door as the sun was rising and smiled a little apprehensively when Melina jumped in fright.

"Sorry," He bowed deeply.

Melina shook her head and smiled; she pointed to herself and made a silly confused face.

Spitter laughed softly, "Spitter goes now."

Melina shook her head again and made a show of being out of the way.

Spitter smiled, "No—Spitter has work," He bowed again, the rags that covered his waist and chest—passing as clothing—revealed all-over dark-green skin, and left quietly, slipping the door closed behind him.

'*I wonder what's through there.*' Melina pondered a moment, and then was disturbed by the same groans that had awoken her.

She saw her sister rise and lurch to the screen, behind which hid the bathroom. Then came the unmistakable sounds of sickness.

Watching her stagger back a few minutes later, Melina decided Regina actually looked worse than she had when Jerne rescued them.

The long years of starvation had left their stomachs tender and unable to take much food. This had occurred to no one, until very soon after the feast.

Regina, after her indulgence, had spent some time in the bathroom. Melina, having controlled herself more, had simply doubled-over in pain and moaned on the floor.

Spitter had hurriedly mixed a potion to soothe and calm their stomachs and persuade it to digest. Melina had gulped down the dirty-grey gum, grimacing, and felt immediately better. Regina had scoffed, between retches, huffed and thrown hers back in Spitter's face, screaming. For once, Melina was glad her sister had no tongue, but Spitter seemed to understand anyway for he had hidden himself away the rest of the night.

Melina had only slept in-between Regina's bathroom runs, but it was more than she could recall having in a long while. So now, she sat and watched the town come to life, not thinking, just waiting to see what would come next.

It was a few more hours before Jerne awoke. Melina had moved only to switch positions once or twice. Now she watched in silence as Jerne stumbled, sleepy and hung-over, through Spitter's door and demanded a draught to cure his poisoning.

By the movement beyond, Melina assumed Spitter's compliance. Indeed, a few minutes later, Jerne walked back in, smiling and flushed from the jolt and carrying a cup in one hand. He nodded 'good morning' to Melina and gently disturbed Regina.

She sat up grumpily, eyed the cup suspiciously. Jerne took a swallow to show it was fine and held it out until she took it. The he stayed perfectly still, watching her, until it was all gone.

Almost immediately, Regina's colour returned and she smiled.

"Next time, love, you might drink Spitter's potions right away," He smiled lopsidedly and snapped his fingers. Spitter entered, "Time for Regina's bath," Jerne ordered, not even bothering to turn his head. Spitter hurried to heat water.

Melina had relished in her tub last night, after the medicine calmed her stomach. She was now clean, though pale due to the dirt having hidden her skin from the sun for so long. Her hair was long and light brown, eyes deep grey. She still wore her old rags—Spitter had refused to wash them for fear they would disintegrate. Jerne, however, had promised them a tailor today—followed by another bath and outfits of clean clothing to wear until their new clothes were ready. So Melina stayed put, watching.

Osmon rose just after dawn to see his son off from the Palace. They had embraced awkwardly; Cinamon told his Dad to watch Cinderella, and Osmon told his son to write.

The boy had nodded, hopped gracefully onto his horse and trotted away, pulling a quarter-full wooden cart behind him, scattering sleepy villagers left and right as he went.

Since then, Osmon had wandered around the many passageways and corridors of the castle. Partly, he was trying to avoid his wife— whether she was still in the same sickly-sweet mood, or her more usual foul one, she was a person he had no desire to see today. Partly, also, in a sort of aimless, alien daze that fell just short of thoughtfulness.

The lack of thought had been a conscious effort. Osmon crushed them, instinctively, knowing it was a bad idea to go wherever it was he wanted to go.

They tried to come nonetheless, trying to creep through his barriers before he snapped them shut, causing barely coherent half-sentences to clatter in a jumble to the floor of his mind.

The truth was, Osmon was lonely. All his life had been spent either preparing for Kingship, or ruling as King. Childhood had given him no real friends—they were all too afraid and respectful. His mother had died giving birth to him and his though his father was attentive and caring, still it was very different from the friendship of his peers. Only Royston had been close enough to see behind the Kingly facade. With him now gone, who was left? The newly discovered son had just departed for an indeterminate amount of time. His wife…was nothing to him. His Nanny had once been a confidante, until he grew up and she grew older. There were no siblings, no relatives at all to his knowledge—aside from the step-sisters-in-law. The Centaurs…he could not feel comfortable going to with such matters, not after the way the Monarchy had treated them.

Osmon was alone, lonely—not even in touch with the people he was meant to love and rule. If Royston remained hidden—or refused to forgive, then what would there be?

Exhausted from his unsuccessful thought-management, Osmon eventually gave in and returned to his bed. At least the physical part of him could be warm and rested, no matter how cold and tired the mental.

"There he is," Whispered a foot-high, pale green, black cloth clad pixie. He twitched his pointed ears, barely visible under his thick black mat of hair. He was pointing to a pipe-playing musician on the music square.

His partner, a yellow tinged girl with fine red hair, nodded, "Go send the Phoenix, I'll watch him. If I move I'll leave a bauble."

"Have fun," He kissed her cheek with thin, green lips, stroked her curiously pointed face and darted off through the crowd at high speed.

She watched him go, longingly, already missing the man who had been her companion since birth. Soon, though, she turned back to Royston's playing and edged closer. Her sensitive pixie ears, used to tuning out the usual discord of daily life, now opened themselves and absorbed each note with glee.

Hermer-hi an Klaan Qualesh was the pixie's full name. Her companion was Rooker-hi an Klaan Qualesh. For short, Hermer and Rooker. 'Hi' stood for History—the highest branch of learning, and their own current scholarly interest. Qualesh was the name of the ancient clan of the Island.

Though very few pixies knew their history, and those that did study it rarely stayed for long, they were still fiercely proud. They prided themselves on their small stature, faintly colour-hued skin, and in inbred loyalty to their clan, their partner, themselves and their race.

Hermer and Rooker were fairly new to their studies in history. They had learned, however, their origin and history of friendship with the Centaur race. Once, the races had resided on the same Island, the Centaurs helping them grow from small animals to the sentient, intelligent beings they now were.

Before history, they had become skilled in magery—something few pixies missed the chance to attempt, but even fewer could perfect. Once their studies in history were complete, there was nothing else for them to learn. Pixies lived for around 700 years, so taking time with study was no big deal—though any pixie could leave when he or she chose to pursue their own destiny.

Hermer and Rooker had, mutually, decided to complete the course, which is why they were in the schooling building when a Phoenix fluttered in and perched on their teacher's desk.

After he read them the note, they both volunteered to take a break and track down the man described. The Phoenix now waited patiently in their house, which is where Rooker was now going to send back word: 'target acquired.'

So now, all Hermer had to do was watch the man and hear his exquisite music of the happy-damned, swaying gently with her eyes closed. Cursed with pixie dancing feet, though, Hermer soon opened her eyes to the realisation that she had been dancing gracefully, but the music had stopped, and the angel-piper was looking at her with narrowed eyes.

"That's all for tonight, folks," She heard an amused voice say, registering through her embarrassment only the knowledge that she would have to leave a bauble to guide Rooker after her as she followed her quarry.

Hermer muttered an incantation, and a small, transparent, white orb floated in front of her at eye-level. When she moved, it would track her. When Rooker returned, he would find it and tell it to follow. Nodding to herself in satisfaction, the darker-yellow tinge of embarrassment fading from her cheeks, Hermer followed behind the piper. Small, stealthy, and dressed in black—she was still glad the fog was thick enough to conceal her. She had a bad feeling about this man.

The back of Royston's neck tingled, each tiny hair standing on end. Repeatedly he stopped short and peered into the gloom around him, seeing vague shadows but nothing more.

Yet the feeling persisted, itching at his brain. Someone was following him.

A picture flashed into his mind—a pale yellow pixie, dancing in happy abandon. Staring fixedly at him in embarrassment...or was it fear? Fear of discovery?

He turned a corner sharply, ducked into a gap between two buildings and watched for a foot-high shadow to walk past.

Instead, he felt a foot-high figure dart into the same gap, gasp in horror, and try to scuttle away.

"Not so fast," He growled, bending quickly and picking it up by a slender neck.

The pixie stared straight into his eyes, trembling with fear.

"Why are you following me?" He hissed, feeling no pity for the petrified figure before him.

"I-I was sent," Came the whispered reply.

"By who," He did not bother to add the question mark; he told the pixie what she would say.

"Centaurs—a Phoenix...letter, described you-" its voice, pitched high with fear, trembled and broke.

"Why, who for, what for."

"I-I don't know. I-I have t-to meet someone. B-bring him t-to you. T-that's all I know!"

Royston let the pixie drop and it hit the floor with a crunch, "Stay," He commanded, as if it could run with broken legs, "Quiet," He ordered, and it stopped the pained whimpers.

'*Osmon.*' He clenched his fists at the thought. '*He comes for me. But it is not yet time, not yet my choice! I will see he never finds me. That Phoenix shall not return.*'

"Where do you live?" He snapped. The pixie stammered an address. '*I will destroy that bird tonight, if it has remained waiting for a reply.*' He decided.

"Tell me anything else you know."

The pixie shook its head, it was dark, but Royston felt the movement.

"Refusal? Or no knowledge?" He demanded.

"I know no more," It squeaked.

"If the Phoenix does not return—what will happen?"

"Nothing. The Centaur will not come unless she knows you are here. The Centaurs will assume their bird dead."

Something occurred to Royston. *'My ex-lover has befriended the Centaurs?'* He stored it away for future use and picked up the pixie, again by its tiny neck.

"Do you work alone?" He hissed. The pixie's eyes widened and flicked momentarily sideways as it nodded its head rapidly. *'It lies.'* Though he knew little of pixies, he had enough information to know that they lived, worked and traveled in pairs. That meant one more, easily dealt with later. And, of course, the absentee would be sending the Phoenix back, and would return to follow him soon.

'Very well.' Royston smiled cruelly. *'The other may meet Osmon at port…and lead him into my open arms.'* He chuckled darkly and felt a spasm in his hand. It was the pixie, shuddering at the evil sound.

"I would have let you live," He told her, "And your man. For naught but a promise to 'lose' me in this fog. When you lied, you murdered the both of you. Understand that, pixie; your lie was both suicide and murder."

The pixie screeched, squirmed, struggled to Royston's amused laughter. Quickly, though, he tired of the game and grabbed the pixie around the waist, holding tighter to its neck. He turned it on its side and twisted his wrists sharply in opposite directions.

The crackling seemed to echo, even in the dense fog, and Royston dropped the shattered pixie to the floor with a mixture of horror and disgust. With a last glance at the twisted head and spine, he stepped back onto the street and continued home—hearing, for a second, an anguished cry cut through the fog.

Rooker had sensed wrongness. When the bauble began to shake and stumble, like a drunkard. When it flickered from white to black. He knew Hermer was dead, but he forced the bauble to hurry, and ran after it to the broken corpse.

In a heap, Hermer lay at strange angles, eyes closed tight and face screwed up with fear. Rooker fell to his knees by his beloved and took her in his arms, and then he threw back his head and howled, an animal cry that cut through the hearts and minds of all nearby.

Footsteps came running from every direction. A babble of voices, a yelp or two as the more sensitive turned from the horrific sight. Someone ran for help.

Quickly, the local volunteer Marshall for the month was on the scene, "Get some cloth and a spot in the apothecary," He ordered to no one in particular, and then gently tugged Rooker aside as people rushed to obey.

Rooker clung to him, small, afraid, sobbing. The big Marshall sat on the damp floor to be the same height, and then hid a surprised smile when the pixie sat by him and leaned on his arm, "What's your name?" She Marshall asked kindly.

"Rooker-hi an Klaan Qualesh," Came the tiny reply.

"Rooker-hi, I need to ask you some things," The Marshall knew well to show his respect by using the full name. He waited for a small nod, and then continued, "Did you see anything?" A headshake, "Hear anything?" Another shake, "Was the lady your Other?" A nod, "Tell me what you know," He said finally, deciding the best way was to let Rooker talk.

The pixie told all he knew. The Centaurs, the Phoenix, tracking the man down by following rumours of a new musician fitting the description. How he had left to return a positive reply. How he had followed the bauble, seen it stagger then turn black.

He ended by letting loose another wail of pain, punctuated by large sobs and thick, shimmering, blue-rinse tears.

Chapter 13

"I-I'm sorry, your Highness!" The guard whimpered, falling to his knees before her, "I gave them their tray yesterday 'n' they said nothin'. But that's normal with no tongue, your Highness, so I didn't think nothin' of it! Only today, the tray was still where I put it 'n' still with the food. So I went in, right away I did, Highness, and it was empty! They was…they was just gone, Highness! Like into thin air!" He cowered as she stood, the assembled court looking on.

The prison guard had entered during Cinderella's weekly session—where members of the public could come and have their voice heard. Usually it was a quiet affair; the public had learned very quickly that having their voice heard usually led to death or other inventive punishment.

Today, however, a prison guard had staggered in and stammered nonsense until one of the Queen's soldiers saw fit to hit him hard enough to break his nose. Now, trying to staunch the blood while remaining prostrate, he looked fearfully at the ground beneath the Queen's feet.

"Look at me," She commanded, "Kneel and face your Queen."

The guard lifted himself up a little higher on his knees and faced her, trembling.

"You lost my stepsisters?" She asked, almost kindly.

He nodded.

"What? Speak to your Queen, do not gesture!" She bellowed.

The guard whimpered, "Y-yes. I'm sorry my Queen."

"Bring me Jerne, that noseless traitor," She told the closest servant, who ran off gratefully, "I believe I have an idea of what transpired. They did not escape past you, wretch, in this you are fortunate. Therefore I am inclined to be lenient."

The guard relaxed visibly before her once-again-kindly tone.

"However. Some people must be shown consequences. And other people must be shown that no form of failure is acceptable. If they had walked past you, I would have had your eyes. Instead, they disappeared. I believe I know how, and I believe that you could have heard the whispered conversation that led up to it.

"Therefore, I shall have your ears. And you may leave my service and live however you can."

The guard was still, stunned. He allowed himself to be manhandled away by the soldier that had hit him, followed by a doctor who stared at the floor and pretended to see nothing.

Cinderella waved her hand and the room emptied rapidly. She then returned to her room to await Jerne.

It was not long before he arrived, appearing from her study and leaning against the doorframe, "You sent for me," he said, "Should I drop my britches now, or later?"

Cinderella gave him a stony glare from her bed, "Whip that thing out in my presence and you'll be two organs short."

He smiled sardonically and stepped over to meet her, "A noseless, eunuch spy. How intriguing a concept. Yet I fear I must pass.

"If not my body, then you want my talents," He hooked a thumb in his belt and waited.

"Talents? Now I know we have moved on from bed talk," She smiled at him, "Yet it is not those I wish for either."

Jerne's face became quickly blank, "Not for sex. Not for spying. Am I, then, useful in some other way heretofore unknown to me?"

Cinderella stood and walked to the window, "My stepsisters are vanished from the dungeon cell I left them in. You tell me over and over how none know those tunnels like you." She left the accusation unsaid, hanging in the air between them, and awaited his reaction.

She heard nothing and chuckled, "You have no defense then," She spun around to face him triumphantly, and almost lost her balance in surprise as she saw an empty room, "Well. I shall take that as an admission of guilt," She pulled the rope that rang the bell I her servant's room. When the maid entered, she bade her tell the Captain of her Royal Guard to assemble a company in the courtyard in ten minutes.

'I know the sneaking bastard will be gone when we arrive…' she mused, making her way down. *'But there is a tunnel in his hovel somewhere, and it seems a good place to begin blocking them all off. As for his spies…well, they can consider themselves freed so long as they stay away from me, and should any find themselves trapped in a blocked tunnel…well…I should think it a lesson to them that they should never have spied.'*

She wafted out onto the courtyard and waited, inwardly seething with fury at being tricked, outwardly composed. A Queen simply trying to round up an unfortunate bad seed.

Jerne flew in from the wall by his bed, not bothering to close it, "Spitter!" He yelled, flushed and panting from his run. Spitter appeared, "It's time."

Spitter nodded and set to packing two large, cowhide bags drawn from under the bed.

"Time for what?" Regina demanded, "Where are we to go?"

Melina, having started from her doze by the window, now spun around, got up and began to toss useful-looking items to Spitter, most of which he caught and proceeded to pack.

Jerne, restlessly hopping on the balls of his feet, turned to Regina, "Cinders—she knows. She'll be on her way. She needs time to make a squad, get down here…I'd say we have less than an hour to get out."

Regina's hands flew to her hips, "You said nothing of this when you brought us here. And what of our plans, hmm? Why do we run, why not simply begin turning the wheels?"

"Regina—surely you knew your sister would not let us go."

"Step-sister," She interrupted.

"Yes, yes, surely you knew she would not let us go. We will begin as soon as we get to hiding—but it cannot be done if we are dead!"

She nodded, turned and watched Spitter calmly, "Be sure you pack all you can," She called, "One day we shall need it to fill up a whole Palace," She turned and smiled at Jerne, who smiled back with a form of dumb admiration.

"You sit well under pressure, dear," He muttered, moving to her side.

"It seems I have a natural temperament for it," she whispered back, "Of course, I am not always so calm and quiet," She winked suggestively then turned away, her face impassive.

"Is that so?" Jerne felt his cheeks heat with blood and his pulse quicken as a hand gently teased his buttocks, "Hmm, I only hope you're nicer about it than your stepsister," he breathed.

"Never compare me to that harpy," she hissed, pinching the tender flesh over his kidneys, "Never do that, and I can be incredibly nice," her hand slipped, now, to tickle the fine hair crawling down the back of his neck.

Jerne shuddered, "No, m'lady," he managed through gritted teeth.

Melina saw all this, while seeming to concentrate only on assisting Spitter. '*So, she plans to use him as a toy then cast him aside, no doubt. Or perhaps marry him, and then bed everyone but him. I wonder where—if at all—I appear in either scenario.*'

Spitter closed the last bag and hooked it shut with a feral grunt, "Sir," he gestured to the bags.

Jerne shook himself from his erotic reverie. Regina smiled softly and spoke first, "Spitter, Melina, take the bags. I shall take one light, Jerne another. He shall lead the way."

'*Now I know.*' Melina thought, accepting the lighter bag from Spitter and dragging it on its wheels behind her. '*I am servant number two. For now, anyway.*' she glanced at Spitter, "You first," she told him, he nodded and moved on. '*But I wonder how well Spitter truly knows the language…and how pleased he is with his situation.*'

She kept her face solemn and took the last—and darkest—spot as she pushed the brick and the wall closed behind them.

Cinderella stood to one side as her Captain ordered his guards to force entry.

With a crash, two shoulders sent the door tumbling in a flurry of splinters and dust.

One-by-one all ten entered, swords drawn, followed by Cinderella and the Captain.

"Well?" He asked.

"Nothing, sir," Came back the short replies.

"Hmm. He certainly looks to have done well for himself," The Captain chuckled, gazing at the remaining furniture and bric-a-brac.

Cinderella shot him a deathly-cold stare, "You think it admirable, honorable, do you? To profit at the expense of other's secrets?"

"I didn't—" he tried to say, but was overridden.

"By blackmail, theft, trickery and devilry is how this and more were gained. Is this a man worthy of your respect?"

"I apologise, liege. I did not mean it so. The furnishings are nice is all I meant to say. In no way do I admire this fiend who fooled you into believing him loyal."

Though his voice grated with anger, his fists clenched and his sword rose, Cinderella took him by the head and spoke into his face.

"You will leave my service. You will lose your place as Royal soldier and your Royal crest. You will fight into old age as but a low hedgeling, with neither master nor apprentice. Then you shall die, and none shall care."

He spluttered, his sword crashing to the ground.

"Kneel!" Cinderella ordered, knowing now that all eyes had turned to her. She removed his cloak, scabbard and breastplate—all emblazoned with the Royal sigil, "Rise," She told him, now, "Rise and leave this place, and may I never see your face more."

The Captain set his face and spoke without taking his stony gaze from Cinderella, "Goodbye liege, my loyal men. I—Skimbradge—shall not travel alone, or die unknown. Nor will you last forever in your tyranny. You have none who are truly loyal to you, none but yourself. Remember this," And he turned sharply on his heel and vanished through the doorframe.

For a moment, Cinderella watched after him, stunned. For ten years, none had dared speak a wrong word to her—and none had ever spoken thus. But quickly pulling herself together, she faced the equally stunned soldiers, "Who was his second in command?"

A dark-skinned, muscled female snapped to attention and turned her dark eyes upon Cinderella, "I, liege, was second to Captain Skimbradge."

"Then step forward and become Captain in his place, with all the honor that follows."

But the woman clenched her jaw and walked straight past to the doorway. In the frame, she turned back, "Unworthy liege—aye, Skim spoke true. He commands my loyalty, not thee." Cinderella, near-gaped at being spoken to in such a way by a commoner, "Remember me, spider-Queen—for I am Vana and I join my Captain in his disgrace."

She was gone before Cinderella could speak. The Queen simply gazed after her in amazement until another voice spoke.

"I will be your Captain, my Queen, and you shall find me more worthy than those ingrates."

The Queen turned and found herself facing another girl. This one a few years older, with a scar crossing one brow and descending through a golden eye.

"I am Suzee, of the Magus. I have no power—indeed few do, anymore, besides the Magus-Pure in the mountain, not after centuries of dispersion. But I am your loyal subject, and a powerful warrior. I would swear you my soul to protect and serve."

Cinderella, by now recovered, studied the stocky form before her. Over average height, locks of silver hair dropping loosely from underneath her helm. Then she spotted the unmistakable rainbow-striped sigil, very small on the corner of Suzee's breastplate.

"You are a Tabby?" The Queen asked, pointing to it.

"No, liege, but my lifelong friend is. She has Magus power and lives with the pure, but I keep her sigil just as she keeps mine," Suzee motioned to her in the center of the plate, a black bird sitting on the blade of a dagger.

"Very well," The Queen sighed, unhappy but sensing the woman's kinship with herself, "You may keep it, but I believe the Captain's cloak you have talked yourself into will hide it."

Suzee smiled and dropped to one knee, "Indeed it will, liege, for I have just the clasp that will angle it so."

"Good," Cinderella tossed the cloak around Suzee's shoulders, "Have your sword hilt recast with the Royal sigil. And take this," she motioned to Skimbradge's, "to be melted down.

Suzee took it up, hefted it, and handed it to one of her new underlings, "I shall, liege."

"Now set your people to search every inch of this place for a pressure plate, a moving ornament…anything. There is a passageway here, and it will be found."

Suzee nodded and began to bark out orders to her somewhat bewildered crew.

'*I believe we may be something alike.*' Suzee thought, watching the Queen surreptitiously. '*I see a great friendship—or mutual partnership—blooming from this new promotion.*' She smiled to herself and thought of the gains and the fun to be had by the near-demon-with-Godlike-powers such as this Queen.

Cinderella in turn was watching Suzee watch her. '*So you think to share my power and become my equal, do you? Well…it is true I have never had a friend…and it may behoove me to encourage some form of loyalty. Perhaps this may be the place to begin.*'

"Skim! Hold!" Vana almost audibly screeched to a stop beside the burly, thunder-browed knight, swinging his arms and strolling casually down a forest path.

"Vana," He rumbled, "What brings thee after me?"

"I am your soldier, not hers. My loyalty is to you. Also, what better way could you have given me to leave the Queen's service and still keep my head?"

"For now," Skim chuckled, "I was thinking I could board a rig and work my way to an Island. If you would join me, 'tis your choice and my pleasure."

Vana slapped his thick shoulder, "I am with you; I always longed to visit the Islands."

Skim smiled his half-smile and shook his shaggy head, "And there's nothing I can say to shake you, is there?"

"Not a thing," She grinned, "Only, what's to be of your vow to see the Queen fall?"

"Vow?" Skim's eyes widened in fake innocence, "For shame! I made only a prediction!"

Vana raised an eyebrow but said nothing. Skim shrugged.

"Well, mayhap one day I'll find a way to take part in that bitch's downfall. If not, then I'll not return here so long as she lives."

"Then let's be off, surely we can persuade some kind skipper to slip us pay in advance to buy working threads and a replacement sword."

"Well, I have no doubt the sword will be returned to the smithy for melting. I think I can ask him to give it to me, tonight mayhap. As for the rest, aye. I say we go the docks tomorrow."

A polite cough came from behind them. Skim whirled, reaching for his sword. Vana's blade was in her hand and her dagger against the stranger's neck before Skim realised he had no sword and reached, instead, for the dagger strapped to his thigh.

"Who are you?" He asked, nodding to Vana who loosened her grip to let the well-dressed man talk.

"I am a friend," He croaked, sweating and pale against his deep-red clothing.

"A friend of whom?" Skim countered.

"Jerne. The Queen's ex-spy and lover turned rebel and traitor."

"How do we know this?" Vana growled.

"Vana, even if the Queen could send after us so quickly, she would not send just one—and the one would not be foolish enough to do what this one did."

The stranger's eyes narrowed as he worked out the meaning of Skim's statement. Then he nodded frantically, "Right, he's right!"

Vana shook him, "Hold thy tongue, or you'll have none to speak with! Tell us proof or gain a new mouth," She demonstrated by making gentle side-to-side movements across his neck with her blade.

"I can show you," He whispered, "Please, sir, lady. I can show you where Jerne is to be tonight."

"Lead us to ambush, he means to say," Vana hissed.

"Perhaps not," Skim held up a hand, "Let him free, Vana. If he moves wrong, kill him. But first let him talk."

Vana grudgingly loosed the spy and let her arms drop, though the curved sword and dagger remained in her hands.

"Now talk," Skim told him.

The spy rubbed his throat where two drops of blood had sprung from under the blade, "Jerne told all his spies that he was to take the stepsisters, and that he would soon have to run with them. He told us all to bring rebels to the few who knew his hiding place, and we in turn would take them to him. Of those few who know his hiding place, I am one. He plans to build an army, kill Cinderella, overthrow and banish Osmon and Cinamon. Leaving the stepsisters as closest heirs, and him as King."

Vana laughed, "And he thinks to truly do this?" She chortled and looked at Skim.

"I like your man about the same as I like that bitch. But if it's a chance to rid us of her, it's a chance I'll take.

Tell us where he hides, and leave us. We will journey there ourselves."

Vana opened her mouth, but shut it at a glance from Skim.

The spy nodded, glad to be allowed to leave, gave them the location of a secret cove and flitted away through the trees. Vana waited patiently for Skim to tell his reason.

At last he did, "I think we can help build that army. Half or more of the guards and soldiers will join us, perhaps the Centaurs could be persuaded…and certainly most of the citizenry. I said I would join a cause to rid us of Cinderella if I could, and so I will. I do not, however, plan to allow Jerne to rule."

"Then who? You?" Vana asked.

"No. The people. There is an Island named Giizintaan where there is no ruler. The people work together and provide themselves with everything they need and want. There is no caste, none higher than any other, and there is almost no crime and all peace. I wish to make this the way of Lamsonia, but first we can use Jerne to rid us of that Queen. Osmon and Cinamon will have to be killed—banishment will do no good-"

"I think they may happily surrender to us, Osmon at least," Vana interrupted, "I have no wish to kill Osmon, he does nothing wrong but follow the ways he has been taught. But Cinderella, she dies."

Skim nodded, "Okay. Mayhap Osmon and son will adapt to being equal. If not, we will have to lock them away. But you're right; I do not wish to kill them. Come, we should find a place for the night, and then I shall fetch my sword. Tomorrow we shall visit Jerne."

He set off strolling again, arms swinging loosely. Vana followed, blades sheathed, easily matching Skim's lumbering stride.

Chapter 14

There is no secret passage! This is what you tell me?" Cinderella shrieked, "Look again, incompetent fools! There is a passage here and I want it found!"

Suzee motioned for the soldiers to continue looking and walked to her Queen.

"Well? Your first task seems insurmountable. Is this a portent of things to come?" Cinderella hissed.

"Liege, I am your Captain. Please don't speak to me as a serf or a slave," Suzee sighed, knowing she was risking her head again not an hour after risking it to get the job, "I cannot work if treated so."

Cinderella opened her mouth to tell Suzee that if she felt this way she could leave, but hesitated. *'This is an intelligent one, a possible ally…even a friend. Treat her well, think before you speak or you may come to regret it.'*

So instead, Cinderella nodded, "I apologise, Suzee. What was it you had to say?"

"Simply this, liege. Is there no other place you know of a tunnel? Somewhere smaller, containing less? Surely in his own home we will never find the trigger, there must be someplace easier to search," Suzee knew the stepsisters had been taken from their dungeon cell, but tact told her to allow Cinderella the glory of having the idea.

Cinderella knew Suzee was giving her the idea. For perhaps a second, she was angry. Then for another second there was an unfamiliar feeling—a good one. Cinderella decided to let Suzee have her moment, and pretended she had just remembered, "My stepsisters were taken from their dungeon cell. Perhaps you could go alone, be sure to test every brick, every crack?"

Suzee nodded, seeing the pretense and being glad of it. *'The Queen does have humanity after all.'* She thought and nodded in reply, "I shall leave my men here. If the Gods show them a tunnel, it is all the better. Would you have me accompany you back to the Palace?"

Cinderella nodded, "I believe so. I will then await your success in my chambers—tell nobody when you find the door, you must come straight for me."

Suzee made a small bow, "But of course, liege. I am your loyal guard. Listen up!" She called to the soldiers, "Hunt till nightfall, then return to the Palace. If you find a door, one of you come immediately to the Queen's chambers and leave the rest to guard. Touch nothing. When you leave at dark, two will remain to stand guard and the rest of you will arrange shifts between all the guards until I say otherwise."

Murmurs and nods of assent came and Suzee nodded for them to continue before turning back to Cinderella and bowing again, "Liege."

"Let us away," Cinderella replied and Suzee fell into step a half-head behind her as they mounted horses and set off at a slow trot.

Almost immediately, however, Cinderella motioned for Suzee to move up and ride abreast with her to talk. Suzee did so with some surprise; Cinderella was widely known and feared for her regimens where rules and tradition were concerned. To ask a mere Captain to ride beside her was as unprecedented at it was surprising.

"Liege?" Suzee enquired warily, "Is there a problem?"

"No, Suzee," Cinderella replied, allowing a small smile as Suzee flinched involuntarily at the re-use of her forename, "You are uncomfortable with my addressing you 'Suzee'?"

Suzee shook her head, "No, liege. Just surprised."

Cinderella smiled, "Well, Suzee, it occurs to me that Skimbradge and Vana spoke some small truth. I am friend to none; therefore, none are friend to me. Hence, my people are loyal only to their own personal comfort—and what grants them fastest peace.

"You were courageous, to step up and tell me to make you my Captain. Is there a lion's heart under that steel, or was that moment a mere anomaly?"

Suzee considered the question, knowing the answer but searching for the trap that would fell her. Cinderella watched with an amused smile that stretched no further than her mouth, "You think I seek to trick you, to fool you so I my strike you down," She finally said.

Suzee knew it was not a question, so said nothing, only looking at the road ahead in expressionless silence.

"Mayhap if you were another, I would. Mayhap in the future, I will. Mayhap today, I simply wish to know you better. Have you an answer to that?"

Suzee opened her mouth, closed it, and frowned. *'Some game? Surely the Ice Queen cannot act this way. Aye, yet what to do but play along? To not will be my death, to do so may allow me to keep my head a day more.'*

Suzee looked sideways at Cinderella and took her chance, "Know me better, liege? Know me at all is surely what you mean."

Cinderella tinkled laughter, a very different sound from the trilling she emitted during cruelty, "Suzee, you credit me with neither ears nor retention. Your feats are known even to your Queen. The scar over your eye I know to be from hand-battle with a Cyclops from one of the unexplored Islands."

Suzee touched her scar self-consciously, "You know one story, liege, I assume you know them all. So I answer your first question—though I think you already know. Yes, I have a lion's heart. And the heart of every other beast I have killed."

"What, you devour these hearts?" Cinderella asked with more laughter.

Suzee grinned, "Aye, liege. Each enemy I defeat, I eat its heart. One from each species—and I've beat almost every species known."

Cinderella's laughter had abruptly quit, "Why would you eat a heart?" She asked, showing a disgusted face but listening with obvious interest.

"It is a superstition of the Magus, liege. The first of each species—except your own—that you defeat, you must cook and eat its heart. This imbues in you all its talents. Bravery, intelligence, stealth, skill. Whatever is theirs becomes yours."

Cinderella turned her face forward and rode silently until they reached the outer wall of the Palace. As the gate clanked and creaked upwards, she said, "I would hear more."

"More what, liege?" Asked Suzee, exchanging a saucy wink with a guardsman.

"More of your beliefs, your life," Cinderella sighed impatiently.

Suzee took another chance—risking her head yet again, "I could do that, liege, if you share yours in turn."

"You think to order me this way?" Cinderella said, "You realise I could have your head for those words—and some others you have uttered."

Suzee nodded and tensed, half-expecting one of the Queen's infamous merciless punishments instead. When nothing was said, Suzee glanced sideways and saw Cinderella looking at her, waiting, "I merely mean to say, liege, I would be honoured to enter into frank discussion with you about my life. I feel, however, that to give away something personal should not be done without at least some small measure of yours in return."

"This is how you feel?" The Queen asked. Suzee nodded and Cinderella pondered as she nudged her horse towards the stables, followed by Suzee.

She spoke again as they entered the castle, "How might you feel if I did take your head for suggesting this?"

Suzee almost smiled, she knew now that her head—and the rest of her—was safe. Cinderella never warned twice. So she bobbed her head, as if testing it, "It is a good head, my liege, and would doubtless look well mounted upon your wall. Nevertheless, I think it may do more useful things left where it is."

Cinderella laughed again, "I believe I shall accept your offer, Suzee. You tell me of your life and thoughts, and I shall sometimes tell you something of mine. For now, Captain, I do prefer your head where it is. You intrigue me. I think I shall appoint you my advisor, for now." And with that, she gave a pleased smiled and waltzed down the corridor.

Suzee looked after her in amazement, "Advisor," She whispered. *'Well, well. It seems the Queen and I may become friends yet. Only she neglected to inform me which cell to search...'* Suzee almost went after the Queen to ask, but thought better of it. *'Best to leave it as it stands, for now. The guard will be in the hospital by now. If I speak close into the stumps of his ears he will be able to tell me where to go.'* And, smiling her own pleased smile, Suzee gave a friendly nod to a passing servant and turned in the direction of the Palace hospital.

"Here we are," Jerne told them, entering a spacious cave residing in the mountains that lay at the farthest edge of the forest, "Our base from now on. There are torches on the walls," he lifted his lamp to show them then handed it to Spitter, "Light them, then we can see if it is possible to make this place livable."

Regina handed the second lamp to her sister, who put down the heavy bag she had carried here with a thump. After a moment, she followed Spitter's example, lighting a wick from the lamp flame and touching it in turn to each torch.

When the walls were lit all around the cave, Jerne smiled, "Well, Palace it is not, but I believe it will serve for now."

In the flickering light, the high-roofed cave seemed to dance ominously. Rats scurried from the light and Regina looked distastefully around, "Am I to assume you are expecting me to live in this place?" She hissed.

"You were expecting a golden tower, perhaps?" He whispered back, "It is for only a short time, be glad it has no bars! Soon you will live in the Palace as the Queen you were always destined to be."

As Jerne and Spitter spent time setting traps and magical wards to protect the cave, Melina took up the slate and chalk Spitter had provided for her for communication.

She scribbled on it and handed it to Regina who read it aloud.

'Sister, noticed you can talk again. Assume this is related to the sounds coming from the bushes when you both left for a short time.'

Instead of the empty space still suffered by Melina, there was a tongue. Tinted silver, it looked as no tongue ever should. Yet it was, nonetheless, a tongue where one had not been the day before—or, indeed, for the past ten years.

Melina took her slate back, wiped it clean with a sleeve, scribbled again, handed it back, waited for a reply.

Regina closed her mouth and read, "You are observant, sister. Yes, my tongue was returned to me by Spitter, on order from Jerne. And yes, it was given as a gift for certain services exchanged while you rested in the forest."

Melina scribbled again. 'So you are his new whore.'

Regina read it and her face darkened, "No, sister. We have an equality."

'You fuck him in exchange for a silver tongue. This, sister, is whoring.' Came the reply.

Regina screeched and shattered the slate against Melina's cheek.

Melina uttered a guttural cry of pain and pressed her sleeve to the largest of the gashes.

Jerne returned, laughing, "Now, now, Melina. It does no good to provoke your sister."

Melina hid her stare of hatred by turning and walking calmly over to Spitter at the cave mouth. She stood silently beside him, waiting for him to break his own concentration, then held out a hand for the slate around his neck.

'Please could you heal me?' She wrote. 'The large cut has slate inside it and will be infected.'

Spitter nodded and tried to put his hand to her face, but she brushed him away and scribbled again.

'You read English?'

He nodded, looked round furtively then took the slate. 'For him I draw pictures. You and I, though, are alike. Keep this secret. We work together?'

Melina nodded and he smiled, "I have another slate," he whispered now, resting his hand on her cheek and drawing it back with a chunk of chalky slate. He then let it hover over her cheek and she felt a tingle and fizz, then a sharp pain. Then it was done. She touched her cheek, rubbed it, smiled.

"Amazing," she wrote.

"I can teach you something," he muttered, facing back to his— apparently unfinished—wards.

Melina nodded, thanked him and strolled back to Regina and Jerne. They were giggling sickeningly with each other.

"Making use of Spitter, I see," Jerne called, allowing himself to be pulled farther back into the cave.

"Make use of yourself, then, and unpack while me and your sister are…busy," he smiled nastily and vanished into darkness as Regina used a metal hood to extinguish all but one small torch in their corner.

Melina's lip curled in disgust, but she picked up the bags and attempted to shut them both out as she unpacked. *'I have an ally.'* She thought, holding that close to keep her spirits up.

At the cave mouth, Spitter sat and looked out at the still forest, thinking in his own language. *'Will we be enough? Are there more? Must we stop these humans destroying all? I do not know how. There needs to be more people to help us. Has to be! The two of us, we will somehow find them. She will learn what magic she can, there is little inside her but I can make her a healer, I believe.'*

A little more satisfied, he rose gracefully and plodded over to help with the bags.

Vana touched Skim's arm and crouched behind a tree, "I see it," She whispered.

Skim looked for a moment; the cave mouth was carefully hidden by magic, "I see it," He confirmed eventually and stood, "Let's go in."

Vana pulled him back down, shaking her head, "It's warded."

Skim grimaced, "That could have been ugly. Thank you," Skim knew from long experience that while Vana had no magical skill, she was extremely sensitive to traces of magic. He waited for her to tell him everything she could glean.

"Seems to be…no more than 4 hours old. About ten feet thick…each foot is a new ward…starts at extreme fear, ends at gruesome death. It starts…" She spread out a hand as if resting it on a wall, "Very strong—the work of a wizarding race, I think, but not the Magus. Theirs has a yellow-tint, this is greenish."

"So how do we get to Jerne?" Skim asked.

She concentrated, "There is a sizer on the wards. Something smaller than, say, a pixie could get through to grab the attention of whoever's on watch. Try a rock."

Skim looked around, realised he was kneeling on a flat rock and hefted it, "All right," He grunted and threw it with enough force to hit the cave wall and shatter onto the ground.

A small, stout, green figure appeared in the cave mouth, "Who?" He asked.

"We are here to see Jerne the spy, sent by one of his men. We wish to join his resistance."

The green thing walked through the wards towards them.

"You cast them," Vana realized, putting together his skin colour with the green-magic, "And you made them backwards working, only coming in do they work."

Spitter looked blank at all of this, "You join army?" he asked, standing two wards in.

"Yes," Skim said and nodded vigorously, "He seems to speak very little English," he muttered to Vana who switched immediately to a different dialect.

"Do you know my speech?" she asked in the common Islandic trader speak.

"I do," he nodded, replying in kind.

"We wish to join Jerne's army. One of his spies sent us here. We have a dream that Monarchy will be vanquished and Government given back to the people," she spoke almost fluently, hesitating only to find a correct word or two.

"Then make your own army," the green thing advised sadly, "Jerne and one of the sisters wish only to vanquish the Queen so they may take her place."

"And what of the other sister? And yourself?"

"We have your dream, but I am bound to serve Jerne and the other had no place, no people to go to. I will teach her healing magic, but can do no more. Perhaps we can help you from our places here. Now we know of you, we will try."

Vana frowned, "Why not simply join us?"

"I am bound magically to Jerne. I cannot leave unless I pay, and I have no gold. Melina is free, and might join you if you tell me where to send her."

"We will, when we know where we are," Vana promised, "And we'll try to get you free."

"There's no person who would pay 8000 nugs to free me," he shrugged, "I am Spitter," he offered a hand through the wards.

"I am Vana, this is Skim."

Skim smiled, bemused, and shook the proffered hand.

Spitter looked behind him, "Go now," he ordered, "I'll send you word of when to come next, so stay nearby and wait for a sign of magic."

Vana nodded and inclined her head to him. Spitter bowed to both of them, Skim bowing back awkwardly. Then the green man skittered back through the wards and into the dark maw of the cave.

Jerne was waiting halfway in, still dressing, eyes cloudy with sleep, "Friends of yours?" he asked bluntly.

Spitter shook his head, "Guards," he said, sounding as ignorant as ever of the language, "Queen's men, were, not now."

"Rebels, you say?" Jerne asked.

Spitter nodded, "Sent them, find more."

"And why did you do that, my friend?"

Spitter was surely glad his master was in such a good mood. Other times there would be no chance for explanation, just punishment with a sturdy switch, "Guards know Guards."

"They say they can send us other Guards?" Jerne smiled when Spitter nodded, "Well, well. For once in your life, you improvised and got it right! Good boy," Jerne flicked his wrist in a gesture of dismissal and Spitter left to do whatever it was he did, "You heard?" he asked the shadows.

Regina stepped out, "Yes. It seems he does have a tiny brain in there after all."

"So, we shall have some Royal Guards on our side, my dear. I feel more assured of our victory even than before."

She smiled lovingly at him, "Do not be too complacent, Jerne. But it does seem as if my stepsister has made rather a few more enemies than is wise. Fortunate, too, as you can no longer be our inside tool."

"Hmm," Jerne said, "But as you say, no matter now. We shall have Royal Guards to be our tools. And then they can conquer her from inside."

"I have a wish, dear," Regina mused, "I would like Cinderella captured. Injured, maybe, but not killed. I wish to visit upon her some of what she gave to us, and make her see those peasants shun her."

Jerne smiled nastily, "If it is your wish, it shall be done," He kissed her outstretched hand and retreated into a dark corner to think and plot a way to take Cinderella alive.

"What do you make of it?" Vana asked after relating the conversation back to Skim.

He scratched absently at his close-cut beard and squatted on a fallen trunk, "Could be a trick," He said at last.

"Could be..." she prompted.

"Could not be," He replied.

Vana gave up and sat down with a sigh. Skim's way, whenever possible, was to say nothing and think quietly for a while, "Hungry?" She asked.

He nodded.

She stood, took his water bottle for refilling, and walked in the direction of the gurgling stream she could hear through the thick trees. Once there, she filled both bottles with water and looked for a shallow pool to catch fish.

When she returned, with wet feet and two large fish dangling from her belt, Skim had already set up a fire for lighting. He could be heard, though not seen, rustling in the undergrowth collecting eatable berries.

Vana sat down and lit the fire with a flint then hunted for the flat metal pan to be used for cooking the fish.

Soon, she had the animals filleted and laid over the fire on a makeshift tripod and was happily breathing in the scent as she laid out camp. Skim returned with a bag full of berries and left them by the fire as he helped.

When the fish were ready, so were they and they sat to wolf it down in silence.

Skim washed the pan with water from his bottle then set it and Vana's on the pan to boil it pure for drinking, "I think Spitter was telling the truth," He said, breaking the silence.

Vana nodded, "I feel that too."

"So, we wait here until he sends for us?"

Vana shrugged, "Why not? He may give us Melina and some advice. Besides, how can we return right now to persuade people to join us? The Queen is certain to have a watch out specifically to chop off our heads."

Skim nodded, "True. Then we wait," He settled back and looked up at the trees, "Not a bad prospect, I think, to stay here a few days."

Vana grinned, "Not compared to some of the holes we've been in."

Before full darkness fell, they had both retired, exhausted, to their bedrolls. They slept until morning, not seeing the slip of parchment that appeared from nowhere, tucking itself under Vana's bag and waiting to be read.

Chapter 15

"The boy should rest," Arison argued as politely as she could, "We have journeyed hard; he is tired and becoming sick. He should rest."

Mueren gestured towards Cinamon, sleeping on her bed, "Then I shall heal him and we will begin."

"Begin? He has been learning nonstop the whole way here. As we traveled, you spent all hours a day teaching. He has picked up the magic faster than anyone I have ever heard of. You can give him a day to rest."

"He learns so fast because the Gods have willed it. And if the Gods have willed it, Arison, there is a reason. My dreams tell me the danger approaches fast. I would rather him be tired than all be destroyed."

"Did you ask him what he would like to do?" Arison threw up her hands, "Mueren, he is no machine. He has magic, yes, he has power. Yet he is still only 9 years old! Give him rest today, tomorrow is soon enough. The boy can be no hero if he is too tired to cast a spell."

Mueren frowned deeply and turned away, "As you will, Arison, but it sits on your head, not mine. Let him sleep," She left, leaving a Arison half-stunned at her anger.

'I did the right thing.' The Centaur assured herself, turning to look at Cinamon fast asleep. 'I know it, as does the old sorceress or she would not have given in.' She watched him sleep for a moment more, then slipped the door closed and left through the front door, meaning to take a walk to refresh herself. A few steps out she was surprised by a loud squawk.

A Phoenix swooped in from the sky and landed gracefully at Arison' hoofs. There was a note on its leg; Arison took it and quickly scanned the words;

All is well with us. Royston not yet found, but this is only the sixth reply. Two guards left Queen's service and her spy stole the stepsisters. I think her reign soon ends. With blessings, Mossan.

The Phoenix pecked politely at her leg, then, and looked up expectantly.

"You want food?" Arison asked and the Phoenix seemed to nod, "Food, then a night's sleep, then may I send you with a reply?" The bird seemed to nod again, "Follow me inside," Arison suggested and it hopped along beside her as she re-entered Pyrone's Tower and headed for the well-stocked kitchen.

Osmon awoke to a Phoenix pecking at his cheek gently. He started and the bird fluttered away and hovered, unsure of him, by the window.

He apologised softly, coaxed the bird to him and took the note, sending it away with a tickle under its beak.

Have found Royston. Come to Centaur Forest. Will appraise you of situation. Do not travel in the open.

He read this, amazed, startled and curious at the same time. '*Situation? Travel in secret? What has happened?*' He began to dress quickly. '*I will leave this minute.*'

He was ready in no time and left by a side door, hurrying across his private courtyard and out. Turning quickly into the wood he made his way at speed to the Centaur Forest where he waited at the far edge of the clearing to be spotted.

Eventually one of the younger Centaurs saw him, nodded acknowledgment and galloped away excitedly. He returned with Mossan, who thanked the youngster and made her way over.

"Into the trees," She told him.

When she deemed they were far enough in, she brought him to a halt and hesitated, not sure how to begin.

"Where is he?" Osmon asked, impatiently.

"Before I tell you that, I must tell you what he has done,"

Osmon frowned, "Did he find his way to one of the intolerant Islands, finish up in jail?"

Mossan shook her head, "Quite the opposite,"

"Then…?"

Mossan bowed her head and thought, "I do not wish to tell you this, and I have hope that you can control your emotions,"

Osmon swore he would and Mossan clenched her fists, released, took a deep breath and began the tale.

Osmon heard the tale in baffled, stunned silence.

"Just after Rooker's first note arrived on the Phoenix, a raven flew in with the second explaining this," She finished and looked at him anxiously.

He slumped against a tree, graying and listless, "Your Pixie may be mistaken," He muttered, without hope.

"I fear he was not," Mossan said softly, "I advise you not to go-"

"No," Osmon cut her off, "I will go to him. I did this, do you understand? I killed that Pixie. I killed her with my cowardice. Tell me where to find Royston."

Mossan scrunched her face up and looked away.

Osmon caught her shoulder with soft hands, "Please tell me, Mossan. I must go there. I must try…something."

"Giizintaan," She sighed, turning her eyes on him, "He plays nightly with the musicians in the Square."

"Thank you," Osmon whispered, damp-eyed and trembling. He gave Mossan an awkward embrace and stumbled off through the trees.

The Centaur thought of following but stopped and returned at a gallop to the field. She found Xyntu, among her birds, talking with Eera.

They greeted each other informally and Mossan told them of Osmon's intent, "I must have a Phoenix to get word to Rooker on Giizintaan," She finished.

"The King still thinks he will find his man there," Eera shook his head in sympathy.

Mossan nodded, "We must find a way to protect him from what his man has become."

"I will go," Eera told them in a tone that brooked no argument, "I will travel with him and remain at his side. Rooker, if he is able, should provide help to bring Royston back here where we can keep him under watch and try to return him to the man he was. If he will let us."

"And if he will not?" Xyntu asked.

Eera bowed his head, "If he refuses our help. If there is no hope once we have tried all we can. Then we return him to Giizintaan and into the arms of the Marshall there. Crimes on the Island are so few that no book is ever closed. If it takes ten years until we have nothing left to try, the case will still be open and Royston will be imprisoned for life."

'*As will Osmon.*' Mossan thought.

'*As will the King.*' Xyntu thought.

"But," Eera continued, "If that happens, we also imprison Osmon, who is neither a bad King nor a bad man."

Xyntu brought out parchment and quill from the small back always slung around her back. She bowed and left to write the letter to Rooker.

"Osmon will not want you to travel with him," Mossan said.

Eera smiled, "Osmon has not yet encountered the force of my persuasive personality. He will allow me to accompany him as his friend and advisor, not knowing that in the shadows lurks a guard for his protection."

Mossan chortled, "Go to it, old wise one! I have known for some time you could persuade the Dark Ones themselves to walk into the fire! Go persuade a weakened King you are his consort," She clapped him on the shoulder, cringing as he winced back slightly. He winked to show he was fine, tossed his head to show off, laughed and trotted towards the trees to pick up Osmon's stumbling path.

It wasn't long before he saw the back of Osmon's head through the evergreens. Too out of breath to call out, Eera simply crashed heavily into a path of bramble.

Osmon whipped around, too fast, and fell into the nearest trunk, "Eera," He bowed greeting, then put a hand to his cheek, which was scratched from the bark.

Eera bowed in return and, knowing better than to fuss over a small scrape, went to the point, "I will be your companion on the trip to Giizintaan," He said in the same firm tones he had used on his fellow Centaurs, "You need friendly support, and you will receive it from me. I simply wish to be sure you are well."

Osmon shrugged in weary submission, "Very well. I know better than to argue. We leave at dawn tomorrow. Tonight we should sleep aboard my ship, come at dusk and I will see my new Captain gives you one of the Master cabins," He bowed shallowly, afraid of falling, and left.

'He is a breaking man.' Eera thought, turning back in the direction of the field. *'No King should submit so easily. I only pray Royston still has enough heart not to break him completely, for he certainly has the ability.'*

Mossan and Xyntu were waiting, and trotted over as Eera emerged, "He agreed," the oldster told them, keeping the rest of his thoughts a secret. *'Why burden them with such worries?'* He reasoned, "I am to be given a cabin on his boat tonight, and we cast off at dawn."

"The Phoenix is sent," Xyntu told him, "I asked Rooker to provide a stealthy guard, in shifts to cover all day, no less then four in each section. They will join you as you disembark, and if Royston returns under and amount of persuasion, they will take jobs aboard and keep watch,"

Eera nodded approval, "I believe I shall retire to my Shaa. I will arise three hours before sundown to be on my way to the ship." He sighed inwardly. *'A ship is not a home for a horseman, most especially an old one.'* he plodded away, feeling somehow infected by Osmon's exhausted dejectedness, to quickly pack and then sink into sleep until it was time to leave. *'This must be my last wearing mission. I grow too old for such nonsense. If I return, some other spry young thing may take my place in this as I sit all day on my haunches and tell stories.'*

"Royston," Dijn said, shutting the door and giving a furtive glance around the weed-filled garden, "You've been acting strange the past few days. Is something wrong? Something you can tell me? Something about, you know, 'Him?'"

"Dijn," came the icy reply, "how do you know if I act strangely? You hardly know how I act normally!" Royston set his face to hostile indifference and folded his arms defensively.

Dijn held up his hands and backed away, "If you say so. I just thought if there was something, you may need a friend."

Royston snorted, "I had one of those. A best one, in fact, and more. No, I think I can do without friends. Dijn, keep away from me, keep out of my space."

Dijn shrugged and turned back to the door, "Your choice, Royston," He opened it and looked backwards, "But if you ever do need one, I'm afraid it can't be me. I leave here tomorrow—for where? Well, that's something I only tell my friends," He was through the door before Royston could form a reply, and it fell shut on his baffled expression.

His face cleared quickly, however, as he chuckled to himself, "See," He told the weeds, "This is why no friends. They turn their coats so easily for any slight reason, and then they stab you in the back and laugh at you in front of the whole world."

He studied a flower for a second. Yellow-bristled and waving with the movement of the mist. Then he stomped on it with grim pleasure, crushing it to the floor and grinding with his thick, wooden heel.

"Unfortunately, a stab in the back is no guarantee of death. Unfortunately, the stabbed one may sometimes rear up and take the head of his so-called friend," He spat the final word in a voice full of venom and disgust, and then he spat onto the withered, flattened flower. Then he stood still, feeling the eyes of the second Pixie upon him as firmly as ever. *'And sometimes he does it when least expected, in a way that no one would ever guess.'*

He resisted the urge to wave sarcastically at the creature spying on him; instead, he spat once more and stomped away, "Hurt me, will you?" He muttered, "Rip out my heart and eat it in front of your entire Kingdom? Well, that was the heart you gave me fifteen years ago, and I plan to take mine back. Traitorous organ it is, I will show it how to stop loving you," He caught the last words and growled deeply, "Loving him. Yes. Yet how can one love a dead man? And how can one kill he who one loves?"

With a groan, he flew into the nearest wall and crashed his head against it repeatedly, screaming all the while.

"I do not love him! Oh, gods, how could I love him still? Why do I still love him?"

The wall was attached to a bar, which was soon spilling out curious patrons. The half-drunken men swarmed him and pinned him, bleeding and raving, to the floor.

"How can I still love him?" He screamed, "I hate him! How can I still love him after what he did? Gods help me—how can I stop loving hiiiiiiiiiiim!"

Slowly he calmed and lay still, fevered and pale, bleeding from multiple head wounds. The bartender tentatively offered a shot of brandy and, carefully sitting up, Royston took it with an appreciative murmur.

Then followed a mug of ale, which was quaffed in haste as the doctor arrived on the scene.

Hours later Royston lay in bed, head bandaged and throbbing, a painkilling sleep-draught in his hand being slowly drunk.

'I still love him…after when he did, and even though I hate him…I still love him.' He thought, half-asleep from the draught. 'Gods, I just wish I could be with him again. He will be here soon, I know it…then maybe…maybe I can stop hating?' He drifted lazily, almost wondering which side of him might eventually prevail. His last thought was of Hermer. 'What did I become?' Before a haze enveloped him whole and took him into peaceful slumber for the first time since leaving Lamsonia.

Osmon knocked and entered Cinderella's quarters to find her sitting on the bed, talking with another woman dressed in the cloak of the Captain of the Royal Guard. As he entered they stopped their conversation and looked up, Cinderella expectantly, Suzee a little irritated.

"I apologise for interrupting," Osmon said to the stranger, who seemed to remember her manners and bowed lazily.

"I will wait nearby," She told Cinderella, smiling, and left without a second look at the King.

"Well, husband?" Cinderella said impatiently, "What is it that is so important you must enter my chambers uninvited and interrupt my conversation so rudely?"

"I must travel," He said simply, "Those relations I told you of, with one or two of the Islands, need my presence to strengthen and repair. I leave tonight and shall return once all is well,"

Cinderella nodded gracefully, though her eyes seemed to glitter, "Return soon, Osmon, your child grows within me and I require your presence once I cannot move so easily."

"I hope to return soon. However, it may still be prudent to appoint a Regent. Someone you trust to speak with your voice while you rest."

"Perhaps," She smiled, and her eyes flicked to the door where Suzee was, no doubt, close by, "Have a safe journey, husband. Please tell my Captain to return to me."

Osmon almost let out a sarcastic retort to this dismissal, but held it back and ducked his shoulders in something that was not quite a bow.

Suzee returned almost immediately and waited for Cinderella to turn over some thoughts.

Finally, the Queen looked up, "You have loyal men?" Suzee nodded, "Then set those you can spare to crew on my husband's ship. It is being readied at the dock as I speak. Their first mission is to make sure that Gods-damned nancy Royston does not return. Their secondary mission is to ensure Osmon returns alone, or not at all."

Suzee nodded and turned to leave.

"Use any means needed," Cinderella told her.

Suzee turned back, snapped a salute and almost hid a sly smile.

Cinderella inclined her head in approval of her genius and settled back onto her bed comfortably, "Return quickly, I wish to see this tunnel you found."

Suzee nodded, "As fast as I can move," And, true to her word, she was gone in a flash.

Chapter 16

A section of wall slid open with a faint whooshing sound and Cinderella stepped back to take in the darkness beyond.

"Ever since I came to this Palace," she said breathlessly, "I have heard of these secret passages. Myths, legends, songs, poetry; everything about them I studied. I truly believed in them, and then that traitorous spy gave me proof. And now…"

"Now you plan to destroy them, block them off, make them no more; before you take so much as a step inside," finished Suzee. The short time since she had joined Cinderella had advanced their acquaintance. Now, no title was expected in every sentence. She was also secure enough that Cinderella was intrigued, if not yet fond, enough to allow an amount of free speech without risk to Suzee's neck.

Now Cinderella sighed, she too had spoken freer than she could recall ever doing, "I would give almost anything to explore and map these tunnels. Yet while I have no compunctions against disposing of those who know too much, I am sure others in the Kingdom know this. So none will volunteer, and most will run if forced. The risk for them is too great; all will know I cannot have any other knowing their way around these places."

"Then how will you call for workers to block and destroy? Surely you cannot allow them life either, so who would work? I think your hands too delicate, and mine too busy and too few," Suzee looked into the enveloping blackness, "There must be some other way. A magic to make us a map, perhaps? A truth potion to make Jerne talk?"

Cinderella considered, "If it comes to it, I will have Jerne talk. First, though, we will try magic. Find the most powerful sorcerer in the land and have them brought under armed escort to me."

Suzee hesitated, and then added on the title in an attempt to ease any wrath, "Liege, the most powerful is she you sent to Pyrone's Tower."

Cinderella groaned sourly, "Then bring me the second most powerful!"

Suzee nodded, bowed and took off at speed.

Cinderella waited a moment longer, studying the tunnel entrance, and then she pressed the high-up brick and the wall slid closed once more.

Eera arrived at the foot of the gangplank leading onto the ship. Seeing him hesitate, one of the crewmen stepped down to him.

"Eera?" The Centaur nodded, "All right, on this way then. Yer legs'll get used to the rockin' in a day or two, if yer gotta be sick do it over t'side then come to one of us fer a cure. There's two big cabins, t'King gets one, you get t'other, it's all set fer yer," The crewman kept up a steady stream of easy chatter as he led Eera to his cabin, close to the bow of the ship. It was large, with a bed, a desk and a closet.

"It's no Palace, and there's naught 'ere made fer a Centaur, but it's t'best we got on t'ship," He finished and smiled at Eera, waiting for dismissal.

Eera nodded, "Thank you…"

"Samson, sir, I'm t'Captain."

"Samson, well thank you for your kindness and hospitality. I hear this is your first time in the King's service?"

"Aye, sir, I got meself signed up a couple days ago. Wasn't expecting to ship out so quickly, but s'my pleasure for the King and a Centaur such as yerself. We know yer reputation even out on the seas, sir."

"Please, call me Eera—and if you could let the rest of your men know that too. I'm glad the good part of my reputation has preceded me," He smiled and received a warm grin in return, "Thank you, Samson, I will rest now, it's been a long day for an old man. Could I please be woken before we set off?"

"Sure thing Eera, I'll send a fella down just before we go. I'd be honoured if yer'd keep me company at the wheel atime, if yer feel the urge. I'd enjoy a discussion or two."

"I will certainly do that, Samson. Thank you," Eera inclined his head and Samson bowed and left, closing the door behind him.

Eera lay down his small pack and hung the few clothes in the closet. As he turned down the covers on his bed, smiling at the warming plate already making it hospitable, a soft knock came at the door.

"Come in," He called and turned to see Osmon, wearing a casual outfit for the journey, entering with a sheepish smile.

"Eera, I hoped you would be here already. I would like to offer you my gratitude for coming with me, but I know you would refuse it. Instead, I beg you to accept my thanks, I need a friend and advisor, and you are willing when most seem to be turning their backs. You are a good man, Eera, the best I have yet known. And I swear that upon my return, with or without Royston, I shall fulfill my promise and release all Centaurs into freedom. And the field and forest where you live will be officially dubbed Centaur Forest and given to you all as a sign of my friendship."

"You realise Cinderella will not allow that," Eera shrugged, "I do this for love of our world, and of you – a good man in more ways than I think you know."

"Cinderella be damned," Osmon told him sharply, and then smiled to lessen the blow, "I have developed a backbone recently, and I intend to keep it. When I return, alone or not, the Centaur shall be freed upon their own land. Cinderella shall be divorced, as I tell the world of my true affections. My son will be known as a great wizard. And I, with the right advisor," he looked pointedly at Eera who smiled sadly, "will make this Kingdom as great as it can be. None shall be poor, or hungry, or jobless. Giizintaan is no paradise, nor is anywhere else, but if the people let me keep the Monarchy once they know who I truly am, then I will give them everything I know how."

Breathless after this speech, he slumped a little and took the chair offered by Eera.

"With such words, how could any citizen say 'Nay'?" The old Centaur said, "But I fear I cannot accept a role as advisor. Unofficially, yes, but not as a full time place. I am too old," He went on, giving Osmon no chance to speak, "Wise, I may be, and as long as I live I will do what I can to help, but I am not so young. This task I have set myself is to be my last, but I am replaceable, and I will give you a young wise one who will protect as well as advise. And if you permit, I would come to live within the Palace, to teach your children and be on hand when I am needed. Also because even the Shaa's in our forest are cold and damp, with hard floors and night animals."

"You have any room you wish for, Eera, customised for your stature, and I will take your recommended and trust them with my life—as I trust you. Until your death you shall live nobly, and have a burial worthy of a King when you are gone," Osmon knew this the highest honour he could give; the Centaur took death as another part of life, a new beginning where they would see old friends. A funeral was a status symbol, the larger and more lavish the better, if themed to armies and battles then the Centaur was a warrior. For Eera, books and scholars would be the theme, with his stories retold by the young ones, and his teachings relearned by the others. And for a burial fit for a King, there would be a feast, a dance, a coffin instead of the usual dirt burial.

Eera took the King's hand and shook it warmly, "Thank you, Osmon," Was all he could say, but it was enough. Osmon rose and left, leaving Eera to shake his head at the turns of life; '*Once banished, now to live inside the Palace and die as a King...*' He mused, dropping the warming pan onto the floor and climbing onto the bed, covering himself as well as possible with sheets made for man rather than Centaur.

It was full dark before Suzee returned. When she did, she brought confirmation of three of her men becoming last-minute crewmen on the King's ship.

"Good, good. Thank you," Cinderella yawned, "And the sorcerer?"

"I sent a message to a mage they call Arguth. From what I've heard, if any can map those tunnels, he can. He has the power of one of the Gods on his side, and may be worth keeping around even after."

Cinderella accepted this advice with a nod, rather than her more usual reaction of throwing the advisor into a cell, "Very well. I think it is time I slept. Return tomorrow at breakfast, I have things to teach you if you are to act as my voice while I am heavy with child and recovering from the birth."

If Suzee was surprised, she showed it only by a slight widening of the eyes, "Thank you," She said quietly, and left the Queen to her bed.

'I am to be the Queen's voice?' She grinned as she headed toward her own prepared quarters. *'I am to be the Queen's voice. What a worthy, if unexpected, position from my new friend.'*

"So you are truly leaving," Royston stopped Dijn on his way out, bag slung over one shoulder.

"It seems that way," Dijn replied coldly and tried to pass. Royston stopped him, moving his body in the way.

"Will you not stay? If I apologise, would you?"

"No," Dijn shook his head and started again for the door.

"Then why do you leave?" Royston checked the anger in his voice and tried again, "Dijn, why if not because of my actions?"

"It's just time I moved on," Came the reply, but Dijn stayed where he was.

"Then what of helping me? What of the friendship you wanted of me?"

Dijn scoffed, "I wanted nothing of you, and if you understood friendship you would know that."

"Well, perhaps I had a bad teacher-"

"Perhaps, Royston," Dijn turned to face him now, "Perhaps you simply never tried to learn. Perhaps you need to move on from this man who hurt you. Perhaps...the advice I gave you was wrong. Perhaps I should not have hurt the people I hurt and moved on myself. That is, anyhow, what I plan to do now; move on. You ought to try it, but first you may need to grow up a little; you are no nobleman now, Royston, and none will love and shower gifts on you if you act like a child."

Royston grabbed his arm again, but Dijn shook him off and went, slamming the door behind him.

"Grow up, move on, learn, bad, bad me," He mimicked in a childish voice, "Ah, but it is too late, Dijn. I made a promise before the Gods on the sea, as I came here, what can I do but that which I swore? Though, maybe, otherwise I would change my plans."

Royston absently rubbed his head, bandaged and throbbing from the beating he gave it on the wall. He was troubled and confused, love and hate meshed together and tearing him apart, though his face to the world was mostly bemused at his actions and otherwise normal. One thing returned to him, however, when he considered the possibility of waiting for Osmon's arrival so he could embrace and forgive. The promise, made to the Gods over the sea. To break such a promise could bring worse on him than he could bring upon himself, Royston knew.

So there it was, all laid out, maybe he wanted to forgive and simply love again, but he could not. So he awaited news of the King's boat, every day returning to the docks to watch, every night playing music that disturbed the listeners into restless sleep. When the King arrived, he would wait for the pixie to lead him to the house, then lure him away and kill him. But not before he told him why, not before he told him one last time that, no matter what things they both did and said, he would always, always love him.

Royston's vision blackened as he sank to the floor, using all his willpower to avoid a faint, The doctor's orders to stay abed were good ones, but abed he could not stay and had said so. Now, then, he found in his pocket an amount of powder to be mixed in with water to heal him faster, or at least stave off some suffering until his uneasy work was done.

Watching him through a crack in the door was Rooker, his normally benign face twisted into a scowl of hatred for the monster stumbling into the kitchen. *'You think to escape, after you kill my Hermer? You think to avoid detection? I think your King will have things to say to you, and I think if he is still the coward he apparently was when he left you that I might have some things to say instead. To the Marshall, or to the Queen of Lamsonia. Yes, I think the Queen could devise appropriate punishment for you, monster,"* Rooker nodded to himself in satisfaction. *'The Queen it is, I am sure the King will take him back to Lamsonia, all I need do is follow; as I am told to assist, it should not be hard. Then I can see the Queen there, and I pray her reputation is truth, for if it is then you, murderer, will regret ever being born and my Hermer will be avenged by the damnation of your body, as well as your soul,"*

Samson oversaw the loading of the ship with food and drink and the belongings of the King. He watched his three new crew members suspiciously, late sign-ups were far from unusual, but something about these three just did not feel right. The way they talked, not of noble stock, but not quite of the general grunt either. Not that that was unusual in itself. Royston, for example, was a noble-born late sign-on. Of course, Samson still harboured doubts about the man's sanity, so there was no good comparison there in truth.

These three, though. It was more than just their speech, it was their whole attitude. Willing to work and fit in, but seeming to hold themselves higher. Samson could tell his men noticed it and were somewhat displeased.

'I warrant those three are in service to someone other than me.' He decided. *'Prudent to keep a close eye out, I'd say. Especially given our destination.'*

Samson had been told where he would travel, though not why, he had guessed the rest for himself. The King, off to the Island where his lover had gone. In this very ship, in fact. The irony did not escape the gruff Captain, and he planned to talk to Royston himself as soon as possible, though common sense told him that he might have to follow the King on his visit there to find the man. Common sense interrupted here, telling him that to stalk the King was death—and for good reason! But Samson pushed it away, resolved, and watched his men talk or wander below decks for an early rest.

Still, it was an uneasy thing for a man captaining his first voyage. Dane Weathers, the former Captain of the Peregrine, had retired after returning from the same voyage that had taken Royston to Giizintaan, leaving Samson the helm. Samson had, on some sort of instinctual whim, signed up in the King's service. Now he knew why.

Chapter 17

Eera had slept restlessly, so gave up, almost gladly, just as the sky began to gray before the dawn. He rose, stretched, feeling his bones crackle and shift. He groaned loudly, disturbing a crewman walking past the cabin.

A knock came to the half-open door, "Sir, y'a'right in 'ere?" came a young voice.

"Just an old man in pain, my friend," Eera replied, "Would it be too much trouble if I asked you to bring me a cup of water?" He had fortunately remembered to bring the powdered painkiller-cum-joint and muscle relaxant Mueren had made up for him. He knew it was the perfect thing for him this morning, though it dried his throat somewhat, and that he would definitely be asking her for the recipe he had forgotten to get before he left.

"Nay, sir, one cup o' water on t'way, just gimme a tick ter go gerrit," The boy replied and shot off before Eera could thank him, his shoes pounding on the wood as he ran at full speed.

Eera plodded painfully around his cabin, loosening up a little, listening for the sound of shoes returning. There it was, slower now the boy carried water in a cup, but still as speedy as he could probably get without spilling.

A knock, "Come in," Eera said, turning to face the door, packet of medicine at the ready.

The boy entered. He was young and baby-faced, unsure where to look in the presence of a Centaur wiseman. He held out the water, face averted. Eera chuckled, "You can look at me, son."

The boy slowly raised his head and smiled slightly, "Sorry, sir, 'tisn't you, I know you're an elder and I was told t'respect yer…"

"Respect isn't paid to the likes of me by avoiding my eyes, son," Eera smiled, "Just be nice, polite, can you do that?"

"Yessir."

"All right, and I think you'd be safe to do that with the King also. It's the Queen you might want to avoid eye-contact with," The old Centaur winked and the boy laughed.

"Mayhap I'll be turned to stone if I do, sir," He shot back, a cheeky grin making his young face look near childlike.

"Call me Eera," The old one chortled, "Thank you for the water, young man. You have a name I presume?"

"Aye sir-Eera I mean, they calls me Stocke."

"Stocke, thank you for the water, I'm sure you have jobs to do. If you could let the Captain know I will be joining him at the wheel in a few minutes you'll have well earned this dragg I have in my hand," Eera grinned as he said this, the smile widening as the boy's eyes fled wide. A tip was rare in a job like his, and he had probably never actually owned a silver dragg in his life.

"Thankee!" He gasped; taking the dragg like it was a block of gold.

"Don't tell everyone, now, I have no wish to be robbed blind," Eera smiled.

"No, sir-Eera, sorry. There's none I know'd rob yer, but I'll keep it safe. You be sure t'call on me if yer ever need owt for the journey, eh?"

"I most certainly will, Stocke," Eera flipped the dragg into the air. Stocke caught it easily, formed a sloppy bow and ran off to deliver Eera's message to Samson.

Eera chuckled to himself. '*The boy is clever.*' He swallowed the medicine. '*I think maybe he'd suit a job in the Palace when we return, I know I will need someone to help me unless a miraculous recovery occurs to make me young again.*' Thoughtfully he sipped the water and smiled, "A toast to you, Mueren, to you and your medicine!" He said to nothing in particular and took the rest of the water down in quick form as his muscles felt easier.

After a few more moments of pacing around the cabin, the cramps began to quickly loosen and fall away. With a sigh of relief, Eera stretched again, this time not grimacing at the expected crackles, and set out to the top deck, closing his door carefully behind him.

Samson thanked the boy for the message and waited at the wheel for Eera's arrival. The sky was deep purple and lightening when the oldster arrived, apologetic for his tardiness.

"No tardiness, Eera, 'tis not dawn yet. Asides, I know how it can take the old bones a minute to get warmed up of a mornin'—my old Captain was t'same way."

"Where is he now?" Eera enquired.

"Retired, just a few days past, left me t'ship and all," Samson shrugged, "Been doin' the jobs awhile before anyhow, Dane was an old man a couple years past, but stubborn as a mule, 'e was. T'whole crew had to persuade 'im to take rest afore 'e killed 'imself!" Samson laughed at the memory, and Eera smiled as he had a sense of this man's good nature.

"Do you travel to Giizintaan often?" He asked now.

Samson looked out to sea, "Not really."

Eera sense his avoidance. '*Curious…*' He thought and pressed it, "When was the last time?"

"Last time I was out we stopped off there a day."

"I have never been there; I have never been away from Lamsonia in fact. I hear Giizintaan is akin to a Utopia."

"Something of the sort. There ain't no ruler, no politics, no crime, no poor," Came the reply, a little more open now. Eera backtracked.

"What did you do the last time you visited?"

Samson shrugged idly, "This 'n' that. 'Tis a nice place, if foggy."

'*Trying to divert me?*' Eera wondered and stayed stolidly on track, trying to get hold of whatever Samson wanted to hide, "Do people ever visit and simply stay? It sounds the sort of place one might visit and never leave."

Samson shrugged, "Mayhap."

'*Aha, here it is…but what?*' Eera studied the man's profile for a moment, "Did you ever wish to stay there?"

"Most times I go. 'Tis a good place."

"Is there someone you know living there?" Eera sighed inwardly at himself. '*I sound like a coppiceman of some sort, trying to force confessions.*'

Samson turned to face Eera; face set deadly straight, eyes cold, "Why do you ask such questions? Have you a wish to accuse me of something?"

Eera forced himself not to take a step back from the man, "No, sir," Eera bowed his head with his arms across his chest, a sign of guarded deference and respect, "I feel you are protecting some knowledge you have. I feel it is related to this journey, somehow, though I am trying not to think how."

Samson softened and patted Eera's shoulder, "Stand strong, man," Eera straightened, "I do know something," The man hung his head and sighed heavily.

Before he could speak, though, the call came from a crewman that they were ready for push-off. Eera looked at the sky and saw it was almost light, "Dawn comes fast," He commented.

Samson nodded, "When I'm done at the wheel I will talk with you. Once we're clear of Lamsonia."

Eera nodded, "Than I shall leave you to think what to tell me," He bowed graciously and left, planning to watch his Island, the only place he had ever known, move farther away and grow smaller and smaller until Samson was ready to talk."

Samson spun the wheel, steering the ship out of the dock and setting course for the open water. It was a task he had done many times before; living on a ship since he was 6 years old had given him many opportunities to become proficient at every job, however awful, before joining as paid crew at the age of 15.

While he steered, he thought of Eera and what to tell him. *'He knows something, he knows I dropped off someone at Giizintaan...and if his reputation is all it seems, he'll know if I lie.'* So, resolved to truth, he turned his mind to anything else; for to plan what he would say would only make him fumble his words later; and he turned the ship slowly out to sea, waiting until the main course was set and he could hand the reins over to another.

Suzee opened the door quietly and made to creep in, balancing a tray of breakfast foods on one hand, before realizing that Cinderella was already up and dressed.

"Good morning, Suzee," The Queen greeted her with a smile, surprisingly chipper though it was barely light yet.

"I thought to wake you to breakfast," Suzee smiled and set the tray down, "Now I know I must arise before the greying of the sky to do this."

Cinderella laughed her musical laugh, "No, usually I do not rise until the sun is fully up and the streets are aired and warmer. Today, however, is a special occasion," She pulled the tray to her and began to pick out the foods she wanted, "Please, join me," She invited.

Suzee sat down and proceeded to pick at the foods Cinderella was not eating, "And what occasion might that be?"

"Why, today you become my assistant in truth. I will teach you the ways and means, and then we shall announce you as my voice while I bear this child."

Suzee smiled, glad the Queen's fickle temperament showed no signs of emerging; at least where she was concerned, "I am still honoured for this position, liege," She bowed her head, swallowing down a chunk of bread and grimacing.

"I believe you may call me Cinderella. So long as you never tell another soul and only do so when in private, the two of us."

Suzee smiled warmly. *'It seems whatever charms I thought never to possess are working on her. She is to be my friend, first and only. And I hers.'*

Cinderella thought she saw some of Suzee's thoughts in her scarred face. *'You are happy to be familiar with me? Why, when none until now can bear to be in my company for so long as you have. Even my own husband keeps as far away from me as possible. Yes, I am glad I chose you as my acquaintance. I think…I think maybe we can enjoy company and do some good things to show the serfs of this Kingdom who is in charge.'*

Suzee, meanwhile, was now hiding her thoughts. *'And maybe I can persuade you, sometimes, to be more lenient. If the people are less scared, this Kingdom will be much improved.'*

Eera heard a step behind him and turned, squinting against the sun, bright through the morning sea mist.

Samson was moving toward him, slowly, as if with great weight on his shoulders. He smiled sadly as he came close, "If yer still want me ter talk, I kin do it now."

Eera nodded, "I would like to hear what you know. I feel it may be important."

Samson nodded, "I think mebbe it is," He jerked his head in a 'follow me' motion and took Eera down and into his cabin without a word. He laid a blanket and straw pillow on the floor for Eera's seat, and took his wooden chair from behind the desk, "Fergive me, Eera, if I stumble a mite," He said, sitting down, "I'm not sure how ter start…"

Eera inclined his head graciously, "Take your time."

Samson smiled, "Thankee, friend. Well…yer know I dropped off someone at Giizintaan…" He began, and talked through the story of Royston's arrival, their friendship, his promise to the Gods that had scared Samson enough to avoid his sight for the remainder of the trip, and then the ship's arrival at Giizintaan; the last time he had seen Royston, leaving the ship as he watched from a corner, sadly.

Eera took this all in without a word, and kept his silence for a time once Samson was done. The Captain shifted nervously, trying to see through the blank expression on the Centaur's face.

Finally Eera spoke, "Thank you, Samson. This is good to know. I must tell the King, with your permission. And I would ask you to, perhaps, accompany us to Royston when we arrive on the Island."

Samson nodded, "Truth be told, Eera, I were gonna follow yer to 'im and talk to 'im anyhow."

"You would no doubt have been spotted by the stealth guard I have arranged to be waiting for us."

Samson laughed, "Aye, I would at that! Then I'd be in the crapper, eh?"

"Not really, the King knows nothing of the guard. They would simply have asked you to leave, possibly with a bruise or three to remind you."

"Would yer like me ter come to the King meself?" Samson asked, fidgeting again.

"No," Eera smiled, "I think you have been brave enough for one day. I can relate the story to him. Also, he may take it better from one he knows."

"Aye, good point," Samson conceded, visibly relaxing.

Osmon reacted quietly to the story, sitting with his head bowed and saying nothing for some time. Eera, with more practice than

Samson, could wait in patience for whatever reaction was brewing inside the King's tousled head.

What came was unexpected, "Turn the ship around," Osmon lifted his head, teary-eyed and flushed, "Turn it around and we'll go back home. Everything still stands, but there's no point going on with the journey."

Eera was too shocked to speak for a moment; this was a reaction he had not considered, "Osmon, why?"

"Because if he hates me enough to vow to the Gods to see my ruin, then where is the point in me begging him to return by my side? Even if he has cooled some and simply never wishes to see me again, tell me, where is the point? Where will be the crack in all that hatred?"

"The crack is the hatred itself, Osmon. Think! If he cared little for you, what would he have done? Shrugged and moved on. Such a vow is a terrible thing, but it shows the pain he felt after what you did, which was also a terrible thing. If his mood has cooled some, then he may give you, me, or Samson the opportunity to talk through it. At the root of it, Osmon, is all his love for you, and that is something which does not evaporate overnight."

"Perhaps, and yet a vow to the Gods is more lasting even than true love."

"The Gods, yours and mine-"

"Not mine," Osmon shook his head. I may have use for magic and the natural forces, but I have none for these Gods."

"Very well, though I must agree with you a little, this is a conversation for another time; with alcohol and a deck of cards," Eera smiled, trying to coax another from the dejected figure before him.

It worked, Osmon cracked a small smile, "Yes, and indeed we will continue sometime. But go on with what you were saying."

"If the Gods are not real, it does not matter. But Royston believes, or he would not have vowed so. He is an intelligent man, however, and must know that the Gods of legend, in which he puts his faith, are known to be lenient with vows made in a situation like this. Think of the ballad of Artisero and Shanka. Shanka, cast aside by her man because he was pressured into marrying one of his own race. She vows revenge on him and his family, but he returns to her and begs her to come back to him; prostrates himself as a fool and cries that he loves her still. She cannot agree because of her vow but the Gods release her from it because they are true lovers."

"And this, you think, will help?" Osmon raised a skeptical eyebrow.

"If Royston believes in these Gods, then yes. But first, we must break through the exterior. Osmon, we cannot forget that he has killed once; to escape from such a trap is not easy. This is why we must coax him back with us, no matter if he wants to or not."

"To rebuild him, then he can remember he loves me and the Gods can release him from his vow," Osmon sighed and slumped backwards in his chair, "Please, kill me now if this is our only hope!"

Eera rose and flexed his front hoof, "As you wish," He said, deadpan.

Osmon leapt up and shook his head, holding his hands protectively out in front of him, "Okay, okay, I know you never would—but please don't! I didn't mean it!"

Eera shrugged, smiled and sat, "I would have, if you truly meant it. My race will not preserve life at all costs, no matter the consequences or wishes of the person involved. If the person wishes death with all their heart, they will find it. If the person is unable to indicate a decision to us through continuous unconsciousness, then they will find whatever afterlife there is at our hands, and go there with all our love."

Osmon stared thoughtfully, "Interesting."

"Yes, another discussion for ale and cards," Eera pressed on, "Osmon, tell me now, will you continue our journey? Find Royston with the aid of Rooker; take Samson and myself with you? Bring Royston home and try to bring him back to who he really is?"

Osmon nodded, "I will. How could I not? Where he is, in his head...it must be so cold. I will help him any way I can—including tying him to a chair if I must."

Eera bowed his head, "It may come to that. But first we will try conversation."

Osmon chuckled, "Yes, we might try that first. Thank you, Eera."

Eera bowed and left the King to his thoughts.

Osmon rose after a while, singing to himself a snatch of the Balled of Artisero and Shanka.

Come, listen to my tale of
Artisero and Shanka.
Of different race were they, you see,
But fell in love to the chagrin
Of those around Artisero...

He stopped, forgetting the words for now, and carried on humming the tune to himself as he walked upon deck and looked around. Seeing a man watching him closely, he smiled and waved. The man returned a curt nod and went back to what he was doing with his back turned square on Osmon.

Chapter 18

Jerne paced, quick and angry, "They are supposed to be here by now! Where are they!" He growled at Spitter who flinched back, to the amusement of Regina.

"They will be here," She assured him, "They're peasants, serfs; they can barely tell when the sun is up, much less where it is in the sky!"

"They're the Queen's Royal Guard," Melina pointed out on her chalkboard, Spitter had tried to persuade Jerne to give her a tongue, but he refused.

"So they can wield a sword. This is no basis for assuming brainpower," Regina replied, sickly sweet.

'She is Cinderella herself, and yet she would never know nor hear of it!' Melina realised. *'So, then, there is no use to talk with her, about anything.'*

Regina had obviously never entertained the thought of repenting her deeds before Cinderella locked her in the cage. On the contrary, she seemed eager to add on; and make up for the lost years by causing death instead of mere pain.

Melina, on the other hand, had quickly recovered from her anger at being caged. It was all she deserved, came the realisation, for what she had done to her stepsister. Not only taking her innocence, her childhood, her father, but also turning her into the sort of monster that, she soon realized, herself and Regina were.

So Melina had accepted Cinderella's little tortures with no angry thought or sound, though this often tended to make her the main target.

Now, out of the cage, Melina, allied with Spitter, had arranged a meeting with Skim, Vana and some of their friends in the Palace Guard. So here they stood, Jerne pacing, Spitter dark green with nerves, twisting his neck in all directions to look, Regina watching the birds with a hunter's eye, Melina watching everyone else and listening for a step.

There was a slight movement in the undergrowth. *'Serfs, are they?'* She thought, hiding a smile and waiting, *'Well, I have a feeling that the peasants are about to give you a small fright.'*

Spitter had stopped nervously twisting his head around; he had obviously heard the small noises coming from the left of him.

Still Jerne paced and Regina eyed the birds lustily.

Until from every side of them stepped an armoured, sword-in-hand Royal Guard.

Jerne stopped dead, pale and said nothing. Regina let out a scream of terror and held her heart for a moment, before recovering with the red blush of embarrassment and rage on her face.

'She'll give them a hard time today.' Melina knew, feeling almost sorry for the Guards, but knowing that they were, in fact, working with herself and Spitter, and would barely need encounter the other two.

Skim and Vana led the small parade fully into the clearing for all-round introductions.

Regina, becoming her frosty self again, introduced herself and Jerne, dismissing Melina and Spitter with a flick of her hand. The only reason the two had been permitted to come was to be sure the Guards made their return to the town via a different route—which only Spitter and Melina knew; or so they had argued.

Skim bowed and introduced himself and Vana. Then one by one the other Guards stepped forward and Skim introduced each: Jonsa, Aara, Tintil, Ronson, Tohmas, Blese, Ooran and Mame. Squad leaders for the Royal Guard.

"These are our loyal squad leaders, and in turn the men and women in their squads are ours. Skim explained, "It was easier and safer just to bring these eight, but be assured that they speak for each member of their own squad."

Jerne nodded and began to speak, but Regina took over, "Very well, Skim, you have done well. Our two servants over there," she gestured once more to Melina and Spitter, who kept their silence and acquiesced, "Will lead you out of the forest by a different path."

Skim turned and smiled at them, showing a flicker of recognition in his eyes then turning away as if he thought them as servants, unworthy of attention from such as him, "That was indeed thoughtful, I had in mind a path but I am sure your servants will show us one much safer."

"Indeed," Regina smiled tightly.

'Must be killing her to be around such lower beings.' Melina thought and couldn't help but smile. She turned away to hide it, unused to being invisible, and saw a figure shifting in the trees.

Feigning composure, she straightened her back and walked over to tug Regina's arm. 'Somebody watching in the trees.' She wrote.

Regina shook her off roughly and Melina tried again.

Skim took the board and read it. He nodded, thanked her and casually waited for a minute or two, glancing from the corner of his eye to catch the listener.

Shortly, he excused himself from Regina's statements of grandeur and took himself off in the opposite direction, ostensibly going to wet a tree trunk.

Regina waited impatiently, unwilling to continue unless all were here to admire her.

Minutes passed and Skim did not return, "Where is he?" Jerne growled, and then started as scuffling came from the trees behind Melina.

Spitter leapt into action and dived headfirst into the trees with a yowl.

A moment later, Skim dragged a paralysed, roughed-up figure through clinging branches. Spitter followed, wiping faintly green spittle from his lips.

"Thank you, Spitter was the name?"

Spitter nodded.

Skim turned to Regina, "Your servant, here, used some sort of poison to paralyse this spy."

"He has poisonous spit," Jerne growled in explanation, "I've been wanting to test its effect on a human. Interesting. Now who is he?" Gesturing to the limp, groaning figure, "I vote we slit his throat and string him from a tree by the Palace."

Skim dropped the form on the floor where it groaned loudly for a second then lay still, curled into a ball where Vana could not reach the wounds inflicted by Skim's knife.

Skim held her away and shrugged, "Hoy, spy, show your wretched face."

They all waited, crowding the clearing with their anticipation. Finally, a stranger's face rose and looked at them. It was gentle, young, blonde hair peeked from under the black hood and the stranger's eyes flickered between each armed soldier.

"Please," He had an almost musical voice, "I am no spy, simply a coward. I wished to join you but was afraid to step forward," Skim helped him struggle, still half-paralysed, to his feet, gripping gently, afraid to injure the slim, delicate arm held in his meaty hand, "Thank you," The stranger said and leaned himself on a tree.

Now Vana stepped forward with her kit of healing herbs and the stranger allowed her to examine the blood seeping from his chest.

"'Tis but a scratch, stranger," she told him and he nodded.

"I only wanted to bring him in, not kill him," Skim said, "Else there would be no use treating the wound—you would be a dead man."

The stranger nodded, wide-eyed, "I felt the sharpness of your blade, sir, and I thank you for my life though I know you will scoff."

Skim scoffed, and then caught himself with a frown.

Vana stepped back after applying a thing coat of crushed herb and covering it with a leafy bandage, "Leave this on for two nights, you will have no scar," She told him, "Now if you can talk, tell us who you are," She offered him water and he took it and drank, greedily yet somehow with a gentle nobility.

"I wish to join you in your quest to overthrow the evil Queen. She has injured a friend of mine, injured him so much that he has forgotten who he truly is. As for the King,…he is weak enough to step aside once Cinderella is dead. I wish to join you, I have no real fighting power, but I have a voice that may hypnotise, and I can sneak and spy a little. I will learn to wield a sword, but would prefer a knife."

Skim looked him over, "If you can swear your fealty by the soul of your most beloved, then you may join us."

The stranger knelt, "I swear my loyalty to you, by the soul of the one I killed in a jealous insanity. I swear by the soul of the man Dentoi."

"A doll!" Regina sniffed, "What an asset."

She was ignored as Skim took the stranger's hand and shook it, "Then you may travel with me and Vana, for we are outcasts of the Kingdom. We will train you as we can, and you can put to use those skills you know of, and any others you may find."

"Thank you, sir," The stranger smiled for the first time.

"Call us Vana and Skim," the female soldier told him, shaking his hand also, "But one thing remains, stranger. Your name."

"Of course," The stranger smiled again, wryly, "I should have given it to you earlier but I was a little paralysed and afraid."

Spitter stepped forward and touched the man's shoulder; the man accepted it as an apology, "You have good spittle, friend."

Spitter stepped back and the stranger looked again to Skim and Vana, instinctively taking them as his leaders instead of Regina and Jerne, who saw this and steamed quietly in the background.

The stranger gave a small waist bow, "I am a singer and ex-nobleman, lately of the Island Giizintaan from where I recently rushed in the fastest boat I could find in the hopes of finding a rebel resistance. My name is Dijn."

Royston could feel Osmon's boat drawing closer every minute. It would be here soon, the King's shippers only built or hired those ships of the sleekest, lightest and fastest build, the type that might cost another man a four-month of hard work and no refreshment to pay for a journey aboard.

His bones seemed to harden, his teeth seemed to grate, and his skin seemed to prickle and stand on end as if a storm approached. It was almost unbearable. Almost, because still there was the calming thoughts that twirled in his brain. Tempestuous as they may be, at least both sides of his being argued solutions that calmed a little. To kill and be rid, or to love and be with him. Each choice had near-same appeal, and none was yet ahead of the other, except in his dreams.

But the boat came closer, it would be another day or so yet, evening tomorrow was his guess. Giizintaan was only a short trip as the crow flies, but the way was blocked by two small islands, those encircled and joined together by jagged rocks, so even the speediest schooner was forced to tack widely around one or the other before veering back in to this Island's only port.

That port was where Royston sat now, the large, single port, bustling now the time drew close to lunch, hot with high sun and sweat and loud conversation. He came close to suffocation, sometimes, a sweating, gasping, panicking sensation that drew him into the alcove he always kept behind him while he waited. Sitting and bowing his head, calmly out of reach and sight of any other, until he recovered and waited for the throng to die, before returning to his post.

All day he sat there, knowing Rooker was watching him and would report this, not caring, knowing that Osmon would come to him anyway: for otherwise, what point the journey? He thought, also, that Rooker may know Royston be the murderer of his half-soul, Hermer, and therefore so would Osmon. What to think of this, Royston did not know, would not until he saw what Osmon made of it. One thing he knew, with a knife he was no match for any soldier Osmon might bring. But with his new weapon, bought years ago as a souvenir from a more violent and deadly Island, the odds would be more than tilted in his favour, even when they knew of it and returned prepared.

As a figure, Royston no longer cut such a dashing, seductive, one. Since he had left Lamsonia eating had been something of a necessity, when he was otherwise too weak to move, rather than the enjoyment it had been as a nobleman. Shortly afterwards, drinking had taken its place; in moderation, mostly, he remained constantly tipsy but never quite drunk. Now, however, though he could force away the conflicting thoughts while he was awake simply by concentrating fully on others, it was not so easy at night. When he tried to rest, the voices came back, arguing, screaming. There were fading scabs, some of which would doubtless heal into small scars, from the night he had knocked himself into half-oblivion on the bar wall and the memory of it was only barely enough to keep him from repeating the episode.

Instead, Royston had speedily taken to drinking more, and more, spending each day's music money at the bar every night. Taking a bottle or two with him when the bar closed, so eventually he could fall unconsciously into bed and awake early, unrefreshed, groggy, aching, but unable to think of anything but curing the pain with more alcohol and groping his way to the dock to wait.

His fellow musicians worried that he no longer spoke to them, barely looked at them unless they accidentally walked into his line of view. They saw him drink, thought he was trying to kill himself with it. Two nights ago they had formed a group and prevented his leaving, tried to talk. Royston had roared angrily and, finding strength from somewhere that was not his jug of whisky, tossed them aside and stormed to the bar.

The musicians had, unanimously, nursing bruises, agreed to leave him alone for as long as he played the music well—which he still did without fault. When he began to falter there, they would call for the help of police and drag him into a cell at first light some morning, when he should be less able to fight.

No longer was this man, this being who played music of both God and Demon, their friend. He was a ticking time bomb, and they had no idea how he would explode.

Back in the Lamsonian forest, the meeting between rebels was over. Spitter and Melina led the soldiers and newly recruited singer a winding trail.

'This leads to Centaur's field.' Melina explained in chalk. 'We think they join us. Not to knowledge of J and R though.'

Skim grinned, "Very cunning. Who are we to see?"

'Palace Centaurs said to see Eera.' Came the scribbled reply. 'And Arison.'

"I believe both are away," Dijn spoke up, "Eera travels with the King to find his man Royston. Arison guards the boy prince at Pyrone's Tower," He looked around at surprised faces, "Did I not say I had a little spying ability? Also, I have other ways of gaining information," He smiled cheekily, an odd look on the young face.

"What else can you tell us?" Vana asked.

Dijn thought, "Cinderella's new Guard Captain is one named Suzee, who is also her friend and advisor."

'Friend!' scoffed the chalkboard. 'She doesn't know how. Advisor? She trusts none."

"Truth, but this one she does for some reason I know not."

"I know Suzee," Skim said, "Hard-bitten, tough, ambitious. But not all bad, she may do the Queen some good."

"Or the Queen may do her some bad. Either way it is too late," Vana shrugged, "But perhaps we will spare her life if she finds the meaning of change."

Melina halted the conversation by stopping and pointing through the trees. While talking, they had come upon the Centaurs; standing between them now was just a thin line of brush.

Skim stepped forward, "Is there one here the Centaur know?"

All heads shook negative, "Then I shall take Vana, Spitter and Melina to find whoever may be able to speak to us."

Melina tugged his arm and wrote. 'Do you know the Centaur customs?"

Skim shook his head.

'Give our names, but never ask theirs, they'll give it when they trust us. Bow and be polite. Never touch them. These are the basics, anything else they'll forgive.' Melina scribbled, wiped and scribbled again before finishing, 'Always be polite, wish long lives and the like.'

Skim nodded, "Thanks Melina. The rest of you, find your way home, do not all leave the forest in a large group, or all at the same place. Dijn, remain here, we will return and take you to our hideout"

The squad leaders departed, muttering between themselves, leaving just the four conspirators and Dijn, who backed away to hide. Prepared with deep breaths and straightened clothes, they stepped out from the forest in a line.

All Centaurs slowly stopped what they were doing and looked curiously at such a number of strangers trespassing here. Eventually one stepped forward and beckoned.

The four nervously moved to her, trying not to look around them, Skim and Vana fighting to keep their hands from defensively holding their sword hilts. A Centaur made an imposing figure to any, so many in one place made a fearsome sight. Some with banded tails, all large, but with peaceful faces.

The one who had called them bowed as they neared. She had red fur and hair, her torso covered in red leather.

All four stopped and bowed almost simultaneously and they saw her hide a smile at the comical image.

"It is unusual for four strangers to visit our field," She said.

"We wish to ask your aid," Vana said, automatically taking her known role as ambassador, "I am called Vana; with me is Skim, ex-Captain of the Queen's Guard, Melina, stepsister to the Queen and Spitter, servant to the spy Jerne."

"An unusual crowd indeed," The Centaur said, "What is it you come to ask for?"

"We are a rebel alliance," Vana told her, "We come to ask your aid to overthrow the tyrannous Cinderella; we know of your great warriors and your slavery, and the Queen's cruelty to those in her service and ask you to join our alliance."

The Centaur considered them for a moment, "I know of your downfall, Skim and your loyalty, Vana. I also know of your imprisonment and previous torture of Cinderella, Melina. I know of your master, Spitter, and will never join such as he in battle for any rule by him would not be a boon."

"We do not truly ally with Jerne and Regina," Vana explained, "They may be of use in our task, but they will never take rulership."

"This is good news indeed, yet I have no cause to trust neither you, nor you me, though you entrust me with your names."

"We know of the Centaur's loyalty and greatness. One in the Palace told us to seek out Arison and Eera, but our spy who remains in the trees knows they are not here."

"Indeed?" The Centaur mused, "If you were sent here by one of ours I must assume your worthiness. What is it you would have us do? You wish us to fight with you when the time comes?"

"Yes," Vana nodded, "To join and command in battle with us and free the Kingdom from Cinderella's grip."

"If you will give me leave, I will discuss this with the other freed Centaurs. Return tomorrow evening through those woods, and bring your spy for I wish to see him."

"As you wish," Vana bowed and the other three followed suit.

The Centaur bowed also, "Remain safe and hidden. I know we will not hinder your battle, but whether we join you is to be decided."

"Thank you," Vana bowed again and the four turned away and returned to the forest, forcing the pace of a calm stroll.

Chapter 19

This time Cinderella was sleeping when Suzee entered bearing a tray of breakfasts. Suzee silently applauded herself as she placed the tray on the nearby table and gently shook Cinderella awake.

The Queen awoke, stifling a yawn, and looked around, "Suzee…the sun has barely risen over the hills, why do you wake me?"

"I was to wake you later, I know," Suzee replied, "but the sorcerer you sent for has arrived and I was also ordered to tell you the second he did…I took the liberty of presuming the second was most important, but I can tell him to wait if you wish."

"My, my," the Queen shook loose her blonde hair from the nightly bun and sat, breathing deep of the breakfast smell, "you have quickly developed a pretty way with words haven't you?"

"I have learned from the best," Suzee smiled, "Ah, but if only I had such a face to match."

Cinderella smiled, "You know how to flatter me. I shall be down to our sorcerer when the sun is risen and light comes in the windows. Feed him and have a room for him, and let him come to me in the private room close to the cellars."

Suzee nodded and took her leave. Cinderella watched after her. *'Learns fast she does, aye and as she learns from me I learn from her. Who might have ever guessed that one day someone 'nice' would befriend me? Not a one, I wager, and yet…here she is, a nice person. Oh, a hard one and one willing to do anything it takes, but still…far from being a bad person. And I know enough about that.'* She sighed inaudibly and forced down the food in front of her before rising and dressing in her casual finery. She waited until the sun was shining in on her, waited a few minutes more—to make the sorcerer wait—and then swung out of her bedroom in her most Queenly fashion to greet this strange magic-man.

And strange he was. A wizened, wrinkled old man, barely reaching stomach-height on the tall Queen. His face was both wrinkled and, seemingly, set into an expression of permanent screwed-up distaste. He held a staff of black wood, topped by a bauble of resin, in the center of which was a single drop of blood. He wore equally black robes, with a hood cast down behind him while he was inside. He smelled faintly musty, exuded an aura of barely-thereness, yet seemed to be more there than Cinderella or the walls around him.

When he rose to greet the Queen, hiding her astonishment in a welcoming smile, he did so fluidly, as a strong young man might, and smiled knowingly to himself as he shook her hand, seeming to peer directly into the very depths of her mind.

The Queen resisted the urge to shrink away and simply took her hand back as soon as she politely could before closing the studded oak door and taking a seat opposite from him in the cold room.

"I apologise for the coldness," she began, "The Palace walls have pipes running through behind the initial, thin walls for hot water to be pumped, but I normally have all but the rooms being used cut off and neglected to order this one open again. It should heat up soon enough; already I can feel the wall warming slightly."

The wizened wizard shrugged, "I feel very little in the way of heat or cold."

Cinderella nodded her favourable impression at this and settled herself more comfortably on the padded stone seat carved into the wall, "I am sure you are wondering why I asked you here…"

Seeing she awaited a reply, the wizard merely shrugged again, "I was curious, yes."

She nodded approval, "I wish your aid, sir—"

"My name is Arguth," He interrupted.

"Arguth then, I wish to enlist your aid in a small venture."

"I am willing," He replied deferentially.

"There are legends of tunnels that pass throughout most of Lamsonia, underground and in walls, each with a secret entrance," She paused to gauge reaction, but the man simply looked at her impassively and waited, "I have found an entrance to these tunnels in one of the castle's dungeon cells, and I was informed by my advisor—Suzee—that you may be the only person capable of using magic to map them for use."

The wizard stood and shuffled back and forth in the small room, muttering to himself. Cinderella watched with one eyebrow raised.

Eventually the wizard sat again, "I just cast a seeing spell on the tunnels to spy out magical barriers. There are some, but none strong enough to keep me out. I would first need to break them throughout before I could map. This means spell-casting at strategic places in the city, could you arrange this?"

Cinderella nodded, "Anywhere you need."

"I will give you a list of items I need for this. After the barriers are down, I will erect my own to keep out any but those you give permission to enter, again I will provide you a list of needed supplies. Lastly, again using these strategic places I will need more items, a list of which I shall write up, and at this point I will be able to map the tunnels for you. In all it should take but a small number of days: a week, perhaps. Is this acceptable?"

Cinderella nodded, "You certainly seem to know what you are about, Arguth. I will have for you any items you require, and only let me know the places you need and my Guards shall ready and stand watch over them."

Arguth nodded and hopped once again from his perch, "I will return later with my three lists of supplies. I expect to start the day after tomorrow at sunup."

And he was gone in a flash before Cinderella could speak, not through the door—which was still firmly closed. Simply gone. Her mouth stood open a moment longer before she shook herself and stood to take her leave in silence.

So it was that out of nowhere, while eating lunch in her den, a thin roll of parchment appeared on the table before Cinderella. She paused, chunk of bread in her hand halfway to her mouth, while

Suzee—sitting opposite and giving a surprised inhale at the unexpected appearance—choked and spat up a wad of meat.

Cinderella calmly put her bread down, "Breathe, Suzee," She said, absentmindedly, to her red-faced advisor who gave her a stony look and continued to slow down her panicked breathing, "This must be the requests from Arguth," The Queen went on pleasantly, oblivious to any radiating waves of irritation from her scorned eating partner.

Looking through, Cinderella's eyes alternately widened and narrowed at the items requested:

For all tasks the following items are needed in each place.
2 scented candles—unused!
1 small wooden bowl
1 small knife
1 bowl of water
materials for fire
1 mirror
salt
1 rabbit (or other small woodland creature)

Places required:
Five (5) locations, each dark, roofed. Set aside from people, but not too far.

Four (4) must be on the outskirts of Lamsonia, set so a line drawn on the outside between them would create a square.

Place five (5) must be set directly in the center of those four (4), this place is to be found by drawing lines inward, diagonally from the four (4) points so they meet in a point at the very center.

Each place must be private, fully enclosed, with nothing on ground ceiling or walls. A tent of canvas will suffice if no building it to be found in the right spot.

Guards must be situated at LEAST out of earshot and NONE must be allowed to come closer as long as I remain inside.

I will contact you tomorrow in person, Queen Cinderella. As I believe I said, I plan to begin at sunup the day after tomorrow, but my tasks cannot be accomplished without everything I have asked. Once everything is ready and I enter the first location, all my work will be accomplished within 3 days, then you shall be presented with a complete map of the tunnels. The tunnels will be secured, so that none who attempt to enter without a special mark I will give you (and any you choose) will be forcibly expelled.

I hope this is to your approval, and I know it is within your power. With my regards until tomorrow evening, I am your faithful subject. Arguth the Unseen

Cinderella finished reading aloud to Suzee who raised her eyebrows, "He certainly is most forthright and superior, isn't he?"

The Queen nodded, "You speak true, but he has much reason to be, and I believe I have no doubt for his loyalty. He is simply who he is, a superior wizard. What gives me worry are the items he requests. Multiply all he asks for by 3, for each task, then by 5, for each location," She considered, "I can easily get enough wooden bowls, small knives, bowls of water, mirrors, firewood and salt. But scented candles…they become rarer each day, and as for unused! I declare it impossible!"

"I think there is a place that may have 30 unused scented candles," Suzee spoke up quietly, "I would ask you not to ask me where, for I know to hoard them is illegal. But this man hoards them for such occasions and people as this, and if I may go with the favour of the Queen he will be sure to sell me all he has, which I wager amounts to more than 30."

Cinderella narrowed her eyes, "Very well…but let him know from me that if he receives any more shipments of these candles—or anything else similar—he is to report to me. He has my word of immunity if I have his vow to report, and so make these things available to me at little cost."

Suzee nodded, "You know the value of such a deal could be high, this man will be most pleased to assist."

"He had better be," Cinderella snapped and went back to eating.

Suzee bolted her food down as fast as she could and reached for the parchment. Cinderella slapped her hand with the tines of a heavy silver fork, "Do not take the original. If it should be lost? Stolen? Damaged?"

Suzee drew back her smarting hand and saw it welling blood, "Apologies," She said tightly, feeling the hand burn and turn red.

"You may go," The Queen waved her away with the same fork, and then stabbed it into her food.

Suzee turned and left, her face twisting with pain and anger and her hand held close to her side, where the other covered it with a cloth.

Basha visibly cowered as Suzee entered the shop, clearly word of her new rank and proximity to Cinderella had spread well.

"Calm down, little man," She smiled reassuringly downwards at the small, chubby figure, "I have a request from your Queen."

"Anything," He squeaked.

Suzee nodded approvingly, related Cinderella's message, and need for candles.

Calmer, now he sensed no imminent danger, Basha nodded and scuttled off behind a dank, brown curtain into the rear of the shop.

He returned in a moment, sweating profusely, with an armful of red candles, which he hurriedly packed into a leather sack, "No charge!" He squeaked and pushed the sack across the counter, simultaneously backing off to press himself into the section of wall uncovered by curtain.

Suzee shook her head, "No, the Queen pays her subjects. People may call her many things, but thief of a man's livelihood is one I will not allow," She tossed a handful of silver drags onto the counter, swept up the sack under one arm, and left with a jaunty salute from a gloved, still painful, hand.

Amazed at his luck, Basha greedily hid the drags under the counter. There they would remain until closing time before most would retire behind a board in his house, and one would buy all fortunate enough to be in his local alehouse a decent meal and a drink.

Suzee moved at double-time back to Cinderella, still in her den, waiting.

"I have the candles. And the man was very pleased to accept your offer."

"He is intelligent," Cinderella smiled cruelly, "I will have the other requirements assembled soon. If you could give out the instructions for the five places Arguth needs to your men, that would be most helpful."

Suzee nodded and left once more.

Cinderella watched her go with a somewhat heavy heart. The fork she had used as her weapon still lay on the table, polished clean, but to her it near dripped blood. *'She needed to be taught a lesson…cruel as it may seem, I am still her Queen, not her equal.'* She told herself, repeatedly, eventually grinding her teeth in anger and storming from her rooms.

Walking in the courtyard, she came close to the Centaur stables. Usually quiet, its inhabitants stalwart and stony-faced, this time there was a current of babble reaching out to her from within.

Refusing to hold her nose against the smell of the rarely cleaned building, Cinderella moved closer, listened.

"I am sure Mossan will accept," Said one voice, female, young.

"And when the time is right we will join them. None can prevent our escape if we all go at once," Said another, male, deep.

"And break our vow of servitude? A beastly vow it may be, but it is yet a vow," Came a third, gravely and stubborn.

"We vowed to the family of our current King. He has promised us freedom on his return, in exchange for Mossan's locating of his man. What? We cannot simply take it early?" A fourth voice this one high-pitched and wavery.

A fifth voice hummed for a moment, "Perhaps if we got a message to Osmon, requesting him to grant our freedom now…"

A babble of approval. Then the gravely voice spoke over it, "And then? You would have us war against the Monarchy? Aye, she might be a bitch and a tyrant, but we are Centaur. Above such petty squabbles as humans have."

"Aye," mimicked another voice, "And yet we still fall prey to them. To this one anyhow, and are we not 'allowed' to 'interfere' in our own lives?"

The stubborn voice was drowned again in general rabble. Eventually, though, it spoke one last time:

"I'll go with you, you know I'll not desert my race, and I'll be fighting at the front the same as the rest of you. But make sure you recall what I said when our Gods frown on our interference."

A small crowd of dismissive jeers, and Cinderella heard metal shoes clopping towards her at a slow pace. Quickly, she withdrew into the shadows and watched a brawny, fiery-red Centaur stomp away, muttering dark thoughts to himself.

"Centaur!" She called after him, "Stay where you are. Do not turn."

He obeyed.

"The Queen knows of the Centaur's imminent betrayal. Rest assured your Gods will frown upon you!"

The Centaur turned now, ready to throw angry words. But the speaker was gone, melted into the shadows and hurrying back inside in a furor!

He looked back into his stable, returned in a hurry to relay the promise.

Shouts of anger and terror rose from within, followed by an overflow of disbelief.

The Centaur returned outside, dejected. As the only objector, he had not been believed by those inside. But he hoped, prayed to all his Gods, that Mossan would listen, if he could only get past the Guards at the gate to see her.

Inside, Cinderella fumed and stormed the corridors, "Get me Suzee!" She screamed at all who came close, "Get me Suzee!" She screamed at the walls, "By the Gods I'll paint the castle in their blood and decorate the turrets with their heads! And him—release them, will he? I'll show him who has the final word! Yes, when he returns...this Queendom will be a *very* different place!" Then once again to all within earshot, "GET ME SUZEE!"

Suzee was found instructing her men, but finished in a hurry as messages came from all sides. The Queen was insane! Calling for her! Steaming with fury!

Afraid, still hiding her hand in a glove, Suzee hurried to the castle where she followed the sound of echoing shouts to its source. Warily, she approached the Queen.

Cinderella was distraught, her face wrung and pale, her hair falling loose, her clothing twisted and torn.

"Liege?" Suzee whispered, but it was enough. The Queen spun to face her, controlled her bloodshot, rolling eyes.

"Suzee!" Cinderella mouthed, and collapsed in her Guard's arms.

Suzee carried the limp, moaning woman to her chambers and called for hot water and a sharp drink. Once these arrived, speedily, from pale and worried servants, she kicked the door closed and locked it before bathing the Queen's forehead with a cloth.

Slowly, tenderly, Suzee encouraged the lady awake, finally dripping a cap of reviving drink down her throat. At that, Cinderella was wide-awake and gripping Suzee fiercely by the shoulders.

"The Centaurs…" she gasped, "Osmon…rebellion!"

Shocked into action, Suzee leapt up and paced the room, "Calm down," she said in the most soothing tone she could muster, "Tell me everything."

Cinderella waited until her advisor had seated herself close by, then with deep breaths told her of the conversation she overheard, and of her words to the Centaur who had disagreed.

Suzee listened with wide eyes, "A mutiny," she breathed at the end of it, "The Centaurs! Osmon in on it too…and who else?"

Cinderella shook her head, "I have enemies, Suzee. Skimbradge, Vana, Jerne, my stepsisters…half the Kingdom. Gods, Suzee I only tried to be tough, I only wanted…not to be hurt again!"

"I know, Cinderella," Suzee used the name for the first time, and it seemed to be what was needed for the Queen relaxed and slumped.

"You…call me as a friend," Cinderella said quietly.

"I do," Suzee replied, "I thought…we could be one day. Perhaps the day is now."

Cinderella nodded, bowed her head and leaned in Suzee's shoulder, "Yes. Friend…I have…never had a friend. I apologise…for the fork…"

Suzee winced to be reminded of her hand, but only nodded and accepted it, "You've been treated worse than anyone could cope with. None blame you for how you have been, but yes, they do hate you for being it."

"Is it, then, too late?" the weakened tyrant looked up with large eyes.

"Perhaps...if we can crush this, show the people that the rebellious are the tyrants...then once crushed, we can work on how you rule. But...can you be vicious, at least publicly, until we crush this thing?"

Cinderella thought a moment...straightened up and put on her cruelest smile of cold, burning hatred, "Oh yes, I can do that. I say we take the Centaurs first."

'And still her hatred of another breed overtakes everything...perhaps it's not so shocking, she was treated as an alien being herself.' Suzee thought. *'We must crush this, for they will not allow her to live even if she tries to flee and never return. But then...?'* she left this unanswered for now, placed survival firmly in her mind. For if Cinderella was to die, who would spare Suzee? *'None...not now.'* she answered herself.

Cinderella was looking at her searchingly, waiting for advice.

"I am your advisor?" Suzee asked, "Most trusted in all things?"

Cinderella nodded.

"Then you must listen to me. We have an army of soldiers, plus the Royal Guard. We have Arguth. They have Centaurs, perhaps a few of your traitors...if we can surprise the Centaurs, attack the Palace and the Field in one blow, then what is left?"

"A handful of hiders," Cinderella replied, nodding, "Who can be picked off at will."

"Following which," Suzee continued, "Your image can undergo something of a change, after you have banished Osmon and Royston for good, of course."

Now a cruel smile slipped into place, "Yes..."

"But, Cinderella...you can pretend to still be cruel for a while, but you cannot forever pretend to be nice. This is your choice. I will stand by you, but choose now—once the threat is crushed, will you let our citizens be free and rule with a loose hand? Or will you draw them in tighter?"

Suzee held her breath, either way would give her power, and power was all she wanted. That and the friendship of this troubled and gloriously cruel Queen.

Cinderella stood; her posture was straight and her head high, "I will...draw these peasants tight to me. None shall step foot onto or off this Island without my personal leave. All shall work or die. And all shall give penance for their treacherous ways."

179

Queenly once more apart from the wrinkling and tearing of her dress, Cinderella turned to Suzee and smiled her cruel smile, "And you, Suzee, will be by my side."

Suzee stood, "I will m'lady. For always."

The Queen nodded, "I shall knight you, Suzee, once the Centaur threat is crushed. And now...tell me, how will we do this? How will we take the heads of every single Centaur on this miserable Island?"

Suzee smiled, her course was set, and began to sketch out a plan of annihilation.

Chapter 20

Samson squinted in the afternoon mist, a sure sign they were drawing close to the foggy island of Giizintaan, even if the call of 'Land Ho!' Wasn't still ringing in his ears. Sure enough, there was a faint line crossing half the horizon. A small Island, this, but large to take the one or two problems that were readying themselves to disembark from his ship.

Samson remembered Royston's tale. He had listened intently to the man, before his story turned to insane-sounding ramblings and vows of revenge (at which point Samson had made a speedy exit). He thought Osmon would get no warm reception from the man, possibly even a violent one, for after killing that pixie who could know where his brain would be now.

He felt Eera and Osmon come to stand close by him, watching the flat line of the island grow as the boat sailed closer.

"How long?" Asked Eera, sensing Samson's apprehension.

"'Bout an hour, these fogs're tricky, mebbe less."

"Will he be waiting for us?" Osmon asked quietly, almost rhetorically.

Samson kept his silence and Eera frowned a little, but replied, "He may be watching for us, but I doubt he will still be there when we put in. I think…it will be up to us to go to him."

"A power game," Osmon nodded, "Then he is a new man, the one I knew played no games."

Eera put a gentle hand on the King's shoulder, "Maybe a game, maybe fear of what we are here to do, maybe fear of meeting you once more, maybe shame, maybe hatred…his absence could mean much or little."

Osmon sighed and bowed his head, "I want to see him play tonight; we can go to meet him after that."

Samson nodded, "Aye, word is he's t'best Giizintaan ever saw."

"He used to play to me…happy music; full of love…I doubt he plays like that any more," Osmon turned away, "I'll be in my cabin until we dock."

"Aye, liege," Samson grunted, steadying the ship to run a straight course through the mist.

Before an hour was past, the ship was docked and Samson clearing his crew for leave, "I know you'll all be sleepin' on t'ship," He told them, "So I'll leave notice when we're ready ter leave. G'arn now, 'ave some fun," He waved them away and they scattered down the plank and quickly disappeared in their different directions, soon out of sight in the thick fog.

"A'right, so where d'we go now?" Samson asked Eera and Osmon, once the ship was clear of all others.

Eera looked up at the barely visible sun, "I find it hard to gauge time in this fog, but I should say it is late afternoon. The musicians on the Island usually put on their show before dark…this time of year it will begin to darken early. So I recommend we simply move to the square and find a bolthole from which to watch and listen without Royston seeing us."

"Smart 'un inn'ee?" Samson grunted, amused, "Sounds a'right by me, liege?"

Osmon was pulled from his reverie, staring into the swirling mists with blank eyes, "Hmm? Oh, yes, thank you Eera."

The three trundled down the gangplank and Samson waited while Eera stomped his hooves on the ground and took off on a small, circular run.

"Good ter be back on t'ground, eh?"

Eera nodded, "It certainly is. I have been on ships before, but am never able to get used to having no solid ground under my hooves."

Samson guffawed and clapped Eera on the back.

Osmon looked at them faintly, once again lost in his own world, "Do we go?" He asked, once Samson had finished chuckling.

Eera nodded and Samson set off slightly ahead of them, leading them to the square, a journey he knew better than either of them.

A short walk and they were there. Already a small audience milled around, chattering quietly, waiting for the show to begin. They heard names mentioned, Royston's among them, his usually steeped in complimentary awe.

Eera left the two alone and scouted for a good spot. Returning, he took them to an alcove large enough fit them all comfortably, where they could look out as they chose while being hidden behind the growing crowd.

Samson leaned back on the wall and proceeded to stuff his battered old pipe with tobacco and smoke it, "Aaaahhh" he commented after a puff or two, "Nowt like the good ol' weed from some o' these Islands. Pure Arasin weed, this stuff, best there is."

Osmon ignored him, or rather didn't hear him. He was too busy watching the small stage in the centre of the square intently, waiting for the smallest sign of Royston's arrival.

There was not long to wait. Soon a ripple of cheers ran over the audience, and clapping followed as the troupe of musicians came into view. Most settled around the stage, heads bowed the way they normally did. One other, a middle-aged man with a small paunch, carrying a smooth, rounded stone, stepped up onto the stage and let the applause continue for a moment before raising a weathered hand.

He launched into a well-practiced speech while the audience waited patiently, knowing this was for anyone new.

"Good Afternoon, ladies and gentlemen of all race and species," He began, "For those of you new to our little performance, allow me to introduce ourselves. I am Ellis, on the moonstone," He paused for applause and cheers before indicating each man in turn, halting each time for the noise to die, "Tanton, on the hand-harp…Hesuit on the viola…Zane on the sitar…Royston on the pipes…" here he was forced to quell the raucous crowd before continuing, "And our newest member, to replace dear Dijn on vocals, Pexem!" He stood back and finally let the crowd show their full appreciation.

When finally they quit, he spoke one more time, "Without further delay, let us begin," He grinned and raised his moonstone, enveloping the crowd in a soft, mournful melody.

Eera and Samson watched each musician with interest. Osmon stiffened each time they changed players, but he could see they played in order of introduction so it was not until Pexem followed Zane that he spoke to ask when Royston would play.

Samson grunted and turned to him, "They play 'em in t'order they stand mostly, but when there's a clear favourite they play 'im last."

Osmon nodded. *'Next, then. I could have guessed that...I simply wondered why they skipped him.'* He resumed his watching, letting the sweet vocals of Pexem wash over him unheard, as he had the music of all the others.

When finally Pexem finished, Osmon stiffened to rigidity and waited. Royston stepped up on the platform and finally raised his head.

He was sallow faced and pale, Osmon could see from his distance the bags under his eyes and the way his dark clothes hung loosely. Royston lifted the pipe almost carelessly to his lips and a hush fell over the crowd.

Royston scanned the audience quickly. *'I know you're there, Osmon...I saw your ship arrive, I saw you disembark. Listen. Listen well. See how it feels to be me.'*

The crowd was still silent, waiting, and Osmon was breathing in short, quick gasps. Eera and Samson watched him carefully, ready for any reaction, but Osmon simply stood and waited, feeling he knew what he was about to hear.

A note flowed from the pipes. Slender and kind, it was, followed by more. For a moment the tune was love, happiness, then sadness of a kind. It went up again, to guarded pleasure and secrecy, remaining so for a long while.

Osmon groaned and his legs wobbled, but still he stood and listened, playing their 15-year relationship in his head as it fit with the music.

The guarded pleasure faded and a silence hung in the air, apprehension...then it built, going towards...something?...Building higher and higher...until at it's peak, it crashed into a downwards spiral, taking Osmon to the floor with it, uncaring of the damp seeping through to chill his bones as he had been chilled inside from the day this event took place.

Royston still played…anger, hatred and tears fell from his pipe, a faint shanty hovered in the background as he spoke to the Gods themselves. Then faint tinkles as he arrived on the Island and fell into a new life.

Apprehensive anger followed, dueting with Osmon's groans…he knew what was to follow, something he had tried so hard not to think of.

And here it came; anger and nervousness, scurrying and looking around, the pipes twittered angrily and then came to a halt. For a second…two…silence…then a blast and a crack of sound!

Then nothing. Royston bowed and left the stage.

Applause from every direction, cheers and whistles from all but three in the crowd. The three who knew what the tune truly meant.

From two of those three came no sound, but from the third came a shaking denial, a groan, tears falling to lose themselves on the dark ground.

Eera and Samson dragged Osmon bodily away, almost threw him into an enclosed alley and pushed him down to the end of the deserted path. There he sat, huddled to himself, curled into a corner of the wall. Whimpers and small cries fell from his shaking face, tears ran in a stream to wet his clothes, but Osmon heard no pleas, no words from his two friends, only the tune…over and over, replaying with each note the event that it told.

Able to take it no more, Samson reached out and, with a hoarse apology, picked Osmon up and slapped him twice, quickly, shaking him back to the present.

Osmon stared at him for a second, hardly knowing what it was that had brought him back, eyes blank and wet. Samson let him gently down and the King stood on both feet, shaky but firm. But then he collapsed to his knees and tore at his hair, and from his mouth came an animal howl of grief and pain.

Samson and Eera looked behind them; one or two people looked in and started to ask questions. Eera cantered over to them, leaving Samson to calm the now silent King.

Sending them away appeased with his gentle intelligence, Eera trotted back to the two shapes on the floor. Osmon was shaking in Samson's arms, but quiet now, neither seeing nor hearing anything.

185

"Royston..." He murmured into Samson's chest and closed his eyes, a small smile playing upon his lips.

Samson looked at Eera and shrugged with his eyes, "I tried to tell him I wasn't," he whispered in a gruff voice, holding back a lump in his own throat, "But it seemed to help if he thought I was...for now, anyhow."

Eera nodded, "Put him on my back," He whispered and turned sideways on. Samson lifted the sleeping King and placed him sidesaddle on the Centaur. Eera grunted at the weight. *'I believe I am too old to do this on a regular basis.'* He thought wryly, *'But this man...I would carry until my back broke.'*

With Samson holding the lifeless body on, cupping his hand and bringing it to his lips whenever someone looked at them strangely — the universal symbol of too much drinking — Eera carried Osmon to a hotel close to the musician's shared house.

The place was dark, indicating they were not yet home; but they would be soon and so it was best to hurry inside.

Samson spoke to the innkeeper and took a room at the front, with beds for three and a bathtub — which, the innkeeper promised, would be filled with hot water whenever they needed it. Samson grinned and slipped the man yet another drag, "And if anyone comes askin' if we're 'ere?" He quizzed.

"I've never seen you in my life!" The chubby old man replied convincingly.

"Good man," Samson nodded, "And that means anyone, mind, anyone at all. If we want a visitor, we'll be bringing 'em ourselves. Ye ken?"

"But of course," The man nodded and palmed the coins like a pro.

Samson held out his rough hand and the innkeeper shook it, smiling at his good fortune.

Skim, Vana, Spitter and Melina stood in much the same spot as they had the day before, on the edge of Centaur Forest. This time, however, they had with them a fifth. Dijn, their newest recruit, who the red-haired and furred Centaur had asked to see.

Dijn looked fearfully around him, as had the others the day before. But the Centaurs were ignoring them, so it seemed, none looked their way after the first few glances and the five waited impatiently, wondering whether they should walk further in.

Eventually, however, the red Centaur seemed to notice them and came over. Behind her walked another, with a fiery-red mane and pockmarked face. He twitched his moustache and looked down at them.

"Follow me," The female said and took them through a bramble that looked deceivingly thick, and into an enormous enclosed clearing, "None will see or hear us here," She told them, "I had thoughts that you may like to bring your men here, those who are sleeping elsewhere that is. Though I refuse to have the traitor-spy and his woman," She smiled knowingly as if to say 'Yes, I know things too.' And Skim nodded.

"It is certainly more than large enough. Most of our allies are still within the city, seeming to be loyal to the tyrant. But there are some, and there will be more before the day is out."

"Does this mean you will join us?" Vana asked, glancing a little nervously at the stone-faced male standing directly in front of her.

"I had talked with the other Centaurs," The female said, "And we had decided that yes, we would join you."

"Had? Would?" Vana asked.

"Now it is imperative that we join you, and lay our plans as speedily as is possible."

"What...what happened?" Skim asked.

"First," the female said, "As our allies you—and only you five— may have our names. We have yours, and now give you ours as a symbol of our bond."

Skim drew his sword and knelt in front of it. Vana followed suit. Melina, Spitter and Dijn simply knelt.

"Your others shall call me Red-Huntress," the female went on, accepting the tribute wordlessly, "And the man beside me they shall know as Dark-Star. They shall need to interact with no other Centaurs. My name is Mossan. Beside me stands my loyal brother, Micx."

'I thank you for your names and shall keep them always safe.' Melina was the first to answer via her chalkboard, more instinctively aware of the Centaur traditions than the others were.

The four quickly followed suit and rose, Skim and Vana sheathing their swords.

Dijn stepped forward before anyone could speak further, "You do not yet have my name, not from my lips. I am Dijn," He bowed.

"Thank you for your name, Dijn. We shall keep it safe," Micx growled.

Mossan nodded to him and he carried on speaking.

"The tyrant, the one you name Cinderella, knows of our alliance. She knows the Centaurs would join with unnamed rebels to throw her from her throne. She heard our argument in the Palace and spoke to me, the one voice who spoke in disagreement for fear of failure," here he bowed his head, "and as I left the stable she spoke to me, telling me the Queen knew and would destroy our race. I ran from the Palace, fortunately I am a rarely used beast," he spat the words bitterly, "And often come and go for a day or two. The Guards let me go with a smile and a nod, and I ran here swift as I could. We would have joined you anyway, even I would have overcome my cowardice, but now it seems destined. We must lay plans immediately, for the tyrant works speedily with her new advisor to run around for her. She will attack the Centaur, but we do not know which group. We must prepare for both, and if we lose we shall die before becoming her prisoner. If we win, then the way is open to be rid of her," He finished in a gruff growl and looked around, challenging any to speak against him.

Skim was the first to reply, "I am sorry you were brought to this," He said, simply.

Micx shook his head and stomped a hoof, "It is time the bitch was brought down. Vows, we do not break, but Osmon was to release us upon his return. As it is, we shall simply take our release sooner, in fact when I return we shall privately release ourselves, thus leaving us free to fight. It is time the Centaurs recalled how to fight for what is right. I forgot this in my cowardice, long years of work can easily break courage, but now I see the time has come to repay this so-called-woman for all she has done and will do. Not just to Centaurs, but to all creatures on this earth," He drew himself up proudly, "Once we were the greatest warriors the world had ever seen! It runs still in our blood, and now is the time to recall it!"

Mossan interrupted with a small shake of her head, "I believe they are already convinced, brother, therefore what the need to pontificate?" She smiled, and gained a frown in return, "A great potential warrior—though untried as are most of us before we leave the Palace—sadly, my brother has yet to develop one of those more advanced personality facets...namely, a sense of humour."

The four humans and Spitter stifled their giggles, still somewhat nervous of this towering Centaur with the gruff face.

"We must have a way to get a message to the Palace. Micx cannot forever come and go, and most of the others will not be allowed," Mossan went on, deadly serious again, "We can talk to you, as you will be here, but it is impossible to get to the stable through the normal route—even should we get inside the grounds, the stables are off-limits."

All were quiet for a minute, trying to think of some ingenious, reliable and reuseable way of swapping notes. Eventually Dijn raised his head and spoke tentatively.

"I am a spy...but not a great one. There is one, however, who knows all the routes, all the tunnels..." He faltered as Mossan turned to him.

"You speak of Jerne, the traitor who thinks we serve him?"

Dijn nodded, but elaborated no further, preferring to shrink back behind Skim and Vana.

But Vana had understood, "He thinks we work for him. He is proud of his skills, and none can deny that he has them..." she mused, "Perhaps he may be of use. So long as he believes we are on the same side, where the harm? Send him in with a note; tell him to return with another. He will believe that the Centaurs will only speak to those who first contacted them, because that's true...he's fast, we know that...I see no harm in making use of him."

"Is this what you were thinking, Dijn?" Asked Micx, as kindly as he could manage for the spy was still almost cowering in the background.

He nodded, "Yes, sir."

Micx reached out a great hand and patted Dijn's shoulder, "Good man, you have a brain worthy of a Centaur Master, I'll warrant!"

Dijn looked up in pleased surprise; even one unversed in Centaur ways could recognise a great compliment when he heard one.

'But how to stop him reading the notes?' Melina scribbled and showed around the circle.

"The Centaur still practice the Old tongue," Mossan replied, "I can write notes in that language, and have replies the same way. If the spy asks, say it is simply extra security against the unlikely possibility of his capture, or that the note should be taken by one of the Queen's loyal."

"Not that there's many of them left!" grunted Skim.

"Who do you have?" Micx asked.

"We have all her squad leaders and Guard but one—that being her Captain and advisor, Suzee. She treats none of us well; to say nothing of treating us badly, and not even one has quailed in the face of our task. There are us," he indicated the group, "The Palace Centaurs and the freed. This is all so far, but the workers will rise with us when asked, of this I am certain."

Mossan considered this carefully, "Perhaps I have three others to join you."

"Three!" Scoffed Micx, "How about a three hundred, sister!"

"These…" She sighed at him, "May well be better than a three-ton. Cinderella's old godmother, Mueren is in her Tower with Cinamon, the young Prince, and our most powerful, Arison. I shall call them back immediately to prepare for battle. I know Mueren's power from the words of Eera, and of Arison's with my own sight. Cinamon…is untested, but if the notes we receive are true, he learns with the speed of thought and excels as if he were a miracle."

Micx bowed his head in acquiescence, "My apologies, sister," He growled.

Mossan acknowledged with a nod of the head, "So we have a good army, and now…we wait…set our plans for the tyrant, whether she attacks the Forest or the Palace Centaurs. It will not be long. I would wager you that. And when she does…" Mossan shrugged, "We'll be ready. To win, to knock her down, and to free this once-lovely Kingdom from her forever."

Micx grunted a laugh, "Now who pontificates?"

Chapter 21

Arguth entered the large, canvas tent and scrutinised it, taking in everything in a quick glance.

It sat over solid earth, which had been meticulously cleansed of all grasses, weeds and possibly even bugs. He smiled a little at this; he had not been so specific. Sitting in the center, upon no table, with no gentle thing for him to sit on, were the objects he had requested.

He nodded to himself, looked back and sent out his telepathic thoughts to probe the two Guardsmen. They were well out of earshot, smoking and chatting with each other, and the occasional acquaintance. But neither gave away their mission, and most knew better than to ask

Satisfied, Arguth seated himself in front of the pile of objects and arranged them into a comfortable order. Ready, now, he closed his eyes, took a deep breath and prepared his mind, clearing and purging it of all things but the barriers around the hidden tunnels.

Done, now, he dimmed the overhead sun, climbing in through the canvas, with a thin shroud of Darkness, leaving just enough light to see by.

He struck a flame using the tinderbox provided, and lit the kindling, which in turn fed the small fire that would heat the bowl of water already placed over the top. Now he waited, watching the water. He could boil it himself, oh yes, but it was purer when boiled naturally, so he waited.

When the bubbles were fierce and the steam was rising thickly, he removed it—leaving the fire on for warmth—and placed it on the ground before him. Using the tinderbox again, he lit the candles, which were set on either side, surrounding his objects.

Taking the mirror, he placed it carefully on the surface of the water, careful not to wet it. Instead of sinking, his magic kept it afloat as he poured salt on it to create an unbroken circle.

Now he took the knife and small bowl and, setting the bowl on top of the still-floating mirror, he drew the knife slowly across his palm. Even the hardiest of men would grimace and cry out at the deep cut, from which he dripped blood into the wooden bowl, but Arguth remained stony faced; though indeed his insides cried out. With pleasure.

Prepared, now, he let his hands hover over the water bowl, slightly to each side so he could see the mirror and bowl of blood below them.

Softly he began to chant, words unused by the White magus for centuries, taken in secret by the Black magus and forced into meanings of power.

He chanted, softly, voice rising and falling, all the time watching the center of the bowl of blood intently, unblinking, unmoving, barely breathing.

There was a flicker and a small figure appeared, growing larger as he moved his hands away and stood. The figure grew only up to the height of his hands, but no further. Arguth could have kept it small, but found them more willing to talk and assist with a little height.

The figure was stocky with red-tinted skin. His eyes were yellow and blue, matched by baubles of jewellery. His clothes were finery, baggy trousers and tight jacket, each woven with fine threads in all the colours the eye could see and likely more. On his head was a black turban, fastened with a burnished copper clasp in the shape of a sword.

Now, keeping the figure small enough so a quick word could put it down again, Arguth spoke.

"There are barriers around secret tunnels in this Kingdom. I want you to remove them, and replace them with ones of my own construct."

The figure scowled, "Why?" It muttered.

"Because I, Arguth the Unseen, command it!" He told the figure firmly, "Because to disobey me will be dire for you."

The figure grunted, shrugged, "Okay, where's the barriers and what d'you want me to replace 'em with?"

Arguth smiled, nodded, "Good choice. The barriers are covering tunnels which run through these lands. I will call you five times, each time to weaken the barrier, and the fifth I will also ask you to erect a new one—which will be similar, but composed of my magic, and concentrating on a specific sigil which any who enter must wear on their person, or be cast out. Once you have proved yourself in this, I will call you five more times—this is to map the tunnels, which you will do for me on parchment I bring."

The figure sighed, "As you request, I shall do."

"And I would like a little more willing cooperation," Arguth growled, "Or your punishment shall be the same. You may be a dark Genie, but you are still in my power, and I always keep a lamp or two handy…"

The Genie changed instantly, stood straighter, bowed low, "Yes, my lord. Sorry my lord."

"Good, better. Now let us begin," Arguth told him.

Cinderella reclined in her bed, grimacing in the general direction of her stomach, "A girl," She muttered in disgust.

Suzee entered and gave her a puzzled look, "Cinderella?"

The Queen looked up, "Suzee…the practitioner was just here. He claims my child is to be a girl," She spat the word in disgust.

"A girl may follow in your footsteps," Suzee pointed out, not seeing the problem.

"A girl may be cruel and overtake her mother, who wishes to be remembered rather than overshadowed and poisoned one lonely night by a girl too alike."

Suzee sat on the edge of the bed and mused, "There is nothing to say you must bear the child…even now, there are ways to be rid, and only a small white lie need be told the serfs." Seeing the Queen's face darken, Suzee tried again, "And of course, there is the current popular trend among those unable to take care of their children, it is called adoption. They hand them to the rich who cannot bear themselves, and the children are raised better than the poor original parents could have ever done."

Cinderella looked a little brighter at that, "Someone might take away this child, so it might never know me for its mother?"

Suzee nodded.

"This is something I will think on," She nodded, pleased, "How are things coming?" She asked now.

Suzee cleared her throat, "Arguth is in his first tent now; he says he can be done in two days if he gets the reasonable power," The woman shrugged, "I have no clue what that means, but I wished him luck in it anyhow. I have split up and rearranged all the Guard squads, if there are any rebels left behind by Skim and Vana they are now split apart. Men are travelling to Giizintaan to...obstruct...the King's return, should he attempt to bring anything...unsavoury...Back with him. The Palace Centaur are being watched at all times, but as you requested no watch is set upon the forest tribe."

Cinderella nodded, "And do you wonder why I request this?" She asked.

Suzee nodded, "I did,"

A crafty smile lit up her face, "These Forest Centaurs are intelligent, sneaky. You know as I do the history of their race, the greatest warriors and thinkers ever known have emerged from within their ranks. They would know, the banished ones, they have had time to hone their talents once more. But our Centaurs, they are kept tired, a little hungry, on edge, a watcher will never be noticed among their misery in that too-small stable. And that is also why we attack them first."

"But surely an attack on the defenceless will anger the trained Centaur more!" Suzee protested, "I tell you, Cinderella, we need to strike on the strong side first, take that down then the small handful of human rebels and Palace Centaurs can be dealt with in our own time."

"Yes...but to go man-to-beast against a trained tribe of those creatures is suicide. Angered, they may be stronger, yes, but also more willful, more careless, ready to run headlong into a sword. They may have honed their talents, but the war skills of the Old Centaur are long lost by now. They will crack under anger and pressure, and give themselves to us," The Queen settled back, shifted painfully and waited for Suzee's reply.

"I believe we both show logic," She said finally, smiling, "But I will follow you anywhere, Cinderella, only allow me to lay my plans and instruct my men and we will be prepared for what you say."

Cinderella smiled and closed her eyes, "Good," She yawned, "I feel I must sleep…please wake me when the kitchens call that food is prepared."

Suzee smiled to herself. *'Still a Queen, even as a friend, but nicer about it — to me at least.'* And still grinning ruefully, she left, closing the door silently behind her.

Cinderella smiled to herself, "Get rid of the child…conquer the Centaurs…be rid of my girl-like husband, and his bitch…yes, this will be a good time, full of blood and victory — for me! And then? Who would presume to question my rule? Who would presume to offer me their head? None and none that I can see," She settled into a drifting doze, faint smile sliding off her relaxing face as she wondered. *'But what have I missed? I feel…something I have forgotten…something which could ruin my plans…'* But the thought was gone as the darkness overtook her and pulled her gently into dreamless sleep.

Mueren smiled widely as the ball of fire rose in the air hit a target 100 metres away.

Cinamon, still concentrating, created between his hands a ball of water and hurled it at the flame, which was extinguished as soon as the water hit.

Now he turned and grinned his pleasure, "Did you see? I did it! My first try!"

Mueren hugged him and nodded, "I saw, young one. That trick took me near 12 years to fathom! Ah, but the Gods are on your side, Cinamon."

"I know," He nodded, "It is soon, I feel it, when I will be needed to help my Kingdom. But be it the Gods, or that I was born under a magical star, these spells are as childsplay to me."

Mueren studied him and noticed again how he had grown noticeably in just the short time he had spent at Pyrone's Tower. Not within, but without, he was older, more intelligent, and looked out with soulful eyes upon a world he was training to defend. A hard burden for one so young. Yet, somehow she knew he could carry it and much more on his slender shoulders.

Arison, watching from the side, was thinking much the same thing. Only her thoughts were darker. '*One so young, so innocent…yet he is being trained to kill some unknown enemy, and I should simply watch his childhood fall away, and call it the will of these cruel Human Gods? And I must, for I am ordered to protect his body, not his mind. Though what use his body will be if his mind breaks, I do not dare think. He is powerful, aye, but…power corrupts, and the battle is soon. How will he fare when faced with a sword? Can he kill, or will he be killed? And if he kills…what then? To take a life, for one so young to do that, and have so much power…I fear this could endanger us all.*'

She snapped herself out of her sorrow as Cinamon raced over to her and flung his arms around her muscled neck, "Did you see, Arison?"

"I saw, Cinamon. You are a powerful one, for sure," She forced a smile, and knew Mueren, walking towards her, was not fooled.

"Inside now, child," The old witch ordered, "Time for you to make your old teacher a meal."

He nodded and ran in to make whatever came into his head.

"So you still doubt, Arison," Mueren shot to the point.

"I doubt none of his power," The Centaur shrugged, "I doubt not his intention, or his ability, or his strength."

"Then what?" Came the frustrated reply, "You doubt something, you fear something, but never tell me what it is that affects you so much. Am I but a foolish girl, prone to giggling and gossip? And if I were, would I be teaching this young child as I am?"

Arison sighed, "I cannot say, Mueren, you know I cannot. I am ordered to care for the boy, and this I will do until my last breath. That is all you need know."

Mueren snorted, "I already do know that, if only because you are Centaur. I also know it because, though you tell me nothing of import, I know you in some way. You care for him as a mother, as do I—and any he meets, I don't doubt! He'll not come to harm while he's himself that I know."

Arison smiled faintly, "You speak truth. So let it rest, sorceress, and yourself with it."

Mueren scowled, shook her head, shrugged, "As you will, warrior," She mimicked with a cheeky smile, "But whatever it is that eats you up, I wish you would tell me," She sighed and took Arison's arm, leaning on her slightly as she limped back to the Tower.

"Your pain grows worse," Arison commented.

"It does, by the day or near enough. I think I'm not long for this world. But Pyrone knows I've prayed for release many-a-time. This will be my last work on this Earth, I think, and I plan to visit my grave knowing I trained a good wizard, who will ever battle the forces opposed to the Light."

Arison nodded, "You train him well, Mueren, and you shall have any burial you wish—you earn one worthy of a Centaur, or of a warrior, or any other you choose."

"My wishes are written," The woman replied, "You shall have them before we depart this place."

Arison would have dropped to one knee and begged her elder to say what Arison feared she was trying to say, but could only pat her arm gently, "You are one of a dying breed, Mueren, and the world shall be much less without your light in it."

Mueren smiled faintly and looked away towards the falling sun, "I'll watch you from Pyrone's Court," She promised, tears glistening in the dying light, "And I'll be sure you fare well."

Arison bowed her head, with nothing more to say she simply walked on at Mueren's tottering speed into the Tower, where Cinamon was singing snatches of old songs as he prepared some unknown feast.

Mueren sat herself with a grunt of pleasure on her chair, made in her younger days of soft leather and feathers. She looked thoughtful for a time, and sad, and then finally spoke her mind, "It is possible, Arison, that I may leave you and the boy sooner that I hoped. His teaching is finished and all that remains is practice. I feel…weary, and my heart sputters. If I should go before word comes that we are needed, please take the parchment from the drawer beside my bed, continue to practice Cinamon here, and let Eera and the other Centaur know of my passing," She breathed heavily and settled herself as air whistled in and out of her lungs.

Arison felt a weight lie on her heart, "You cannot die, Mueren, you are still needed here."

"No, the boy is well enough and you can practice him as well as any. I...I hoped to see him in battle against whatever trouble comes, but each time my heart sputters it does so for longer, and seems harder to start up again. I fear it is my time, and Pyrone has finally finished with me. I beg of you only one thing; to visit my grave sometime and tell me how things go." She dropped her head back to close her eyes, "Could you light the lamps, Arison?" She asked, a hitch in her voice, "Wake me when Cinamon is done making a mess of my kitchen."

Arison nodded and moved around the room, lighting a lamp with the tinderbox and touching it to the others. She touched Mueren's pale forehead and found it cold and damp. Her breathing was ragged, though deeper in sleep, and Arison gently kissed the wrinkled forehead, "I fear this is the last time you wake, wise one," She said, a tear dropping onto the chair.

Arison fought with herself, wanting to shake the witch and bring her round, but for what? *'If she is to pass away the next time she sleeps, let it be at a peaceful moment when she has said all she needs to say.'* The Centaur thought, wiping dry her eyes, to no avail as tears dripped over her fingers. *'Go in peace, Mueren. You belong wherever your Gods are, as their equal, for you were a Goddess among Humans.'* Arison turned her face away from the chest, rising slower now, and entered the kitchen where Cinamon was whistling now, stirring soup over a fired hob.

He looked around, smiling, "Hungry?" He chirruped. Then the smile fell from his face as he saw Arison's red eyes and bowed head.

He had seen Mueren's decline, though none had spoken to him about it, and known she was to leave him soon. But in the way of children, and all men and women, still it hit him like a hammer.

He raced into the room where Mueren lay, looking peaceful, only the still chest and wan skin to disclose her newfound absence from the world.

Cinamon fell to his knees and wept on her hands, "Mueren!" He cried through his tears, "Wake up, Mueren, you're okay! Muereeeen!" The last was a wail of submission and he slumped to the floor and sobbed, "I—didn't—even—get—to—tell—you—I—love—you!" He sobbed, the words barely making sense to Arison who watched from the kitchen door.

She drew back within and continued stirring the soup, directing her silent tears to the sink. The way of the Centaur was to leave new grief to become old, and the one who suffered would come for comfort when they were ready. So Arison stirred and said a silent farewell to her old friend, *'Stubborn though she was.'* She commented to herself, but could not even force a smile.

Cinamon rose to the smell of the soup, chest hitching, eyes sore, and nose running. He found Arison in the kitchen, slumped over her bowl with no more tears to cry. She spooned some out into his and pushed over the loaf of Mueren's special-recipe bread.

"Now she'll never tell us the recipe," Cinamon whispered, remembering all the times he begged and jokingly threatened to get the recipe for the tastiest bread he had ever eaten.

Arison nodded, "Now she can never tell us anything. But she did tell me this. Your training is finished, and I'm to practice you," She saw him begin to protest and held up a hand, "Do it for Mueren, Cinamon, do it for the Kingdom she loved even after she was cast aside. And do it for the future you still have. But do it…after we…"

Cinamon understood, "I'll do it, and everything I do will be for Mueren," He whispered, "From this day on. And her God will be mine, and this Tower will belong to me," His words grew strong as a vow, "And whatever this evil is, I will kill it for her. And I will rise and rule this Kingdom in her name! With you by my side, Arison, who knew and loved her as did I."

Arison nodded, "I will serve you, my lord."

"You will be my equal," He corrected, then tentatively; "What…what do we do with…with her?"

Arison looked up, "We do whatever she wished. There is a parchment in her bedside drawer that will tell me. But Cinamon, in there…is Mueren's body, do you understand? She is…elsewhere, I hope she is with her God or mine, but she is not inside her earthly figure anymore."

"I know," He nodded, "For earthly shells crack and decay, but the mind and the soul go on," He quoted Eera, and Arison smiled faintly and nodded.

"Eat your soup," She commanded with little force. But Cinamon obeyed and broke off a chunk of bread.

He looked at it a moment, his deep, dark eyes seeming to pry into its very secrets, "I feel…very little," He confessed to it.

Arison answered, knowing this was a textbook answer from Eera, "You feel numb, as do I. Those who go on often do, the force of feeling at the loss of a loved one often causes the brain to cut it off for a while, before letting it out in controlled bursts. You will cry, you will mope, and you will feel as if you cannot go on. But you must, and you will."

Cinamon smiled a small smile, recognising the mind behind the answer, "Yes," He said, "I will go on. And so will you. And there will be one great lady, at least, whose life will never be forgotten."

Arison bent to her soup, hiding her surprise as such words falling for the mouth of one who was so young, and looked so innocent. But he saw and shrugged lightly.

"You know who my mother is, I presume," he said, and both broke into peals of guilty laughter.

'The sea of emotion is well on its stormy course.' she thought to herself later, after gently wrapping Mueren in sheets and placing her for the last time on her own bed. *'It is as well we do not travel alone.'* And she pulled Cinamon a little closer, where he slept on her bed, afraid to be alone tonight. *'I only hope I am enough…'* She sighed and drifted into restless sleep, with her doubts drifting through her mind.

200

Chapter 22

Eera woke with a small groan, cursing his stiff muscles, "Another two or three decades of this and I'll be ready to lie down and die!" He muttered grumpily, oblivious to the fate of another.

He drew himself up and searched for the curing cream, noting Osmon standing by the window, staring out blankly, "Find him yet?" Eera grunted, rubbing on the cooling gel.

Osmon looked back, "Mmm?" He asked, "Oh, no. He's not been out."

Eera nodded, "So how do you want to approach him?"

Osmon shrugged and turned back to the window, "I don't know, Eera," He sighed, shoulders slumped, "I don't know."

Eera took his arm gently, "You should sleep. For a while. I'll watch."

Osmon looked up at him through bleary eyes and nodded like a child, "OK," He yawned and allowed himself to be lifted by Eera's aching arms and put into the unused bed. Eera smiled, seeing he was asleep before his head touched the pillow.

Eera sat before the window and continued rubbing the ointment into his joints, relaxing slowly as they began to work, loosening the muscles and cooling the bones. He looked out of the window when he saw movement from the corner of his eye, seeing only traders and citizens, but none from the house across the way, and none of them Royston.

Soon, Samson yawned and flopped over in his bed, waking suddenly from a deep sleep, as was his habit. Wide-awake, he hopped out of bed, shivering, and changed into some warm clothes, instead of his nightdress of long johns and a thick shirt.

"By the Gods it's cold in this place!" He grunted, and then sat himself in front of the fire, which Osmon had kept going low all night, and threw some more wood on the faintly glowing coals, "When's the grub?" He asked once heated.

Eera looked at the faint light visible through the thick morning mist, "Soon," he guessed, "The sun is hard to read…but I think soon."

"Good enough fer me," the sailor replied and scooted away from the fire a little, his face and hands rosy from the heat, "Any movement?"

Eera shook his head then sat up straight, and nodded, "Door opening," He said, "Coming out…looks like all of them? No, just three. The Moonstone, the singer and the sitar."

Samson grunted, "Gotta gerrim on 'is own," He muttered, willing the remaining two to depart.

They sat in silence for a while before Eera nodded towards the house again, "Hand-harp leaving."

Samson jerked, woken from the doze brought on by the warmth of the fire, "Eh?" He started to his feet, "Oh, hand-harp. Just viola left then. 'Ere, lemme sit 'n' watch a-time, afore I fall 'sleep agin."

Eera grinned and moved aside, "I will go find the innkeeper and ask about breakfast," he decided.

"Good man," Samson grinned and patted his potbelly, "Could do wi' a fillin'," he turned back to watch the slowly filling streets and kept his eyes carefully on the door, watching for one of the remaining two to exit.

Soon a small knock came at the door, "Food," Samson rose and opened the door with a smile, "Uh?" he grunted, seeing nobody there. Then a small voice spoke.

"Is this the place of the Wise One, Eera?"

Samson stepped back, looked down, "Aye, aye. You must be t'pixie."

Rooker nodded and smiled.

Samson noticed the small shivers emanating from his tired body and hurriedly stepped aside, "Come on in, set yersel' in front o' t'fire. Eera went ter see 'bout some grub."

Rooker came in and gratefully seated himself close to the fire. Samson took back his place in front of the window, "Osmon's asleep o'er there," he pointed, "Eera'll be back when 'e's chased t'innkeeper up 'bout some breakfast."

Rooker nodded and smiled as his teeth slowly stopped chattering.

"So, what yer bin doin' ter make yer so cold!" Samson asked, curiosity finally getting the better of him.

"I have been watching Royston. I did not know where you were to be staying, until I found a small note from Eera telling me to come here as soon as I could."

"Aye…" Samson nodded wisely, realizing now why Eera had decided to go for a walk before bed the night before, "'Ere, I'm sorry as 'ell ter 'ear about that girl o' yours."

Rooker bowed his head, "Thank you, Samson. It is enough for to know that Eera will try to bring this man back to himself, or see him punished for that which he did."

"Surely yer'd prefer 'im punished," Samson said, surprised at the gentleness of this one's speech.

"No…" Rooker shook his head, "For what could bring Hermer back? If this man can be brought back to himself, then that is all I can hope for. Mine may be no more, but this one has a chance of continuing life."

Samson had to force his mouth shut as he gaped at this small thing before him, "I ne'er 'eard such a thing in all me life!" He exclaimed eventually, shaking his head, "By t'Gods, Rooker, we must seem barbarians next to yer."

Rooker smiled, "A little."

Samson slapped his knee and roared with silent laughter, careful not to wake Osmon, "Aye, yer a trig un, Rooker. And 'ere's Eera now I'll wager," he said as he heard the door creak.

"You guessed me by the creaking of my old bones," the Centaur guessed with a rueful smile, "Breakfast is being prepared and will arrive shortly, on a tray outside the door, left by the landlord."

"You have the staff of this inn well trained, Eera," Rooker grinned up at him.

Eera picked the small pixie up and gave him a small hug, "Rooker, my deepest sincere apologies for Hermer. You look almost bare without her at your side. Rest assured I will give this man the life she cannot have."

Rooker nodded and let himself be put down, "I wanted to kill him, at first," he said sadly, "I am ashamed of how I felt, but if I had come across him then…I think I may have tried. Of course I know it would never have been him to lose his life!" the small one smiled, "But then…I realised that one beautiful life was already lost…how senseless to take another."

Samson lowered his head, "I never thought it like that," he confessed, "Revenge is revenge, and I grew up wi' it. I'm a sea-dog, never got taught like you. Mebbe I'm learnin' at last."

Rooker smiled at him, "Then I am glad."

A knock came at the door, "Food," Eera guessed and waited a moment for the knocker to leave.

When the stairs finished creaking, he opened the door and brought in a large tray, packed with food.

"Should we wake the King?" Rooker asked.

"Never mind!" Samson leapt to his feet, "Viola's leavin'!"

Eera looked out of the window, and together they watched the door close behind the final musician.

Rooker was already shaking Osmon gently, "King Osmon, wake up," He called into the sleeping man's ear. But there was no movement.

Samson grinned, "'Ere, I think I know this trick," He stood by the King and brought his meaty hands together in a deafening, hollow clap.

Osmon started awake with a yowl, saw the three trying to conceal their laughter and grinned himself, even as his heart hammered with the shock.

"Royston is alone in the house," Eera said eventually.

Osmon leapt out of the bed; still fully dressed he quickly straightened his clothes and smoothed down his hair, "Let's go," he said, simply, and the breakfast was left to cool as the four went down the stairs and out of the inn.

Osmon led them to the front door of the house and knocked. He shook visibly, and his three companions gathered around him to give what comfort they could.

The door slowly opened on the sunken, weary face Osmon had seen the night before, playing him into a fit of agony with his pipes.

"Osmon," he said, matter-of-factly, "I was waiting for your arrival."

Osmon opened his mouth to speak...but came out with nothing but a hoarse sigh.

Royston bowed his head and Osmon suddenly saw how tired and drawn he truly looked. Eyes black with sleepless nights, cheeks gaunt and face pale. His slumped shoulders held none of the confident majesty that was once his alone. He looked less a killer and more a tired old man, waiting for death's door to open and take him inside.

"Come in, Osmon. Leave your friends outside," Royston said at last, seeing Osmon was yet no closer to speaking sensibly.

Samson moved a little in front of Osmon, "We ain't gonna lerrim inside with ya," He grunted.

Royston lowered his head, "Please," He sighed, "I swear not to hurt him," He seemed to notice Rooker for the first time, "I am sorry about your other half, sir. I...I don't know what I was...I-I still don't."

"We want to help you remember who you are," Rooker said, simply, "When you are who you were, the true you, then you will have my forgiveness."

Royston nodded, "I had heard much of the pixie views of death. I will ever be sorry for what I did, and if I can repay in any way..."

"Just let your friends help you," Rooker said, "If you wish to truly repay, in any way, then you will let yourself be helped, by one who loves you more than any other, and by others who care for you both."

Osmon gently moved Samson aside, "Stay out here," He told them all and stepped inside, past the almost shrunken figure, who closed the door behind him, leaving Osmon's three protectors out in the street.

"The Guards I employed are around," Rooker promised, "All it takes is a wrong move...and Royston will be taken. But...I do not think it will be necessary."

"I 'ope you're right," Samson sat himself on the cold ground, leaning his back against the wall, tensed and ready to move, but relaxing at the same time.

Eera bent his front legs and sat beside him, on the sparse grass. And Rooker set between them. All three with their heads bowed, looking relaxed, but physically tensed for sudden action, and mentally agitated, straining their ears for the slightest wrong movement.

While in the shadows of the mist, secreted Guards watched for the smallest sign of danger. Telepaths, with no vocal chords, they were able to speak while remaining hidden. Their men on the docks had told them of certain crew on Samson's ship that would betray the King, and they were well aware of Royston's recent volatile behaviour. Unseen, they were the faceless mercenaries for good, though most who knew of them feared different due to the mysterious atmosphere around them.

Hired by Rooker to watch Royston and protect the King, there were troops of them invisible in the fog, here, at the docks, and by the sailor's main tavern area, watching and waiting for those traitors to show themselves. As Osmon returned to the docks, with Royston, the troops here would follow, never revealing themselves except in lightning-fast strikes against any who might hurt their charges.

Inside, Osmon had no knowledge of the faceless telepaths, only of the wood and stone between himself and his friends. But Royston was slumped and slim, no longer slim and athletic; simply slim, and his eyes were dull. Though perhaps they had grown a little brighter, since Osmon arrived, since the promise of rehabilitation. Osmon hoped.

Royston motioned to a chair and took one opposite as Osmon seated himself, "I knew you would come," Royston said quietly.

Osmon said nothing. *'Let him talk…for sure he has things to say.'*

"I couldn't decide if that was good or bad…one moment I wanted to kill you, too, the next I would throw myself into your arms and beg for help…another would have seen me running for the hills and shipping off to the farthest Island I could find. Those…and many more options I had. Instead, I stayed, and my mind broke," he touched the scabs on his forehead, "but now I see you and your friends, offering me forgiveness?

Telling me to rebuild myself? And suddenly…I almost want to forget all the things I wanted to say."

The silence was Osmon's to talk into, "I think…you said most in your tune last night."

Royston smiled, "Aye, a pretty ditty was it not? I seem to have made myself a favourite here, with my tunes of sadness and rage...yet still, this isn't where I would have been...you put me here, Osmon," Royston raised his head and looked, truly looked, at Osmon for the first time, "But I see you know that as well as I. Your face tells me you've seen a similar torment to me. I see I need not lash you with my tongue, if I had the energy to do such."

Osmon held the man's eyes, "You could give me no more pain than I gave myself. I came here to return with you, to throw Cinderella down and raise you as my new Queen," Osmon's eyes glinted and Royston threw back his head and laughed.

"Aye, and should I wear a pretty dress too?" He chortled, breathing heavy with the exertion.

'Gods, but I remember a time when I made him pant with more than laughter...' Osmon thought to himself. *'But he is so slender now...I would be afraid to even hug him, for fear he would break.'*

Royston knew his thoughts; the 15 years they had shared developed a form of telepathy between them, and this short time apart had done nothing to dull it, "Thin...aye. I am. But nothing that cannot be rectified."

Osmon's heart pounded in his chest, he dared himself to ask the final question, dared himself to go to this man he loved...but dared not. Not yet.

Royston saw it and held himself back too. *'Only when he is ready...then I will decide what to do.'* he promised himself, while small parts of him argued for and against each option.

They sat in silence a while; nothing need be said of the events leading up to this, they had said it all to themselves many times.

Royston waited for his decision to arrive, for the moment of instinct which would arrive when Osmon asked him the one question he needed to hear.

Osmon wrestled with himself, daring not to ask the question he knew they both needed him to ask, fearing not the question itself, but the answer.

So they sat...neither moving, neither coming closer nor moving farther from their goal. Until Royston rose and took a clay jar, with a small lip, from a shelf. With it, he brought two glasses, and filled them with amber-coloured liquid.

"A Giizintaan special," he said, raising his glass to Osmon, "Guaranteed to loosen a tongue."

Osmon looked at his for a moment then raised his glass too, "For sure it is what we need right now," he replied, and tossed back his in a single slug.

Royston, sipping his slowly, laughed as Osmon coughed and spluttered his drink, "I should've mentioned its potency," he said at last, as Osmon stopped coughing, bright red.

He shook his head, a wry smile on his face, "But it did the trick," he said.

Royston smiled, "Wait," He said, and threw back his own drink. With a little less coughing due to his tolerance, he was done, and the effects were making his head pleasantly swimmy.

Osmon came and knelt on the floor before him. Royston shifted, uncomfortable with the position of prostration his King and lover had put himself in, "Don't sit so," he said after a second.

Osmon shook his head and refused to move. Royston slid from his chair and knelt on the floor opposite him, "There," he said, "Now we are as equals."

Osmon opened his mouth, praying the effects of the drink were enough to finally let him speak.

Royston watched, gazing into the other's eyes. *'Ask it!'* He willed, finally knowing his answer. *'Ask the damn question and we can be done with it!'*

Possibly hearing an echo of his thoughts, possibly his resistance simply coming to an end...Osmon opened his mouth.

"Royston...we are agreed not to hurt each other for the past things I have done. I am sorrier even than you can know, and so I came to find you. My friends came with me to protect me, and to bring you back and rebuild you, but I see there is no longer a criminal in you, so whatever you decide will be final, and your decision alone."

He paused again, licking his lips.

'ASK IT!' Royston screamed in his mind, tensing for the final question...for the final answer, for the rest of his life to be made.

Osmon took the man's hands and held them in both of his. He looked into the deep eyes of the man he loved and spoke:

"Royston, I love you more than any man loved anyone. Return with me. Return with me and Cinderella will be cast aside and you placed as my King—or Queen—and together we can take care of Cinamon, the child you always wanted, and rule the Kingdom as well as those before me have. I was a coward and I ran from you, but now I've run back to you, risking more than ever before. Please, Royston...I love you with every inch of my heart...return with me, and be mine as the stars once decreed we ought to be."

Osmon ground to a halt, the words finished rushing from his mouth, and he cringed as Royston opened his mouth to answer.

"Osmon..." Royston's voice broke and tears fell from his eyes. Osmon held back from wiping them for him, knowing it was wrong unless Royston was his man again.

Royston sniffed, shook his head a little and braced himself, "I love you, Osmon. I wish to return and make my life with you, and now you have asked my only answer can be yes."

Chapter 23

The Centaurs in the Palace stable were jerked awake, almost as one body, by some unidentified presence. Together they looked around, ready for battle, and gaped as they saw a man emerge from a large, black hole in the stone wall.

He was deformed, they saw, then picked out just what was wrong; he had no nose.

"Who is your leader?" He hissed, "I come on urgent errand from Mossan, as leader of the rebel troupe.

None stepped forward. Jerne threw up his arms.

"I apologise, I forgot your equality. Then who is able to read and write in the old Centaur language?"

A few shuffled, but one stepped forward, "I am most able," She spoke in a low voice, bowing her pale head to him. Her hair and fur were grey, streaked with snatches of blonde, and she held out her hand for the note.

Opening the scroll she saw the familiar letters of the old language, penned by one who has studied them as she did. She began to read:

> *I do not know which of you will read this, but read carefully and reply on the reverse of this parchment. Tell nothing of its contents to our messenger, he believes he leads our rebel cause and will rule as tyrant in his own right, but he will be proved wrong once we have no more use for him.*

The Tyrant Queen knows of our rebellion, and will attack either the stabled Centaur or the banished Centaur first, as she knows we must be the main force.

In our Forest, we have still hidden the ancient Horn, which called us to battle centuries ago, now it may be used once more.

If you, in those stables, are attacked first, do not fight, only mow down those in your way and come at full gallop to the Forest, where our stand will begin.

If we are attacked first, then the horn will blow and you must come at full gallop to join us in our battle.

I fear that the stables will go first, Cinderella will attempt to part us and make us foolish with anger, so be ready at all times. And remember—make no fight, but run through the line and to the Forest where we will be waiting. Upon your arrival, the Horn will sound and call the Humans to join us.

Many will die, but some will live, and victory must be taken for us, cost it everything we have!

I can say no more; to plan too much is to fall at the first hurdle. Come if you are attacked, or come when you hear the horn, make no fight but make all haste to the Forest to fight.

Tell the would-be tyrant that secret plans are laid, we have told him similar ourselves, and bid him return with your reply. He is ordered to give it to the Humans we trust (those who will be in our front line at battle) to give to me

May the field of battle once again be fertilised with the blood of the enemies of both Centaur and Human alike! And may a new friendship and Order spring from our certain victory! Gods bless you all, prepare for war.

Mossan.

The grey-yellow Centaur turned the note over, "Brought you a writing implement?" She asked of the noseless would-be tyrant, "I must reply to confirm the secret plans for battle."

Jerne sighed, "Still I am to know nothing of these plans? Though I lead the fight, I am kept in the dark.

The Centaur shrugged, "Centaur are a secretive race, as you know, simply trust that the good will win in the end, and that the Centaur are prepared to fight for it."

Jerne nodded and took a quill and ink jar from under his cloak, "Reply as fast as you can, I have a way to go and must return this message with haste."

The Centaur nodded and scrawled only a short paragraph.

We prepare to return to the days of glory. Our hooves are hard, our legs are limber, and we await with eager anticipation the first attack or the sound of the Horn. Victory is assured.

She folded it and gave it back to Jerne who bowed slightly and began to speak. But the Centaur had already turned away and, scowling, he simply turned and vanished through his dark door, which closed behind him silently.

Micx stepped out of the crowd of Centaurs, most of who had been conspicuously studying everything but the noseless Human.

"Well?" He gruffed, still sleepy from his hasty return, before anyone could grow suspicious; especially the Queen, with her newfound suspicion.

The grey-blonde Centaur related the contents and her reply, speaking loud enough for all of them to hear.

Reaction was fast and powerful. Not a one would be left out or fall behind, watches would be held at all times from now until the Big Moment, to catch any troupe of Guard unawares as they attempted to take *them* unawares, or to strain ears for the Horn's booming call. And always, always would each of them be fully clothed and armed however they could, limbered and ready for the escape. For sure, Cinderella wouldn't have them used as workhorses anymore, so they were free to sit and wait, and be ready whenever the time came.

Cinderella was waiting also, though pacing rather than sitting, "When is that wizard going to bring me my map?" she was growling at Suzee, for the umpteenth time.

Suzee, once again, replied; "He sent the note only a few hours ago saying he'd be done in about 6 hours, he was lucky enough to find a cooperative and very talented genie so his estimate of a week, which came down to a couple of days, dropped to little more than the travelling time—and as we know, he can do that quite speedily. He'll be here with the maps any time now, I should think."

"Well, he had best hurry!" the Queen snapped, yet again.

And this time Suzee had enough, "He will be here!" she snapped back, "Shouting at me will make him come no faster, and make me go elsewhere to wait."

The Queen stopped dead in her tracks, her mouth open and gaping at Suzee, before she realised it was unseemly and closed it, but still stared.

Suzee gazed back, her eyes glittering with defiance and suppressed anger.

Cinderella laughed! "Well now, you are a fine one! I apologise for my behaviour. Now and in the past. You must tell me in future when I treat you wrong, you know as I do that I have nothing to compare to when it comes to a friendship."

Suzee nodded, "Be sure what you say, Cinderella, I've grown fond of my head and don't want to lose it by telling you not to order me about and try saying please."

"Please…" The Queen mused and nodded, "I give you my word that your head stays where it is, and no other punishments will be forthcoming," she added this with a smile, before Suzee could speak, "I have no knowledge of how to be anything but slave or…tyrant, I suppose it what they call me. If I treat you wrong, I need to know."

Suzee smiled and nodded, "I promise to always be honest," She said.

A knock came at the door and Cinderella strode to it, "It must be him."

Suzee tilted her head, "I don't think Arguth is much disposed to the standard scenario of walking to a door and knocking to gain entry. I think you'll find one of my squad leaders there waiting for orders."

Cinderella threw open the door with an impatient sigh, and sure enough there stood a Palace Guard. Dull in muted armour, he snapped a salute and entered by the Queen's leave.

Unsure who to face, he remained at attention and waited to be told.

Suzee cleared her throat, "At ease," She told him, and he relaxed a little, trying not to observe the Queen from the corner of his eye as she watched.

"Your squad is ready for duty?" she asked.

"Yes ma'am," he replied smartly.

"How many?"

"15 ma'am."

"Good. I wish you to set each man to copy 10 of these notices," she gave him a scroll, "then place them around the city, and the Palace, in equal measure so all can see. I wish this done by first light tomorrow morning, which means you will work through most of the night, I know, but it must be done. Understood?"

He took the scroll and his hand slipped behind his back to hold it, "Yes ma'am."

"Come and see me when all the posters are up," she told him, "Dismissed."

The soldier, in a flash of genius, saluted Suzee, turned sharply, saluted Cinderella, turned once more and marched out of the door, discreetly closing it behind him as he went.

He ambled down the corridor, opening the scroll. His mouth gaped as he read its contents, and rolling it up once more he set off at a run.

Cinderella smiled wickedly as Suzee grinned, "Should be a fun day tomorrow," Suzee remarked, and Cinderella smiled more wickedly still.

"Indeed," Agreed a voice, making them both jump and whirl to it, Suzee with her sword drawn, leaping in front of the Queen.

"It's just the wizard," Suzee said, a little disgusted at her own reaction, and slipped her sword back into its sheath.

The wizened old man smiled innocently, "Didn't mean to startle you. I have your maps, and your sigil," he said to Cinderella, holding out a fur bag filled with parchment.

"Thank you, Arguth," she placed the bag on her bed "Tell me, what really happened to make this task go so much faster than you thought?"

Arguth shrugged his bony shoulders, "I called a dark genie. He was sullen but incredibly powerful, and easy to bring to heel. It happens rarely that I find one so powerful, I was lucky, and so the time needed was greatly reduced."

"Hmm," Cinderella mused, still no wiser, "I thank you, Arguth, you will be repaid well. In fact, if you wish to ally with me against a great threat, you shall be repaid with a title, and a great plot of land."

Arguth raised a hairless eyebrow and his yellow-brown teeth showed in a grimace that was meant to be a smile, "I am interested," he moved closer.

Resisting the urge to take a step back, Cinderella smiled at him, "There are those who plot against me, and we wish to bring them down. With a wizard as powerful as you, how may we fail? And I promise to you a high title and all the land these rebels currently occupy in the Kingdom."

Arguth grinned now, an even more hideous sight than his smile, "I am yours to command, my Queen," he gurgled.

Cinderella smiled and patted his shoulder, gently for it seemed so fragile, "Then sit and Suzee will let you in on her strategy."

Arison held Cinamon close as they watched the funeral pyre burn lower, signaling the end of Mueren's earthly vessel.

'But her memory and deeds will never fade. Through me, they will live on.' Cinamon promised himself, yet again.

Arison's attention was elsewhere, however, as a Phoenix landed and waddled as close to the fire as it dared.

In its message pouch was just a small, red square of cloth, with no sign or sigil, for the Centaur swore themselves to each other, rather than a symbol.

Arison turned to Cinamon, face fiery, and held out the cloth, "We must go," She said simply, gave a last bow to Mueren's flames and trotted inside.

"What…?" Cinamon asked as he raced after her, "Where? Why?"

Arison stopped in the living room, "Pack everything you wish to take, for we may not be back. It's time."

"Time for what?" the boy exclaimed.

"Time for you!" came the stern reply, "Time for all those powers to be out to use. Time for me and mine to be what we were, centuries ago: warriors for the good. Time for the final war against the tyrant who rules even the King himself with an iron fist and a sword for beheading!"

Cinamon turned pale, "You mean…you want to…my mother…?"

Arison stopped dead in her packing, "I-I had forgotten, Cinamon. You are so different to her in every way…"

"I will not go," he shrugged and sat down, "I'll not be party to the murder of my mother! And I'll be no friend to any Centaur who joins in!"

Arison bent herself to the floor in front of him, "Cinamon…I'm sorry, but I have no time for soft words. Your mother is tyrant, a dictator, a torturer and she is driving this Kingdom to ruin. The Centaur have been peaceful, because of the vow they made to serve. But Osmon has released us from service, you know this, and so now, we refuse to bow and scrape. Instead, we fight for ourselves and every person who has been touched by this evil Queen—because evil she is and you know it as much as anybody! This is bigger than one person, Cinamon. If the Centaur lose your friendship by fighting for what's right, then so be it. We'll be sad; none more so than I…but this is what must be done, for the sake of now and for the future! Come with me, you'll not have to face your mother, only those few loyals she has left."

"And what would you do with my mother, Arison?" he demanded, "Kill her outright? Lock her up and give her an unfair trial then kill her? I'll be no part of that, though you know I'd join you in a second if it were anyone but my family."

Arison rose, shrugged, "Then you have chosen. Your training was for nothing, and your people will be freed without your help. Understand that you give up any right to succession, or friendship of the Centaur, or those riches and servants that you've had. All of that goes now, while you sit and sulk because mummy is never wrong!"

She packed in silence, waiting, hoping, and taking as much time as she dared.

Cinamon watched her, openly sullen, inwardly wracked with indecision. *'To fight against my mother? I know how she is…I do…I know it's for the good…but my own mother! I want to fight on the right side, and I have the power to right all the things gone wrong…but Gods it's my mother!'* and so there it all came back too. Still a boy, Cinamon was grown in every way but one; still he looked to his mother as one who could do no wrong, against all evidence, and how could he fight her? Even if he had the strength, surely a look or a withering word would bring him down with a crash!

Arison tried one last time, bag on her back, giving the boy last chance, "Come with me, Cinamon. We fight not your mother, though if I can I will have her life spared. We fight the tyranny and oppression she stands for. You say you love us. Then join us and fight for what we, for too long, forgot. Freedom and justice, and the right to be whoever we want to be. Fight not your mother, Cinamon, fight the dictator she has become."

Cinamon looked at her with tears in his eyes, "I'm not...strong enough to fight her. I believe in all you do, truly...I want to fight what she does...but..." he sighed, "I'm weak, Arison, a stern word and I'll be lost, and she'll make no bones about having my head displayed on a spike!"

Arison sighed and hung her head, "Oh Cinamon, if only you could see the strength that I see. Fear makes you a coward, but overcoming fear makes you brave, do you see that?"

"I...I can't!" he sobbed, "I want her to stop...but...I...I-I can't stand before her and fight, she will wither me!"

Arison turned away, "Then your choice is made. The Tower belongs to you, as Mueren said. Take care of it and live well, for the Centaur will no longer allow you on their land; those who fight not at all, fight for the wrong side."

Cinamon watched her through tears as she trundled away, looking back, giving him time to follow. But his legs would not run, and his voice would not shout...and so he sat where he was, crying and hating himself for a coward, torn between blood and heart, wailing for something to give him a sign.

As he cried, he saw the Phoenix step inside the Tower, looking for food after its flight, finding a small dish of grain left by Arison. It ate, and then walked up to him, seeming to see his pain, and rested at his feet.

It was morning when Cinamon awoke, face stiff from dry tears, the Phoenix still at his feet, alert and watching him with curiosity, seeing him awake, it stood and tugged his sleeve.

He climbed to his feet and followed the bird, wonderingly, to the door where he looked up...

...And saw a copper-coloured horse gallop from the forest onto the barren land around the Tower.

The Phoenix flew away with a squawk, but Cinamon hardly noticed.

The horse drew near and stopped, quietly stood and watched Cinamon. It seemed to glow in the growing dawn light, silver rays lifted from its fur and filled the countryside with a faint, warm glow.

Cinamon took a step closer.

The horse took a step back and tossed its head.

Cinamon tried talking, "Come on horse, you came to me, right? Come on, I won't hurt you…"

The horse simply looked at him in a vaguely amused way and idly flicked its tail.

Cinamon took small step forward.

The horse took a small step back.

Cinamon sighed, "You want food, horse? Will that make you my friend?" He asked gently.

The horse bobbed its head and Cinamon gaped.

"You understand me!" he exclaimed, a little louder than he intended.

The horse bobbed its head again.

"Are you sent to bear me?" he asked.

The head bobbed.

"Why will you come no closer?" He held out a hand.

The horse looked at him; the question was not one he could answer with his head.

Cinamon thought for a moment. *'I cannot go close to him, which means he doesn't trust me yet. So no point asking him to let me ride. But I know, now, where I must go, and I know I must be strong enough to do this, or the Gods would never have sent this horse. But how to gain its trust?'* he mused. *'Food? Comfort? Friendly talk? All three?'* the boy shrugged. *'All three it is.'*

"Would you come inside, so I can feed you and you can rest?" he asked.

The horse bobbed its head, but didn't move.

"Then come in," Cinamon tried.

Still nothing.

"Oh, you want me to move first?"

The horse nodded.

Cinamon shrugged, "You'll have to get used to having me near, it's a small room we have to live in."

The horse bowed its head as if in thought, then seemed to shrug, and trotted over. Cinamon moved aside and the horse ventured warily inside.

In the main room, it stood, looking around.

"Here, this is where Arison slept," Cinamon pointed, "If it is a bed for a Centaur, I hope it is a bed for you?"

The horsed replied by wandering over and sitting on it. It whinnied approval and waited.

Cinamon went to find it food. Then, after the horse had eaten— neatly and carefully, as if more Human than Animal—Cinamon asked it if he could put some questions.

The horse nodded and shifted a little.

"You are sent to bear me to the battle?"

Nod.

"You must trust me before you allow me to ride you?"

Nod.

"Are you beginning to?"

Nod.

"Do you know who sent you?"

Nod.

Cinamon thought…then in a flash it came to him, "Are you a friend of Mueren?"

Nod. Nod. Nod.

"Do you have a name?"

Nod.

"Can you tell it to me?"

Instead of a nod, the horse stood and looked around. It saw parchment and pointed to it.

Cinamon incredulously fetched a quill and ink jar and led it in front of the horse.

Using its mouth, the horse wrote a word on the parchment and slid it over to Cinamon.

"Nuisance," the boy read and laughed aloud, "Nuisance! Really?"

The horse nodded and seemed to smile wryly.

"An accurate name?" Cinamon queried.

The horse looked away and bowed his head.

Cinamon clapped his hands, "Nuisance it is, certainly so far you have been! Tell me, Nuisance, how will you bear me to this battle I must help win if you refuse to let me near you?"

Nuisance seemed to frown and his back straightened.

Cinamon held up his hands, "My apologies…but I think I understand the name. Very well, but you had best trust me fast, Nuisance, or all is lost, and I'm not the only one who will be angry…"

The horse cringed, but made no reply. After a moment, he held out his copper head to Cinamon who stroked it and talked gently.

"There we go, see, I'm not a bad guy, Mueren would never have sent you if I was. But you have to try hard, Nuisance, because I need you. And you best be the fastest horse in the world, or it will be too late. Will you bear me, Nuisance? If so, I give my word that you will be the best looked-after horse the world has ever known!"

Nuisance raised his head once more and considered. After a moment, he nodded.

"Great! When do we go?" Cinamon was on his feet.

But Nuisance stayed put and yawned.

"Oh…after you sleep," Cinamon sighed and sat again.

Nuisance nodded, put his head down and slept, while Cinamon marveled at his mere existence—and the fact that he slept like no true horse he had ever known

"Tonight it is then," he murmured, "For I'm sure you'll sleep for hours, then expect food and time to digest," he shook his head, "Nuisance, yes you are…but Mueren sent you for a reason, so you must be speedy enough to get me to the battle."

While in the centre of Lamsonia, posters had appeared like a plague.

By order of the Queen Cinderella, and enforcement of the Palace Guards

All areas where the Centaur live are hereby declared off-limits, on pain of death!

Any interaction with Centaurs who venture out of their areas will be dealt with similarly!

Repeat—ANY form of interaction with ANY Centaur is punishable by death!

They are hereby declared no longer a part of this Kingdom, and will shortly be dealt with accordingly!

In her Palace, Cinderella laughed gleefully, "That ought to confuse and worry them a bit…" She grinned.

Suzee's brow was dark, "Perhaps…but still I think that goading them on is the worst thing we could do."

"Ah, well we'll see soon enough," Cinderella grinned, "For just before dawn tomorrow, the Palace traitors will be sacked, and then we'll see how the banished ones react!" She went back to watching the city, bustling in confusion.

Suzee simply sighed and left the room. She had plans to perfect, and a nasty feeling to drown in ale.

Chapter 24

"Won't you join us, Rooker? For a time?" Osmon asked before they left the inn, then the Island, behind.

Rooker shook his head, "I have not yet performed the Ceremony of Souls of Hermer. I could not…not until I know her released spirit will be free of torment," he looked up at Royston and smiled, "I think, now, I can tell her to be at peace."

Royston smiled wanly back. He had slept better the previous night than he could recall doing since leaving Lamsonia, and suspected it had just as much to do with the warmth of Osmon lying close to him, as with the new freedom his mind had found. But he was still pale and thin, something Osmon had vowed to begin putting to rights immediately.

Rooker looked back to Osmon, "But should that perhaps be an open invitation, I shall visit someday, when things are settled down."

"Any time, Rooker, you are welcome wherever I am," Osmon answered and squeezed the pixie's shoulders in a gentle hug.

Rooker bowed low as the group rolled out of the inn, watched by their faceless Guardians…who were aware of more watchers, in the shape of the Queen's 'crewmen', now preparing to follow orders. Namely, to kill he and Royston before allowing them to return together.

The Guardians followed, silent and invisible as ever, waiting, they would know the strike was coming a second before it did for one of their number scanned constantly the mind of the leader who would call for action.

Oblivious, the group said their last goodbyes to Rooker, who departed in a sort of peaceful sorrow, back to his house to prepare for Hermer's final ceremony. They moved on swiftly, then, eager to be away, talking little but moving as fast as the fog would allow.

Until just before coming within sight of the dock, a man swung rapidly out of the fog and sent a knife flying to the centre of Osmon's heart!

Without time to duck, Osmon could only stand in horror…as a black shape swept in front of him and caught the knife in one hand, before sending it back to puncture the neck of the thrower.

The protected group were bundled close together by black-cloaked men who faced outwards in a protective circle.

From out of the mist strode 12 men, decked as sailors, but with malice in their eyes and murder in their minds.

The Guardians standing in the shadows behind them stepped forward and took two at a time, slicing a knife across a throat with each hand.

Without a sound made, or a blow struck, the would-be killers were themselves killed, and as the protective circle broke away the protected stared around in astonishment.

One of the Guardians stepped forward and gave a sweeping bow. Speaking to all of their minds, he told them; *'You were under our protection from the second you stepped onto the Island. I am at liberty, now, to reveal that we were hired by Rooker, at command of a Centaur who remains nameless to me. Those men were hired by the Queen Cinderella to be sure King Osmon and (King?) Royston did not return together. There are no more, at this end at least.*

If you still require our protection, we will accompany you to Lamsonia; if not then we take our leave.'

Stunned, it took them all a moment to digest. Osmon spoke first.

"Thank you, sir, sirs! You saved our lives. I-I could never have known Cinderella would do such a thing…yet I know how terrible she is, and she knows that if Royston returns, then he will be King with me, and she will be nothing…" Osmon mused a moment, distraught and amazed.

"I was one of those who asked for your protection," Eera spoke now, bowing low as he did so, "I felt Cinderella would do something…I thank you for your protection. I fear things are…unsettled…in Lamsonia, and we may need you to join the good fight. But I feel it is right to leave you to protect those others who need you."

'*Then we shall take our leave. If you are in need, we shall return.*'

"How may I call you, a name?" Eera asked.

'*You need not. Simply trust I will be there when you have need of me, and that all under our protection shall ever be safe. Only allow me a suggestion; that you stay together and do not part, or we will be spread thin.*'

Osmon nodded, for the leader had again spoken to all of them, "We will follow your advice, for now we remain as one, in a group."

General nods and agreements.

The leader bowed once more, and in a flash all Guardians were gone, leaving the small group blinking in surprise once more.

Samson clapped Eera on the shoulder, "Well, yer bleddy good at keepin' secrets, eh?"

Eera smiled a trifle innocently, "Me? Oh, well, maybe a little."

Samson laughed loudly, if a little forcedly and set off back to his ship, ""Come fellas, lerrus be off 'ome. I gorra bad feelin'…I gonna be tiltin' along full sail, we gorra get back 'ome, and quick!" He hurried along, exuding a strange form of anxiety and dread unknown to him before.

The rest followed, noticing his fear matched up with their own private, niggling, gnawing thoughts.

'*The Faceless—that must be who they were.*' Osmon thought, now. '*Speak with their minds, unseen, unequalled, never lost a man…indeed, if my bones are correct and there is a storm brewing in my Kingdom, they may be needed, perhaps, to settle things at the finish.*'

But, for now turning his mind to pleasanter things, he moved a little closer to Royston and took his bony hand. Royston looked down and smiled. '*I did right.*' He was thinking, '*There was no other decision I could have made. But perhaps…perhaps we need not be Sovereigns…it's a bleak role, and stressful, and Osmon will grow old early from it…but that is a later conversation.*' He smiled to himself and watched Samson's ship come into view, this time with an abundance of pleasure, tainted only with that same dread.

"How long at full tilt, Samson?" Royston asked, speaking in front of them all for the first time.

"Well…" Samson scratched his head, "I'm gonna do a cut through t'center of t'Islands, on a course through t'rocks some of us old 'uns remember…there's a clear course there, but only used for emergencies…s'dangerous, s'why we go round mostly…"

"So how long?" Eera prompted.

"At full pelt and through t'rocks? I cin 'ave us there by late tomorrer mornin'," He said, finally.

"I hope it's soon enough," Osmon muttered and sped up to match Samson's lumbering, but agile and speedy, stride.

The banished (or freed) Centaur were gathered around, furious, but listening despite their urge to do something.

"This is what she wants," Mossan was saying—to the agreement of those whose blood was a little cooler, "It is an aggravation, an invitation, an attempt to anger us and make us lose to her. She will attack tomorrow at dawn, so says our friend who spies, and she will attack the Palace Centaur."

As this settled in, Mossan tossed her head and drew herself up to her full height, an imposing sight even to those of her own breed.

"But we will not be foolish, and we will not be angered by the words of such a woman. If woman she is worthy to be named!" She went on, "We will wait, and she will attack the Palace, but they will be ready—for even now that untrusted spy goes on his final mission for us, to tell them the attack will come at dawn tomorrow. They will break out and join us, and we will fight. The Humans are rounding up the villagers; those on our side will join us at dawn. Those placed to attack the Palace stables…are mostly our men, and will stand aside—then follow to our side! Arison—the greatest warrior we know—is by now traveling at full speed and will be here at a gallop, hopefully in time to take a breath before the fighting. And Cinamon! Blessed with the power of those Human Gods, will fight by our side!

"At dawn, my friends," her voice dropped low, "At dawn…comes the stand. No war, this, no ongoing feud or siege…one battle, bloody and painful, but just one…and we shall have our win, and we shall—us and those who stand with us—we shall return this Kingdom to the people who live in it, be they Centaur, Human…or the humanoid Spitter!" she grinned at this last, realizing she had never asked where he came from.

But no matter. The cheers rose triumphantly, so that a blind bystander—one who could not see the still-pristine land, the grass not red with blood—might think the battle already won!

And in the town, bustle and action! Armorours had been working day and night since Skim and Vana had spread the word of, someday soon, a battle against the Queen. Villagers swarmed in, fought each other over the best weapons, newly forged or newly emerged from storage. In each place was left a bulky soldier to quell all squabbles, so that, eventually, when no weapons remained, all were well—and no worse than a bruise had been put upon another in the hustle.

"Before dawn…" was the unspoken murmur, "Just before the sky lightens, we go to the Centaurs who will provide us with what armour they have, and will place us beside them to fight! We, us, are to stand beside the Centaur to fight with them for common goal!"

And in the Palace, similar movement—except each fighter here had his own weapon and armour, so the fights broke out through tension, knowledge of imminent treason, fear of possible loss of life—for if they won, still some would die. And if they lost…loss of life was the most pleasant punishment they could conjure!

Yet all this kept quiet as Suzee and Cinderella, with their new consort, Arguth, watched the preparation.

"Not much really going on," commented Suzee, "Just a lot of movement. Mostly, they are checking weapons and armour, limbering up—for most, it has been a while since a good fight, and never against a Centaur. They'll get their heads down for 8 hours before muster, be fresh to attack. But I think the Centaur will be waiting, Cinderella…" Suzee tried one last time to voice her fears.

Before the Queen could reply, Arguth broke in, "Not so, Suzee…oh, they may suspect, but though I cannot hope to break through their thick hides with some powerful spell—for I would send them to sleep, if only I could—I think I may have a trick or two…" He smiled knowingly and Suzee tensed, then relaxed.

'Well…he can only be right…' she decided, and moved off to separate two relatively new soldiers who had gotten too far in each other's way, and decided to sharpen their swords on the other's flesh.

While in the stables, Jerne had just left with a reply to the warning note, holding an injured shoulder and creeping in the shadows—

mightily angry that he was forcibly expelled from his tunnels. The Centaurs inside were preparing to rest and sleep, as well as their jittering nerves would allow, anyway. One last word from Micx before they slept;

"Mossan is right; this can be easy if we let it be. Most of the Guard will let us past, then turn and follow us to the final fight! The rest…can be killed instantly, or tossed aside to deal with later. Cinderella…will eventually be taken—but alive—by some of our more experienced. There is a wizard, the spy says—apparently a spy they trust has found this out, one who gave me his name—so I trust him also. The wizard will be out of our way, I am certain, but should you see a chance, do kill him! Otherwise…the plan is the simplest it can possibly be.

"Run! Run as fast as you can! Trample down any swordsmen who stand in your way and ignore any cut or bruise you may fetch, they matter not! At dawn, Mossan says—again from the trusted spy. So before dawn, we will be awake, ready, and at their signal—their signal of attack is our signal to go! I know each one of us can run, and each one of us has twice the legs any of they have! It's time for a stand, friends, to be strong and fight for the good—which we have all but forgotten how to do.

But now we must remember…search your blood, it was in your ancestors, it is in you! It's time to remember who we are…and we are not slaves to a tyrant bitch! We are free, and so are all—Human, Centaur or any other race! And now the time has come to reclaim it, for us and them, for all our generations to come!"

He spoke only quietly, his voice somehow still strong, and the Centaur were afraid. But his message hit home, and they silently rejoiced and lay down, some to sleep, some to search their blood, some simply to shiver in fear…for the time was nearly at hand, and they must rest the sunshine away, this day, and awake in the light of the moon to begin a stand for the things they were supposed to believe in.

Cinamon watched Nuisance sleep, looking awkward on his bed, but resting comfortably enough. *'I never saw an actual horse sit down…'* The boy mused absently. *'Humans, yes…Centaur, yes…other animals, of course. But a horse?'*

Nuisance stirred and snorted and Cinamon jerked back out of his reverie. But the horse settled again and, impatient, knowing he would be troubled with grief for Mueren if only his mind was clear for long enough, the boy stood and strolled outside.

There were targets still remaining, most of them battered and burned now, but they stood and so were good enough. There was much Cinamon had not had time to learn, the powers he could control were those of assistance in battle. Fire, water, wind, to move objects without touching, to move himself short distances, to make himself grow dim enough to go unnoticed—or invisible, on rare occasion. He could call up beings, three at one time if he did nothing else, to do his bidding—and they would come willingly at a thought, without stubbornly requiring a ceremony, for he was polite and gentle. And more.

Mueren told him Pyrone was helping him, unlocking all the doors in his mind so he could access these skills in haste. Cinamon himself...did not know, or much care at the moment. He had the skills, and would use them—the arrival of Nuisance had determined that decision. So now, Cinamon wandered over to the funeral pyre, nothing but a handful of smouldering embers remained but he saw it as it had been. Blazing tall and hot, with the body of one he loved slowly peeling away from itself to be consumed.

"Thank you for Nuisance, Mueren," he told the glowing coals. He expected no answer, and received none, but he knew that if Mueren was listening—which she was, he was sure, else there would be no Nuisance—then she had heard.

He turned to the four targets, double the distance now than he usually would be for practice, and narrowed his eyes.

The first burst into violent flame and was gone within five seconds.

The second rose into the air and dashed itself on the hard ground, again, again, again until only small pieces remained, seeming to bounce on and wrestle each other like cubs at play.

The third simply spurted up into the air, hovered, and slowly crinkled itself smaller and smaller...until it vanished into nothing.

Now he opened his mind and called for one of his genies. The figure came forth, knew what was wanted, drew himself to great height and zapped the fourth target with an outstretched finger. It fizzled, sparked, crumpled and collapsed into dust.

The genie turned to Cinamon and brought himself to the boy's height. He dressed in large, baggy, colourful clothes, woven with threads of silver, bronze, purple, red, yellow, blue…all the colours Cinamon knew and many he did not. On his head was a white turban, held together by a grey-gold clasp in the shape of a wisp of smoke.

"I apologise," Cinamon told him, unable to use a name—for the genies gave their names only to those who forced them, and who were then forced to incant that name in ceremony of blood to call them. Of course, the white genies would simply ignore anyone calling their name, or show themselves and cause devastation. While the dark would groaningly go forth, evil since time immemorial, they had been stripped of their own powers and could only come forth when their name was called, and then could only direct the powers of the one calling for them specifically, or by being dragged forth in pain by a call for any of them.

The genie smiled, "No apology, child," in return, Cinamon had held his name a secret, and should one of the genies mistakenly hear it they had trained themselves to forget it completely, "I see you practice, and see the results! I gave you no help to call me, but was pulled willingly to your needs."

Cinamon smiled, "Really?" for before the genies had always confessed to hearing Cinamon's wordless call, and coming to him.

The genie nodded, still smiling, "Try to call the three of us at once. I will not tell the others anything, see their surprise," the genie blinked and was gone.

Cinamon relaxed, closed his eyes, picturing the three genies assigned to him by…whatever power it was that did such things.

He opened his eyes and there they were! All three clapping, two looking somewhat amazed.

"He did it!" exclaimed one.

"Good job boy!" said the second.

"I knew you could," grinned the third.

Cinamon took their congratulations and smiled. But eventually, "Could I ask a favour?"

Three nods.

"When my horse awakes…" he cast an annoyed glance to the Tower, "I must ride with all speed into a battle. I have to stand with the Centaur against my mother who is…evil?…" he paused, "I need you, all three of you, more than ever during this battle. If my horse wakes in time to get me there." Another annoyed glance sideways.

"Ah," came the combined acknowledgment.

The first smiled and nodded, "For my part, simply call me and tell me who is your enemy, they will be killed. I know you understand that to kill is a great evil in itself, but I trust you boy and know you would not do this were it not for even greater good!"

After a moment came the second, "Aye! I, too, join you! Against the three of us, even an army stands no chance!"

The third shifted in the air and looked away. He was young, or at least looked that way—though Cinamon once made the mistake of saying so to be greeted with guffaws and a comment of how he knew nothing of time. He finally looked at Cinamon, "I can kill none," he said slowly, his eyes full of sadness, "There are some of us who simply…find themselves unable to fight in battle. I am yours for practice, for private spells…but I am one of those weaklings who can produce no magic in a crowd. You asked me once how young I was…I am, in truth, more ancient than you could guess, but among my kind I am still young, and not yet matured enough for a war."

Cinamon smiled, if a little faintly, "I understand," he said, "In my time, you would barely be out of your mother's stomach. I will call on you for more private magic, then, but for this I will call only those two who are able to come."

The third smiled weakly, "Thank you, boy. In which case…my leave is to be taken," he bowed to Cinamon and was gone.

Cinamon thought for a moment, "Do you need information? Tactics? Anything?" he asked the two.

The first nodded, "Only tell us who your friends are, and we will destroy every other. Or, if easier, tell us who to destroy and we will do that and no more. Names we do not need, just an impression will suffice."

Cinamon crinkled his pale brow and thought hard, "My mother— if you are able you must take her away, somewhere she cannot be killed. She is in the wrong, but I want her to live."

Two nods of confirmation.

Cinamon frowned again and was lost, "The Centaur are on our side…Arison said there were to be Palace Guards and villagers too…how can I separate them for you?"

The genie bowed his head, "We will know," he said, simply, "The minds of each side will be different."

Cinamon relaxed, "Good," he nodded.

The second genie cocked his head, "There is one thing even you, Cinamon, have not thought…yourself!"

Cinamon looked shocked, and then shrugged.

The second genie grinned, "Fear not, young one, the second you are in danger or injury, we will both know, and those who put you there will be in the afterlife before they realise they are dying."

Cinamon nodded sadly, "I wish there was a way to save all these lives…"

The genies joined him in sadness, saying nothing, knowing the ways of human nature all too well. What is good can be corrupted, and what is corrupted can rarely be turned good again, must be lanced so good can grow afresh.

Eventually Cinamon recovered, shook himself a little and smiled, "Thank you both. I'll call on you as soon as I have need. And if we win or lose, I know I'll be in your debt."

The genies shook their heads negative, "We keep no tally," they said as one, grinned and went.

And Cinamon trudged back along the fields into the Tower, where Nuisance was still snoring softly on his bed.

Cinamon repressed an urge to kick the animal awake and took himself to the kitchen to set about making a meal for when he awoke, to set off sooner, and hopefully not arrive too late.

Chapter 25

Jerne returned, breathless, to a meeting place in the forest near his cave-hideout. Waiting for him were Regina—impatient as always—with Melina and Spitter.

The latter two had left the cave when the Centaur offered the clearing to all the rebels—except Jerne and Regina. The reason given was that if they should be discovered, at least Jerne—the powerful leader—would remain hidden.

Flattery being one of Jerne's many weak spots, he accepted this with a smile—even more so when told he would have to be the messenger between the two bands of Centaur, because no other had his knowledge or talent.

So despite the scowl he placed on his face, he was pleased when he entered the clearing and thrust the note at his two servants, "Just a confirmation I suppose," He told them, "Go give it to the Centaurs and be quick about it."

Melina and Spitter merely bowed, they would be unable to speak in any case—Spitter still pretended to Jerne and Regina that he could speak no English. Melina, however, had gained her tongue; using the same magic Jerne had ordered Spitter to use for Regina's silver-tinted muscle, Melina now had a fully working tongue for speech. Jerne, however, could be kept in the dark—not least because he would be furious!

Jerne, oblivious as ever, turned to Regina, also oblivious. Both so secure in their own fabulous power they failed to sense the eyes on them, or see the occasional shadow whose shape was not that of the natural forest.

But the shadows saw them. And their cue, the absence of Spitter and Regina carrying the note, was almost upon them. Giving the two another moment to be farther away, Skim held his breath, the moment before the surprise attack was always the tensest. To be discovered, or find that the surprise was already expected! To fail, to make one small mistake and be killed instead of the victim. To fail and escape, but never have another chance because your hand has been revealed.

Vana nudged Skim and they moved silently through the trees, making no more rustle than the gentle wind, following the pair back to their cave. They must have them before they passed Spitter's barriers—for the green creature dared not to remove them, "They'll know," he had argued, shaking with fear, and would say no more.

So it had been accepted, and the two assassins must seize a moment before they passed the first charm.

Dressed in shades of green to match the forest, without armour for this task, carrying a dagger in each hand, they crept forward, stealing ever closer to the strolling duo and their planned place of ambush, listening in to the last conversation they would ever have.

"Soon, my love, the whole Kingdom!"

Regina giggled, "And the world, someday..." She tinkled, more like Cinderella than she could ever admit, yet worse, because even after her actions there was no regret.

Jerne took her arm and moved closer, "And if they thought the 'Tyrant Queen' was bad..." he chortled, moving his hand around to her breast, "Wait'll they see Jerne and Regina! They'll have to invent a whole new word, just for us."

Regina grinned and pushed Jerne against the nearest tree, hand moving straight for the fastenings on his trousers.

But stopping, face frozen in surprise and lust, as two figures stepped out; one on either side of the tree. They raised daggers, waited for their victims to make their move.

"Traitors!" Regina hissed and left Jerne to work his blood back to his head, "Traitorous wretches!" she hissed again...

...And dived at Vana!

Vana saw the move in Regina's eyes the second before it came, and her dagger was already lifting, so the slender, wiry body hit no flesh, though the sharp nails raked a weather-roughed face, as the dagger found it's way into the stomach and up, angling to the heart.

As Jerne stared in utter disbelief, Regina collapsed to the floor, sliding down Vana's clothes, leaving a trail of blood. Her eyes burned with one last spark of hatred at her killer, before they slowly blanked as the wounded heart stopped pumping blood.

Jerne backed away, held up his hands in surrender, "Give me no trouble!" He begged, "I'll leave; you'll never see me again!" He tripped over a root and tumbled to his back, crying in pain as his head hit a stone and his vision went blank.

Skim stepped forward, "Unconscious," He said.

Vana nodded, "Good, he'll feel nothing."

Skim looked at her, "You wish him mercy?"

Vana shrugged, nodded, "He's still a person, after all. Just a normal man, who couldn't resist the call of power and money. It happens to many of the best."

Skim nodded and bowed his head, "It could've been different," He told the prone figure, sprawled before him. Then he bent and quickly brought his dagger across Jerne's exposed neck.

Vana sighed and went behind the nearest tree. She returned carrying two spades, having cleaned her daggers and dropped them into the holders strapped around her thighs, "Now we bury them."

Skim nodded, "Even an evil man deserves a grave, if he is to lie in it forever."

They shook out their arms and shoulders, stretched their backs, and began to dig—a shallow grave each, one for each of the would-be tyrants, lost from the side of good, like so many, by the call of wealth and power.

Later, weary, grimed and sweating exhaustion, regretting the digging now—so close to the battle, Skim and Vana returned to Mossan and gave her the nod of confirmation.

"Good," she replied, "Or rather, helpful? Not such a good thing, but nor is any of this we do…" she shook her head sadly, then shook herself and looked at them sternly, "Now, you will go back to your tents and sleep until night. Everyone else will be doing the same in a few hours, when dark arrives. I understand why you needed to dig them graves, and you have my respect for that," Skim and Vana smiled at that, though they barely had the energy—recognising it as a great compliment, "but if you would keep it, go now, wash and rest. You will be woken with everyone else when it is time."

They both nodded mutely and stumbled off to do as they were ordered.

Mossan turned to Xyntu, "Are we almost ready elsewhere?"

Xyntu started, she had been in a daydream, stroking the head of her favourite Phoenix regretfully. But her eyes cleared, and she nodded, "The Phoenix are primed," she showed Mossan steel barbs on the feet of all the birds, and pointed to the already-sharp beak, "They'll work in two groups. One attacks in a wave, the other tries as well as they can to heal and take care of our injured or…others. They switch over when the attacking wave begins to tire, whenever that may be. And keep doing this…for as long as they last," Xyntu stroked the Phoenix head once more, and it nestled itself lovingly into her shoulder.

Mossan smiled sadly, "I know, Xyntu…the Phoenix are the most loyal of friends, and showed no argument or reluctance when we asked them to help. But they can fly, remember that, and they are strong, many will survive. And the others…will be given the same burial as our Centaur fallen—and even the humans who fight with us," she hesitated, but needed to ask, "How goes the rest?"

Xyntu straightened her shoulder, put down the Phoenix and watched it return to its kin, "Well. Our armoury, strengthened these years by our friends in the smithy trade, was full to bursting and with all of the Forest Centaur fully armed and armoured, we still have much left. We will have enough for the Palace Centaur, and the smithys will be bringing with them whatever they have in storage to pass between the villagers who are without weapons. After that, strong boughs of wood, stealing from those already fallen, or fist and foot," she proudly showed her own new mode of dress. A sword slung on her hip, simple iron, but well made, in a black leather sheath. A breastplate of iron, covered by mailed silver—this last an old parental heirloom. She carried a helmet, hooked onto her belt, and her feet and body were covered in thick, tough leather. In all, she was almost the very image of the Centaur warrior.

But as Mossan admired, and showed off her similar attire, a thundering of hooves sounded and shouts of happy greeting as another figure raced into the Forest, lathered in sweat, pale and looking ready to collapse.

Mossan gasped, her hand flew to her mouth as she and Xyntu raced over and excused themselves through the gathered crowd.

Arison stood in the center, dripping and shaking with exertion, "Much faster journey…at full pelt," she gasped, and then she did collapse. Her legs folded under her and down she went, but her eyes remained open as she smiled at Mossan, "I got your message," she said.

Mossan looked around, "Cinamon?"

"Not coming…refuses to fight his mother."

Mossan frowned.

"I tried…" Arison panted."

"Mueren?" Mossan said, hopefully.

Arison hung her head, "She left us…just before I had to leave we made her a funeral pyre as she requested…"

Mossan bowed her head too, followed by every Centaur who heard. But after a moment, "All right, everybody you have work to do, and the sun begins to leave," Mossan ordered, "Or if you finished, help someone else! Get everything done, get equipped, get the spiked balls dug into the ground—and for the Gods' sake remember where the line is and don't cross it! You all have chores! Arison needs peace."

The crowd dispersed quickly, heartened at the arrival of their most decorated fighter, despite that she looked now less capable than a newborn baby.

Arison smiled wearily, her breathing had slowed and there was no new sweat on her coat. Slowly, she stood up, and Mossan realised why the mood had risen.

Arison wore her finest armour, finer than that which she had worn when leaving. A studded sword-sheath hung from a red-leather belt, inside it—Mossan knew—would be her sword, engraved above its hilt with the Centaur God of war, Throu, it would glitter cruelly—almost gold in the daylight, moon-silver at night. She had discarded her tail-bands, trophies of her wins in tournament; instead, she would replace them with one for each person she slew in the coming battle. Her chestplate was matt-black, forged from the wizard metals no longer remembered in this world. The rest of her body was covered first in double-thick leather, then a mithril suit, which shone bright silver. For her head was a heavy iron cap, with no face guards. Each piece had been passed down among generations of her family, given to the greatest warrior when the elder would retire, and Arison indeed looked the part.

'*Or she will, when she is rested.*' Mossan put an arm around Arison's shoulders and led her gently to an unoccupied Shaa where she led her down to rest and left a cup by the soft-hay bed. Arison made her promise 8 times to be sure to wake her, but she was asleep before the final answer could be given.

Mossan crept out as quietly as she could and shut the door.

Xyntu came over with a questioning look.

"She will be fine, and ready for the meeting with the villagers," Mossan promised, "But that journey takes three days at a stroll; none should be forced to gallop the whole path. She must rest, but she will be ready, I gave her a cup of Uret, it will restore her to full health and energy quickly."

Xyntu nodded, "That is good, for a while I was afraid she would collapse before us and never rise! And what of Cinamon and Mueren? Did you ask?"

Mossan nodded, "Mueren passed on. Arison and Cinamon burned her on a pyre, something she requested. And Cinamon...refuses to fight his mother."

Xyntu nodded, "I can understand the boy's reluctance...they will both be sorely missed in our fight, though. And Mueren forever after."

Mossan sighed, "The magic would have given us an unexpected edge. Be only thankful that the woman has no black wizards in her pay."

A throat cleared itself behind the two Centaurs and they both whipped around in surprise.

Dijn made a bow and timidly spoke, "Mossan, Xyntu...I wish I didn't have to correct you...Cinderella has allied with Arguth," he cringed as both started in horror.

"Are you sure?" Mossan cried as quietly as she could.

Dijn nodded, "I saw them talking...he is promised power, money, land...he has already mapped the secret tunnels and attached a barrier to them which will only allow those bearing a certain seal to pass through."

Xyntu grasped him, "They will use the tunnels?"

"For the Palace, yes," Dijn nodded, "There are none here, but they will take the others by surprise…they won't be watching the walls for the attack."

Mossan groaned, "Gods, why did I have Jerne taken down right now!"

Xyntu patted her comfortingly, "It was that or…a lot of trouble we cannot deal with."

Mossan nodded, a pained look on her face, "But for it…our friends are to be slaughtered!"

"But the soldiers are in our alliance!" Xyntu protested, "A surprise, yes, but death from our own proclaimed friends?"

Mossan shrugged, "There are many who are not ours, and the wizard, and Cinderella and her advisor…"

Dijn cleared his throat again.

"If you wish to speak, do so and leave the tiresome noises elsewhere!" Mossan snapped.

Dijn cringed and backed away.

"Dijn, stay," Xyntu shrugged, "You are not the one this anger needs be directed at," she gripped Mossan's arm tightly, "And if he is a little nervous of us, is this his fault? And can you now expect him to be reassured?"

Mossan was nodding and she gave Dijn a sorry smile, "I apologise, Dijn, and I beg your forgiveness."

Dijn nodded, "You have it," he said, as quickly as he could.

"Please tell me what it is you wished to say?" Mossan asked.

"I…I followed Jerne through the tunnels to the stable that time," the small man blurted then turned pale, as if expecting punishment.

Mossan laughed loudly, "Why Dijn—I do believe you could be as much a danger to us as Jerne, should you choose!"

"But now there is the barrier, and we do not know the sigil to wear," Xyntu pointed out, "So what use is this, Dijn? Though how you ever managed to follow Jerne to begin with, I should dearly love to hear!"

Dijn smiled faintly, "It was simple…Jerne is too confident in himself, I just tiptoed behind. And the sigil…was on the parchments of maps that Arguth gave to Cinderella..." he trailed off and waited for the idea to clang in the Centaurs heads.

It did simultaneously and both were clapping him on the back and calling him as many nice names as they could think of.

"And you are willing to do this? For...soldiers may be in the tunnels already," Mossan warned.

I'm willing," he nodded, "I just need something to draw a sigil with..."

Soon, he was equipped with a note and a sigil drawn in black ink on his arm, and slinking off through the trees to do his task at speed.

Mossan watched him go, "Be glad only that he is indeed on our side," she grinned.

Xyntu laughed, "And with a mind for deviousness to beat the Queen herself!" she replied.

All around, Centaurs were finishing their tasks in the gloomy twilight. In ones and twos they would stretch, look at the sky and head to their usual sleeping spot to rest until the dawn. All were armed and armoured, ready for battle, and willing to put their lives— however terrified they might be—on the line. Mossan watched them for a while, a tear or two forming in her gentle eyes, but then they hardened, became grey and stony.

"Time to rest," she ordered Xyntu with a slight smile.

Xyntu nodded and yawned, "Time to rest," she agreed.

Cinamon waited with ill-disguised impatience for Nuisance to finish his food. He had put together whatever cold food he could find, ate himself, then filled a large bowl with the rest. Now Nuisance was rapidly emptying the same bowl, though not all of it went into his mouth. Cinamon was forcibly reminded that this creature, intelligently annoying as it might be, was still a horse—and had a horses eating habits if nothing else!

"Are you done, Nuisance?" he asked again, the horse ignored him and carried on eating, "Apparently not," the boy sighed and paced the room some more, "Please hurry, Nuisance! It's dark, and I have to be there! You had better run faster than you eat and sleep!" he growled and Nuisance looked at him in surprise.

He climbed to his feet and stretched languorously, then bowed his head to Cinamon's face and nuzzled him.

"An apology?"

Nuisance nodded and, looking back to be sure Cinamon followed, went outside where the clouds obscured what would normally a star-filled sky. But no clouds could hide the fresh night air, and Cinamon breathed it deeply. *'This could be the last time I ever know this place...'* he thought, looking around sadly.

Nuisance nudged him and turned side on.

"Bare-back?" Cinamon questioned nervously.

Nuisance nodded.

The boy fidgeted, "Well...I suppose if you trust me I have to trust you...and Mueren would never have sent you of you weren't going to help me..."

Nuisance nodded and stamped his foot impatiently.

"Oh, now you want to be quick!" Cinamon laughed, "But...how can I get on? You're twice my height!"

The horse cocked his head then knelt, his forelegs folding under him.

Cinamon grinned, shrugged and climbed on—holding onto Nuisance's mane for dear life as he leaned far forwards, then relaxing a little the horse rose again.

Only to hold on tighter as Nuisance, without warning, sped off!

And now, from his new vantage point of being buried in the copper mane of his new friend—Cinamon realised why Mueren had sent him, and why he had seen no reason to hurry! When he dared a peek out, he saw the trees and the ground flashing by in a daze of speed, dizzying him until he was forced to bury his head once more.

The steady gallop continued, Nuisance knew where to go, and Cinamon found himself lulled into a doze. Not a sleep, not with the thundering hooves, but rocking with the steady—if speedy—rhythm, he felt his eyes grow heavy and snuggled to the horse tightly to escape from the whipping wind. And so Nuisance sped through the night, just a flash of copper light, there and gone so fast no animal had chance to run, nor could any human—were there any there—have seen it long enough to see what the light was.

Suzee paced as usual, annoying Cinderella to distraction.

"For the final time, will you sit!" the Queen cried.

"For the final time, will you let me go and fight with my men?" Suzee retorted angrily.

"No! You may be the chief of my Guard—reason in itself not to let you get yourself killed!—But you are also my advisor and my friend. And I need you for tactics and instruction just as I need you for friendship," the Queen told her sternly.

Suzee softened, "You need me as a friend?" she asked.

Cinderella opened her mouth, closed it, obviously surprised at her own words, "Well...I rarely say things I don't mean—and then only with prior planning...so yes, I suppose I do need you as my friend," she nodded to herself and smiled brightly, "So therefore, I wish to keep you safe as long as I possibly can."

"I'll have to fight in the bigger battle," Suzee told her.

"I know, Suzee...but at least this one can pass you by?" the Queen was almost pleading now, without realizing it herself. Suzee saw and kept it to herself, but was appeased.

"Very well," she smiled and sat down with an exaggerated flourish. But in her mind, still everything whirled. *'There are men in the tunnels, waiting—half of my force in fact! The other half is ready to creep up to the stables and ambush the cowards who run...they'll do this the second I blow the battle-horn. These plans are simple...but the Centaur in the Forest...ah, but they will be incensed, and I fear not to distraction but of greater effort!'* she sighed inwardly, still hiding her tumultuous thoughts. *'But what can I do? Naught but be there and follow my own instincts.'* she made to rise again and pace, but stopped herself just in time; before realizing with a wry smile that Cinderella had taken the convenient strip of floor.

Suzee grinned, "Now who needs to sit?"

Cinderella started, looked at Suzee, laughed and sat herself down, "I barely realised what I was doing."

"Are you afraid, Cinderella, of the fight?" Suzee asked daringly, expecting the lashing of her friend's tongue.

But the whip seemed to be lacking tonight. Cinderella just nodded, "You may be right or wrong about the Centaur of the Forest fighting better with anger...and by the same, so might I. And it occurs to me they may have other allies."

"Me also, which is why I split up and reformed the squads," Suzee reminded her.

Cinderella nodded again, "I know. Still...I have this feeling of doom over me..."

"But we have our secret weapon!" Suzee spread her hands, "We have Arguth! Who do they have?"

The Queen relaxed a little, "Right! They cannot have more than an amateur schools magician!" She chuckled, "And will they be shocked? I believe they will..."

"So we are all prepared..." Suzee muttered, mostly to herself.

"We are," Cinderella agreed, "All that remains is to rest until the dawn."

Suzee nodded, "I rested all day, so can remain awake and wait. You should rest. I will be in your study, if I may. And I'll wake you in plenty of time."

Cinderella yawned and nodded, "Thank you, Suzee," she said, for once entirely lacking her Queenly airs.

Suzee smiled at this. *'She truly is my friend...and I hers...we may do many bad things in the future, but only to those who work against us...and what an unbeatable team we will be!'*

She left Cinderella to sleep and sat by the window in the study, pretending to read a scroll, instead running through all possible scenarios in her mind as she watched for the first dark grey of dawn.

Chapter 26

Inside the tunnels, men shifted and grumbled to themselves, the cold seeped through their armour, through their clothes and into their skin and once in a while someone would get up and stomp around a little, to assure his circulation that he was still alive.

Tension filled the air, for some it was simply the before-battle nerves, waiting to be released in a fury from the sharp end of their sword.

For others—indeed most—it was more than that. For, though they had a battle to fight also, they knew it was a different one...

Each man sat alongside two others, not knowing whether one or both of them was on his side or the other. The only things they knew for certain were these:

Each squad Captain was going to fight for the rebels, but only the Captains knew which soldiers were involved.

Should the rebels be defeated, the soldiers would not be given a hasty trial and execution, as most of the other fighters would. In fact, running around many minds were petrifying ideas of what the Queen's deranged mind might think up to punish them for betraying her.

They knew, also, that dawn drew closer with every thought, and that soon enough those on the other side would know of the betrayal of so many...they would know, indeed, by the way those 'traitors'— or so they would think of them—would be running at speed in the same direction as the forewarned Centaurs.

A young soldier at the far end of the line, farthest away from the entrance to the stable, dozed unhappily. He was loyal to his Kingdom, and felt guilty that today would be not only his first battle, but also his betrayal.

He mused on this deeply, and so was startled when a shadow moved just beyond the reach of his lamp!

He raised it and stood. The man next to him grumbled, "Wha?" in his half doze.

The young man shrugged, "Stretch my legs," he muttered.

The other was already back into his sleep, and the young one moved forward. Just beyond his lamp, moving backwards with each step he took forward, he knew—just a feeling in his gut, he knew!— There was a figure.

'*The spy? The one who brought the warning to the Centaur?*' He thought and crept forward faster, to be far enough from any other ears to speak to the figure he knew was there.

Finally, "'Ere, who's there? Cinderella's man, or the Centaur's?"

A relieved sigh and Dijn stepped from the shadows. Though he needn't have bothered—he was swathed in black clothes, his small and slender figure made flowing by the thin garments wrapped around every inch of him, "You are whose?" he asked, cautiously.

"Eh? You the one in a place you shouldn't be," came the gruff reply, "But, er, here's a clue—I'm on the same side as my squad Captain."

Dijn nodded, "You are with me, then. Tell me, friend, how many soldiers are seated between here and the stables?"

"Half of the whole. You'll never get past."

Dijn thought for a moment.

"And outside?"

"The other half, but they won't be out yet—just before dawn they'll move in and watch, now they're no doubt eating and donning their armour."

Dijn smiled behind his covering, "Thank you, friend. I have to let the Centaur know where the attack will spring from—is there more you can tell me?"

"Eh? Not me, I only know there's us in here, and there's the others'll be getting in their places soon. You best hurry."

Dijn nodded, "I will, thank you, friend."

"All right, be careful now," the young man blinked, but the shadowy figure was gone. He shook his head, wondering if he was still dreaming, and went back to his seat where the one beside him snored softly.

In the village, movement was rife and stealthy. Though mostly sure Cinderella would not be watching them this night, still the villagers moved slowly from their houses and crept in the shadows the moon and clouds gave. Some armed, some unlucky enough to be late to the smithys with only a sturdy stick or a kitchen knife, a few armoured. All gave each other suspicious, nervous glances as they moved towards the Forest where all was quiet and the Centaur slept.

All but Mossan. She was up and waiting for them, and held up a hand to tell them to stay still.

"There are barbed chunks of wood in the ground just a few steps beyond the border," she hissed as loudly as she dared, pointing to the edge of the grass where it met the dirt road, "When you get to me, you must step or jump as far as you can,"

One by one, showing their understanding by doing as they were told, the villagers leapt or strode as over some invisible barrier. One or two caught glimpses of wickedly sharp metal and shuddered to think of how many would be brought down by them when they came to attack.

"The barbs will not get them all, or even very many if they are lucky, but they will get some, and confuse the rest. The line is not straight, so we hope so disable some in the first few lines before they reach us," Mossan told them all in a low voice, barely loud enough to be heard by straining ears at the back of the crowd.

The town was a small one, though before Cinderella it had been bustling and crowded, and almost every able-bodied citizen had turned up. But even in near-full number, the deceivingly small size of the town was obvious. No more than 300, Mossan estimated, with perhaps 100 weapons of note, and a pitiful few with armour. She gestured to a small pile of arms.

"Some of you can arm yourselves better, do so. But be silent, and argue none!" she ordered.

The first few ranks filed forward, the rest stayed where they were, knowing there was little point. Some tugging ensued, but quickly owners were found for all the weapons and all had been done with minimum noise and trouble.

'*And a good thing, for the real trouble is nearing...and it's big!*' Mossan thought, "Good," she nodded, "There are enough arms put away for the Palace Centaurs to be armed, and those without must remain to the rear until you can borrow a weapon from one of the fallen—on either side," she said this coldly, watching for hints of shock, but none came—it seemed this idea was already thought of, or at least too obvious a solution to dispute it. Mossan noted this with a measure of contentment. '*No soft-headed idealists wanting to play at war.*'

Skim appeared from the shadows behind Mossan, causing a gasp of recognition to flutter through the audience. He smiled, "I always wondered how well I was known outside of the Palace, and so now I know. I hope you also know how and why I left the Queen's service?"

Nods and mumbles.

"That's good, perhaps I will tell you after the battle the story unembellished by rumours. However, as you know me, you should also know Vana."

Vana stepped from a different shadow to noises of recognition, though less shocked for they all knew they left together.

"Good. Then you know to listen to us, and listen well," Skim went on, "We have plans, tactics...all simple and easy to do—I just want to put you all in the picture and let you know where I expect you to be— at least in the beginning—and offer a suggestion or two to help as many of us as possible survive."

Gratitude radiated out and he grinned to himself. He was armed and armoured, as he had been the day he left. Only now, his armour shone like new after hours of polishing, his cloak was mended where the forest had torn it, and his sword had been given back to him by the very underling who was ordered to have it melted down, as sharp and level as it was when it was first made.

Vana, likewise, had polished, mended and set an imposing figure side-by-side with Skim. Together they might meeken the hearts of many a crowd of bandits, and together they strengthened the hearts of every willing fighter standing before them. Even more so than the Centaur could, for these were of their own race and ran with the old warrior halflings, and they had experience, something which none of the Centaur could truly claim no matter how imposing he or she may look.

Nobody noticed a young boy on his copper horse watching from the gloom beneath the trees.

"Good boy, Nuisance," he whispered into the horse's ear, "Forgive me for nagging you; if I'd known you run so fast…I would not have done so."

The horse tossed his head amiably and waited.

Cinamon strained his ears to listen, somehow not wanting to show himself—not yet, anyway—but trying to find a place where he could fit in.

"Now here it is," Skim began, once a large piece of parchment was pinned with knives from two trees, he pointed to each section in turn and waited for confirmation—or questions—before moving on.

"On the right flank—at the front will be half of the Palace Guards we have on our side; that makes about 100. Right behind them will be half of you, we don't want you as fodder for the first of Cinderella's lot, so about 150 of you will be right behind the Guards. Beside the Guards, just to the side, will be Melina—she is one of our commanders and you'll meet her later. Commanding you villagers on that side will be Dijn—he is also our spy, and a damn good sneak, so obey him and if he vanishes just trust he'll be sabotaging someone without them knowing and will be back," Skim paused and looked around. Nobody moved. He grunted to himself and went on.

"On the left flank, the same basic set-up. In the front will be the other half of the Guards, about another 100. Behind them will be the rest of you—about another 150 there. And to stress—if you do not have a weapon, make your way to the back and pick one up the second you can without getting yourself killed! Clear?" there was a small roar of approval, "Good, now commanding the Guards on the left side is Spitter—he speaks better than English than he pretends," Skim grinned, "And if you keep out of the way of his saliva you'll be fine," questions came then, but he quelled them, "You'll meet him soon enough, then you'll see. And commanding the villagers will be Xyntu—she will also be looking after the 18 Phoenix that the Centaurs have equipped for fighting. More on those in a minute, any questions?"

Nothing, so he continued, somewhat pleased, "In the center will be the bulk of the Centaur—again, the less armour and protection they have the farther back they will be. They have no commander as such, but will follow the lead of Arison, Micx and Mossan. Who…" he pointed, "Will be directly in front of them. On the same row, on the left in front of the guards will be myself, and on the right in front of the Guards will be Vana. We'll be grouped close together at first, and far enough back to see how many of the opposite side get themselves impaled on those barbed chunks of wood you all stepped over—because you knew they were there," his eyes glinted cruelly as he said this, "I think we'll disable quite a few with this. Any questions?"

Still not a sound, "Everything sunk in and you have not a single thing to ask?" he called.

A few mutters, but still no one spoke.

Vana piped up, "People, if you have a question you must ask it! If one tiny thing is a little unclear, we need to know or it could kill you!"

Finally someone moved, "Sir, I have a question," a voice said meekly.

"Call me Skim, and go ahead," he gave Vana a grateful look.

"I think we all got everything, where we gotta stand and everything…but what about Her? What's she got? And…and what happens at the end, when we win or lose?"

Skim sighed, "Okay, first to Cinderella's forces. I estimate she has about 800 City Guards—who, as you know, will do anything for her as long as they can beat people up for their money. Plus about 120 Palace Guards who we didn't get to because I don't know them well enough to try, or because I know they would have turned us in. Also, there is Suzee—Captain of the Palace Guards now, and the Queen's close advisor. Lastly there is Arguth…"

Now there came a rabble of noise! Every person there knew Arguth as the darkest of the dark wizards, and every person was scared enough to hide in their house at the merest hint of his presence in the area.

Vana held up her hands, "We know he is a powerful wizard!" she shouted over the noise and received a barrage of disgusted agreements and curses. She raised an eyebrow, "But you won't defeat or escape him by doing that!" she retorted.

This time a few laughs came back, and the noise faded.

"Thank you," she said, "Now, we know all about Arguth, but do you know all about dark wizards?" mostly silence here, none knew much aside from how to keep out of their way, "I thought so. Well we do!" she called, "In fact, Arison has spent some time with Mueren, the very lady who helped a poor, tortured slave-girl escape from her life. Unfortunately, she was no future-scryer, and was banished before Cinderella took her power too far! Arison knows something about dark wizards..."

Arison had been waiting silently in the darkness and now stepped out. Added to the spectacle of Skim and Vana, she caused a rush of awe. *'May as well use it.'* She laughed inwardly and flexed her muscles, making her armour flash and glint cruelly in the moon and torchlight.

After a moment she stopped and smiled at Vana and Skim, who were laughing.

"Thank you," she rumbled and the noise abated speedily, "I know something about dark wizards from Mueren. Arguth has two ways of doing things. For many, he is forced to call up a dark genie. He can call up only one, for he must hold it by force and threaten it until it obeys, and its power is limited because of this. Two, he has his own power. Which is great, yes, and there is no bar on that aside from his own strength. I can only tell you that he will probably not bother with a genie, and will be somewhere off to the side but close to the front of Cinderella's group. I hold out little hope that he will be disabled by the barbs, and even if he is, until he is dead he has power. All I can advise is that none of you tries to get to him! You will die if you do, and quite nastily. If you see a bolt of something coming towards you, duck and dive and you might avoid it, but whether he will concentrate first on your commanders, the Centaurs, the Guards or yourselves, I have no way of knowing. I wish only that I had better advice," she shrugged regretfully and moved back to let Skim and Vana continue.

"The Queen will-" Skim began but was interrupted by gasps from those in front of him.

All who were facing the wrong way spun around and saw a copper light walking towards them.

As it came closer, they discerned the outline of a horse, strolling peaceably to them, giving off a glow that no normal horse could ever do.

Entranced, none noticed the figure riding it until he hopped off and walked towards them.

"Cinamon!" Arison was the first to recognise him and raced over to hug him. She carried the boy back and set him down in front of everyone before addressing them proudly, "I think, my friends, that we have found our secret weapon."

Cinamon grinned and bowed to the mutters and rumblings of "That's the Prince!"…"He's on our side?"…"We should trust the spawn of that witch?" and more.

Eventually it died down as everyone waited to hear him speak.

Nuisance trotted up and down a short distance away, his light giving all present an eerie glow. And Cinamon was no exception, his height made him no less remarkable as he spoke.

"I apologise for arriving at such a late hour," he said, "I was reluctant to come…it is my mother we fight against, and though I hate the things she does as much as you—nay, more, for she does them to me too—I could not bring myself to fight her. But…my teacher, Mueren, had passed away, and was unable to look at me sternly and order me to come!" he grinned at the memories of various confrontations, "Instead, she sent me Nuisance," he gestured to the horse who stood still a moment and whinnied, "He runs like the wind, and so here I am. Afraid, yes, but Mueren would not have sent me Nuisance just so I could sit in a corner and turn yellow!"

"But you're a boy! What can you do?" someone shouted and gained agreements from all sides.

Cinamon thought then broke into a mischievous smile, "Who spoke?" he asked.

The crowd moved away and pushed a burly man to the front. He grunted, "Yeh, it was me."

Cinamon examined him a moment. Thick-muscled, with a generous layer of fat, he was tall with gentle eyes and a gruff manner, "Let me show you," the boy shrugged and held out a hand.

The man, unsure, took a step forward…

…And rose up into the air!

Cinamon grinned and lifted him higher, until he was above the highest head, then set him slowly turning around on his belly.

He blustered, groaned, screamed, kicked, and begged to be let down, "Gods, I'm sorry Prince! Put me down, put me down!!!!!" he screamed.

Cinamon shrugged and let him gently down, even placing him feet-up before letting go his invisible hold, "A small demonstration," he explained, "I can do much more than that—though I hesitate to tell you all those things—and so can my genies. Two of which will come to me the second I call, and being good genies will happily fight on our behalf without interference from me."

He stepped aside to let Skim retake the villagers attentions, only to realise that he, Vana, Mossan and Arison were close to hysterical laughter and unable, just yet, to say anything!

Cinamon shrugged and took over again, "I heard the questions you asked. At the end…if we lose, those who survived will die—simple and quick for most, for you villagers at least. The rest of us…especially those who lead you, will be far from lucky in that respect. But the only answer to that is…do not lose! She has Arguth, yes, but they do not know you have me, whom the Gods themselves have given power and learning to," he showed no sign of boasting, only shrugged and went on, "As for what happens when we win," he gently accentuated the 'when', "Cinderella will be captured—I'll have none kill her out of hand," Now he looked around sternly to be sure the message hit home. Once happy that it did, "She will be given trial and so will all survivors who fought with her, and we will treat them well and fairly. Then a new system will be ordered, one that benefits us all, one that will be spoken of more fully when we have won."

He looked at Skim again who nodded and shrugged apologetically, then stepped aside.

Skim stepped up once more, "Finally, from what I know of the Queen and Suzee, they will spread their army wide, no more than 2 or 3 rows, to try and surround us. We will begin as a close group, as I mentioned, to see who is picked off by the barbs. Those that are leave them until the end, for you'll not get close enough to that line for them to do any harm," this was a well-concealed order that everyone understood and nodded at, "Once the rows are over the barbs, listen to your commanders. They'll call to spread out, do so, but not too far—and keep to the back if you're without weapons. We'll be far enough back to move forward as we spread, and by the time we meet the Phoenix will be picking off the ones to the outside. And of the Phoenix, there will be two waves of nine controlled by Xyntu, one will be attempting to help and heal our injured, the others will be attacking—and they will switch off as needed. You need not concern yourself with that unless you are injured—in which case look for one and ask it to help you," he nodded satisfaction as everyone in front of him nodded theirs.

"Now to meet your commanders," Vana gestured and more figures came into view, bowing as they were introduced, "First is Melina, stepsister to the Queen and commanding the Guards on the right flank. Dijn—commanding the villagers on the right. Xyntu, commanding the Phoenix and the villagers on the left. And this small green fellow here is Spitter. Former servant of the traitor-spy Jerne, he is from Rumazane and his spittle is poisonous to animals, and paralysing to men and women of good health," Spitter bowed to awed gasps from the crowd, his green tinged slightly red with embarrassment.

"And that's all we have for you," Skim concluded, "If you have anything for us, ask it now, for in just three or four hours we'll be in formation and there's no time for question then!"

No questions came.

"Okay. Then…do what you will, but do it restfully. If we don't call you beforehand, then gather to us when the Palace Centaur and Guards begin arriving, and do it quickly! For that is when the true fight begins," He waved them away and turned, with his commanders, to walk to Cinamon, who had returned to Nuisance.

"I'll be on Nuisance," the boy told them, "He says he'll watch for Arguth trying to get me, and move me. Plus my genies will help, they said.

"The horse talks?" Vana asked.

"No, but he understands, and he can nod or shake his head or do other things to answer," Cinamon shrugged.

"Well go get some rest, lad," Skim told him gently, "We'll be doing the same, and you'll be woken the same time as us."

Cinamon nodded and led Nuisance off to find a spare patch of grass.

Chapter 27

Royston tapped his fingers on the table as he tried to say the words he had planned so well the night before, lying awake while Osmon slept.

Osmon waited with a patiently bemused look, wondering what was so important and hard to say—but happily assured by Royston that it was nothing bad.

"How would you feel about...not going back to Lamsonia?" he finally asked in a rush of words.

Osmon opened his mouth, then closed it, then opened it again, "Well, I mean...I'd not really..."

Royston nodded, "Well I have. I'm not sure I could be any sort of King or leader; I don't want to be, for a first. I'm not one for that sort of attention...when I'm playing that's a different matter, but in charge? I don't think I could, Osmon!"

"To be truthful, I only do it because I have to," the King grinned wryly, "I can do it, I'm well trained and I really do want to do what's best for everyone...but my choice of career would have been much simpler given a chance."

"You'd've made a decent rentboy," Royston grinned evilly.

"Wha-! Hey now!" Osmon guffawed, "And you would have been my main customer!"

Royston giggled, nodding enthusiastically. Then, "So what would you have done? Given the chance?"

Osmon shrugged, "I don't know…something simple. A trader, perhaps. Or…maybe something more hands on," he gave a sly wink but continued before Royston could interrupt, "like, well you like to play music, but I always liked to see how music worked…perhaps I could have made instruments," he shrugged, "But I have this responsibility, I was too cowardly to refuse it gracefully when I could have done, and now…I can't leave my people with Cinderella. Or whatever comes of this big thing that was can all feel happening over there…I can't abandon them through it. They never hated me, I don't think, they pitied me, maybe…but they seemed to like me."

"Few people can help that," Royston replied, smiling to himself, "But what about afterwards? When this 'big thing' is over, if Cinderella is gone? What then? Maybe that would be a good time to step down with honour, and honesty."

"Honesty…" Osmon laughed sourly, "Now there's a thing much easier to use if you're brave enough."

"But you are! You came and got me, didn't you? You're taking me back, you want to kick out Cinderella and put me in her place, right?" Osmon nodded, "Well then, it's no braver to get rid of Cinderella, leave them in the hands of someone capable then take your leave to live elsewhere, be something else—something you choose, for once in your life."

Osmon bowed his head, nodding, and gave a resigned sigh, "But…I have a responsibility to these people…and who will lead them if I go?"

"Let them lead themselves!" Royston gestured behind them, "It works on Giizintaan, and your people are peaceful folk…or leave an advisor to bring Cinamon into his Kingship when he comes of an age."

Osmon took Royston's hand in his and stroked it lovingly, "I want to leave," he confessed, but his head was lowered in shame.

"Who can blame you? Forced into something so big?" Royston lifted Osmon's head and looked into his eyes with a wry smile, "Not like you've had a choice about much in your life so far, is it?"

"Some things I would've made the choice about anyway," Osmon replied, "But…I can't simply go, vanish into the ether, you have to accept that."

Royston sat back and nodded wearily, "I understand. But once you get there…will you be able to leave? Or will this same force keep you there?"

"I got past it to come and find you, did I not? Even after everything I did and knowing what you did," he spoke carelessly and winced in sympathy as Royston gritted his teeth.

It was not anger at Osmon, but at himself, and would be for a long time to come—perhaps forever. Both knew this, also knew there was nothing to say…not yet, anyhow. Osmon went on:

"I can do it. I'm not the lily-livered, yellow-spined fool that…that everything and everyone had done their best to make me. You kept that one spark of bravery alive in me, and now…it's growing. I just never willed it to before, not really. Let me return once last time, see how this…big thing turns out, let them know I'm leaving…I'll not just abandon them, whether they care or not," Osmon shrugged, "I can't, and it's not due to any duty. I love each one of those people, because I know them, in a way, and I know them as my fathers and mothers have all made the effort to know them. So, whether they take notice or not, or care that I'm going, I have to at least go back and tell them."

Royston nodded, "Then we leave?"

Osmon grinned, "Then we leave," he promised and leaned over to give a quick kiss.

"Then we will return, for a short time…before deciding where in this wide, wide world we should go," Royston spread his arms as wide as he could, "Perhaps…perhaps we could even see it all!"

"Perhaps," Osmon nodded, "Though hard it will be to see any sights more beautiful than the one I see right now."

Royston blushed and grinned shyly.

"Just a few days," Osmon promised, "To see everything is fine, and then we travel—in style, for I am a King and will take some of that treasure that none have bothered to touch before and show this wide, wide world just how much I love you!"

Royston clapped, "Excellent! I must say, however much I came to love Giizintaan…it compares little to being somewhat noble…though I never did miss the fuss people made over me. Except you, of course, the more fuss the better."

They planned their journey, for a time, as the ship sailed at full tilt to its destination, Samson and Eera on deck praying that they would arrive in time.

Eera was musing about the yet undiscussed feelings of he and Samson, the urgency to leave which had rubbed off on the others, the feeling of something big happening…that they were probably going to be too late for! Now, he decided, was the time to talk.

"Samson," He said quietly from behind the man's shoulder, where he watched the dark sea rush by. Past the stony Islands now, where Samson had guided the ship carefully through the rocks without damage, one of the other seamen had the wheel, and the Captain was thoughtfully watching ahead of him. At Eera's voice he smiled.

"I knew yer were standin' there," he said and turned around, "An' I know what yer wanna talk about."

Eera inclined his respectfully, "I had thought you may."

"Aye, yer one o' them few who don't unnerestimate me," Samson grinned, "But I think yer know what I'm gonna say anyhow."

"There were always those in my race who could scry the future, few, to be sure, and most of it was oneiromancy, or vague visions—impossible to interpret most until the event itself. As it was diluted in the blood, it became just a feeling—an urge to do something, or to avoid something! My grandmother of, perhaps, 8 generations ago was a powerful scryer. She had it all, dreams, visions, feelings, and once in a while she could interpret them right away—often she could do so just before. But she always told us that to not see the future is the best way…for if she foresaw a death, the death would happen no matter what we did. It is unchangeable…and everything comes to pass whether we know it or not. Her blood came down to me, diluted, and all I feel occasionally is…a certain something," Eera smiled a little, "I felt something of a tug that night of the legendary Prince's Ball, when I drew the pumpkin-shaped carriage of a poor slave-girl to the Palace…"

Samson chuckled, "Well, I'd say yer got than 'un pretty accurate!"

Eera nodded, "And this feeling is the same. It is just as strong, and had been tugging at me for a while. I assumed it was related to our mission of finding Royston…but once we found him it was as if the gates were opened and it came flooding in, ordering me to return home immediately…"

Samson nodded understandingly, "I can't say my family history, I was a bastard born and raised on the ships. But there musta been summat somewheres, cos I always foller me gut. And like yer said, it was tellin' me summat before, and I thought it were just the Royston thing…then we caught 'im and…bam—I had to get 'ome right now cos summat were goin' on! Thing is, Eera, I think we're gonna be too late…"

"You are not the only one…" the old Centaur said gloomily, "I think we are going to be just too late to catch, and help with, whatever is going to happen…because it is about to happen any second now—in fact, I think it may have already begun."

"Well yer certainly a mite more telling than me!" Samson snorted, "I on'y know summat's gonna go soon, an' that's so far as I get! That Granny o' yours was a powerful 'un and no mistake!"

Eera nodded, "So we will be too late for this…thing, whatever it is…and the two things I am unable to tell are the most important—who is involved, and who will…win? Win, I suppose, a fight of some kind?" He furrowed his greying brow.

Samson patted his arm, "Nothin' yer can do, Eera. Just gotta get there soon as we can and see what went on. An' if it were bad, mayhap we can put it back tergether agin."

Eera nodded and sighed his frustration, "If these old bones have the strength," he muttered.

Samson heard, "There's time in yer yet, Eera. If yer think o' our different races an' how they age—yer no' much older than I am! An' I know damn right I got a few more years to frolic in t'snow wi' a pretty young 'un yet!" he gave a toothy grin, intentionally lecherous, and Eera laughed despite himself.

"I'd know very little about that!" he confessed, "Other than what others have told me."

Samson gaped, "Yer mean…yer never…well I'll be…"

"I was a professor, a teacher, a student…" he shrugged, "There are those among the Centaur who are like children to me. And that has seen me through."

"Aye, but it in't all about the kiddies tho is it!" Samson put back his lecherous grin, "Sometimes yer gotta 'ave some fun, relieve the tension, like."

Eera chortled, "You will always be an old fool, Samson," he declared.

"Aye, but so long as I'm an old fool up ter 'avin' a bit o' fun, I'll be an 'appy old fool!" the man guffawed.

Eera joined him, though his laughter was perhaps a little less untroubled, for those dark feelings were drawing in closer as each second passed. *'Soon...so soon...but what! And how will it end!'* he begged of his watered-down talent. But there came no reply, unless it was a faint clashing of swords, or a vague tumult of pain that lost itself in the lapping of the sea against the boat.

Lost in thought, Eera didn't see Royston and Osmon arrive on deck until they appeared beside him, making him jump in surprise.

"Calm down old one," Osmon smiled, "That heart of yours shouldn't get itself so worked up."

Eera smiled and shook his head, "Just what I tell it myself..." he shrugged and smiled a little, "But you know how hearts are; they won't listen to what they're told."

"That I know," Osmon nodded solemnly, "They just live their own lives, and sweep us along with them. But we have news," he gestured to himself and Royston.

"Oh?" Samson was interested now, "Havin' a babby are ya?" he chortled and patted Royston's belly.

Royston grinned, "Looks more like you're the one with a 'babby' Samson," he replied, patting the other man's beer-belly.

"Aye, at that yer could be right," he grinned, unfazed, "So what's it then fellas?"

Osmon looked at Royston, took a breath and; "After we've been back to Lamsonia and sorted out...whatever it is that needs sorting, I plan to renege my Kingship to Cinamon—and a trusted advisor..." he glanced at Eera "and take Royston and myself traveling."

Eera nodded, "This is not unexpected," he smiled.

Samson chuckled, "Sounds like a plan ter me. Ah, but if only we all could do such things, eh? Long as yer return sometimes an' feed us plenty o' tales to whet our appetites! And, o'course, if yer see me on meh travels come an' ave a bite wi' meh."

"But of course!" Royston spread his arms, "To both things! We don't plan to abandon the place entirely, just spend most of our time elsewhere…"

"Eh, and did I tell yer I'm right glad to see yer together an' 'appy? T'pair of yer!" Samson grinned, "Nowt like 'elpin' a coupla luvvers get wi' who they meant ter be wi', eh?"

Osmon hugged Royston and smiled, "And did I ever tell you both thank you so much for everything?"

"Yer did now!" the burly seaman laughed and clapped them both meatily on the shoulders, "A'most makes a man like mesel' wanna sit down and find 'isself some good 'un ter be wi'."

Eera raised an eyebrow but said nothing. Samson caught it.

"I said a'most!" he guffawed. And the three others joined in laughing as the first thread of grey began to lighten the distant sky.

"It's happening," Eera said in a low voice, grimacing with his diluted seers blood.

The laughter stopped, cut off as with a knife, and an apprehensive, gloomy silence descended as the four of them strained to see land, to arrive in time for…whatever. But there was no line on the horizon, and as Eera seated himself painfully on the floor, trying desperately to make sense from the turmoil inside him, each other in turn watched him, and the horizon, and the growing light in the sky. Only this dawn seemed less an escape from night, and more like the light leading the defenceless into the abyss.

Chapter 28

As the four companions on the boat watched the horizon lighten, so Suzee, still staring from her window, saw the darkness give way to a thin line of grey.

She had awoken Cinderella, who was now dressed and grumbling about the protective clothing Suzee had forced her to wear—thin mail over thick leather, trousers covered by more leather, and a dagger to one hip.

"If you insist on being there with us, you will be protected," Suzee had told her, sternly, "By myself, by some clothing, by yourself if you must!"

Cinderella had relented, knowing Suzee had her best interests to heart, but she still frowned a little as she adjusted the uncomfortable cut of her new-style of clothing.

Shaking her head, amused, frustrated, and afraid, Suzee took up her royal battle horn and put it to her lips.

Once the deafening note had sounded, without waiting to see the obedience she knew her army would give her, she took Cinderella by the arm, talking as she half-pulled her along, "Come on. Time to get saddled up; the City Guards will already be congregating on the edge of Centaur territory. If we want to join them while still in relative safety, we move now."

In the Centaur stables…the 'secret' door had opened before the horn finished its note, and half the Palace Guards rushed in, swords brandishing, ready to strike down any non-human they saw!

Then, those loyal to the Queen stopped in amazement.

The second the horn sounded, the Centaurs had thrown themselves as orderly as possible to the door, trotting out in twos and threes, before galloping down any men in their way, not looking back as they made the short journey to Centaur Forest.

Following behind them or squeezing through the door with them, most of the Guards were slashing left and right at their own fellows as they followed on as fast as their feet could move!

Some Centaurs stopped and picked up a passenger, some dawdlers fell as the rest of the Guards found their minds again and attacked.

But foremost in every mind was, *'They knew! They were waiting! And…there are men with them! Guards! Traitors!'* Followed quickly by, *'Gods help us; the Queen will string us all from the Palace walls!'*

Some dropped their fight and ran; finally glad to be free of the Queen — or glad, at least, that their last act would be to die in freedom.

Micx, had allowed himself to be one of the last to run from the stable, but he had left it a moment too long — so he saw as he emerged at full gallop, to run directly over one screaming soldier, and into the swords of three others.

Bleeding and screaming his pain, Micx reared and pounded the two swordsmen to the ground, leapt over them and stopped a yard farther on when he saw one man reaching for him, seeming to plead.

"I am Skim's man!" he gasped, and Micx saw he bled brightly from his mouth. Trampled under the rush of escapees, but not dead, leaning closer Micx heard his breath whistling in and out…but not from his mouth.

"Your airways are broken, man," Micx growled, looking around, seeing the remaining men group together, and five start carefully towards him.

The bleeding man nodded, "I would die with honour, not torture," he gasped, his hand resting on a sword that lay near him.

Micx nodded and took the sword from him.

The advancing men took the opportunity and rushed forward, swords out.

The dying man croaked a warning and Micx turned, drew the sword up in a flash and took two of the men before glaring at the others.

One dropped his sword and backed off before the terrible glint in the Centaur's eye.

The other, realizing he was alone, but too afraid not to even run, raised his sword shakily, "B-by order of the Queen Cinderella, I p-place you under arrest..." he trailed off, staring at Micx who edged closer, becoming more imposing with every inch.

Without warning, the sword flashed again and the soldier was dead.

"The price of bravery," Micx growled, "Any of you move, you die too," he turned back to the dying man, '*A little sooner, anyway.*' he added grimly.

The man looked up with half closed eyes, he was dying, Micx could see, but painfully...and slowly.

"Please..." the man begged.

Micx nodded, bent and touched the man's clammy forehead a moment, "Go in peace, friend," he growled and raised his sword.

"Thank you..." the man sighed...and his own sword cut through his neck in a flash of bloody silver.

Micx performed a quick rite—something usually done after the battle, but this ally had died at his own hands, by request, and he must hide his tears, and apologise for the words he would speak next before dealing with the remaining soldiers. Bowing his head, he rested the sword point-down in a pool of blood and muttered a quick prayer to Throu, Centaur God of War.

Then he threw back his head and laughed, "See how one of your own begs me for death!" he whipped around and chortled cruelly as the men, eight of them now, still standing in a huddle, cold and afraid, flinched.

"B-b-b-by the..." one of the others tried, with his eyes squeezed tightly shut.

"By the authority of King Osmon of Lamsonia, the Palace Centaur are free!" Micx roared, "And by the authority of the People and Centaurs of Lamsonia, Cinderella and her rule are OVER!"

The men had no time to unfreeze and run as the fiery red, maniacally cackling brute bore down upon them with his sword, the battle-history in his blood coming out as he took each man in easy strokes.

"And for those of you who ran to join the assault on the Forest…" he growled at the sky, as he threw his head back to revel in the coppery smell, the thick feel of blood, "You will die too!" he finished, turned and galloped from the Palace and towards the trees, to take the longer but safer route to the Forest.

Formed into ranks, arranged as ordered by Skim, the Centaurs, the Villagers and their commanders waited for the rest of the Centaur and the Guards to arrive. The horn had sent a shiver through all of them, and Arison paraded now in front of the villagers, talking to them powerfully.

Mossan nudged her and nodded towards the edge of the small grassy knoll, which told the beginning of the Centaur region.

Arison turned, hearing the gasps of those who also saw.

Gathering, barely in sight but growing clearer as each second brought the sun closer to rising, were men. City Guards. All clad in blue and grey, scowling but silent, armed and armoured.

Arison turned back, "We expected this," she reminded them, "The City Guard are all with Cinderella, for so long as she lines their pockets and allows them leave to beat up innocent people they will be with her. Or…for as long as we LET this happen! For tonight, friends, comes the end of her regime!"

"But how will the other Centaurs get through?" piped up one small voice.

"They will come through the Forest behind you," Arison smiled, "We assumed the Queen would gather here in advance, for she would assume any escapees would travel this way. See how some of the City Guards face away from us? That is why we traced them a route through the trees to us. And if I am not mistaken, I can hear the thundering of many hooves right now!"

Every head turned to face the Forest as the thundering grew louder, closer. From a sea of green exploded a mass of movement as the sheer force of those escaping drove the villagers back a few paces to half-cower behind each other.

Breathless, the Centaur quickly formed a center rank under instruction from Arison and the villagers tentatively moved closer to reform theirs, growing braver as they caught the eyes of a few who smiled warmly and uttered friendly greetings. Trickling in as fast as their legs could run, or climbing down from the backs of those who carried them, the Guards formed too, a barrier of armour and swords in front of the untrained villagers.

"Micx?" Mossan asked a Centaur close to her.

The Centaur shrugged apologetically.

"Micx?" Mossan called, "Did any see my brother?"

"He helped us all out of the stable," came back on small-ish Centaur—a youngster, at the back, "He told me to go ahead and he would follow behind," she looked around, "But I did not see him follow," she caught a hitch in her throat as she looked behind her, searching, but only finding another group of soldiers, panting as they fell into line.

"It's okay, young one," Mossan told her soothingly, looking anxiously into the trees, "But—"

She was cut off as Micx came pelting into the clearing, covered in blood, still holding the sword, eyes blazing fire. He came to a stop at the front of the group, who all turned in awe to watch this bloody warrior stand before the clean, almost shining, Arison and the relieved Mossan. He carried three men on his back and let them down gently before turning to his sister and hugging her tightly, without words.

"I had to relieve one of our friends of his burden..." Micx said sadly, his eyes glowing a little less, "He was dying slowly, and he gave to me his sword," he held it to Arison, "As the greatest warrior in our tribe, I ask your blessing for this weapon."

Arison laid a hand on it, and then crossed it with her own shining blade, "Blessed it shall be, and blessed it is. No enemy shall stand before it, nor harm come to its owner shall he remain true."

An old blessing, one proved many times wrong, but one so ingrained into these once battle-blooded creatures that little thought was given to the meaning, only to the sentiment behind it.

Micx's eyes brightened cruelly once more as he told of dispatching the 12 soldiers who dared remain behind.

A moment later, as Micx took his place in the front rank, the City Guards began to shift, somewhat nervously, and all now were looking behind them.

The sun was higher now, and the two figures could be seen clearly, as they rode to across the front rank and took a position on the left-hand side of those watching.

Across the battle-lines, the two sections had discovered a twin-emotion. Fear of Cinderella, who sat regally despite her unusual clothing, atop a well-groomed, white horse. By her side sat Suzee, in the white cloak and polished armour of the Captain of the Palace Guard.

And even at all stared at the two, even as the fear became tangible in the air, another figure appeared in front of the Guards on the right side of the Centaur's army.

"Arguth!" came the gasp, seeming to rise from the ground like a clammy mist, exhaled from the mouths of the fighters on both sides.

Hearing this, Arguth smiled and gave a small bow, chuckling to himself darkly. He then bowed to Cinderella who inclined her head. Now, he stepped aside to reveal a dark genie, already conjured, who moved grumpily to the fore and folded his arms.

A silence fell…

Before the tramping of grass was heard behind the villagers and Cinamon appeared.

He had been dressed in loose-fitting armour, too big for him, but it sat well upon his frame. Gold, he shone now, plated on head, chest, arms and legs. But his glimmer was outdone—even in the golden dawn—by that of Nuisance, who snorted and pawed at the ground, giving off his brightest copper glow. Cinamon clapped his hands and on either side of him appeared a genie.

Both turned to him, bowed, ignored the gasps of both sides—Arguth included, Cinderella especially, then moved backwards to swirl around behind the ranks.

Cinamon moved back also, behind Xyntu and her Phoenix, all raring to go, pleading to be sent on the attack—or the healing.

Cinderella finally found her voice, "Cinamon!" she screamed, and the sound echoed in the trees. Birds departed, and each man and woman—Human or Centaur—flinched, cowered and waited for this Prince to be brought to heel.

But no, "Mother," he replied amiably.

"Cinamon, to me right now! You have no place in a fight such as this!"

"On the contrary, Cinderella," use of her first name sent her purple with rage—there was no older, nor easier way, to distance yourself from a parent than to use their first name, "I am placed here by the Gods themselves. With a little help from my Fairy Godmother," he smiled.

"And where is that treacherous bitch?" Cinderella replied harshly.

"She is dead, Cinderella. As I'm sure you will be glad to know. After all, why else would you have sent an old woman, one who made you everything you could have become, to such a place as Pyrone's Tower? If not so she might sit there and rot."

The silence was broken only by a short, sharp laugh from Arison. But it was enough to turn the Queen on her.

"You! You dare laugh?"

"I dare," Arison agreed, "In fact, we all dare. You are nothing, lady, and you have nothing but a handful of guards, a single grumpy genie, and a stack of pot-bellied misers who like to beat unarmed people without cause. Go now, and perhaps we will save you a ditch to sleep in."

Suzee put a hand to Cinderella's arm and shook her head softly, "Cinderella...we will show them the truth, only give the word to attack."

Cinderella closed her mouth and nodded, "So be it!" she called.

"What!" came Skim's voice, "You use the language of the Gods? Aye, but surely you're naught but a fallen demon!"

Now his own army was laughing, chuckling to themselves, and Cinderella was spluttering with rage.

"Say the words, Queen Cinderella," Suzee urged, reminding her who she was, "Say the words, and these...traitors will die."

"Not all of them, I hope...I have plans for those that are unlucky enough to survive..." the Queen ground her teeth and nodded tightly. She drew her dagger, to more amused chuckles from the opposite side.

"What, you plan to tickle us?" came a shout from one brave villager.

Cinderella gritted her teeth, raised the dagger on high: "Forward! Forward for Lamsonia!" she cried, "Trample these traitors and bring them to death or destruction for your Queen!"

The army surged forward, roaring. The front rank hit the barrier of barbed wood and many fell in agony to the floor, disabled or tangled, to be trodden on by those behind—barely giving thought to what might have caused their fall.

Those that missed the barbs kept their line, filled it from the rank behind—also depleted with moaning stragglers on the ground. They advanced, slowly, as the villagers, Centaurs and Guards spread out their line, but by bit, until they were in three ranks.

Arguth slunk forward a little, ordered his genie, "Attack!"

"Attack who?" the genie protested, "There's lots of them!"

"All of them!" Arguth growled.

But the genie was too late. The first of Cinamon's had come, and even now was covering it in a spell to bind it to Arguth. The genie was disabled, and Arguth's powers were seriously hampered as the genie tried to free itself.

"Get out of here!" Arguth cried.

"I'm bound to you, you old fool!" the wretched growled, "If I go, you come too!"

Arguth backed off as a smile came to the dark genie's lips.

Cinamon's genie watched with a half-smile, "I remember you," he told the genie, "You got ideas of power and went to the dark side."

The dark one nodded, "I wish I had never…" it groaned.

"Then redeem yourself!" the good genie cried, "He is bound to you—if you take him back to the dark place…"

"He will go mad…and never escape," the genie grinned.

"No! Genie, stay still and let me deal with your trap later!" Arguth hissed.

But too late. The dark genie bowed once to Cinamon's laughing aide, and vanished, taking Arguth with him.

Cinamon's genie roared laughter, "Well done, old friend!" he called into the ether, "Perhaps you can be redeemed yet!"

Meanwhile the Phoenix had been let loose, nine birds pulling hair, striking their barbed legs into faces and eyes…more of the enemy fell, many bled but remained standing.

Cinamon's second genie was busy turning swords into dust, joined by the first he grinned, "Saw that!" he said shortly, pointing at another sword held by an advancing City Guard; who moaned as it crumbled, and moved himself hurriedly to the back of the ranks.

Before the army even reached the three ranks of the Centaur force, it was depleted, with less arms, and low morale. But even the Genies dared do no more as they drew too close. They returned to Cinamon, "We can pick off a straggler, but in the middle of this…we have no hope."

Cinamon nodded, "Same with myself. Thank you. But I can deal with stragglers…if you both could capture my mother and her advisor, hold them somewhere, unharmed if possible, until the end…" the genies were away before he had finished, and Cinamon's eyes were drawn to one with a sword, sneaking towards him from the middle of a group. As Cinamon pulled the now terrified man helplessly towards him, and tied him in magical bonds, so the Centaur force finally dived into the fight.

With a great roar, each commander ordered his own into the battle with cries of 'Fight for your country!" "Freedom from tyranny!" "Last one to kill is a yellow-spined lizard!" And from the Centaur's at the front, "For the past, the future and the present of all! Centaur's fight again!"

Outnumbered now in people, but far ahead in trained fighters, the City Guards threw their swords left and right, their shields stayed up. The villagers brave enough to jump into the fray were speedily overwhelmed, and their weapons lost to those behind them or those disarmed by the genies.

Skim and Vana joined together in a hurry, back-to-back they faced down any that looked their way and soon surrounded themselves with a circle of the dead and dying.

Arison galloped back and forth, riding down those that stood in her way, her strong arms slashing with glowing sword those that tried to escape. None could touch her, for she sped to fast, and never slowed down—after recalling Eera's lesson in stamina, she had trained hard.

Mossan and Micx galloped around to the back and those that turned to them quickly turned back, usually leaking blood But Micx was tired, the injuries he sustained at the stable had kept bleeding, with none to treat them, and no Phoenix has ventured in his direction.

"Brother, sit!" Mossan cried.

"No!" he roared, and slipped. His sword missed the Palace Guard who was trying to escape. Seeing his chance the Guard plunged his sword through the Centaur's heart.

"Brotheeeeerrrr!" Mossan screamed and struck the head from the offender. She turned to him, caught him in her arms.

But another had seen his chance and Mossan's head rolled. As he rejoiced, he turned and met a Phoenix. Sent by Xyntu to heal Micx, instead it squawked and pecked out the man's eyes.

Spitter had met with Melina and formed up. He let out gobbet after gobbet of saliva, paralysing each fighter that came close enough. Melina stood by him, darting forward to catch the paralysed and relieve them of life. She collected the weapon each held and handed them to villagers, then darted out once more and release the next.

Dijn worked alone. He snuck up behind a soldier who stood aside from the others, panting exhaustion. Singing softly into his ear, Dijn caressed the man's head to relax him. Soon he grew weak and Dijn, catching him gently, slit his throat with a slim dagger and moved on, keeping to the right side, looking for the next exhausted enemy.

Xyntu stood in the same spot, ordering her healing birds to those she saw injured, swapping the waves of attack when she saw them begin to tire, resting those to tired to go on. She saw some die, taken down by a quick-thinking City Guard, who laughed as he caught her eye. She drew her sword and beckoned him.

The man, still laughing blundered his way through, shoving aside any that got in his way.

He missed the glance she gave to Cinamon, riding the outsides on the left, looking for any who ventured far enough from the crowd.

Xyntu raised her sword and pointed at him, "Now!" she shouted and grinned. The last thing the burly man was to see before his face twisted and he burst into a fireball of white flame. A second later, and his dust was floating to the ground.

Cinamon bowed his head to Xyntu who blew him a kiss as a thank you. Grinning, the boy rode on again, watching carefully for any foolish enough to look for a breathing space.

Arison took place of Mossan and Micx. She saw their death and, fast as lightning, sped to the jeering man who had been Mossan's downfall. She tapped him on the shoulder and he turned, wide-eyed.

Arison simply nodded a greeting, plunged a spare sword in his belly to its hilt and left him to bleed, crying in pain, as she patrolled the area once taken by Mossan and Micx, taking each man who dared turn his face towards her.

Meanwhile, Cinamon's genies had turned themselves dim, and, invisible to all who were not looking, they had circled and come around behind Suzee and Cinderella, who were watching the battle, torn between emotions, unable to say who was winning—or unable to admit the worst.

Becoming visible again, the genies came up close and, simultaneously, shouted "Hello!" into the ears of both victims.

The effect was to cause Cinderella to whip around, unbalanced, before falling as her horse reared its annoyance. Suzee whipped also, but riding a war-horse, was not thrown. Instead she was bound by magical cord while Cinderella was picked from the floor and also bound. The genies carried them into the trees, remaining just in sight of the battle, and watched over them carefully.

Cinamon saw this after a moment and, relieved, smiled his approval and thanks at his genies, who simply bowed and waved, and carried on guarding.

Stepping back, Cinamon looked carefully on the battlefield. He saw blood...blood in puddles and pools, blood covering the swords, shields and armour of everyone there. Saw bodies, piled two and three in height, saw more appearing by the second, Saw his friends, Mossan and Micx, lying on the floor and screamed his agony.

As he watched, a group of Guards—some City, and a few remaining Palace, circled Vana and Skim and moved in closer as a group. Cinamon watched, his mouth open, as they advanced...closer, closer...and finally pounced!

Skim killed two before being tackled to the floor by four. Vana barged her way through the group, turned, sliced at as many as she could handle. But more had caught the idea, and she was knocked to the ground.

Realizing his stupidity, cursing himself, Cinamon raised his hands and directed narrow beams of fire at each man who pinned them down.

But too late for Skim, for as his beam hit the last man, so that man dropped a war axe into Skim's already-ravaged face.

Vana cried out and surged free of her captives. She knew Skim was no more, but she had seen Cinamon and her mind worked fast. She shot towards him, waving at him to back up.

He did, wondering, then saw the soldiers following behind her. He raised his hands, backed away more, and waited.

Vana broke free and sped past him, praying he had understood and would do what was required.

She was followed closely by five men, so intent on their chase they saw nothing of Cinamon until a ball of fire lit up the grass in front of them.

They turned, tried to return, but the fire spread into a circle and trapped them.

Cinamon looked for Vana, who had looked back and seen. She returned to him.

"This one is your revenge," Cinamon told her.

Vana brandished her sword, "Kill them," she growled menacingly, baring her teeth.

Cinamon nodded, obeyed, and all five crumpled like paper, smaller, smaller until they were gone into nothing.

"Thank you," Vana sighed.

Cinamon looked, found Xyntu, called for a Phoenix. One flew over speedily and attended to Vana as Cinamon guarded her until she rose once more, picked up her sword and flew back into the center of the battle, this time forming a team with Arison.

Melina and Spitter realised the Guards were giving them wide berth. Killing could be handled, but Spitter's personal trick had done more than enough to keep them away. Yet Spitter was not just a one-trick magician. He drew a sword and strode into the blue and grey wall of Guards, short and somewhat squat he was, but strong and fierce. Melina watched him with awe, before realising that without his spittle she was a target.

She turned and sliced through the armour of one who snuck up to her, growled her fury and followed Spitter through the bloody gap he had left in the crowd.

He turned to come back, saw her, grinned a battle-smile, "Kill them all," he grunted.

"Surround them, pick them off," Melina advised. Spitter nodded and she raised her voice to all the Centaur army, "SURROUND THE

OUTSIDES! LOCK THEM IN AND TAKE ALL WHO REFUSE TO SURRENDER!"

The Queen's men laughed at orders coming from a mere girl…until they saw the circle drawing around them. Some 450 left, Guards, villagers and Centaurs, pinning them in. Of the Queen's army, only some 300 remained, fighters all, but beaten down. By Centaurs, recalling the fight in their blood. By Palace Guards, the elite trained, the best of the best. By Cinamon and Dijn, giving none a resting space. By Melina and Spitter, with their quickly devised plan of paralyse and kill. By Skim and Vana, by Mossan and Micx, by Arison and her newer partner—Vana. By the villagers, fighting for everything they lived for, everything they dreamed of, and freedom from Cinderella's iron fist, these villagers that remained, and those that had fallen, had found a superhuman strength in themselves, repressed and oppressed; they had risen to the calling and not found themselves wanting.

Surrounded, now, some tried to break away, only to be taken down by their captors, or by Cinamon if they got too far. Finally, they stood still, surly and angry, expecting to be killed anyway, or worse.

"You have been under the treatment of Cinderella too long!" Arison told them at last, "You will be imprisoned, yes, alongside your captured Queen!" she gestured to the genies still guarding Cinderella and Suzee.

Cinamon grinned, "Bring them here," he called.

The genies snapped their fingers, and the two bound figured, struggling still, floated towards Cinamon where he sat astride Nuisance, who was whinnying gently.

"This is your oppressor," Arison pointed to Cinderella, "And her advisor, recently installed, but no less a part of this than all of you. None of you will be killed out of hand. All of you will be imprisoned and given trial by these people here today. There will, however, be no execution, no torture, and no 'inventive punishment'. Surrender now and you will live—in a cell, yes, but one day perhaps you will be released. That last, is only up to you.

Arison finished and waited. Some, grinding their teeth furiously, stepped forward, "Kill me!" they said, and they were killed. But the few remaining Palace Guards were the first to fall to one knee, cast their swords at the feet of whoever was closest, and give surrender.

Most of the City Guards followed, crying their shame at the way they had acted when given free reign by Cinderella. Some fell to one knee, threw their weapon furiously and surrendered, simply to live.

But all were bound by Cinamon and his genies and cast into cells, with up to four in one, because even Cinderella had never kept so many alive at one time.

Chapter 29

Outside, in the town square, those who had fought cheered the Commanders who remained, with gaps left between them to signal those who had fallen.

Nuisance had left sadly, called back to…wherever he came from, and Cinamon stood in the center. As Prince of the realm—at least until a new format could be discussed (and implemented, or not), it was for him to speak in the absence of his father.

But as he opened his mouth, a shout went up from Arison, who pelted down from the stage and raced to four figures, walking towards them from a distance.

She threw her arms around Eera then stepped back and bowed respectfully to the other three.

"I am Osmon," the King introduced himself, "This is Royston, and this is Samson. I give you our names in trust."

Arison smiled, "You found him, I see," she said, "And love has found its way. I am Arison."

"Our finest warrior and Commander!" came Vana's voice from behind them, "My King." She knelt, "I am no longer a Palace Guard, nor is Skim…and Skim is…no longer. But we staged, today, a revolution against the Ex-Queen Cinderella. You are returned, however, and we give over the Kingdom to you…and accept any punishment you give to the leaders. But please, only not to the other Guards and the villagers, for they only fought with us when they knew there was no other choice."

Osmon chortled, "I think you'll have to take all that back," he smiled, "But let me speak."

The Commanders removed themselves from the stage and Osmon walked up, alone, to cheers from his people.

"As fate would have it," he told them, "I was returning to try and remove Cinderella from the throne anyway. And I feel there would have been such a battle, between you and hers, to come anyway. I humbly apologise for leaving you in her clutches, and for my absence in this time of need, but I know most of you will understand when I say that it was for love," he held out his hand and Royston stepped up to join him, "I went to find the man I let down. That day when I stood here and told you of my second child, I was too afraid to tell you what I really wanted to say. But no more!" he looked around and smiled warmly, "This is the man I love. His name is Royston, and we will be wed before leaving Lamsonia. I willingly give up my Kingship, and hand it over to my son—who shall have a trusted advisor by his side always; this position I offer to Eera and any who my son also chooses. I will return, this I promise you, but never as your King. I simply wish to travel, to see the world," Arison had cleared her throat and looked up, asking to come up and speak.

Osmon nodded and moved over.

"My liege—Osmon, now," she smiled, "We fought this battle for freedom, and I believe it is up to the people left here in Lamsonia to decide what that freedom will be. Monarchy is but one option. We wish the people to decide, however, which they will choose."

Osmon looked at Cinamon, "I think that is up to my son," he grinned and Cinamon joined them on-stage.

The boy thought, "I think...if you all trust myself and your Commanders, plus my fathers," he smiled at Royston who blushed a little, "And my advisor—Eera, that we will retire and discuss the forms of rule—or lack of rule," he shrugged lightly, "There will be a vote, and each one of you of age will be able to cast yours for the type of living you want. We will name these types, and explain them in full, and you—the people—will decide."

A cheer rose, and Cinamon beckoned all those he had named on-stage.

"But first," Samson roared from his place at the front of the crowd, "Did I 'ear a mention o' a weddin'?"

The cheers were earsplitting as Osmon and Royston nodded in tandem, "And each one of you is invited, in three days time," Osmon said above the noise, a Royston grinned and hugged his future-husband to the whistles, cheers and happiness of the citizens of the newly free Lamsonia...

...while Cinderella and Suzee sat grumpily in a cell of their own, listening.

Cinderella huddled close to Suzee for warmth. Suzee wrapped her arms and cloak tightly around her friend and shivered.

"What went wrong?" the Queen asked dully.

Suzee shrugged, "We should never have tried the Centaurs...we should never have tested Osmon and Royston...we should never have done it this way. Secrecy, this is the key...we should have done it quietly."

"Will they kill us?"

Suzee shook her head, "I doubt it. Cinamon set his genies to watch us, remember? He won't let anyone hurt us."

"I'd rather be dead than here forever," Cinderella growled.

Suzee smiled, "That's the friend I came to know, there's that fighting spirit! We won't be here forever. Cinamon will pity us eventually...or someone else will...just be nice, gentle, beg forgiveness and a chance for redemption. If you can be patient...they will free us in the end."

"I can be patient," the former-Queen nodded, "If I could sit inside my cold self all those years before I was taken away by Osmon, I can do it again with a smile. But when they let us out, in years to come...then what?"

Suzee gave a cruel smile, unseen in the darkness—except perhaps by the passing rats, "We have plenty of time to plan, Cinderella...plenty of time to plan..."

Cinderella chuckled, "All the time in the world...and where better to plan than in here, the place I shall lock, bolt, chain and execute every single person who betrayed me," she let her head drop for a snooze. '*Oh yes...plenty of time to plan...and as the Gods are my witness, I shall personally rip the steaming entrails from each man and woman who fought against me this day.*'

Her dreams were pleasant, murderous, and Suzee sat still, listening to the occasional guttural chuckle, making her plans—

making their plans. Waiting...then waiting...then secrecy, yes...secrecy was the key. And not soon, but one day, they would be more powerful than ever before. Suzee smiled and settled more comfortably on the cold floor—as cold as the hearts of the two cellmates—and fell asleep to the calm breathing of her co-conspiratorial friend.

The End

Printed in the United Kingdom
by Lightning Source UK Ltd.
115959UKS00001B/293